of

THREADCASTING

(and spinning chaos)

Also by S.T. White:

Tales of Unraveling

The Way of Water (and drugging dragons)

The Way of Tyranny (and breaking bonds)

The Way of Warfare (and throwing tantrums)

Squid Mark (release date 2025)

The WAY *of* THREADCASTING
(and spinning chaos)

S.T. WHITE

H & B
ENTERPRISES

The Way of Threadcasting (and Spinning Chaos)

First published in 2025 by Huxleyi & Braarudii Enterprises
The paperback edition published 2025
The hardcover edition published in 2025
The ebook edition published in 2025

Paperback ISBN: 978-3-9526205-2-6
Hardcover ISBN: 978-3-9526205-1-9
Typeface: Garamond, originally designed by Claude Garamond, modernized by Monotype Corporation. Licensed by Microsoft Corporation.

Front cover design and illustrations by © R.S. Pioli.
www.stwhitebooks.com
www.huxleyiandbraarudii.com

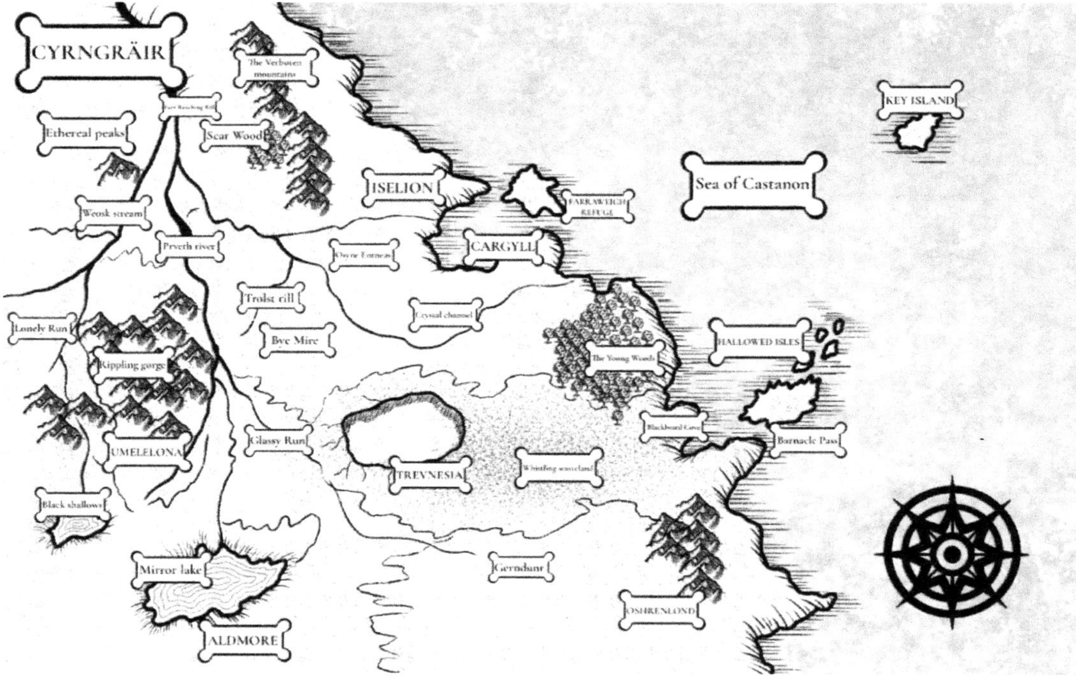
CYRNGRÄIR
The Verboten mountains
Ethereal peaks
Scar Wood
ISELION
KEY ISLAND
Sea of Castanon
FARRAWEIGH REFUGE
Weosk stream
Pryeth river
CARGYLL
Trolst cill
Crystal channel
Lonely Run
Bye Mire
HALLOWED ISLES
The Young Woods
Rippling gorge
Blackbeard Cove
Glassy Run
Barnacle Pass
UMELELONA
TREVNESIA
Black shallows
Mirror lake
Gerndanr
OSHRENLOND
ALDMORE

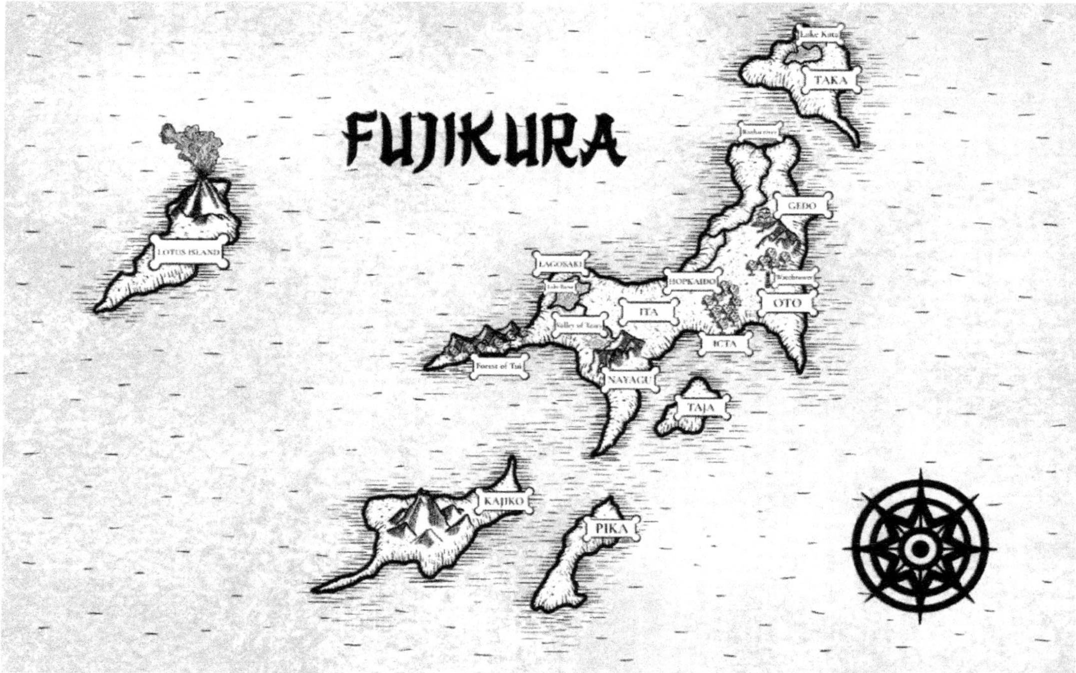
FUJIKURA
LOTUS ISLAND
Lake Kata
TAKA
GEDO
LAGOSAKI
HOPKAIDO
OTO
ITA
Valley of Tears
ICTA
Forest of Tui
NAYAGU
TAJA
KAJIKO
PIKA

To my mother who opened the doors to
Narnia and Middle Earth.

PROLOGUE

MR. FABER

Mr. Faber had arrived at *the Bedraggled Cockerel Inn* moments earlier, scattering the remaining stragglers like leaves in a gale. But one particularly brave—or colossally foolish—man still lingered, leaning against the door, his gaunt frame illuminated by the flickering lanterns lining the cobblestone road. Mr. Faber brushed his arm against the man's shoulder as he reached for the brass chicken foot that passed for a handle.

"Excuse me, good sir," said Mr. Faber, his tone crisp and clipped. "I will be needing to get in there."

The man didn't move. He stared at the door as if it held the answers to the universe, and only after an awkward silence did he seem to realize he'd been addressed at all. "It's closed!" he barked, jabbing a filthy finger toward a wooden sign swinging precariously on rusted chains. "Says so right 'ere! That blasted fairy, Mr. Caligan, tossed me out on me ear!"

He stumbled mid-gesture, catching himself on Mr. Faber's sleeve. Mr. Faber's nostrils flared as he carefully pried the man's fingers from his fine velvet coat, his expression one of distilled disgust.

"If I ain't allowed in, neither are you," the man slurred, his words colliding in a haze of mead-soaked breath.

Mr. Faber straightened his cloak with deliberate precision. "You are aware of who I am, are you not?"

The man squinted, his head tilting like a puzzled crow. "Mr. Faber, I s'pose."

Mr. Faber opened his mouth, then closed it, his lips pressing into a thin line. "Quite."

"You think bein' Principal of that confounded Heron Academy means you can ignore all them rules, eh?"

"Well technically my official title is Leader of the Order of Threadcasters," Mr. Faber replied, adding a polite 'my good sir' to remind the man of his impeccable manners.

"Big whoop. And I'm Karl, leader of the people who've bloody had it with yer caterwaulin'."

Mr. Faber's brow lifted, an elegant arch of skepticism. "A very big whoop indeed young man." He reached for the knocker again, but Karl swatted at him with the enthusiasm of a cat swiping at a dangling string.

"Ha! I ain't been young for decades, fairy boy."

Mr. Faber's laugh was soft, almost pitying. "Try living for four hundred thirty-five years and then tell me you're not a young man."

Karl's eyes narrowed as if he were attempting—and failing—to solve some complicated equation. "Bah! All you fairies think you're special, just 'cause you've got your fancy magic. Think you can rule all of Cyrnghräir, don't ya?"

"We Threadcasters," Mr. Faber said, his patience

fraying at the edges, "are not concerned with ruling Cyrnghräir."

"Oh, so now it's all Narthor you've got yer eyes on, eh? Cyrnghräir not enough?"

Mr. Faber sighed, brushing an invisible speck from his immaculate collar. "It has never been about ruling. It is about sharing chronomagic with those capable of understanding it."

"Rich, comin' from you lot," Karl spat. His finger jabbed toward Mr. Faber but missed, colliding with the inn's wall instead. He yelped, clutching his hand like a child denied dessert.

"I do beg your pardon."

"Aye, you should be beggin'! If you wanna share yer 'precious' magic, why not teach us?" Karl's words dissolved into a garbled mess as he gestured wildly, nearly toppling over.

"Humans," Mr. Faber said, his voice tinged with exasperation, "have never been able to wield chronomagic. Your time is too fleeting to grasp its complexities."

Karl's face twisted in rage. His fist curled, rising with agonizing slowness. Mr. Faber rolled his eyes, and the crystal embedded in his collarbone began to hum. Threads of pink light unfurled from his fingers, weaving through the air like living silk. They coiled around Karl's arm, glowing with an otherworldly vibrancy.

Karl's fist swung—and hit nothing. He stumbled forward, snarling as he tried again, and again. Each time, Mr. Faber was effortlessly out of reach, his expression bored.

"Enough of this nonsense," Mr. Faber murmured. With a snap of his fingers, the threads vibrated, locking Karl in place. The fairy inspected the frozen man with a clinical detachment, circling him as if he were a peculiar art installation—and not some inebriated guy on a random Tuesday, whose greatest accomplishment was adding pickles to a grilled cheese sandwich.

He turned to the edifice of the inn, grabbed ahold of an oversized potted plant from Mr. Caligan's fine collection, and planted Karl's outstretched foot beside a prize-winning lemon tree. He wiped the dirt from his hands on Karl's shirt, gave him a solid poke for good measure, and then snapped his fingers again.

The pink threads vanished. At which point Karl realized two things. One, he was falling, and two, his foot was stuck in a pot.

"You think you're funny, eh?" Karl growled from the ground. "Well, you're a right git, that's what you are."

"A 'git,' am I?" Mr. Faber produced an embroidered handkerchief, unfolding it with the care of someone handling priceless relics. He dabbed at an invisible spot on his sleeve. "It would seem even my handkerchief is more articulate than you."

Karl fumbled for a retort, his gaze drifting upward as if the night sky might offer him a witty comeback. Finding none, he slumped back against the wall and muttered, "Magic folk, thinkin' they're all high 'n mighty."

Mr. Faber sighed, a soft, silvery sound like leaves stirred by the wind. "Good sir, it is not I who am 'high and mighty'—it is merely that I am, quite simply, skilled."

Karl opened his mouth, then shut it, retreating into sullen silence. Mr. Faber sighed and stepped toward the inn's door, only to pause. "Do pray to Amriel that I do not run into you again, Karl. Fairies are not the callous sycophants you think us to be, but insult me again, and you will wish I were half as ruthless as the stories make me out to be."

The man laughed but was cut off by a series of burps and hiccups which shuddered through his body with such ferocity that Mr. Faber had to wonder if he was not instead suffering from some alcohol-induced seizure. Before he could think to do anything about it (he was not overly inclined to do anything at all), Karl was fumbling around in his pot mumbling, "Them bloody fairies, believing Amriel is real. Next, they'll all be waitin' by the water's edge for the sea dragons to return."

"Karl!" shouted a voice from somewhere up ahead.

What now, thought Mr. Faber. Soon enough a face could be assigned to the voice, and it was neither a pretty nor especially proportionate one at that. The newcomer was clearly several steps removed from sober, yet he still managed to appear positively abstinent compared to Karl. "Karl!" he repeated as he arrived at the weather-beaten doorway, "there you are! We've been—"

His eyes widened as he took in the imposing figure of Mr. Faber. "Mr. Faber, sir! My apologies, sir," he stammered, settling for a clumsy bow that looked more like he'd dropped something on the floor.

"Karl," he hissed, grabbing his companion by the tunic and tugging. "Do you have any idea who this is?"

Karl fixed his friend, *we'll call him Fred shall we*, with a stupid grin, "That one made sure of it," he pointed at Mr. Faber, a gesture which off-balanced him to such a degree he fell to the side, bringing the lemon tree down with him.

Fred hauled Karl upright, muttering apologies between gritted teeth. "Please, sir," he said to Mr. Faber, lowering his voice as though imparting a state secret, "you'll have to forgive him. He's a few heifers short of a herd, if you catch my meaning. We try to keep him from the drink, but here in Cargyll, that's like trying to banish rain—you understand?"

If Mr. Faber did understand, he gave no inclination as such and instead glanced between the two men while straightening out his cloak.

"Well anyway," continued Fred, a nervous titter now seeping into his voice, "we meant no disrespect. We'll be getting out of your hair—"

"Mighty rude, draggin' a man from a perfectly polite conversation," Karl slurred, wrenching against Fred's grip. "I was just about to tell him we'd all be better off if 'em bloody fairies stayed in Iselion where they belong. It's unnatural, this—this—"

"Enough!" snapped Fred. "Good eve to you sir!" he shouted at Mr. Faber as he quickly pulled Karl into the cover of the night.

Mr. Faber smiled ever so softly as he caught Fred's words sailing over the evening mist, "How many times do I have to tell you Karl—you can hate Threadcasters all you want but keep that foolish talk to yourself! Mr. Faber has flected people clean in two for less than you just did. It's a miracle you haven't been banished to Selsmire Keep!"

Mr. Faber, left with the fragrant wreckage of the lemon tree and the faint echo of Fred's frantic scolding, sighed the sigh of a man too acquainted with the absurd. Shaking his head, he turned on his heel and entered *the Bedraggled Cockerel.*

Inside, warmth and the aroma of stale ale enveloped him. The innkeeper, Mr. Caligan, emerged from behind the bar, his sharp eyes gleaming even in the dim light. "So, the cat's dragged you back through my door, eh?"

Mr. Caligan did not need to see who had caused the *Bedraggled Cockerel's* door to ring. He already knew who it was. There was only one man (or fairy as it were) who it could be. Mr. Caligan was not what one would describe as 'traditionally handsome' but nor was he unsightly (indeed, that description could seldom be used to describe a fairy with any degree of truth). Perhaps his exuberant personality was simply too flamboyant to be contained within a single vessel, which gave him a somewhat drained appearance. Like a colored picture forced to conform to a restrictive monochrome.

"And I see *you* have still not learned the meaning of the word 'hospitality'."

"Ha! I thought it was you lurking outside the door," exclaimed Mr. Caligan as he tossed down the stained rag he had been using to clean the bar counter. His slightly puckered face gave way to a broad smile as he clamped a strong hand onto the other man's shoulder, "it's been too long my friend."

"Hardly," said Mr. Faber, unamused. "It's been exactly the amount of time I intended since our last meeting."

"Ah, still a regular riot, I see," said Caligan, pouring two drinks with exaggerated flair.

Mr. Faber tossed his long coat and rain-drenched hat beside him and sighed, "You really do entertain the most curious of clientele. Perhaps you should try knocking some sense into them rather than telling them the tall tales of your various escapades."

Mr. Caligan chuckled as Mr. Faber shut the window behind him, hiding them from the pink and yellow gloom of the twin moons. Tonight was the dawning of Narthor's second moon. One might think this was some momentous celestial occurrence, but in Cyrnghräir this was no more unusual than a regular full moon. That is to say, a monthly occurrence.

"You must have met Karl," Caligan replied, plopping into the chair across from him.

Faber grimaced. "That wreck of a man is a regular?"

Caligan groaned, his expression resigned. "In a manner of speaking."

Faber swirled the contents of his glass. "Curious how you keep this place afloat with such sterling patronage."

The innkeeper shrugged. "I manage. Besides," he added with a knowing smile, "I have you."

Perhaps it is surprising that Mr. Caligan was not at all put out by the monthly evacuation of his sole source of income, but what one must know is that Mr. Faber was a gentleman in more ways than one. What I mean to say is, he was wealthy. And not in the enjoys a selection of fine wines and caviar kind of way but in a 'say the wrong thing and I'll make sure you never see the light of day' sort of way. But even if Mr. Caligan were not so generously compensated for the inconvenience, he would have tossed his other customers out with his own hands for less than a copper. For Mr. Caligan and Mr. Faber were confidants. One might even go so far as to say friends.

Despite what the years might imply, the table was not occupied by two wizened old men this evening, but by two positively youthful specimens of a respectable middle-age. The Fae are a tall and rather ethereal race, whose primary characteristic is a thinly veiled superiority complex. Of course, they would never be so vulgar as to make this sentiment explicit and instead adopted a general air of condescension.

Mr. Faber's lavish velvet shirt barely masked the muscular frame of his shoulders, broader than the finest barrels in the inn's cellar. Across the table, Mr. Caligan's cloak draped around him, its extravagant patterns shimmering in the flickering firelight, adding a touch of mystery to his debonair appearance.

"So, tell me, old friend," said Mr. Caligan, setting down the glasses, "what dark tales bring you back to this here dull little inn?"

"Ah, you know me," Mr. Faber replied, swirling his drink thoughtfully. "Chasing rumors. I heard whispers of a nefarious magic taking hold in the East, and I thought I'd investigate. But it appears I've only stumbled upon a drunken fool with delusions of grandeur."

"It's an age of drunken fools, Actinus," Mr. Caligan quipped, leaning back in his chair. "The land is infested with them. You'd think it a plague."

"Maybe it is," Mr. Faber countered. "And perhaps I've joined their ranks. Though I must say, you wear the role quite convincingly yourself."

Mr. Caligan chuckled, a low, velvety sound. "Ah, just wait until the early crowd arrives. You'll see true artistry."

Mr. Faber raised an eyebrow. "And how early might that be?"

"Early enough," said Mr. Caligan.

"Then I suppose I ought to speak quickly," Mr. Faber

replied, raising his glass.

Mr. Caligan clinked his own against it, and the two men exchanged knowing glances before retreating into the warm, welcoming embrace of their drinks and the flickering firelight.

For a moment, the two men retreated into the embrace of their drinks, the warmth of the fire wrapping around them like a familiar old cloak. Then Mr. Faber set his glass down and pressed his hands flat against the table, grimacing as a sticky residue clung to his fingers. The next moment, he began to glow. Not like a torch or a lantern but more like the night sky: a soft turquoise light that seeped from him in shimmering waves, swirling through the collar of his robes.

Threads of light spiraled down his arms, curling around his fingers like playful serpents. Mr. Caligan groaned, plucking at one of the strands now winding around his wrist.

"I wish you wouldn't do that," he muttered, absently fiddling with the glowing blue thread, its warmth palpable against his skin.

"Why ever not?" asked Mr. Faber, as another thread intertwined with his own. "Back at Heron Academy, you would vanish into your thoughts for days, like a shadow slipping through the cracks of time. I'd be hard-pressed to remember you as anything but a flicker in my peripheral vision."

"It's been a long time since those days," mumbled the Barkeep, his fingers tracing the outline of his collarbone, where a thin wisp of purple light peeked from beneath his tunic, "I'm no longer that man."

"Clearly," said Mr. Faber.

Mr. Caligan yanked the thread taut and let it snap back against his skin. "It's disorienting when the flection stops. Feels like hours pass, but it's only seconds."

"That's kind of the point, Caldred," sighed Mr. Faber. "But by all means, let's allow the whole world to eavesdrop while we discuss classified information regarding the Order just to spare you a mild discomfort."

The Barkeep let his hands fall to his sides, the weight of the moment pressing down. "Very well, then get on with it," he grumbled, frustration simmering just below the surface.

Turquoise light curled off Mr. Faber like morning dew as he toyed with one of the glowing threads. The strands began to hum, and though to the two men nothing seemed to change, to any curious onlooker peering into *the Bedraggled Cockerel*, they would have seen only two blurred shapes—a pair of fairies seemingly darting about, an impossible fourteen times in two minutes.

A heat radiated from Mr. Faber, a warmth that seemed to pulse with urgency. "I have a troubling feeling—"

A heavy silence wrapped around them like a shroud, thick and suffocating. Yet, Mr. Caligan sensed that no further pressing was needed.

And lo and behold Mr. Faber continued, "I have not kept much from you about the Order. Perhaps I should have a stronger hold over my tongue, but I do not see the point in starting that now. It concerns Fujikura."

"The island you've been sending Threadcasters to?" Mr. Caligan asked, his fingers tracing the rim of his glass.

The Fairy pinched his fingers beneath his chiseled chin, an action that might have implied the presence of a beard- but his smooth skin belied any trace of facial hair, and the absence seemed to bother him not in the least. In truth, his chief concern at the moment appeared to be his quickly diminishing glass of mead. Though, being in a bar, this predicament was remedied before he could even think to voice his unease.

"Well, most have been sent by orders of Sadhrin, she is responsible for our teaching missions in the East," he corrected, after he was once again heartily nursing his glass, "I have only sent a small number myself, Calder, Klaus and Frenick among them."

"Forgive me for the misspeak," Mr. Caligan said. "But surely you must approve of her endeavors being the leader of her Order?"

"Theoretically sure. Practically, Sadhrin has perhaps grown a bit too complacent in her position. She thinks because she has the ear of the Lord of Urwil I would not dare challenge her."

"Is she wrong?"

Mr. Faber grew visibly uncomfortable at the comment (understandably so) and began to fidget quite uncharacteristically. An outsider might have thought something sharp, or perhaps slimy had found its way into his trousers. Fortunately for him, no such unpleasantness had occurred; yet it was hardly conclusive that he wouldn't have preferred it to the line of inquiry now unfolding.

So, as any polite gentleman would do, when asked a question he does not wish to answer, Mr. Faber simply ignored it and moved on as if it hadn't been posed in the first place. "I never thought much about the increasing number of Threadcasters Sadhrin has sent to Fujikura. I assumed she was merely following the flow of opportunities. After all, who was I to question her if she had found such fertile ground there?"

"Well, only the leader of her Order, but do carry on," murmured Mr. Caligan, his smirk firmly in place.

Mr. Faber pressed on, ignoring the quip. "But several days ago, Kilie—you remember Kilie, don't you?"

Mr. Faber didn't pause for an answer—nor would it have mattered. Mr. Caligan, for the record, did not remember Kilie.

"He received a letter from Brother Calder. At first glance, it seemed entirely mundane. Calder rambled about the food, the culture—you know how Calder is. Never knows when to shut up."

Mr. Caligan's pointed look at this comment went entirely unnoticed.

"But here's what struck me: Calder insisted he'd

remain in Fujikura indefinitely. Now, Sadhrin has sent dozens of Threadcasters there, and from all accounts, the Fujikurans have been receptive to our teachings. There's no reason for him not to return. I confided in Kilie, and we concluded Calder might be trying to send us a message."

"That does tend to be the point of sending a letter," Mr. Caligan muttered, leaning back in his chair.

"You know what I meant," sighed Mr. Faber with a lazy eyeroll that betrayed his frequent exercise of the motion.

"Do I?"

Mr. Caligan shrugged and then poured another round of mead. "You know, I've never quite understood why Sadhrin was even allowed into the Order of Threadcasters. Isn't the whole point of it that women aren't permitted?"

Mr. Faber cleared his throat, "Not the whole point, no," he sighed, "the Lord of Urwil insisted she be allowed on the Council. I had little say in the matter."

"Yes, because we all know what you would've said in the matter," said Mr. Caligan, "but even if she holds a seat on the council, why allow her so much power?"

"Because the Lord of Urwil—"

"Requested it, and you crawled to his every whim," Mr. Caligan interjected, amusement dancing in his eyes. "Ah, Faber, the mighty Actinus Faber, bowing to the will of a mere lord."

"I did not crawl," muttered Mr. Faber, his cheeks coloring.

"Do you prefer grovel and beg?"

"Do keep your jests to yourself," Mr. Faber replied, though the corners of his mouth twitched. "It's not so simple. There are more threads at play here than even we can comprehend. As long as Heron Academy resides in his territory, his requests are less requests and more decrees."

"I'm surprised you haven't relocated."

"I would, if it were possible to move the Sanctum," Mr. Faber muttered, his voice tinged with frustration. "Why she couldn't just train at Iselion like every other woman is beyond me."

"Perhaps," Mr. Caligan said, his tone contemplative. "But as long as she continues meddling with powers she barely understands, we risk drawing the ire of forces beyond our control."

"And what would you have me do? Challenge the Lord's decree? Expel her from the Academy?" Mr. Faber shook his head. "Sadhrin has potential, I'll grant her that. She's tenacious—fierce even. But sometimes I wonder if her ambition blinds her to the dangers lurking in the shadows. But you distract me, Caldred. Sadhrin's aspirations are not the topic of interest here."

"Very well," said Mr. Caligan. "So, you think Calder was sending you some hidden message?"

"No."

"But is that not what you just said?"

"Yes."

Mr. Caligan sighed. "Why do I feel like I'm missing some crucial piece of information?"

"What an astute observation, Caldred, I was not sure you had it in you." Before Mr. Caligan could voice any more of his growing frustration Mr. Faber continued, "Calder's refusal to return to Cargyll, struck me as odd-"

"So, you've said."

"So of course, I investigated further," continued Mr. Faber.

"Of course," added Mr. Caligan.

"And I discovered a crucial detail. The letter—it's not Calder's handwriting."

"What's not *whose* handwriting?" asked Mr. Caligan.

"The letter! It's not Calder's! The angles of his g's, the indentation of the vowels—it's all wrong. Completely wrong!" Mr. Faber exclaimed, exasperated. "Do endeavor to keep up old fellow."

"Perhaps doing so would not present quite such a challenge if you explained yourself more clearly," muttered the Barkeep his leg beginning to bob under the table. "Have you considered that perhaps he simply changed it?"

"Changed what?"

"His handwriting of course," replied Mr. Caligan.

Mr. Faber scoffed, "And tell me Caldred—how often do you decide to change your handwriting? Handwriting is not like a breakfast preference or one of your women, it does not simply change along with the seasons."

"I suppose you are right."

"When am I not?"

The Barkeep sighed and began playing with a coaster sitting on the table, "So you think it was forged?"

"Yes," said Mr. Faber, "there are select few in the Academy who would have had sufficient access to intercept Calder's original letter before it reached Kilie, and the skill and means to replace it with the forgery.

"And I take it Sadhrin is one of those people."

"Indeed."

"Have you confronted her?"

"If there is something nefarious going on here, and Sadhrin is involved, it is better she believes I know nothing of it."

"A fair point."

"Caldred," Mr. Faber's voice dropped, his face ashen. "If my people are in danger and Sadhrin has kept it from me—or Amriel forbid, caused it—I will ensure she begs for death a thousand times over."

"I hope for her sake you're wrong," muttered Mr. Caligan. "What will you do?"

"I will send two of my own men to Fujikura. Men I can trust who have no connection to Sadhrin."

"Is that wise?"

"Almost certainly not."

"Then I take it you've already done it."

The red patches on Mr. Faber's cheeks darkened further and his jaw became as tight as a snared marlin, but the one thing Mr. Faber was not, was a liar. Sure, he was no stranger to the gymnastics one could do with the truth and a little bit of wit, but outright deception was a shade too rich for even his blood.

"Who did you send?"

"Kilie and Kallae."

The threads snapped, and the markings on Mr. Faber's body disappeared as suddenly as they had appeared. A cool night's breeze swept into the room, ridding it of all warmth.

"Oh, and Caldred," said Mr. Faber, "you might want to look into acquiring a new pot for that lemon tree of yours."

"For the love of thread, Actinus," muttered Mr. Caligan, "I just had it repotted last week!"

ONE

KALLAE

Being aboard a ship, with his insides twisted like a pretzel made by someone with a personal vendetta against humanity, was about as appealing to Kallae as eating a fried tarantula—extra crispy, legs still twitching, because why not heap misery upon misery? To make matters worse, Kilie, his annoyingly cheerful, chronomagically glowing companion, was thriving, as though he'd somehow misplaced his invitation to afternoon tea with nausea and despair and had wound up at supper with ostentatiousness and unearned enthusiasm, clinking glasses with reckless optimism while Kallae sat marinating in his own misery. Naturally, because of course he had.

"Floating is cheating," Kallae muttered, head tilted just so to stave off another wave of nausea. He had perfected the art of appearing statuesque in discomfort, though anyone observing might think he'd suffered a catastrophic neck injury. Hours of sitting on the open deck of *The Ploughman's Revenge* had reduced him to this—a mime frozen mid-sneeze.

Kilie drifted nearby, a glowing orb of ethereal blue light swirling around him like a celestial firefly rave. The threads of chronomagic emanating from Kilie's skin twisted and looped in mesmerizing arcs, scattering sparks as they coiled. Beautiful, if you liked that sort of thing, which Kallae emphatically did not. What rankled most wasn't that Kilie could float or that he resembled an enchanted chandelier, but that Kallae couldn't. Not anymore.

Once, wielding chronomagic had been as effortless to Kallae as breathing—not that he'd ever mistaken either for a noble pursuit. But since his most recent escapade, one involving a plunge into the ocean and events he preferred not to recount without the proper amount of liquor, he was as magicless as a rock. A bitter, seasick rock, currently stranded on this splintering excuse for a ship en route to Fujikura—the 'distant shores of utter doom,' as Kallae liked to call them. And that only if they managed to make it there on this godforsaken piece of decrepit plywood, otherwise known as a ship (his words, not mine). The ship's name, *The Ploughman's Revenge*, did little to inspire confidence. Revenge for what? Terrible craftsmanship?

Kallae swiped at a stray thread of light that had the audacity to graze his cheek. Kilie's precise motions conjured more threads, their glowing tendrils snapping in and out of existence with infuriating ease. Kallae sighed dramatically. Meditation, he decided, was the only way to avoid hurling his breakfast into the sea—a sacrifice he wasn't willing to make, even for the fish.

"Show-off," muttered a gruff voice. Kallae cracked an eye open to see a sailor whose name he suspected was Bill. Or perhaps Bob. Some monosyllabic nonsense, anyway.

"You're not wrong," Kallae replied. He gestured vaguely toward Kilie. "It's one of his many flaws."

Bill (or Bob) grumbled something unintelligible.

"What was that?" asked Kallae, finally deigning to open his other eye.

Bill sighed, "Your friend's threadcasting is making some of the other men nervous. It's unnatural this thing."

"Friend is a strong word—"

"Never mind. No use talking sense into you and your kind," Bill grumbled before disappearing below deck, leaving Kallae no chance to mutter so much as a 'my bad,' which, of course, he wouldn't have said even if given half an opportunity.

Kilie's eyes opened, serene as a monk who'd achieved enlightenment specifically to annoy others. "I heard that."

Kallae clapped his hands against his mouth in mock surprise. "Blessed Amriel! I humbly beg for your forgiveness, oh wise sage of the skies. Surely my words are unworthy of your ethereal ears!"

"Oh, bugger off."

"I would if I could," said Kallae, "but in case you hadn't noticed, we're on a boat. There are precious few places to bugger off to."

"There's always the bottom of the sea," said Kilie, shifting his glance forwards again.

"Tried that, can't say I'm keen for a repeat performance just yet," Kallae replied, crossing his arms and leaning back against the railing, the boat swaying beneath him like a drunken dancer.

Kilie drifted to the left putting as much distance between him and his quarrelsome companion as was possible, which was not terribly far at all given the physical limitations of the ship.

Kallae shrugged again, glanced up at the sky and then shut his eyes. Despite his general dissatisfaction rearing its head every few minutes, it took decidedly less time than expected for his mind to drift to happier times and places. Which was, admittedly, not a hard thing to achieve. A cesspit, being scourged by a pack of rabid raccoons with vampiric tendencies would qualify as a happier place than here. Unfortunately, for Kallae, the nefarious plans of his own mind soon seized back control, insisting on dwelling upon the series of events which had brought him to this unholy wreckage of a cesspit in the first place.

Three Months Earlier: Heron Academy

In these halls, appearances were paramount—so important, in fact, that they had been elevated to a near-religious status. The horror of someone wearing a green velvet cloak with a silk pocket square—can you imagine the scandal?—was enough to send reputations crumbling faster than a house of cards in a windstorm. To prevent this tragedy from unfolding, the dress code had been distilled to its most basic and safest choice: the simple, unforgiving black cloak. No exceptions. Ever. Kallae, begrudgingly dressed according to code, stalking through the marble halls, his mood as dark as his cloak.

Naturally, Kallae's pupils were dressed impeccably. Not a hair was out of place—though Kallae wondered if that was more a result of a case of obsessive compulsive disorder rather than actual effort—and not a seam was loose. All was as it should be... well, when it came to their robes anyway. Training-wise? Chaos still reigned supreme with an iron fist, and judging by the scene in front of him, that reign would likely go uncontested until the end of time.

The classroom was a cacophony of noise, a chaotic symphony of chatter and clattering chairs. Kallae stood at the front, arms crossed, his brow furrowed like a storm cloud. He surveyed the room with a disdainful eye, as if the students were a particularly unpleasant strain of fungus.

"Brother Kallae?" came a hesitant voice from the corner. Kallae sighed, uncrossing his arms with the kind of dramatic flair characteristic of overwhelmed mothers or overly caffeinated teachers who had successfully lost the will to live. His hover descended, ever so gracefully, like a raven descending onto a battlefield.

His black cloak, which pooled to the bottom of the floor, billowed around him in that effortless way which was normally reserved for criminal masterminds with a flair for the dramatic, or societal screwballs trying to sell knock-off products under shady bridges. No fewer than seventeen designers had been enlisted to perfect this effect, and a solid twenty-seven mental breakdowns had been required to meet Mr. Faber's (some might call it unreasonably exacting) expectations.

Novice John, the timid boy who had summoned him, wore a much simpler version of the distinguished black cloak, decidedly lacking in the criminal-mastermind flair.

Kallae's sigh deepened as he was forced to abandon his leisurely stroll to the back of the room as several more hands shot up demanding his attention.

"Brother Kallae," began Novice John, eyes wide, "I know the Particulars are important, but Brother Barick said we could start learning about the Crystal Trials. Maybe try for our chronocrystals by the end of the year?"

Kallae's brow arched, the expression both disapproving and slightly amused, like someone who had just been told that a rancid peanut was an appropriate metaphor for the human condition. "Did he now?" Kallae asked. "Do you know what happens if you miscalculate the Particulars when using chronomagic, Novice John?"

"Uh, is it like knowing a knitting pattern but... magical?"

Kallae's lips curled into a sardonic smile. It was so rare, it might've been considered an endangered species. "Oh, very astute. Why don't you go ahead and sew a tapestry of your ignorance? It'll be far more useful than what most of you will achieve in this class."

John's face reddened with an intensity that could be classified as 'alarmingly dramatic' given the context. A ripple of nervous laughter passed through the room, but Kallae wasn't done. Not by a long shot.

"Threadcasting is an art and a science, and you lot are starting with neither. The threads you manipulate have the potential to weave time and reality itself—if only you could muster a modicum of talent."

Kallae muttered under his breath, his eyes scanning the sea of formerly bright-eyed (and now, utterly defeated) students. One might've thought the exhaustion was a result of predicting moon, star, and wind patterns for the entire afternoon—but no. This was the look of people who had completely forgotten what rest even felt like. Kallae wasn't worried about it, though. On the contrary, he promised himself a tall glass of mead at the end of the day in celebration of their collective failure.

He raised a hand. The room groaned in unison, a sound so harmonious it could've been mistaken for a spell itself. Kallae relished the moment, leaning against the wall with an air of dramatic contemplation.

"So, in light of Novice John's spectacular failure," Kallae announced, clapping his hands together for emphasis, "we're going back to the basics! Can anyone tell me what the first principle of threadcasting is?"

Silence hung heavy in the air, thick enough to slice with a knife. Kallae surveyed the room, eyes dancing from one novice to another, feigning exasperation. "Come on, people! This isn't a game of hide and seek! We don't have all day."

John had averted his eyes so severely, they would have rolled out of his head and walked out of the door if the laws of nature did not prevent them from doing so.

"Nothing good," muttered a burly student.

This earned a few brave snickers, which were quickly

silenced in a manner that suggested they hadn't truly existed in the first place.

"A miscalculation of the Particulars makes chronomagic unpredictable."

Kallae walked over to the small boy who had spoken up. Unwilling to spend the minimal amount of energy to actually verbalize the syllables of '*go on*', he instead simply raised his brow.

"If threads are cast without considering the correct celestial alignments, and even factors like weather and terrain, they can become unstable," the student continued, eyes wide. "The desired outcome could be over or under-cast. If under-cast, one might fail at what one was attempting, but over-casting can lead to permanent stasis if warping, or complete draining of chronomagic if flecting."

"And what would happen if your chronomagic is drained?" asked Kallae, his face still expressionless.

The student's eyes flitted from one end of the room to the other, clearly calculating his chances of escaping without anyone noticing. "If a flector over-casts, they might drain their crystal, drawing on their own chronomagic. If that too is drained, a flector will undergo rapid onset aging, their body decays, and they die a gruesome, painful death."

Kallae shrugged, completely unimpressed. "A touch dramatic, but nevertheless true."

He let the silence stretch, a deliciously uncomfortable pause, just because he could. By the time he bothered to break it, the students had begun to fidget, their nerves crackling through the room like a lightning storm trapped in a jar.

Several blue threads hovered behind Kallae's shoulder, the faint undulation of light casting ominous shadows across the poorly lit room. He reached back, effortlessly grabbing one and letting it settle on his palm.

Kallae walked forward, the threads trailing behind

him like a reluctant chorus line. He positioned himself behind the massive oak table, which looked as though it had been designed for someone who thought hosting banquets for a hundred people was just a hobby. Yet, all that sat upon it was a single, lonely green apple. The burlap sack containing two dozen more apples lay discarded on the floor beneath the table, creating a potential tripping hazard that would make the most seasoned acrobat wince. But asking why the apples were there, or why the sack had been discarded with such causal indifference, would likely lead to a conversation about Kallae's mental state that was best left untouched.

Kallae raised both arms, sending his long sleeves into a flurry of motion, before nimbly plucking the apple from the table.

He paused, gathering his thoughts. Then, focusing on the apple, he began to weave threads of energy around it. "Watch closely. I'm going to let this apple decay before your very eyes. It represents the inevitability of failure."

His hands slipped around it, eyes narrowing as he examined the apple, and with a smirk—brief and sharp—he tossed it into the air. A thin band of blue thread wrapped itself around the apple's body. His forefingers made a circular motion, and with each passing second, the thread flickered, becoming unstable under his watchful gaze. Moments later, the structure collapsed in on itself silently, almost anticlimactically. The apple was now nothing more than a pile of seeds and some unidentifiable goo that could probably cause severe food poisoning if anyone was foolish enough to taste it.

"This is what happens when energy is misused," Kallae continued, his voice steady. "But from decay comes the potential for rebirth." He wove a different set of threads, and grabbed ahold of one of the seeds, wrapped the thread around it and reversed the motion of his gesture. He watched with unfettered apathy as it sprouted and grew, until a small sapling had appeared. Its most provocative feature being a blackened leaf to the right of the stem.

The novices, having seen this little stunt a thousand times before, stared at Kallae as if he had just demonstrated how to make a sandwich, not fast-forwarded time itself.

"I'm sick of the sight of these apples," muttered Novice Hari. Clearly, he had misjudged the acoustics of the room for he looked about ready for the floor to open up and swallow him when he realized whispering, like threadcasting, was a skill he had yet to fully master.

The pupils exchanged glances, confusion etched on their faces, coaxing a rare smile from Brother Kallae. He leaned back in his chair, legs crossed, and asked, "Well, wise guy, if you're so sick of apples, tell me this: how did I ensure that the effects of flecting didn't also transfer to me?"

The blank stares were so satisfying, they almost made the entire lesson worth it.

Novice Hari shrugged, looking like he'd rather crawl under a rock. At that precise moment, Novice Pulder's hand shot up, but Kallae ignored it, choosing instead to focus on the nervous wreck in front of him.

Hari shrugged again. "We're Threadcasters," he said, "the crystal fuels life. So even if you accelerate time, it doesn't matter. You're practically immortal."

Kallae sighed, his gaze piercing. "So much of what you said was incorrect that I don't even rightly know where to begin," he said, dropping into his seat and propping his head on his hand. "First off, you are not a Threadcaster. You are a novice. Secondly, although our lifespans are vastly extended by our chronocrystals, that does not make us immortal. Threadcasting can steal enough of your life that even what the crystal grants will no longer compensate for your stupidity."

He let that sink in, then turned back to Hari. "Now, would you like to try answering that question again?"

Hari sighed. "You mitigate the effects of Threadcasting on yourself by knowing the Particulars. Knowing them allows you to shield yourself, but also be susceptible to them, depending on what you want to do."

Kallae raised an eyebrow. "And Novice Hari," he asked, flipping his legs up onto the table, "how do we know the Particulars?"

Hari grumbled, "By studying the alignments of the moons and stars."

Kallae twirled his finger idly, spinning in his chair. "Well then, I suppose you'd better get back to it, shouldn't you?" His tone was half a question, half a command, and all sarcasm. The collective groan from the students was almost musical.

Kallae caught a twitch of movement in the corner of his eye, and his gaze snapped to the hallway. His brow furrowed as he caught a glimpse of Kilie, lingering in the shadows just outside the classroom. His irritation flared instantly. With exaggerated effort, he rose to his feet, waving his hand dismissively at the students, who probably still hadn't figured out that a rhetorical question wasn't a real question. "That might have been phrased as a question," he said, voice as dry as week-old bread, "but I figured, despite your other shortcomings, even you lot could grasp it was rhetorical." He made his way to the back of the room, his feet dragging in a deliberate fashion, and paused at the door. "By the time I return, I want the full set of Particulars for flecting an apple when the yellow moon is waxing and when it's waning," he added, letting the words settle in the air like an unpleasant fog. He left before the inevitable groans could follow.

It seemed every year the novices were worse than the ones who came before them. Out of the two dozen in the room, Kallae judged perhaps five would descend to the Timeless Realm and stand the Crystal Trials within the year. If they were lucky, one of them would become remotely useful. As for the others, it would be a miracle if they underwent the Crystal Trials within the next decade. Why did he even bother? Ah, yes, of course. He had pledged to the Academy, and apparently that meant something. At least that's what Mr. Faber so kindly reminded him of on a bi-weekly basis, in the same tone one might use to inform a small child that they've forgotten their lunch.

Kallae stepped out into the hallway, his expression already weary, his footsteps dragging as though he'd been awake for days. He halted at the threshold, his eyes scanning the shadows. There was no mistaking it—Kilie was there, leaning casually against the wall as though he'd been waiting for far longer than was strictly reasonable.

"Kilie," Kallae muttered, his voice low and annoyed, "what do you want this time? You lurking around in the shadows like some half-wit, do you not have anything better to do?"

"So, I take it it's going well?" asked Kilie, tilting his head, a mischievous glint in his eye.

The other fairy was shorter than him and his hair was several shades lighter than his own. He held himself with the assured confidence of someone who never questioned his position in life. But he was not one of those lucky bastards who had everything handed to him on a silver spoon, his was more of a platinum plated encrusted in diamonds and dusted with gold powder sort of spoon. Despite that, he was one of the most down-to-earth people Kallae knew, and somehow, that made him all the more insufferable.

"About as well as can be expected," Kallae sighed, adjusting his coat as though the weight of the world was resting on his shoulders. "Given this lot have faced about as much adversity as a palace doorknob."

"Well, I trust once you're through with them they will have ample adversity to last them a lifetime."

Kallae shrugged and turned away from his companion, who had casually propped himself beside him, arms spread wide as though he owned the entire hallway. Kilie always did everything—sitting, standing, breathing—with the unshakable certainty that no one would dare question him. It wasn't cockiness, though. More like the ignorance of a man who simply could not entertain the notion of being uncomfortable in his own skin. The idea was as foreign to him as a chicken potpie was to a fish. Kallae, uncomfortable with Kilie's proximity, folded his arms across his chest, the fabric of his coat wrinkling under his grip as if the very cloth disapproved of the situation.

"I heard you had returned from Ethnia," Kilie said softly.

Kallae's jaw tightened, his gaze flickering to some suddenly fascinating point in the distance.

"No time to drop in on an old friend?" Kilie pressed.

Kallae grunted. Kilie, having been well acquainted with Kallae for nigh on half a century was no stranger to the fact that Kallae, was a fairy of few words. And though no fairy, no less a Threadcaster, was overly prone to emotional displays, Kallae showed about as much emotion as a rock.

"Where's Mandrick?" Kilie asked, slinging his arm behind his head in a casual display that was somehow both graceful and utterly annoying. "Did he stay behind in Ethnia?"

"In a manner of speaking."

Kilie fixed him with a quizzical look, which Kallae chose to ignore. Instead, he pushed himself to his feet with a groan. "I really must be getting back to—"

Kilie placed a hand on his shoulder, the touch making Kallae's skin crawl, as though something soft and warm had just pressed against the edge of an icy mountain. Kallae slumped back to the floor, his voice a whisper. "Mandrick did not make it."

"No," Kilie said, his voice dropping to a breathless whisper as his hand fell from Kallae's shoulder. "Cassian?"

Kallae shook his head.

"What happened?" Kilie's voice wavered.

"He was killed by the Ethnians," Kallae said, his voice thick with a strange mixture of rage and resignation. "Just like everyone else."

"But why?"

"Because some people simply should not be taught chronomagic," Kallae snapped, his voice rising as red flooded his cheeks. "The Order should return its attentions to Cyrnghräir. It was a foolish mission. And I was a fool for thinking otherwise." Kallae hung his head, unwilling to meet Kilie's questioning gaze.

An uncomfortable silence hung between them. Outside, rain hammered against the building with relentless fury, as if the heavens were mourning too. Kallae could hear the rising chatter of the novices, who, no doubt, had already started bemoaning their predicament the moment he'd stepped outside.

Kallae sighed. "I trust you did not come here merely to see how I was doing," he muttered. "So, you'd best spit it out before I lose my patience."

Kilie laughed, his corkscrew tresses skimming over his pale eyes as though they couldn't help but join in on his jubilance, despite the somber mood. "I was quite unaware you had any patience to begin with, my friend."

Kallae inhaled sharply but held his tongue.

"I'm sorry," said Kilie softly.

"For what?"

"For Mandrick, for Cassian—all of them."

"Why?" Kallae asked bluntly. "You didn't kill them."

"Very well," Kilie sighed, throwing his hands up. "I do come with news. From Mr. Faber himself, if you would believe it. Though, I'm going to go out on a limb here and say you're not going to like it."

The mention of Faber did nothing to elicit the awe or interest that Kilie had hoped for. If Kallae's chest hadn't been rising and falling with the rhythm of life, Kilie might have wondered if the other fairy had suffered a stroke or been turned into a vegetable by some horrific magical misalignment. But instead Kallae's stare remained as empty and still as the vast emptiness between two stars.

Kilie cleared his throat, attempting to hold onto his grin but losing it halfway. "Anyway. Brother Calder, in Fujikura, has sent word." With that he tossed a thick letter, bound tightly with red string onto Kallae's lap, who flicked through it with as much ceremony as if it were a ream of blank pages.

"What of it?"

Kilie shifted uncomfortably, his eyes narrowing with rare seriousness. "There's not much in it…" He let the words hang in the air like an unfinished puzzle.

Kallae's expression remained stony, but his eyes flickered, just for a moment. "So am I right in assuming this is all just a colossal waste of my time?"

"Mr. Faber has his suspicions. He thinks Caldred—and all the Threadcasters on Fujikura, truth be told—might be in danger. He suspects there's unrest—more than usual—and he's interested in getting to the bottom of it."

Kallae's mouth twisted slightly. He had always thought 'interested' was a little too soft a word for the kind of obsessive fixation Faber had on these things.

"Good for him," he muttered.

Kilie raised an eyebrow. "I take it the notch above your baseline prickliness means you've guessed why I'm here?"

Kallae fixed him with a gaze that could have wilted flowers. His eyes were normally dark—some would say they held the gloom of twilight—but now, even that faint light was missing.

"I am not leaving Cyrnghräir," Kallae said, his voice low and firm. "Never again. I will sail for Carfu as planned. Meet with Lord Gallent Whitmore."

Kilie's jaw tightened, muscles working beneath his

creamy skin like ropes under tension. "Mr. Faber has asked for us personally."

"Well, he might have asked you personally, but my last orders were to go to Carfu. And I intend to follow them. I will not hand another loaded bow to a bunch of infernal savages only to watch as they turn it against us. If Mr. Faber refuses to learn the lessons from Ethnia, I cannot force it down his throat, but so help me Amriel, I will not repeat the same mistake."

"Others can go to Carfu," Kilie said, undeterred, as though he'd not heard a word of Kallae's melodramatic outburst.

"And others can go to Fujikura."

"Mr. Faber will not be pleased."

"I fail to see how that is my problem."

"Kallae, please see reason. If Calder is in danger, we must help him."

Kallae scoffed, his eyes narrowing. "The way I see it, either Mr. Faber is just being a bothersome worrywart, and Calder is, as he himself said, perfectly fine"—he shook the letter for emphasis—"or Faber's suspicions are correct, in which case Calder is as good as dead already. Either way, there's no reason to send more of us to that forsaken island to be butchered by a bunch of savages."

Kilie frowned, leaning in, his voice low but unyielding. "Or perhaps the people there truly are receptive to the Walk of the Threadcasters, to the Way of the Light. Have you considered that?"

Kallae met Kilie's gaze with a cold, unwavering stare. "You weren't in Ethnia. You haven't seen what I have seen."

"The people of Fujikura are not the same."

"They may as well be," Kallae said, his voice a cold whisper.

For a moment neither one spoke. Then Kallae began to laugh. Kilie hesitated, the startling juxtaposition of the sound immiscible with the heavy atmosphere of the hall, but then Kallae's mouth clapped shut with unshakeable resolve. The sound morphed as all the mirth was squeezed from it, till what remained was only a desecration of what it once was, of what it should have been.

"I was a fool for going to Ethnia. Don't make the same mistake I did. Some people simply can't be saved—the people of Fujikura, and those naïve enough to think they can change them. There's no point throwing more lives at a fire that will never be quenched. The fact I managed to escape is a miracle I'll never understand. I'm under no illusions that I could do it again. I will go to Carfu as planned. I bid you a good day, for I doubt you'll have many left if you insist on undertaking this fool's errand."

Kallae began to rise, but Kilie's hand—steady, unyielding—landed on his knee, forcing him back down.

"You know it's the right thing to do," Kilie murmured, his tone both insistent and calm. "Speak with Amriel. He will tell you the same."

Kallae brushed the hand away with a sharp motion, but he could still feel the weight of it long after it was gone. "I bid you a good day," he repeated, more coldly now.

Kilie sighed and rose in one fluid motion. Even though his strides carried him off with swift efficiency, his steps were soundless. As if they too had been bid a good day by Kallae.

As soon as Kilie disappeared around the bend, Kallae's resolve faltered. He slumped to the floor in a heap, collapsing in on himself as his self-pity surged forth. He was so absorbed in his misery that he nearly missed the feather drifting down from the ceiling. Feathers didn't fall from marble slabs. That was a simple fact. But this one—this brilliant ice-blue feather—defied every rule he'd ever known.

He blinked and then blinked again. The feather was gone. Not just the feather—everything. The marble walls, the floors, the door to the classroom—everything vanished, replaced by an overwhelming light. It started gentle, almost soothing, like the warmth of a fire on a cold night, or the soft glow of a firefly caught in the twilight. But it quickly became something else. Something much, much worse.

A light that probed, that searched with no mercy. It sifted through every thought, every word, every secret Kallae had buried deep. He tried to scream, but no sound came. The air around him vibrated with an intensity that drowned everything out.

And then, as if the light itself had decided it was time to break him, he felt it: the burning, searing pain in his shoulders, deep and relentless. He cried out, but his voice was swallowed by the deafening thrum of air. When he looked up, his worst fears were confirmed—his body was not his own anymore. Talons as long as his head sunk deep into his arms, their grip tearing through him like claws in soft fabric. He could feel the ribbons of torment unfurling inside him, growing ever more tangled. The flames flickered around him, feeding on his suffering, but they never wavered.

The bird—a phoenix—was there, cawing with a fury that could have shattered bones. But the blue flames were worse. They burned without reason, without master. They obeyed no voice but their own.

The bird screamed again, a sound that should have broken him, but Kallae held on to something deeper. A quiet desperation, the desire to escape this torment.

He could see his limbs hanging limply by his side, and he knew without even trying, that they would no longer obey his commands. They were no more his own than he could have laid claim to a mountain or the fish of the sea. He shuddered and tried to close his eyes as the phoenix fixed him with a gaze of molten lava, but he could not. Kallae could not be certain if it was simply because he had lost all bodily autonomy, or if his eyelids lay melted in a puddle somewhere beneath him—he found either option was equally as likely and was rather at a loss at deciding which one was preferable.

"What do you want from me?" his voice scratched out, hoarse and shredded.

The phoenix rose higher, breaking through the clouds, sending wisps of mist raining down behind it. Embers of ash, still cloaked in an unearthly glow intermingled with the rain, their fleeting dance entrancing all, until their passionate romance became too much for either of them to bear, leaving them both hollow and entirely ordinary once more.

"Make it stop," Kallae whispered through lips that were cracking with pain. "I can't take it anymore. Someone else. Anyone else. Not me."

The phoenix's gaze was molten, and its voice—low, almost sad—whispered through his mind. *They need you, Kallae.*

"Choose someone else. Please. I cannot do this."

You are not alone, Kallae. The voice carried a strange comfort with it, as though the world had not broken him.

The blue before his vision cleared enough for him to make out an island in the distance. It appeared small at first, no more than a blimp on the map. He rather thought that had he blinked at an inopportune time, they would have flown past it without him noticing at all. But as they flew closer, it grew larger in size. So large that it seemed to take on a pulse of its own. A heartbeat that flushed out darkness and blood with every beat of its ruinous valves. The waves swelled to awesome heights, swallowing everything before it indiscriminately, forging a jagged coastline in its wake. They neared the island, and the beating intensified. The earth began to sing, and at first Kallae was captivated. Her voice was alluring, as clear as a songbird and as haunting as the call of the whales. But then it shattered. Becoming gnarled and filled with discordance it began to scream. And it screamed with the sounds of something ancient. Of something that should have never seen the light of day.

The phoenix dove. Kallae screamed. But his voice was overshadowed by the cries of those that passed them by. The many voices wove into each other, their pain wrapping itself around in such intricate knots that one could never untangle them. Their pain became a person, a shapeless form that overtook the entirety of the land, till not a thread remained free. The tapestry was frayed, and in the center a great fire was coaxed. Its flames flickered, but all around it, faceless figures danced about, chanting, and coaxing it higher and higher. Its hunger grew as the crescendo rose, its tendrils grew greedier, bolder as it consumed more and more of the tapestry.

Kallae felt the heat across his face, he could sense its lust for more. Its undying need for that unattainable more that could never be satisfied.

It must be you Kallae, said the phoenix, *they need you as much as you need them.*

"Amriel, please. Send someone else," Kallae whispered, his words trailing like smoke into the night.

You will not be alone Kallae, came the voice again, as the skies of fire cleared to blue and pink, *you think the world has broken you, but it has not. They will help you remember the light, and then you will show them the truth.*

Kallae squeezed his eyes shut, and when he opened them again, he was back in the hall. The marble walls, pristine and untouched, stood before him as if nothing had happened. His back no longer ached, his side no longer burned. But the weight of what he had seen lingered.

Had Kallae been slightly less absorbed by his own misfortune, he might have avoided accumulating some more. But as it were, he did not, which resulted in him losing his clothes that day as well. For as the feather finally found its destination, it landed on his lap and promptly burst into flames.

"Bloody birds," muttered Kallae.

The memory dissipated as *The Ploughman's Revenge* jolted on a wave, snapping Kallae back to the present. He opened his eyes to find Kilie staring at him, glowing magic strands swirling lazily around his head like he was auditioning for some sort of ethereal shampoo commercial.

"Feeling nostalgic?" Kilie asked.

"Feeling seasick," Kallae corrected. The ship groaned ominously, and Kallae glared at the horizon. "With a generous helping of doomed."

TWO

KALLAE

Kallae was yanked from his reverie by a sudden, unceremonious jolt to the head, courtesy of a particularly enthusiastic wave. *The Ploughman's Revenge* lurched across the water with all the grace of a newborn giraffe attempting ballet. Kallae thrust out a hand, attempting to grip the slick railing as the ship pitched and rolled beneath him. The howling wind whipped his hair into an ungodly mess as he concluded—rather decisively—that this was, indeed, a tropical-level storm. Lucky him.

Battling nausea and the freshly acquired fear of being pitched headfirst into the sea, Kallae clamped his fingers tighter around the railing and screwed his eyes shut. A valiant attempt at denial, one might say—if only it were enough to stave off the gnawing sense of impending disaster. But of course, it wasn't. That was the problem with denial: it was far less effective when someone like Kilie was around.

"You alright?" Kilie's voice barely cut through the howling wind, but Kallae could deduce its content by tone alone. Kilie was certainly not asking if he fancied a round of cards, considering the circumstances. Undeterred by Kallae's lack of response, Kilie repeated his question, this time through a mouthful of seawater, spluttering and coughing in a manner that would have been deeply satisfying—if Kallae weren't clinging to the railing for dear life.

Kallae found it rather disappointing that he could not enjoy the spluttering Kilie, finding the entire scene rather therapeutic, but decided mere amusement was probably not worth risking being tossed over the ship to continue his glee at the depths of the sea.

And before you say don't dismiss something before trying it, I can confirm Kallae was somewhat of an expert in this topic, having been tossed into its depths, not more than a few moon cycles ago- under similar but slightly more sinister circumstances. This time aboard a different, but just as miserable vessel called *the Sea Herder.*

Two Months Earlier: Aboard the Sea Herder

Carfu was not, by any stretch of the imagination, what one might call a "destination city." If anything, it was a collection of people with nowhere better to go and nothing better to do, which didn't so much constitute a city as it did a pile of half-decrepit plywood. If you squinted hard enough, you might be able to imagine a plague-infested rat hole, but even that might be giving Carfu a bit too much credit.

So, naturally, Kallae was excited to be going there.

No, I'm not being facetious. Though Kallae would

probably prefer to deny it, Carfu—despite its seventeen kinds of incurable diseases and pickpockets to boot—was a huge step up from Fujikura. It wasn't paradise, but it wasn't Fujikura, either, and for Kallae, that was all that mattered. He had a special kind of talent for finding the worst places possible to escape the worst circumstances.

The trip to Carfu, however, was proving less than restful. The weight of anticipation pressed down on him, as though the journey had grown impatient and decided to settle in early. Alone with his thoughts—never a place Kallae enjoyed visiting—he attempted to distract himself with the limited diversions available on a ship that had been designed for cargo rather than creature comforts.

Meditation was his first attempt at escape, but it was a failure almost as soon as he closed his eyes. His mind, of course, refused any respite, preferring instead to indulge in its usual chorus of snide commentary and acerbic regrets. Threadcasting, his fallback, was out of the question. His chronocrystal, nestled in his collarbone since his Crystal Trials, was as dull and lifeless as a tavern on judgment day. Its opal color had dulled to grey and refused to be filled despite the many hours spent in the Sanctum of Heron Academy before setting off for Carfu. Opal was considered one of the most powerful attunements, granting Kallae access to the whole host of chronomagic alignments. Though now all it granted him was an uncomfortable bump on his collarbone. Fat lot of good that did for him. And out in the middle of the Sea of Castanon, thousands of nautical miles away from the nearest Sanctum, there was more chance of him laying a golden egg than his crystal recharging.

He retreated to the berth, hoping sleep might offer some form of relief, but the dark, lonely depths of the ship were far more conducive to dark, lonely thoughts. After tossing and turning for an hour, counting all the miscellaneous farm animals he could imagine, he finally drifted into that unsettling space between sleep and lucidity, that hazy void that plagued those with too much on their minds.

At first, he welcomed the silence, preferring the company of darkness to his bleak thoughts. But soon, a light—far too bright, far too harsh—burst into his vision, threatening to scorch Narthor's surface. Now, light could be quite a lovely thing in moderation—without it, I'm sure we wouldn't have gotten very far at all. But this wasn't the delicate light of the morning sun, nor the gentle glow that nurtures life. No, this was the kind of light that unearths long-hidden skeletons—secrets best left undisturbed.

To say his sleep was restful would be a grossly deceptive statement to make. When the choppy waters and raucous shouting woke him just two hours later, he almost felt a sense of gratitude. Expecting chaos, he was mildly surprised to find himself alone, still rocking precariously in one of the ship's hammocks. But before his surprise could settle, the ship gave another jolt, and Kallae found himself flipped upside down and inside out, crashing painfully to the floor.

"I just can't catch a break, can I?" he muttered, pushing himself up on one arm.

Muttering curses under his breath, he crawled to his feet only to be introduced to the walls in rapid succession, as the ship tossed him from one side of the berth to the other. After bruising nearly every square inch of his body, he managed to stumble up to the deck, only to wish he hadn't.

The sight before him was not what he'd hoped for. Storm clouds, dark and bloated, loomed on the horizon, their color so deep that, had it been night, one might have mistaken them for the sky itself. The tides responded in kind, their waves reaching ever higher as they tried to reason with their brethren above. They yelled, their voices reaching their zenith, yet the storm could no longer be reasoned with. No matter how many words were exchanged, how many ultimatums or sweet nothings were whispered, it was too late. All of them, whether kind or filled with anger, fell upon deaf ears.

Kallae shuddered as the wind lashed across the deck, sending a chill deep into his bones. He scanned the deck, puzzled as to why none of his so-called companions had noticed the celestial battle unfolding before them. Of course, that mystery was soon solved—though whether Kallae was better off not knowing the answer was debatable. Answers, you see, were a funny thing. We crave them, but we seldom think about the consequences of actually receiving them.

Sometimes I envy the fools and the drunkards, perhaps they truly are the wisest of us all.

Kallae cast a disdainful look over the scene: five drunken sailors slouched against the mast, sharing the deck with a trio of women who bore more resemblance to overpainted mannequins than anything else. Their garish attempts at makeup had left smears of rouge and smudges of lip stain scattered across their faces with the haphazard charm of a badly assembled jigsaw puzzle.

Finesse was a word that was seldom used in conjunction with sailor, unless it was also accompanied with the word 'lacking', and these water-logged sea rats were no exception. All of them were around three drinks past drunk, and two layers removed from respectably clothed. Kallae might have entertained the thought of intervening, but the raucous laughs and stumbling pawing of the women, soon dissipated any notion of this. His lip curled, and without fully meaning to, his thoughts drifted to Kilie. He wondered for a moment if he had already set sail for Fujikura. A swift jostle of *the Sea Herder* soon vaporized all such reflections, and Kallae continued to stumble along the deck, expending much of his willpower in keeping his stomach from exiting through his mouth.

"Well, if we're aiming for elegance tonight, I'm afraid we missed the mark," Kallae muttered under his breath, casting a scornful glance at the scene.

Before he could take another step, a sailor stumbled toward him with a blissfully ignorant grin, vomited over his boots, and offered him a drink.

"Hard pass," Kallae snapped, his voice dripping with sarcasm. "I'd sooner drink from a mop bucket, thanks."

The sailor, oblivious to the insult, stumbled back to his circle of 'merrymakers', apparently delighted by the spectacle of sloshing ale. Kallae gave his now-soaked boots a final curse and straightened, casting his gaze out to sea. Whatever awaited in Carfu would have to be an improvement—or at least, he hoped, less drunk.

Finding himself entirely bereft of words to accurately convey his disgust, Kallae returned to the berth, where the company of rats and half-starved cats was suddenly far preferable to anyone else aboard. He spent a few moments attempting to get back to sleep, but his efforts were perfunctory at best. If not for fear of another nightmarish encounter with the fiery bird, then for the nauseating pitch of the ship, which had him questioning whether he even knew up from down. He held his arms tightly across his chest—the pressure, though painful, was comforting in some small way.

A sharp whistle ricocheted through the room, uncovering anything ungrounded before leaving again unsatisfied, still hungry for blood. The door was ajar, and Kallae contemplated shutting it but knew the crashing waves could not be stopped by a mere slab of half-rotten wood. No matter how much he pretended otherwise, he couldn't stop the storm.

The scent of the sea, once a familiar comfort, had taken on a sickening quality. It wasn't the clean tang of petrichor but rather the damp fetor of things long forgotten in the depths of the sea. Tonight, they would not be forgotten. Tonight, they would seize their day in the light, whether they were wanted there or not.

Kallae shut his eyes, willing the sounds to go away. But there was no hiding from the roar of the storm. Above him, the cheer of joviality began to morph, to deform into something far more familiar. His hands rose to his ears, pressing so hard that the rush of blood began to echo in his head. But it was not enough to block it out. Not enough to overpower the sound of his name whispered on the wind.

He turned in the hammock but miscalculated and tumbled to the floor. His hip hit the ground painfully, a sharp crack accompanying a bolt of lightning. He cried out, but his voice did not reach anyone; he was alone. The ship tossed like a leaf in the wind, and Kallae felt like he was being torn apart, wondering if that fate would be preferable to this descent into madness.

The murmuring of his name subsided momentarily. It was still there, its taunting voice tunneling its way through his head in places he had never allowed anyone to enter. But it quieted somewhat, seemingly preoccupied with whatever dark secret it had uncovered. In the brief interlude, Kallae could hear the shuffling of feet above him, rhythmic and growing louder. The spirited thumps were soon accompanied by chanting voices. Their chants intensified, breaking through the roar of the storm, which responded with equal vigor. Kallae could not make out what they were saying, but he could feel the weight of their words. They settled around him, oppressive, like a blanket laden with the tears of heartbreak.

He heard a scream and wondered for a moment if it was his own, but it was too distant for that. Too filled with life. His own cries were submissive, more of an apathetic indulgence, for he knew they would do little to change his fate. But this… this was a cry of acceptance. Of sacrifice.

The door burst open with a force that knocked it clear off its hinges. Kallae squinted at the figure that stumbled in—a tall, wiry man with wild eyes and hair slicked with blood. Kallae resisted the urge to ask, already half-aware he didn't care to know. The man moved with frenetic energy, circling Kallae half a dozen times, muttering feverishly and tossing salt haphazardly in his direction. Tears streamed down Kallae's face—not from any spiritual epiphany, but because a good portion of the salt had landed in his eyes.

Kallae observed (with some difficulty, thanks to the salt) as the man ran around the room lighting long rods on fire. Under normal circumstances, Kallae might have objected, finding pyromaniac tendencies somewhat incongruous onboard wooden vessels. But this time, he held his tongue. There was something poetic about burning to death while surrounded on all sides by water. Kallae found himself willing to accept it at this point. He'd had a good run; this was as good a time as any to kick the proverbial bucket.

Unfortunately for Kallae, the long rods turned out to be incense, which soon filled the small room with a cloud of smoke so noxious that Kallae began to wheeze. Without saying a word, the man ran out of the room, his arms gyrating in impossible circles—circles Kallae doubted could be achieved without fully dislocating one's shoulder. Kallae thought it best not to ask.

At this point, the smoke had reached a level that was entirely inconducive to supporting life. Had Kallae possessed even an iota of reason, he would have fled. But as it were, he did not. He merely sat in the corner of the room, trying to avoid being set on fire. Meanwhile, the whispers intensified. He could not make out what they were saying, but that was mostly because he didn't want to. Even without listening, he knew. He knew what they said. He knew what he had been called to do. And yet, he simply did not want to. And by Amriel's beard, he wasn't going to unless he was dragged out of this infernal room, kicking and screaming.

As smoke choked the room, he folded his head into his lap, wondering if he squeezed his legs hard enough, he might simply crush himself out of existence, when someone else came through the door. Kallae recognized him as the Captain of *the Sea Herder*, yet that did not stop him from shouting, "What do you want?" without bothering to raise his head.

"You're a Threadcaster, aren't you?" the Captain asked.

Kallae was forced to abandon his feeble attempts at burying his head in the sand at this question, for it was somewhat of a loaded question. It wasn't anything unusual to assume anyone with even remotely fae-like features was also, by mere association, a Threadcaster, and yet it grated Kallae all the same. It made little difference to him that the assumption, in his case, was entirely accurate.

"And what if I am?"

It was at this point that he finally met the Captain's gaze. Only a moment later, he wished he hadn't. The man's face was covered in a film of sweat so thorough, the entirety of it appeared to gleam as if he represented the next step in the evolutionary march toward becoming a glowworm. The glare was interrupted only by streams of blood dripping down his face, settling around his eyes. Blood had congealed around his eyes, streaking down to his chin in thick rivers. The crimson gleam in his eyes made Kallae's skin crawl.

"We have prayed to our gods," the Captain said, gripping both hands tightly to his exposed chest in what Kallae could only assume was his idea of a reverent pose.

Another wave crashed, sending them both careening into the wall, narrowly dodging a cascade of loose objects.

"Clearly, they're listening," muttered Kallae.

The Captain tried again, "You *are* a Threadcaster?"

Kallae shrugged.

"Do your gods not heed your cry?" The Captain's words were almost swallowed by a crack of thunder that sent shockwaves reverberating through the wood with a sonorous baritone. Kallae half expected a humpback whale to emerge from the depths and answer him.

"It's *God*, singular," Kallae corrected with a sneer.

"Amriel. But let's just say he and I are not exactly on speaking terms at the moment."

The Captain, fear now radiating in pernicious fumes from his very pores, placed both hands on the fairy's shoulders and began to shake him so violently Kallae had to wonder if several of his marbles would be found rolling around the floor for years to come. That was, provided *the Sea Herder*'s floor still existed come the morning (the jury was still very much still out on that one).

Kallae could only tolerate a few moments of this display of desperation, before he raised his own hands in mock salute and muttered, "Alright, alright."

He stood wearily to his feet, having forgotten that it would take approximately three and a half seconds before another wave knocked him off again. "I am indeed from the Order of Threadcasters."

"So, you are a Threadcaster, then—you can save us."

The man's voice carried no hesitation. Even more startlingly, a smile began to tickle the edges of his mouth.

Kallae sighed, the exasperation thick in his voice. "Was, my friend. *Was.*"

The smile vanished.

The hope vanished. "Then surely you still—"

"Does a fish still swim if it's lost its fins?"

"Must your people always speak in riddles! Even in a time such as this?"

A drum half-filled with rum, sloshed across the floor, and had Kallae not had the foresight to jump, would have barreled straight into him.

"This time being?"

The Captain's attempt to form a response died in a splutter, but Kallae cut him off with a reluctant admission, "Alright, I am still a Threadcaster. But my chronocrystal is empty."

Kallae had half a notion to test this notion, but he knew even before his fingers brushed up against his opal that it had not inexplicably filled since last he'd checked.

The Captain's face paled. "Why?"

"That's a very long story—and at the rate this ship is sinking, I'd say we'd both be sleeping with the fishes before I'd even begun telling it."

"Bah!" the man exclaimed, beginning to take his leave, which seemed to be the kick Kallae needed to finally spit out what he'd meant to say, "Because, the Order, and it seems Amriel himself, would have me go to Fujikura."

"And yet you set sail for Carfu with us?"

Kallae hunched his shoulders up again till they very nearly touched the lobes of his ears, "I did not quite fancy going to an island of savages just to be hung up to die. I find if I must die, there are much more enjoyable ways to do so."

"So, you cannot stop this?" The Captain ran a curled finger beneath his eye, leaving a line of red in its wake.

"I suspect I could."

"How?"

Kallae's eyes gleamed darkly. "Throw me overboard."

"What good would that do?"

Kallae shrugged with bitter amusement. "It'd spare you this conversation, for one."

The man scoffed and this time seemed all the more determined to leave Kallae to his own misery.

"I do not intend to mock you."

"And yet that is all you have done."

"Throw me overboard."

"Do not tempt me any more than you already have."

"If it's the only way to make you listen, I'll welcome the plunge," Kallae sneered, eyes gleaming dangerously even in the dim light. Stripped of his connection to the Sanctums, he still felt the power in his blood—a defiance that ran bone-deep.

The Captain hesitated, the weight of Kallae's words pressing down on him, but his gaze stayed stubbornly averted. He shifted his weight uneasily, but no answer came immediately. Finally, he muttered, "What good would that do us?"

Kallae's voice dropped to a low, lethal tone. "This is Amriel's doing."

The Captain's skepticism was clear, but beneath it, there was a tremor of something darker. "How could you know that?"

"Trust me." The words dripped from Kallae's mouth like venom. Even here, in the depths of this damned vessel, cut off from everything he knew, he felt the pull of fate like threads winding around him. Threads he'd rather tear to shreds than follow. "Whatever power I've lost, I'm still a Threadcaster—and that doesn't change easily."

The Captain's eyes hardened, though a sliver of doubt still flickered behind them. "We leave no man behind."

"Do it. Otherwise, I will just toss myself overboard." Kallae's voice was sharp, his tone final.

His voice rang sharp, the finality in it more chilling than any thunder. "Chronomagic won't save you, Captain—not mine, anyway."

Silence swallowed the air between them. The ship creaked again, a low groan that seemed to come from the belly of the world itself. For a long moment, it was just the two of them—two men alone in a universe that had forgotten them. No words. No salvation. Only the howling of the storm outside, the sound of something much bigger than either of them, pulling them under.

The Captain exhaled, long and slow, like a man who had run out of options. He stepped back, his hand slipping from the doorframe as though the very act of turning away was a weight he could no longer carry. There was no anger in his retreat. No relief. Only the quiet acceptance of something that was beyond them both.

Without another word, he disappeared into the shadows, leaving Kallae alone again, suspended in the cold, indifferent silence of the storm. He should have felt something—satisfaction, perhaps. A sense of victory. But instead, there was only a hollow emptiness, a gaping void that even the storm couldn't fill.

And so he stood there, his heart a cold, heavy weight in his chest, the world spinning around him in a blur of shadows and rain, with nothing left to do but wait. The threads were there—pulling, twisting, making their way toward him, wrapping him up in the same tangled mess he had always known. But it didn't matter anymore. Nothing mattered.

THREE

KILIE

The days had begun to blur together like an ill-mixed potion, each sunrise an unremarkable orange disc that was far too cheerful for its own good, relentless in its quest to toast their skin to a crisp. Kilie found himself torn—did he prefer the days when the *Ploughman's Revenge* waddled along on breezy gales toward the elusive Fujikura, or the days when the water lay so uncomfortably warm that he wondered if it was merely an oversized bath? The former at least granted the illusion of destination, something Kilie had half-forgotten; the latter offered a rare and much-needed reprieve from the endless drone of monotony that floated around them like an unwanted guest.

And yet, it was a bittersweet relief, delivered to him by the unyielding hand of hard labor. His arms had always been a tapestry of knotted muscles, a testament to the grueling training of a Threadcaster—a discipline decidedly unfriendly to the faint of heart (and yes, those with any heart conditions were firmly turned away at the door). But now, his black robes had begun to groan in protest, seams straining against his rugged form despite the notable lack of provisions on *the Ploughman's Revenge,* which was luxuriously sparse, like a banquet of air and disappointment.

As for Kallae, true to his nature, he was a walking cloud of misery regardless of the circumstances. When the sun shone, he complained about its unforgiving heat and cursed its certain path. And when the rain came, he muttered under his breath like a disgruntled poet, lamenting the audacity of each droplet as it interrupted his contemplations. What thoughts these were, Kilie could only guess, for it seemed whatever they were, made him only angrier with each passing day. It was a wonder he had not simply become a glowing orb of irritation at this point. Perhaps that would be preferable; at least then they could shove the disagreeable orb into a closet or toss it into the sea, which he would never do, of course—he just thought about it, rather frequently. But if push came to shove, he would not be the one to toss him overboard. But, bribing one of the others to do it on his behalf, why that was still fair game as far as he was concerned.

As the days stretched into weeks, and the provisions dwindled to a sad echo of their former selves, even Kilie's boundless optimism began to wear thin. Neither could remember the last time they had seen the sails flutter, nor even a ripple grace the surface of the water. Its stillness taunted them, beckoning them to drink of its sweet nectar. They once knew it was poison, its words no truer than the song of a mocking jay, yet the truth was beginning to dilate. Where once there was a single destination, a single answer, now it became a soliloquy, a meandering saunter, that grew so convoluted even it could no longer tell what the original intent might have been.

Just yesterday, a man had fallen—his name was Earl,

or perhaps Jahrl (Kilie had never quite caught it)—but the one thing they knew for sure was that he had a fondness for rum. One moment Earl (let's stick with Earl for simplicity's sake, shall we?) was rowing alongside Kilie, and the next, he toppled over, face-first, onto the weevil-infested floor, refusing to be roused. They probably should have suspected as much, for a cracking sound had accompanied his tumble, a sound that made all the right noises to signal 'this is bad' but humans tend to cling to optimism like a shipwrecked sailor to a life raft. Suffice it to say, that idealism wore dangerously thin when Earl was unceremoniously tossed overboard before someone could even murmur a 'goodbye.' Perhaps someone might have objected, but whether their protests melted away in the sweltering heat or the sheer idea of carrying any more dead weight deterred them was a mystery even the infamous Detective Pardegov couldn't solve.

And so they sailed onward. I shan't say with gusto—none of the men (nor the two fairies) had possessed much of that for the better part of a fortnight. They were sailing with all the vigor of a one-winged gull carrying a grand piano, doused in three gallons of oil. It should come as no surprise that the going was slow. There were some vague whispers about an island one of them had been shipwrecked on several years back. A half-hearted discussion followed, and the bearing might have been adjusted, but Kilie could not be certain. Indeed, he was no longer certain whether his foot should be attached to the bottom of his leg, or if it would not be more appropriate to ask it to migrate over to the end of his arm. This occupied his thoughts for several hours, and it is quite possible he asked Kallae for his input as well. He could not quite recall if Kallae had simply declined to answer or feigned selective deafness.

Time was slippery, too. Kilie couldn't tell you how long they had been sailing, nor would he trust himself to hazard a guess; the days had stretched, twisted, and balled themselves into a knot so intricate it was now unrecognizable.

Then, like an answer to a prayer (though not the kind of prayer one would want to repeat in polite company), a voice drifted towards him, meandering lazily like a cloud on a summer's day, so slowly that it was almost a wonder it reached him at all.

"Land ahoy!"

This time, Kilie's ears finally remembered their primary function. He had begun to question the very purpose of his oddly shaped appendages, contemplating their removal no fewer than seven times in the preceding hours.

It took a moment before Kilie's eyes complied, his vision remaining hazy like a lens out of focus. Somewhere, from the depths of his primordial being he rustled up enough strength to prod Kallae. The effort left Kilie panting, and Kallae all but toppled over in his seat. He whirled around (or his best approximation of the movement) and fixed him with a stare that would have had Kilie tossing himself at the mercy of the waves (had there been any, and had he possessed any strength to do so).

Kilie gesticulated widely, his finger trembling, "Look!"

Kallae hesitated, then complied, though his renewed ire suggested he regretted the decision. Before Kallae could unleash a torrent of colorful expletives (and he had a whole arsenal at the ready), Kilie shoved Kallae over and pointed with all the urgency of a child who had just spotted a candy store.

This seemed to do the trick; the harsh lines around Kallae's eyes softened, and he began rubbing the sand and dirt that had conspired to cake his face. I doubt this improved his vision, for the grime clung to him like an unwanted shadow.

Before them, the air shimmered, sending a cascade of motion darting through a riot of colors. If pressed to choose a single hue, none could comply, for it was all and none at the same time—a kaleidoscope bleeding seamlessly into the other. It took them longer than they cared to admit to realize that the ship was moving. Now, this isn't inherently odd; after all, a ship should be moving, but there was no wind (as we've previously established), and while all the men (and fairies) gripped their oars, not one was cutting through the tranquil waters.

Then, *the Ploughman's Revenge* lurched forward as if possessed, the sails billowing and filling with renewed vigor. The ropes creaked; their quiet joy marred by long disuse.

None dared speak, as if doing so might shatter the mirage before them. Shatter the final gift of the earth as it carried them blissfully into her soothing bosom. Several of the men abandoned their post, opting instead to drape themselves over the bow like forgotten laundry. The Captain did not complain; indeed, he was one of the pioneering pieces of laundry.

Kilie was murmuring something to Kallae, neither of them could quite recall what it was, and it is unlikely it was of any import. But suddenly, and entirely without warning, Kallae stood and wandered off to join the other men mid-sentence. Kilie might have been upset by the rude interruption if he had not been so utterly fatigued. Some of the men had begun to dance, and Kallae, as if attached to the same string that flaunted them around the deck, joined them. Kilie was quite at a loss at where they had discovered this newfound well of energy, finding himself rather struggling to keep upright, let alone prance about like a show pony.

He could not say exactly when the mirage began to split. It simply did. It folded in on itself like expensive fabric, forming rivulets of silver that bled into gold and red. At first what lay behind it remained stubbornly hidden, the cloth teasing them with snapshots that gave no more than a glimpse at what lay beyond it. Then the mirage began to shiver and ungulate, as if it had been granted a life of its own.

And then, just like that, it was. Alive, I mean. A woman, dressed head to toe in vibrant red, materialized before them, or perhaps it was more of a hovering situation—think a dramatic entrance with all the flair of a theatrical production. She stood tall, that much Kilie could glean from the distance, but what was truly odd was that he could ascertain rather more than just her height. Adorning her neck was a pearl on a chain that, in all honesty, could have been mistaken for an extravagant accessory from an overly enthusiastic street vendor. It was neither abnormally large nor particularly beautiful, yet it hung from her neck with the weight of a thousand secrets—a burden she seemed either unable or, more likely, unwilling to cast off.

Her hair hung down well past her waist in thick braids, which at first glance were rather impressive, their great heft pointing to something akin to wisdom. But on closer examination, they betrayed something a bit removed from wisdom, something bordering more on mild (if not outright severe) derangement. For they were not merely braided, oh no; they were adorned with a curious assortment of small objects. Even from a distance, Kilie could make out several root vegetables, the tail of what might have been a bat, and no fewer than three frogs. One of them, he was almost certain, had twitched, but he quickly averted his gaze, preferring not to dwell on the possible truth of the matter.

He shook his head, perhaps trying to straighten out his thoughts, though based on the quizzical expression that still remained, this did him little good. The slight look of nausea suggested it actually worsened his condition. Around him, the mood had certainly sweetened, the deck looking more like a dance floor than the soon-to-be graveyard it had been not a moment earlier. Kilie shouted out to Kallae, at least he thought he did, though whether he did or did not is of little matter, for Kallae would not have heard him anyway. His gaze was transfixed on the woman in red, as was everyone else's aboard the now rather erratically faring *Ploughmen's Revenge.*

It did not take Kilie long to discover the reason for their precarious trajectory towards all but certain doom. The Helmsman, a normally quite agreeable chap, was at the wheel, but had rather forgotten what the wheel was for. Instead of using it to navigate, he had decided it was much more preferable to use it as the world's most ill-designed stepping stool.

At this point their path had not only become capricious but positively suicidal. Kilie yelled a half-hearted "Cliffs up ahead!" but he knew before the words had left his mouth that they would go unacknowledged. His voice, alas, fell on enchanted ears, he might as well have yelled *"I am a chicken of the sea!"* for all the sense they had left. The rugged shoreline hurtled towards them at a speed that left his mouth as dry as a desert, despite the humidity soaking through his robes.

His gaze drifted towards the woman, who was no closer than she had been minutes earlier, despite their expeditious pace. She looked much the same as she had when he had first caught a glimpse of her, and yet something about her had changed. She was beautiful, there was no doubt about that (and explained, in part, the moronic expressions of the sailors), and yet the more Kilie looked at her the more he wondered if it was mere cruelty disguised as something less sinister than it was. Her red robes, once fine as silk, clung to her lithe form like a second skin, but now there were frays aplenty, and the antiqued fabric struggled to conceal the shapelessness of what lay beneath.

Her lips, once sensuous and full, twisted into thin, unyielding lines as she chanted. Kilie couldn't decipher the words, but even had they been close enough to hear, he doubted he could unveil their meaning, whether in his tongue or another. Strangely, the winds seemed to respond to the erratic motion of her hands, but he could not be sure. Her fingers beckoned them ever closer, and the ship chugged along without complaint, entirely oblivious, or perhaps uncaring, to the fact that it walked on the cusp of destruction.

Kilie spent far longer than he should have attempting to rouse his companions from their stupor, but it was akin to coaxing a seagull to appreciate the works of Pontiac Cook (one of the finest poets of his time). Having wasted more time than he had to spare, Kilie found himself at somewhat of a loss. He had wrestled with the wheel, and after far more struggle than he had anticipated, given the stupefied grin of the helmsman, he discovered he was an astonishingly poor navigator. Then again, at the speed they were barreling, navigation ranked low on the list of their concerns.

In his mind, he pondered two remaining options. Yell. Which he did, and while he couldn't claim surprise when the Red Lady remained unconvinced by his nonsensical ravings, at least no one could say he hadn't tried. The second option was to hurl everyone—including himself—overboard and pray they weren't gobbled up by a Sea Wyrm (or any number of other delightful sea creatures that I have neither the time nor the inclination to describe).

Just as he was weighing the logistics of this second option, a bird darted past his cheek. Kilie followed its flight until it disappeared into the mist. It took him a moment to realize why he was perplexed; the greater-than-life Red Lady had clearly skewed his perception of reality. The bird, though it was no smaller than your average hawk, hung impossibly still, as if time itself had taken a coffee break.

Kilie's gritted his teeth even as his fingers drifted towards his chronocrystal on his collarbone, "Now?" he murmured under his breath, "with the Sanctum so far away? And the Particulars—" he muttered something about a waxing blue and perhaps pink.

He didn't need an answer to know that was precisely what Amriel intended him to do. "Very well," he sighed. He felt the crystal hum to life, but his mind began to drift, perhaps hoping that losing concentration would free him from this task. Alas, no such luck.

Kilie shut his eyes, and pink light began to shine through his robes. At first, no threads appeared, and he could feel his pulse begin to rise as the ship jolted with increasing frequency. His eyes snapped open, and he was met with the unblinking gaze of the Red Lady. Her chants had reached a pinnacle, or at least he hoped they had, for he rather thought if she moved her mouth any quicker, it would dislocate like some horrific imitation of a python. His hand trembled, and he felt his heart begin to slow as his warping took over his own body. The ship lurched, and his gaze was torn away from the Red Lady. Her voice rose in response, but Kilie barely noticed for the bird had hovered back to the foreground.

Taking a deep breath, Kilie readjusted; the pink moon was waning, along with the blue. He felt his heart return to normal. The pink lines steadied, and threads erupted from his fingertips like horses bursting from the starting gate. Their color was elusive, shifting depending on the time of day, the angle one viewed them, or perhaps the question of whether one had indulged in a morning tea. Kilie's gaze flicked upwards, and he saw the Red Lady's eyes flash. Too far away to see them clearly, but he knew it was true. Her arms began to spin in grander circles, undulating with such energy that Kilie swore they would dislocate any moment now.

Gritting his teeth, he redirected his focus back to the threads, which had grown longer, like they were upset that he had dared to withdraw his attention. He had often found chronomagic had a mind of its own, prone to sulks and dramatic fits of jealousy. Fortunately, this one hadn't yet mastered the art of passive aggression that some of its kin had perfected, so it didn't take long for him to whip it back into submission. His fingers danced faster, quicker still as he shifted some of the chronomagic into blue, using it to amplify his already dexterous motions. Using chronomagic to enhance one's own chronomagic was heavily discouraged by the Order of Threadcasters and could lead to immediate expulsion for novices. Luckily, Kilie hadn't been a novice for decades and was rather content to deal with any potential silent criticism if he managed to escape this situation alive.

It did not take long until the threads began to take on a new form. Gone were the short wisps that had started from his fingertips, replaced with coils of rope which grasped onto the bow of the ship like tentacles. The pink braids flickered, and parts were clearly brighter than others. A bothersome seagull which had sat along the railing and cawed nonsense, landed upon one, defecated and promptly flew away. Kilie would have liked to refine his creation further, but he had long since surrendered his obsession with perfection to the pragmatic realm of reality. Asking one's opponent—or a tsunami—to hold off while he sorted out the alignment of the polar star with the blue moon might sound reasonable on paper but became remarkably unrealistic when a sword (or in this case, an impending rock face) loomed over his shoulder.

So, with as much pomp as if he were playing a game of tug-of-war, he pulled against the rope.

Kilie inhaled deeply; his eyes screwed tightly shut. He did not need them to locate the threads which hovered all around the ship. Smiling to himself, he reached out and grabbed a hold of them. They flickered for a moment, as if deciding whether they wished to remain in this reality or another. Then they relaxed comfortably into his grasp. Kilie thanked them for their trust with a vigorous yank; had they been anything but chronomagic, they would have snapped clean in two. For a moment, nothing happened.

Then the ship lurched so abruptly that, had Kilie not been holding on to the threads, he would have sailed clear over the helm and into the waters below.

The Red Lady's chanting grew louder now, no longer did she whisper sweet nothings, she yelled with the passion of a scorned lover. Her seductive smile having melted into something so sinister, the former could hardly be recalled.

Kilie felt his grip on the threads falter as her voice sent clouds of red tunnelling through his thoughts. The ship dropped a few hairbreadths, and the pink threads began to flicker. Kilie's eyes flared open, and he sought the Red Lady's out with a hunger that could not be quenched. They drifted across the shoreline, and though she fixed her gaze on the horizon, Kilie's own forced her to engage. He felt as the threads bit into his palm, without looking he knew his skin had turned white, which would turn to blue and green come the morning (provided there would be a morning). He did not allow himself to falter now. Could not.

His arms screamed as he yanked the threads backward, throwing his full weight behind him. The motion was so desperate that it seemed as though the ship itself might tip over from his imbalance. He leaned at an angle so precarious it was a miracle he didn't plunge straight into the ocean. The threads, taut and ready to snap, screeched in protest, but for all their danger, they were nothing compared to the agony in his muscles, which felt as if they might tear from their very sockets.

The ship though, still too close to the cliffs for comfort, began to slow. Invigorated by his desperate attempts, Kilie adjusted his grasp and pulled again. His biceps throbbed, and he began to wonder if the air was composed of gaseous acid, for every breath burned. He briefly entertained the notion of not breathing; luckily, his subconscious seized back the decision.

The Red Lady's scream echoed as her form was

violently flung backward. The necklace she wore, gleaming with a strange, otherworldly light, snapped from her neck with a sharp, audible crack. For an instant, time seemed to stretch—her fingers, desperate, reaching for the chain even as it tumbled away from her. The precious necklace spiraled downward, the broken chain trailing behind like a forgotten thread. It vanished into the frothing sea below, lost to the depths with no ceremony, swallowed whole by the ocean.

Kilie watched, eyes wide, as the Red Lady's form became even more distorted, her beauty unraveling in front of him like the necklace that had once adorned her. Her skin, once youthful and smooth, had aged a hundred years in a matter of seconds, her face frozen in an expression that might have been a snarl, or perhaps some deeper, unfathomable expression of despair.

Kilie allowed himself a brief glance at his companions and found, despite the change in scenery, they were just as enraptured by her deranged yelling as they had been by her song. Staring into their dumb and simple expressions, gave Kilie the final burst of energy he needed. He allowed his stance to become slightly less precarious for just a moment, then leaned back in what he hoped was a rather epic fashion, but probably looked more like someone slipping on a banana skin.

The ship, suddenly unburdened by the haunting threads, shifted, tilting toward a safer course. Kilie scrambled across the deck to the wheel, narrowly averting a catastrophe. The ship turned with an eagerness that felt almost human, a relieved shudder of wood and rope as if it, too, had been freed from some unseen weight.

Turning back to the Red Lady, Kilie saw her fixing him with a gaze that might have haunted him for the rest of his life, had he not been so utterly spent. Her eyes glinted with something dark—something deeper than mere anger.

"Fool," she spat, her voice dry and splintered as if it

was made from the very wood of the ship itself. "You do not know what you have done. What you have awoken."

Before he could decide quite what to do, she disappeared just as suddenly as she had arrived. Though rather than an ethereal mirage, it was more of a quiet and rather uninspired *pop*.

Kilie might have given the situation more thought, but his body had reached its limit. The cool, damp wood beneath him was suddenly the most inviting thing in the world, and without hesitation, he collapsed onto it. His robes soaked through with the pervasive chill of the ship's timbers, but Kilie barely noticed. He was drifting, his mind slipping into a sweet oblivion, when the cacophony of voices rose around him.

From his half-dazed position, the sea of heads above him looked odd and amusing. For a moment, he found it the most hilarious sight in the world—so much so that he might have laughed, had he been capable of forming sound.

"What have you done!?" came a ferocious voice—Kilie thought it was the Captain. A glop of spittle flew with the words, and Kilie resisted the urge to bat it away.

"I should rather think, saving your good for nothing backsides. I should think a thank you is in order."

It turned out none of the men could remember what had happened and assumed, upon finding themselves almost impaled on an open rock face, that Kilie had sailed them all to their doom. Though he just about managed to set the record straight before falling into a slumber lasting approximately two whole days, he did not receive so much as a thank you, but rather a begrudging agreement to not have him walk the plank for the unforgivable cruelty of saving their lives.

FOUR

KALLAE

Two Months Earlier: Somewhere in the Middle of the Ocean

They had done it. They had actually tossed him from *the Sea Herder*. Kallae knew he had told them to do so, and yet it still stung, and not just because saltwater was currently infiltrating every one of his orifices.

The waters were so dark it was difficult to see where the waves began and where the sky ended. The bitter cold was as extreme as one would expect for waters as black as these, and Kallae lost all sensation in his limbs almost instantaneously. The storm churned him so thoroughly he had to wonder that he did not turn into a knob of shapeless butter, a fate he found entirely more appealing to his current predicament.

His breaths came out in bursts that were so sharp, it was a toss-up if it was worth it for the meagre reward of continued existence. He did briefly entertain the thought of simply swallowing when a mouthful of water entered his mouth with such ferocity it seemed almost rude to spit it back out. To say he was disappointed when a wave pummeled him from behind, forcibly ejecting the water out of his lungs, would be a vast understatement, on the order of claiming a wheel is an optional component of a carriage.

Kallae realized the only course of action was to surrender. With a final glance at the *Sea Herder*, he propelled himself upward and landed with a firm and satisfying slap on his belly. His legs fought to keep him afloat, that irritating subconscious urge to cling to existence preventing him from sinking to his watery death (not for lack of trying). But Kallae was nothing if not stubborn; he would gladly drag his subconscious kicking and screaming onto the next island if it meant relief from the relentless deluge of the storm. Convincing himself to let his legs lie still was surprisingly difficult, and this despite having had nothing to eat for three days, leaving his muscle mass less diminished and more entirely non-existent. Yet unyielding and vexatious bullheadedness always won out in the end, and this was no exception. At last, Kallae could surrender himself to fate. Perhaps not the one intended for him, but by Amriel's whitened beard, he would sooner accept the dismal one he chose than the one forcefully shoved down his throat with as much finesse as a rhinoceros wielding chopsticks.

No sooner had he welcomed the cool embrace of the frigid water in his lungs than the waters ceased their braying. Kallae just about managed to get out a garbled, "Couldn't even give me this could you?" between violently coughing up lungfuls of biting seawater, which hurt just as much coming up as it had going down.

Despite being a good seventy feet below the deck of *the Sea Herder*, Kallae could still make out the sailors' jubilant cheers, which rapidly morphed into a rhythmic chanting of "Amriel, Amriel, Amriel." Fires flickered to life in various places; whether these were unintentional or some misguided form of worship was unclear. Kallae could not bring himself to do more than mutter (a still garbled), 'go figure' which was so quickly swallowed by a dawdling wave that the only witness was a cowering school of jellyfish- who promptly stung him for his efforts.

The frigid cold was still spreading across his neck and chest when something new caught his attention: a fiery feather drifting lazily through the water. Not sinking, not floating, just sort of existing in its own self-satisfied trajectory, glowing faintly like an ember left over from some celestial barbecue. It shouldn't have been possible, and yet there it was, its edges crackling and popping as if mocking the laws of physics.

Kallae's finely honed survival instincts kicked in immediately: swim away from the flaming anomaly. He backpedaled furiously, the water churning around him in protest. But the feather seemed unimpressed with his display and veered toward him with an alarming level of intent for something so allegedly inanimate.

"Stay away! Shoo! You're not even supposed to be here!" he snapped, thrashing wildly. That's when the feather, with the determination of an angry swan, darted straight into his open mouth.

The heat hit him first, a searing burst that felt like swallowing the sun's misplaced spark, followed closely by a choking sensation as he clawed at his throat. He gagged, he sputtered, he coughed—nothing worked. His attempts to dislodge the damn thing devolved into a full-blown underwater tantrum, complete with wild gesticulations and enough thrashing to stir up a passing school of fish who took one look at him and wisely fled.

But the feather wasn't going anywhere. It burned and

fizzled as if it had become part of him, something he wasn't entirely sure how to feel about just yet. Before he could think further—or, more accurately, panic more—a powerful force grabbed hold of him by the head and yanked him downward.

Kallae barely had time to curse Amriel's name, though it formed vividly in his mind, before he was dragged deeper into the ocean. As his limbs flailed and his vision blurred, he found himself wondering—not for the first time—why this silly thing called fate insisted on adding humiliation to injury at every turn.

He had never been a fan of meandering journeys, finding them a colossal waste of time as a rule, and the pastime of people who were generally an unjustified burden on the rest of society. His disdain for the practice was likely not helped by the fact that Kilie was quite a proponent for random traipses as a way of clearing his mind. The phrase, 'If you clear your mind too much more, you'll have nothing left,' was something that could be heard many a time uttered in the hallways of Heron Academy. This current traipse into the great unknown was doing astoundingly little to change Kallae's mind, who, had he not been so preoccupied with the simple act of not drowning to death, would have been making his displeasure known in quite the ungentlemanly manner.

It was somewhat funny to him that just a mere few feet below the surface there could be so much calm, when above them, a storm had raged not minutes past. At least there would have been calm had Kallae not been thrashing, screaming, and tearing at anything he could get his hands on to with such gusto he was creating somewhat of an underwater vortex.

He was feeling rather proud at how long he had managed to not inhale seawater and promptly drown but found the feeling rather diminished when he finally lost the fight and soon discovered he could now breathe underwater. This wasn't some sort of in-built feature of fairies, nor of Threadcasters (though some passable approximation could be achieved), which left Kallae rather at a loss to what had occurred. He had his theories. Well one theory really. Amriel.

He ceased his thrashing with as little ceremony as he could muster, wanting to preserve the tattered remains of his pride, which now resembled a hundred-year-old linen shirt that had been dipped in acid and then run through a colony of carpenter ants. One couldn't accurately describe the rest of the journey as pleasant, nor was it strictly true to call it uneventful. But compared to how it had begun, perhaps 'uneventful' was indeed an apt description.

The tug that pulled him deeper grew less frantic, allowing Kallae to drift in an almost peaceful manner. Arriving at their final destination was rougher than necessary, as Kallae was tossed into a room with all the subtlety of a sack of garbage flung into a dump.

The room, if one could even call it that, was dark. It appeared akin to marble or perhaps pure obsidian. So reflective was its surface that even the absence of light could not hide his haggard reflection. Kallae might have been more concerned about identifying where he was and why he looked as if he had aged approximately seventy-two years (not that it mattered much relative to the long years of a Threadcaster) had his attention not been monopolized by a glowing orb in the center of the room.

It wasn't so much its size (though it was large) nor its color (it was undefinable), but rather its form. Or perhaps it was the lack of form. For the orb shifted from one thing to another with such speed it was difficult to remember if it had started off as a mountain, or if it in fact had always been a herd of buffalo drinking water by a stream. The buffalo then became a shoal of mackerel, which scattered like a fallen mirror when a shark sliced through their midst. A plume swelled behind the feasting predator becoming a leaping antelope before it could hit the ground. Kallae just about managed to regain his senses and jump to the side as the twin jaws of a crocodile clapped around the animal's hindleg. Before Kallae could process what had happened, the jaws became a book.

The book was held open to some page near the end and a glow even more luminous than the ones that came before it spilled out of it. He could not remember when an elderly man had picked up the volume, or perhaps he had always been holding it. He could not see the man's face, only the long coat which forked at the ends. His hair was grey and short, though decidedly stylish for a man of his age. Kallae could not name an age, only that he was older than Kallae and perhaps older than time itself. His face was hidden, not behind a cloak nor a hood or even a shadow, but merely because he faced away from Kallae. Yet, Kallae knew even if he did turn around, he would not be able to describe the face of the man. It was the type of face that existed only as a memory—one you know you have but can never retrieve, like a photograph you don't want to re-open for fear doing so will fundamentally alter your memory of it.

The old man was thumbing through the book, turning over each page with such care one might have thought the words were printed on the wings of a butterfly. His slender fingers moved with such fluidity that Kallae found it difficult to focus on them; tracking the man's rhythmic pacing proved no easier. The man was slender, not in a way one might mistake for haggard, nor either still the coiled athleticism of the Fae. For the Fae held themselves such that most people found them emphatically unapproachable, which issued forth no shortage of inferiority complexes. But this man was different. It was not that he did not share the Fae's grace, nor their heightened vigor, it was rather that he simply had no need for it. He simply was. And he found no need to hide or augment who he was in any way.

The air swirled around the man, the memory of the orb clinging to the edges. Yet despite his bluish hue, Kallae knew he was real. He knew that if he reached out to touch the man's robes, they would feel just as expensive as they looked beneath his fingertips.

Kallae opened his mouth to say something. What he had planned on saying was lost to the realm of forgotten and unsaid things, for the man interrupted him, and all thoughts left the poor fairy.

"Will you go where I ask?"

The man's back was still toward Kallae, his nose firmly fixed in the book. Had the voice not been so clear, and the room so devoid of sound, Kallae might have wondered if he had spoken at all.

"Do I have a choice?"

"There is always a choice."

Kallae was beginning to grow rather aggravated that the man refused to turn around and had started to edge around the room trying to face him, but found the room, or perhaps the man himself, followed no natural laws of physics. No matter how fast Kallae ran, nor how slowly the other man walked, his back was always towards him.

Kallae panted, feeling ridiculous. "Doesn't feel that way."

"I do not control your perception nor feelings Kallae- only you can do that."

"You know my name?"

"Of course I do."

"Well, it seems only fair you introduce yourself, given that you dragged me here."

"You already know it."

Kallae huffed, and particles of light wavered around him like tiny mocking stars. "I thought you didn't control my feelings."

The man chuckled, and Kallae couldn't tell if it was at him or at something amusing he'd found in that confounded glowing book.

"Truth is not a feeling, little one. You know that."

"I am not little," Kallae growled, though it sounded

more like a petulant whine to his own ears.

The man flickered, his aura swelling until Kallae noticed—disconcertingly—that the room had no ceiling, or perhaps it reached so high that even his sharp eyes couldn't see it.

He opened his mouth to retort, but the air rippled with light, crashing down around him with the weight of a collapsing mountain. His feet left the ground, and suddenly, he was floating—or swimming? No, this was something else entirely, a new and deeply uncomfortable mode of movement he couldn't name but would certainly never recommend.

The light cocooned him, but it wasn't the gentle, nurturing kind. This was the cocoon of a sadistic tailor, shaking its contents like fabric it didn't particularly like. His lungs filled with light, and for a moment, Kallae thought he might burst. He kicked his legs in a frantic, frog-like rhythm, desperate to reach the surface.

When his head finally broke free, he gasped. The waters surged again, dragging him upward into a column that towered higher and higher, the shimmering sides roughening into jagged cliffs. His fingers clawed at the rocky surface, his nails breaking as he fought to hold on. The metallic tang of blood filled his mouth as he bit his tongue in frustration.

The winds screamed around him, tearing at his hair with such ferocity he wondered if he'd be bald by the time this ordeal was over. A jet of flame burst past, grazing his cheek as it streaked into the distance. He swore he heard it whisper, *"Not yet."*

Then the cliff face dissolved. Kallae tumbled forward, landing face-first in dirt that glowed faintly but, unfortunately, still tasted like dirt. He spat it out with a grimace just as the ground cracked open, a thick root nearly lobotomized him before twisting away. He blinked and found himself nestled in the canopy of a massive tree. Another blink, and he was back in the room.

The man was once again off to the edge of the room, his nose still buried in the glowing book, thumbing away as if doing so might reveal to him the very secret of the universe (and perhaps it did).

Kallae wheezed, still on all fours. "You know, there are ways to communicate without mind-shattering visions. You should try them sometime."

"Ah, so you remember me," the man said, not looking up.

Kallae spat out a glob of spittle and hauled himself to his feet. "How could I forget?" he muttered. Then, after a beat, "Not that I haven't tried."

The man tilted his head, his expression unreadable. "Now you see."

"See what?" Kallae demanded, his voice rasping as his heart threatened to punch a hole through his ribcage and make a break for freedom.

"I will never abandon you Kallae."

"I wish you would."

The man didn't respond, but Kallae could feel the weight of his unseen smile. It made him want to swallow a nest of fire ants just to spite him.

"I don't understand," Kallae admitted, his steps unsteady as if he'd just dismounted a galloping horse.

"Some things aren't meant to be understood," the man said. "But even if you don't understand, you know what you must do."

"What if I don't want to?" Kallae snapped, then quieter, "What if I can't?"

"They need you Kallae."

"What, like the people of Ethnia needed me?" His voice cracked under the weight of suppressed fury. "Send someone else."

The man's hum was maddeningly nonchalant. "I have chosen you."

"And what exactly do you expect me to do now that you've sealed me off from the Timeless Realm?"

"I have done no such thing Kallae," said the man softly, "yes," he said firmly, a smile trickling into his voice, "you need them just as much as they need you."

Kallae opened his mouth to argue, the thousand questions clawing at his throat threatening to spill out, but then the man made an odd gesture with his hand—fingers twisting in a way that seemed to defy anatomy.

Kallae froze, his chest seizing. A choking cough wracked his body, doubling him over. He clawed at his throat as something sharp and foreign lodged itself in his windpipe. With a final, heaving retch, he spat out a singed feather that landed at his feet, glowing faintly before disintegrating into ash.

Kallae wiped his mouth, glaring at the man. "Of course, it was bloody you. I should've known. For the love of thread, can you for once just have a conversation like a normal person?"

The man snapped the book shut with an audible *clack,* his expression inscrutable. "Your ride back," he said, ignoring the complaint entirely.

The floor transformed once more, the marble beneath Kallae's feet blazing into red-hot flame. The hues of orange and red merged, then cooled into an icy blue that almost vanished into the air. A deafening *caw* shattered the stillness, and the fire resolved into a magnificent phoenix.

Kallae found himself perched between its flaming wings before he could protest, screaming once again as the fiery creature soared away from the accursed room.

FIVE

KILIE

Kilie woke to the unwelcome sight of Kallae's face hovering above him. It wasn't that Kallae was unpleasant to look at—few among the Fae could claim such misfortune in the genetic lottery—but he had a way of holding his face that suggested he'd either seen unspeakable horrors or was suffering from terminal constipation. Kilie wasn't particularly surprised no one had bothered to move him from the hard wooden deck. Disappointed, maybe, but definitely not surprised. His spine, however, registered several pointed complaints.

"This would have been considerably easier with a seer," Kilie groaned, attempting to stretch out the knots that seemed to have permanently settled in his body.

Kallae's expression soured further, if such a thing was possible. "Then I suggest you take it up with Amriel. I would have much preferred Brother Sinder or even Brother Boster to keep you company. But it turns out I don't get a say in the matter." He made a sweeping, sarcastic gesture.

"You have an opal crystal," muttered Kilie, "you can cast the green seer chronomagic just as well as Boster."

Kallae scoffed. "As well as Boster? That hack gets his predictions wrong half the time. You may as well toss a coin."

"You were the one who suggested Boster!"

"As a hypothetical."

Kilie sighed pointing at the grey crystal shard which sat uselessly on Kallae's collar, "I take it still no luck?"

Kallae shrugged, "By all means, try arguing with the man under the sea, or wherever else he's taking to tormenting me these days. Though I dare say I cannot recommend it."

As Kilie extricated himself from the unforgiving embrace of the deck, a shadow passed over his vision. He glanced up, spotting a bird silhouetted against the sun, far off in the distance. It seemed to hover, fighting some battle against flames only it could see. A smile tugged at his mouth.

"Amriel never disappoints," he murmured, eyes still fixed on the bird.

Kallae regarded him as if he'd suggested they start a swan worshiping cult.

Kilie frowned and pointed towards the bird that still hovered before them. When Kallae's expression did not change, Kilie added, "Do you not see him?"

A huff escaped Kallae as he rose bodily from the floor and disappeared somewhere down in the berths. Kilie thought it better not to prod him further, though it occupied his thoughts for some time thereafter.

The ship had drifted some distance away from the shoreline through a combination of Kilie's earlier efforts, and the tides. Some of the sailors claimed the island itself was pushing them away, but despite their frigid welcome, Kilie did not easily buy into the superstition. Several of the men were lazing on the deck in various states of starvation, fatigue, and general cantankerousness. There was some apathetic talk of what they should do next, but their hearts were not in it. Even the captain, when asked for input, could only manage a vague grunt and a wave in a direction that had no meaning whatsoever.

It was not only that none of them had the energy left to blink let alone think, but more so that they knew they had no choice. They were to return to the island. The island being the one which housed the woman in red who had just tried to drown their entire party with approximately as much remorse as a praying mantis devouring her mate.

"We need supplies," muttered one of the men. At some point in the last hour, he had ripped off his shirt and thrown it overboard. It was difficult to say to what end, for the temperature was not particularly warm nor was clothing a superfluous commodity on board *the Ploughman's Revenge* (not that anything was a superfluous commodity on board *the Ploughman's Revenge*).

Another chimed in, "We need rest." He had, notably, kept his shirt on.

A few heads turned as someone hauled themselves back onto the deck. When they realized it was only Kallae, the interest promptly died, and they slouched back into their various poses of near-death apathy.

Kallae threw himself down beside Kilie without so much as a hand to slow down his descent.

"If you lot are so good at threadcasting, why don't you just magic us straight to Fujikura?" grumbled one of the sailors—Kilie thought his name might be Dan.

Kilie had had his head folded above his knees so could not ascertain who the question had come from, though it did not rightly matter, for he was one of those people who loved having the answer. And the more cryptic the answer could be, the better.

"That is not the way."

"Bah!" (the man probably called) Dan exclaimed,

waving a dismissive hand. "You threadcasters think you're so much better than everyone else just because you can make a gourd grow a little better."

"Not better," murmured Kilie (his head once again buried between his knees), "faster maybe—but not better."

"You want an answer?" interjected Kallae, "you want the **real** answer?"

Some of the men seemed to discover some previously hidden reservoir of energy at this, their faces no longer looking like they had one foot in the grave (maybe just a couple of toes).

"Because magic is a fickle thing, use too much of it, or for the wrong reason and it'll make the Clock tick forward. Become unstable. Blow something up, maybe take a city down with it."

"What clock?" *the Ploughman's Revenge* lurched forward as Dan said this, causing the words to not so much be spoken as fly out of his mouth accompanied by what should have been an anatomically impossible amount of spittle.

"The Clock. The great clockface that separates us from the Timeless Realm," said Kilie, his pale eyes now fixed upon the men before him, "and from our place with Amriel."

Kallae folded his arms, "The Clockturners set the time, day after day they turn the gears, and as they do, chronomagic—"

"They were rebels," Kilie interrupted, head still on his knees, voice laced with disdain. "If they hadn't hungered for power, the Chalidra would still be alive and fulfilling their sacred duty."

"Do you want to tell the story?" Kallae snapped.

Kilie sighed and rested his head back into his folded-up knees, then shrugged.

"Right well, as the Clock turns, chronomagic is released into the Timeless Realm. Portals, called Sancta, in the clockface can be used to recharge our chronocrystals, the chronomagic stored within them can then be used in this realm."

Dan turned to his shirtless companion with a smirk. "See? Nonsense, just like I told you."

"Sure, let's just call it what it is, shall we?" muttered Kallae, "immortality and the ability to control time is pretty overrated."

"Immortality?" one of the men echoed, finally looking a touch interested.

Kallae quirked an eyebrow. "Surprised? Though I suppose anything would surprise a bunch of misinformed halfwits."

"Kallae!" snapped Kilie, elbowing him in the stomach.

"I thought threadcaster immortality was a rumor," someone murmured.

"It's linked to time, isn't it?" Kallae replied, tapping his temple in an exaggeratedly smug manner.

He closed his eyes, apparently attempting some feat of magic, but after a few moments, Kilie raised an eyebrow. The awkward silence grew until Kallae's eyelids almost seemed to twitch from the strain, and finally, he opened his amber eyes with a frustrated grunt.

With a sigh, Kilie reached for the purple crystal on his chest. Ordinarily, he'd go for flair—theatrical gestures were, after all, his specialty—but Kallae already looked murderous, and a little restraint seemed advisable. So, with all the enthusiasm of a child pulling out a lunchbox sandwich, he pulled a few threads from the Timeless Realm.

A few of the men gasped, but most gazed at him as if he really had just pulled out a sandwich out of his lunchbox. It wasn't so much that it wasn't impressive (though it wasn't) nor even that few of them had any energy left to muster any kind of enthusiasm (though they didn't) but more so that chronomagic, though rare, wasn't really anything new to most people. Of course, there are those that only see it a few times in their lifetime, often performed by some street hack in Barncowl Keep or in some other unsavory melting pot of scoundrels. Really, the simple act of pulling a few threads out of the Timeless Realm was almost as impressive as doing a card trick. Sure, it was something, maybe your uncle would feign surprise, or your mother would call you a genius and insist you were 'bound for great things!', but at the end of the day, what good is a glowing tangle of threads if you couldn't do anything more besides toss it around like a particularly uninspired jester?

Kilie did manage to rouse up a little more interest when he stood up and crouched on the floor beside a small burlap sack. He rifled through it for a moment, before reemerging holding a small orange that looked about four days past ripe with a fifty-fifty chance of causing a serious case of food poisoning. He elicited a few shocked expressions when he promptly squeezed the fruit into a rather unappetizing pulp within his fist. He plucked a small seed from the center of the mush, then with a grin offered up the remains to his (rapidly boring) audience, "Can I interest anyone in some freshly squeezed orange juice?"

"Always so dramatic," muttered Kallae.

Kilie, still smiling, wrapped a blue thread around the seed. And then, to the astoundment of everyone—nothing happened. Well other than Kilie looking like a right old ass.

"Can we move this show along?" yelled one of them, who had been lying prone for the entirety of Kilie's performance and seemed in no hurry to remedy the situation.

"Sorry, was I interrupting your appointment with dehydration and starvation? I do humbly apologize," grunted Kilie through pursed lips. But his grimace soon vanished as his hands began drawing outwards. He rearranged the burlap sack, then dropped something in the center of it, tucking the ends around it as if it were a small child needing comforting from the woes of an absentee father figure.

His hands began moving quicker, and without a moment's notice, the threads began to throb, mirroring the patterning on his skin. At first it was unclear whether this had been accidental or not, but when Kilie continued, entirely unbothered by the new predicament, it was assumed this had been an intentional occurrence. He began gesturing upwards, and at first, this looked rather comical, because nothing really happened. If one had merely walked in on the scene with no context, one might have thought Kilie was training to become a mime (and failing rather miserably in this endeavor). But then something green began to emerge from the burlap sack. A glance towards the seed revealed a thin off-shoot of light that was growing bolder with every passing moment. Kilie, now standing, was gesticulating more wildly (far beyond the confines of an acceptable miming box). As he gestured, a tiny green shoot sprouted from the sack, hesitantly poking through like it had serious doubts about this world.

The wind gusted, sending ripples through their flaccid sails, where it drifted down to the small sapling, ripping one of the leaves from the stem.

"That's it?" Dan scoffed. "All that, and your magic can't even grow a tree?"

"Of course it can," answered Kallae.

"So, you mean to tell me you could have magicked us a bunch of fruit this whole time?" demanded Dan.

Kilie opened and shut his mouth, "I—"

"Unbelievable," another sailor sneered, poking the sapling with disdain.

"Can't you just accelerate time a little further, get something useful out of this thing?" asked another.

"What I meant to say," Kilie interjected, a touch defensive, "is that while I *could* grow it into a tree, doing so far from a Sanctum and with what little chronomagic I have left after saving you all from that shipwreck would be foolhardy. Possibly impossible." He gestured to his crystal, which flickered dimly in his hand, a rather pathetic excuse for a glow.

"Well, if you're so short on chronomagic, why put on *this* little display?" asked a balding sailor, eyeing Kilie with a mix of suspicion and irritation.

"I—" Kilie started, but Kallae cut him off with a deadpan, "Because he's an exhibitionist moron. That's why."

Dan, frowning, jabbed a finger at Kilie's chronocrystal, poking it so roughly that the crystal bit into Kilie's collarbone, making him wince. "Then just recharge the darn thing."

"I can't."

"Why not?"

"We are too far away from any Sancta."

Dan turned to the rest of the sailors with a weary, knowing shake of his head. "Always excuses with these people. Who made this blasted clock anyway?"

"Well Amriel of course."

The questions meandered along, as aimless as their crew, until talk of Kilie's failure as an on-demand food larder had run its course, and their imminent consultation with death once again loomed large. Whether it be starvation, thirst, or homicide remained up for debate, though none seemed eager to give it too much thought. And so, they set sail back toward the island. Their tattered charts revealed it had a name: *Lotus Island*—a moniker wholly out of place for a land populated by death traps and volcanic hazards. One sailor muttered about 'another visit from that bountiful lass,' but Kilie, rapidly losing whatever innocence he had left, quashed that notion with a clipped, "Don't wish for things you don't understand."

By some miracle—or sheer force of luck—they arrived without another brush with death (if you excluded the six times they almost smashed into the cliff face). They loaded into the two remaining rowboats—the third having been sacrificed to a sea wyrm—and paddled towards shore. To call the journey arduous would be charitable. Sweat poured down their backs in such abandon that Kilie wondered why none of them had turned into prunes left too long under the Whistling Wastelands sun, then scorched for good measure. Somehow, they made it.

Why they made it, or *what* exactly they'd made it to, was an open question. The island was, in the most technical sense, an island. It was a hunk of rock jutting from the sea, more reminiscent of a mountain that had grown tired of the view and plummeted into the ocean. Their trouble started immediately; upon trying to disembark, they found nothing but jagged boulders to cling to. In their state of near delirium, they could see the island was the size of a modest town, though it was unlikely to hide anything more useful than a few hungry seagulls and a lot of disappointment.

Kallae, naturally, wasted no time in announcing his displeasure. He reminded everyone (loudly, and with all the grace of a cat coughing up a hairball) that he had warned them no good would come of this place. The fact that his being right didn't improve his situation didn't seem to occur to him; it was enough that his superior insight was acknowledged. Kilie, perpetually smiling but with a practiced tact, kept his thoughts to himself—though his silence, as ever, grated on Kallae's nerves.

There were some thoughts of turning around immediately, "No sense risking running into the Red Lady again if all we are to gain from it are some rocks and dead grass." But this notion was quickly overruled, for true as it might be, they saw little sense in not exploring now that they had arrived (it's not like they would avoid potential death by returning to their pillaged ship).

Like the beginning to all horrible tales, they decided to split up. Kilie and Kallae were paired together, but this wasn't so much by choice but rather that everyone wished to avoid Kallae, and Kilie had become somewhat of a pariah since the orange tree incident. The island was, in a word, inhospitable. The question of how the Red Lady survived on this empty water rock came up more than once, but neither could ever come up with an answer that contained any degree of sense. After hours of climbing, slipping, and cursing, their biggest discovery was that some of the rocks were red. Kallae made this discovery firsthand by pressing his palm to one and promptly tumbling from the rock face, clutching his burnt hand as if it were aflame (which it was). They came to the only sensible conclusion that the island was volcanic.

Undeterred, they pressed on—until a sudden blast of steam hurled Kallae from his feet. Being scalded by steam is unpleasant at the best of times; being hit by steam mixed with something viscous and green was three times as awful as anything Kallae could imagine.

Kilie ran a tentative finger across Kallae's cheek, peeling away a sticky green film that clung to his skin like tree sap. "What…is this?" he wondered, lifting it to his nose. But a rancid stench overpowered his curiosity, and he quickly lowered his hand.

Kallae, now on his feet and still attempting to peel the gunk from his robes, grunted, "By all means, let's bottle it, name it, and test it under different environmental conditions."

"Really?" Kilie asked, too absorbed in the slime to notice Kallae's face—now twisted into a gremlin-like scowl.

"No, you cretinous buffoon!" Kallae grabbed hold of Kilie, leaving a thick glob of slime on his shoulder and began tugging him forwards, "last I checked, islands don't shoot slime."

"Curious isn't it," murmured Kilie, stumbling forwards.

"Which leads us to conclude?"

Kilie finally turned towards Kallae and cocked his head not unlike a puppy, "Hmmm?"

"It's not a bloody island!"

It was with this realization that they decided their rapid retreat back to less ornery grounds was most desirable, if not entirely necessary to avoid moving up their appointment with the grim reaper to 'as soon as possible'. The others were informed not so much by a calm retelling by Kilie or Kallae, but more so a garbled screaming of largely unintelligible nonsense as the two of them came barreling down from the cliffs as if their backsides were on fire (a not altogether unlikely scenario in this case).

"Back to the ship!" Kilie managed to yell as he passed by a cluster of men who were standing back-to-back all trying to pull, what appeared to be a small weed, out of the ground with as much force as one would need to separate a rhino from its horn.

Given the amount of concentration this task seemed to require, it was a wonder one of them even had enough processing power left to issue a gruntled, 'give us a second.'

"No second to spare!" Kilie shouted, yanking the poor man by the arm hard enough to nearly dislocate it. The sailor, clutching his shoulder, fell in line without further protest, and so they ran. They ran faster than malnourished, sleep-deprived men ought to run. No one was entirely certain why they were running, and even Kilie and Kallae were beginning to wonder if they'd acted a bit rashly. But there was no turning back, certainly not if the fairies wished to retain the glimmer of respect they still retained (it was not worth much, for the record).

The sight of them—two fairies, a pack of sailors, and a scattering of sticks and possible petrified dung—was miserable at best. But as with all things, it could be worse. And worse it soon became, when the island itself stirred and one sailor was vaporized in a dazzling spray of dust.

Bon voyage indeed.

It turned out the Red Lady, as unhinged as she may have been, had spoken one truth: Kilie did not understand what he'd done. What he had done, in fact, was awaken a dragon from its century-long slumber.

SIX

MR. FABER

Mr. Caligan was a man acquainted with the banal. Yet there was never a day when a customer did not do something so outrageous, he had to thank his lucky stars, that despite his slim prospects, gimp leg, and empty bed, he at least possessed more sense than a good half of his patrons.

Perhaps it sounds hyperbolic to say life in a tavern was ever-changing. Pouring a tankard one day, after all, is hardly different from pouring it the next. True, the clientele varied, but even the most colorful characters—the ones stumbling in with only one shoe or a tongue so loose it defied any loyalty to its owner's mouth—eventually blended into a rainbow of mundanity. And yet, for Mr. Caligan, this was enough. Some live within the narrow margins of the page, never daring to step foot outside well-trod paths. And maybe those are the luckiest people—content with what they have, too settled to dare dream, let alone seek anything beyond.

But Mr. Caligan had one notable exception to this rule: the esteemed Mr. Faber, a man he'd promptly written off as pompous, rude, and wholly unpleasant. Though decades had since passed, it was hard to say if Mr. Caligan had revised this opinion or if their friendship was simply one of those inevitable, begrudging attachments—like a mole discovered on your arm one morning. At first, you scratch at it, curse it, and wish it away. Then, days become weeks, and the mole becomes a minor irritant. Months turn to years, and soon enough, it's simply a part of you. Perhaps this is the most apt way of describing Mr. Caligan and Mr. Faber's friendship. A friendship born out of convenience in the halls of Heron Academy and maintained because of some ill-contrived adherence to the sunken-cost fallacy.

"You're early—by about a week, if memory serves," said Mr. Caligan, absentmindedly swiping the counter with a rag soiled beyond recognition (an action all barkeeps perform, though why is anyone's guess). As it wasn't the scheduled day for Mr. Faber's visit, *the Bedraggled Cockerel* bustled with patrons. Mr. Caligan had been half-heartedly engaged in conversation with a man who seemed to be making an active effort to be dull, his appearance the sole source of intrigue about him. The man resembled a sausage in a casing several sizes too small, stuffed by someone who'd never heard of, let alone seen this delectable dish. To top it off, his hat slumped at an angle usually reserved for either fashionable fascinators or those with a precarious grasp on their sanity.

Mr. Faber entered the establishment with a huff and a sigh and wandered around to his usual table at the end of the tavern. A disapproving '*Hmmmm*' was all it took for the man who had been sitting there to gather up his things and scramble out the door without so much as a second's delay. It was difficult to say if this was because the fairy recognized him as the Leader of the Threadcasters and by extension the Headmaster of Heron Academy or if his mere presence had been distressing enough to want nothing more than to vacate the premises, having consumed no more than two sips of his drink and a mouthful of pie.

"Your memory has always been questionable," muttered Mr. Faber, throwing his heavy cloak over a chair before sauntering behind the bar to pour himself a pitcher of mead.

"By all means, make yourself at home," said Mr. Caligan, tossing the rag aside.

The sausage-man, meanwhile, had moved the conversation to the topic of turnips, interrupting himself (for no one else was listening) to inquire if he might also have a refill. Mr. Caligan grunted, sliding the half-empty bottle his way. "Help yourself. Apparently, that's the kind of establishment I run now."

"Well, if you knew the meaning of service, perhaps I would not find a need to," retorted Mr. Faber.

"Bah!" Mr. Caligan glowered, mock-raising his own glass. "A pleasure as always, my dear friend. Now, what great service have I rendered to deserve your prickly face this fine evening?"

Mr. Faber returned to the round table which had acquired a few new dents since last he'd visited. And by dents I don't so much mean small divots that could be attributed to a dropped carafe or a fallen glass, no these were the deep marks of a knife, or perhaps the talons of a gryphon. In *the Bedraggled Cockrel* both of these options were equally likely, making it a slightly tamer establishment than its neighboring *Prancing Cockroach*, whose most regular visitors were the ogres of the Verbotene Mountains who had the unfortunate habit of slamming their great incisors into the table whenever they were angry (or sad, which accounted for most other occasions).

"I do have a bouncy new lass that I'm sure could knock that frown off your face and then some," said Mr. Caligan with a smile as he poured himself a hefty tankard of ale and sat down beside the other fairy. Most of the other patrons had followed suit after the startled fairy, the intimidating presence of Mr. Faber having largely sullied the atmosphere for the foreseeable future. Though, the man, whose primary qualifier had been his terrible dullness, could now add to his list of attributes, social skills so poor he made Lianthorn (the Lord of the Light Fae) look positively jovial in comparison. Despite Mr. Faber's most intimidating look, the man was rather content with where he was, and seemed to be half considering joining the two fairies at their table (a venture that would no doubt end in blood, sweat, and no small helping of tears), leaving the two fairies to conclude that the man must not only be terribly dull, and socially inept, but also lacking most generally in any degree of sense. They decided to ignore him. Which really, was the only sensible way of dealing with idiots, for any other option made one somewhat idiotic oneself by mere association.

"You ask every time. Have I ever given a different answer?" Mr. Faber replied, waving the offer away.

Mr. Caligan shrugged, downing a third of his pint. "Suit yourself. Only Amriel knows why you Black Cloaks make things so miserable for yourselves."

"If he doesn't want her, can I have a round with her?" piped up the sausage-man.

The two fairies exchanged a look. Without a word, they rose, each taking one of his armpits, and threw him out the door as though emptying a chamber pot—a common occurrence in Barncowl Keep, making it a thriving destination for rats and the more than occasional outbreak of the plague.

The door thudded shut behind him, muffling his incoherent curses. Mr. Caligan slapped a 'We're Closed' sign into place and collapsed into his armchair, which emitted a creak so loud Mr. Faber flinched (an unusually passionate response for the Headmaster, a fairy for whom 'showing emotion' typically involved judgmental sighs and a brand of narcissism verging on clinical).

"It's for Amriel that we do it—to avoid all other distractions," said Mr. Faber, as though that explained everything.

"Do what?"

"Never mind," said Mr. Faber who sighed so dejectedly one had to wonder if Mr. Caligan had not just killed his favorite pet or insulted his mother.

Having finally remembered the topic at hand, Mr. Caligan added, "And yet Amriel does not ask it of you."

"That is the way of the Order. For better or worse. He doesn't call everyone to it. But it's my path, and I'll follow it with the strength he gives me."

With no further insights to add, Mr. Caligan drained his glass, producing an impressive belch. "So, why are you here?"

In response, Mr. Faber downed the rest of his mead, then fetched two bottles of rum. "Tumblers are under the sink," Mr. Caligan called after him, already refilling his own pint.

"Things going that great, huh?" Mr. Caligan asked as Mr. Faber returned, nursing the top of a tumbler.

"Hmmm," grunted Mr. Faber, withdrawing a small object from his cloak—a key, spinning it restlessly in his fingers.

The uncanny scream of a prowling fox drifted in through the gaps in the brick wall, going largely unnoticed by the both of them. The sound began to morph into a soliloquy that seemed to contain a great sorrow which neither could understand, and quickly morphed into the spurned yelps of unrequited love.

"More Brothers have been taken," said Mr. Faber, tying his long hair into a loose tail.

"From Fujikura?"

"No," replied Mr. Faber, his tone weary as though Mr. Caligan should know better. "From here, from Heron Academy. From among our own Brothers."

"Are you sure they've been taken? Have you any proof?"

"No," sighed Mr. Faber, "it's just a feeling I have. I know these men, they would never leave the Order," he scoffed darkly, "not willingly anyway."

The two sat in silence, a thick, syrupy quiet broken only by Mr. Faber's twitching fingers. He stopped suddenly, poured himself another rum, and downed it. His hand shook, though it was unclear whether from drink or emotion finally breaching its iron cage.

With a sigh that seemed too small of a sound to fully encapsulate just how wearisome he found the entire ordeal, Mr. Faber slammed a letter onto the table. Why Mr. Faber always found it necessary to slam items onto surfaces with no explanation is likely something that would require at least three sessions with a professional therapist, and a delving into his childhood that I'm sure would render the poor fairy catatonic for days.

When the fairy finally deigned to remove his palm from the letter, his compatriot saw that it was addressed to Heron Academy.

"I broke into Sadhrin's chambers."

"Of course, you did," replied Mr. Caligan, stealing a sip from his glass. "And this?"

"A letter."

"I can see that, thank you," muttered the Barkeep, "but what does the letter entail?"

"It's a letter from Calder."

"Another one? I am surprised another could have arrived so quickly."

Mr. Faber tapped the letter's salt-stained edge. "The original one."

Realization dawned on Mr. Caligan. "So, the other truly was a forgery?"

"I daresay they all were," corrected Mr. Faber, "at least for some time. I found a stack of these in Sadhrin's office," he patted the top of the letter with the palm of his hand.

"So, what does it say?"

"Frenick has been taken captive, Klaus has been missing for weeks—" Mr. Faber's voice hissed through his pursed lips, the warm air congealing with the coolness of the night, "the Fujikuran Empire has declared all practice of threadcasting punishable by death and ordered a complete rescindment of any former agreements we've had with them. Calder first sent word of this at the eclipse of the blue and yellow moon. Sadhrin has been covering this up for years."

"Thunderation," murmured Mr. Caligan.

"Thunderation indeed."

"But what reason would Sadhrin have for hiding this from you?"

"I do not know," said the fairy, "but I intend to find out." He frowned and then released a sigh that bordered on a groan, "Tarnation!" he exclaimed suddenly, "that woman should have never been allowed to join the Order!"

"I said as much last we met."

"And yet there's nothing I can do about it."

"So, you've said."

"There's a reason women aren't allowed admission into the Order."

"Oh?" Mr. Caligan pressed the lip of his glass against his mouth, his eyebrow arched so high it was in danger of taking flight.

"For exactly this reason."

"This reason being that this particular woman seems to defy you at every turn and has seemingly made it her life's mission to undermine you wherever possible?" Mr. Caligan asked, taking an exaggerated sip from his drink, relishing the opportunity to poke at Mr. Faber's sense of infallibility.

"Precisely," Mr. Faber responded, with a tone that suggested he hadn't realized he'd just walked into a trap.

"Why, that's rather presumptuous of you isn't it."

"What is?" Mr. Faber poured himself another tall glass of mead, the liquid sloshing precariously close to the edge as though matching his rising tension.

"That her poor qualities are a result of her being a woman, and not just a result of her being—well—an utter menace to society in general." Mr. Caligan's lips curled into a smirk as he leaned back in his chair.

"I suppose."

The barkeep let out a laugh so hearty it could've been bottled and sold as a cure for melancholia. "I dare say that's the nicest thing you've ever said to me." His smile faltered, though, as reality nudged its way back into the room. "I take it there's no way of reaching Kilie and Kallae?"

Mr. Faber hung his head, his long fingers curling into his temple as if he might wrestle an answer from his own mind. After a moment, he nodded.

Mr. Caligan shut his eyes, the weight of the moment settling across his features like a heavy shroud. "May Amriel protect them," he murmured.

SEVEN 七

AKIRA

"Kote!" shouted Akira, lunging forward with all the ferocity of a woman wronged, her wooden sword slicing the air in a dramatic arc before missing its target entirely. The target in question—a being so infuriatingly smug that his mere existence was a personal affront—responded with an insufferable smirk.

Ryū Shirai. The very name conjured an image of arrogant confidence, and not by coincidence. Ryū ensured everyone knew what his name meant. 'White dragon,' he'd say, as if it were the most original thing anyone had ever heard. Or 'white noble,' depending on his particular mood. He shared this fact indiscriminately, whether you asked or not. Usually not.

His cropped grey hair didn't help his case. It stood out like a sore thumb in a clan that demanded long, disciplined buns. He claimed the short cut reduced air resistance. Akira suspected it was just rebellion for rebellion's sake. The stark greyness, however, was a mystery, since he was hardly old enough to warrant it. He never revealed whether it was the result of alchemical experimentation or sheer stubborn will.

At least some of Ryū's uniform could be considered standard issue, or at least could reasonably pass as such. They all wore wide-legged trousers, which flowed with such a degree of liberty at certain angles they could almost pass for a skirt, which proved a good, and debatably necessary distraction from their curious choice of footwear. In Fujikura, rather than the clunky boot or slightly more refined riding shoe, they were most often found sporting sandals. Now this in itself would not be considered an oddity, beyond the fact that though an efficient leather saving approach, they did not offer up a whole lot in terms of protection nor support of any kind. But this curious choice was made only curiouser by their insistence on wearing socks, which, though not an uncommon practice, gave off a distinct hint of heightening derangement when paired with the aforementioned sandals, which split the bone-white socks clean down the middle, in a way that could only be described as fashionable by one who had never heard of the word before, and indeed could not be trusted to comprehend anything beyond the notion of mere continued existence.

Their upper attire was considerably less offensive and consisted primarily of tunics which were folded quite pleasingly at a diagonal across their chests. While most wore rather innocuous colors, an off-white, a black, or perhaps a more daring grey, there were two notable exceptions to this rule. Shoji, who alternated colors every day, the only requirement being that the shade was more garish than the one which preceded it. Today they were all being subjected to a dip-dyed abomination that was a headache inducing combination of bright pink and khaki brown.

Today, Ryū was shirtless. Of course he was shirtless.

Despite Fujikura's decidedly non-tropical climate, his torso gleamed in the dim dojo light as if daring someone to comment. No one did, though Shoji had nearly choked on his rice trying not to laugh earlier.

Akira, meanwhile, adjusted her tunic—a sensible off-white, unlike Ryū's bare chest or Shoji's kaleidoscopic wardrobe. She'd tied her dark hair into a ponytail with a red band, and her pale eyes glinted with a mix of annoyance and determination. She hated fighting Ryū. Not because he was good—though he was—but because he knew it. And worse, he made it look easy. Every time he dodged a strike or landed one of his own, he wore an expression of faint boredom, like sparring with her was just a particularly tedious chore.

Ryū leaned back at an angle that defied the laws of anatomy, narrowly avoiding another of her strikes.

"Kote!" yelled Ryū, his voice coming out at an octave so deep it was a wonder whales didn't breach and come looking for their lost offspring. The heavy wooden sword hit Akira's side with a dull thud, and she gritted her teeth in response.

"Oi oi," said Ryū as he spun the sword in a lazy circle, "why the long face?"

Shoji whinnied from the other end of the room, which cost him a strike to the wrist by Jun. Though Shoji either did not care or had not fully come to grips with the general concept of the spar, both of which were equally likely scenarios.

Akira shifted her weight onto the balls of her feet, the hilt of her sword pressing heavily into her palms. She glared at Ryū, who was now leaning casually on his weapon, looking for all the world like a man waiting for tea to be served. Her scowl deepened as he chuckled softly.

With a sharp cry of "Tsuki!" Akira darted forward, feinting to one side before ducking low to the left. For a moment, she thought she had him. But Ryū, in all his maddening agility, slipped just out of reach. She muttered a low, venomous "Chikusho," the curse barely audible over her heavy breathing.

Ryū, ever the gentleman, winked at her.

Sweat pooled into her eyes, and as she shook her head, beads dripped down from her bangs, like the gems of a tiara forged in the great mining fortresses of Iselion. She was just repositioning her legs beneath her when something hit her on her opposite wrist with a resounding clank. She swore.

"Arigato gozaimashita," said Ryū, having straightened himself back up to his full height. When Akira repaid him only with a glare and another huffed, "chikusho," he folded himself deeply at the waist.

"Good match."

"It was supposed to be a one-sword match," she muttered, returning her practice blade to its rack.

Ryū shrugged, "I decided it was a two-sword match."

"You can't just change the rules mid-way through a game."

"Says who?"

"Says basic decency," Akira snapped. "Which, in case you're wondering, is a thing most people have."

"Oi, oi, no need to get testy there, princess."

"I'm not a princess," she shot back, her voice sharp.

"You're the daughter of a Daimyo," said Ryū, "in my book, that's basically a princess."

Akira opened her mouth to retort, thought better of it, and opted instead for a frustrated growl. She balled her fists, glaring at him with enough intensity to make lesser men reconsider their life choices. Ryū, unfortunately, was not a lesser man.

Meanwhile, Shoji and Jun's sparring match had dissolved into chaos. Shoji, ever the strategist, had spent most of the fight eating a bowl of rice, his sword held in his free hand like an afterthought. Jun, visibly exasperated, had landed several strikes, none of which seemed to register with Shoji, who only muttered a cheerful "Chikusho" between bites.

When Jun finally declared himself the victor, Shoji applauded Ryū and Akira instead. "As always," he crowed, "Ryū might have won the battle, but Akira's won the war."

Ryū ignored him. "Oi, oi," he said to Akira. "No need to sulk. You fought well."

"You're awfully smug for someone who had to change the rules to beat someone half his size," Akira muttered. "Congratulations. Truly. A proud moment for any warrior."

Shoji whistled, then clapped his hands. "Well said, Akira!"

Jun, ever the voice of reason—or at least critique—stepped forward. "Ryū," he began, "your left hand is still lagging behind. If you're going to fight two-sword style—"

"Three-sword style," Ryū corrected with a grin.

"Fine. *Three*-sword style. But unless you plan on carrying a third sword at all times, you'll need to refine your technique. Surprises don't work twice."

Akira smirked as Jun turned to her. "You feinted too late," he said. "In a real fight, hesitation will cost you. Never assume your opponent will fight honorably."

"That," said Akira, "is the first thing you've said today that I agree with."

"And Shoji," Jun began, his tone heavy with resignation, "I don't even know where to start with you."

Shoji grinned, entirely unbothered. "Start with dessert," he said, holding up an empty rice bowl. "I'm starving."

"Do you think you could bring yourself to pretend, just for a moment, that you care about anything besides food?" muttered Jun.

"No problem, boss," said Shoji, finishing the last few grains of rice with a decisive snap of his chopsticks.

"I'm not your boss."

"Sorry boss."

Jun sighed, a sound so practiced it felt less like an expression of frustration and more like an art form.

Jun had a particular talent for being the type of person who made reasonable people consider whether tossing someone out on their backside was a valid life choice. The only thing stopping them, as cruel irony would have it, was the infuriating fact that Jun was usually right. Sure, he wouldn't win a battle of strength (unless his opponent was too distracted by a bowl of rice), but a battle of wits? Well, Ryū had abs of steel, but Jun? Jun had a mind forged in the molten pits of Trevnesia, sharpened on Amriel's high sword, and polished daily by at least one hundred metaphorical pixies.

In short: he was very, very smart.

Not that it helped him socially. Jun's intelligence had a peculiar side effect—it made him the conversational equivalent of a poorly timed sneeze. People avoided him as if he were an unpleasant smell, or perhaps someone prone to discussing the origins of advanced calculus at a casual lunch. This eccentricity, however, was why he remained fiercely loyal to Jiro. Jiro's ragtag group tolerated him, which was significantly more than anyone else had managed in Jun's life.

Shoji, on the other hand, was a human—but barely. Despite his mortality, he could easily be mistaken for a Yōsei. The Yōsei, cousins to the Fae, were almost human, if you squinted and ignored the pointed ears, lighter complexions, and irritating superiority complexes. They lived a little longer (about 150 years, if they weren't stabbed or starved), and their magic aligned with the Way of the Water—a type of paper-folding sorcery that might sound adorable but could kill you faster than Shoji could empty a rice bowl.

Shoji, though, was a liability in nearly everything except eating. Even now, he was heading out for a rice refill when he careened directly into Kyou.

Kyou was tall, sharp-featured, and as severe as a tax audit. Half his hair was tied in a bun so tight it probably interfered with brain function, while the other half hung in such perfectly straight strands it seemed immune to the laws of physics.

Shoji brushed himself off, winked, and struck a mock battle pose before skipping out of the room, humming a tune audible only to him—or perhaps the clinically insane. Seconds later, a crash echoed through the dojo, followed by what might have been curses or an impromptu vegetable shopping list. Everyone decided it was better to ignore it.

"Kyou," said Akira tightly, her clenched teeth betraying the restraint it took to remain civil, "nice of you to join us."

Kyou shrugged and began wandering the room, his fingers brushing the gleaming tamahagane steel of the katanas. He inspected his hand, disappointed, then dropped it against his thigh. It seemed Kyou was searching for something to criticize and, failing that, decided to criticize the air instead.

"I take it something is not to your liking," Akira had turned around to break the other Yōsei's path.

"Why do you assume that?"

"Am I wrong?"

Kyou's shrug was noncommittal. "So, are we sparring, or are we going to braid each other's hair like geishas?"

Ryū stiffened, his sneer sharp enough to cut glass. He might have lunged at Kyou right then and there if Shoji hadn't reappeared, balancing a bowl so overflowing with rice and fish it looked like he'd stolen dinner from an entire village.

"If you'd bothered to show up on time, you wouldn't be disappointed," Akira shot back.

Kyou smirked, his handsome face twisting into something decidedly less so. "I'm surprised you haven't challenged me yet. You usually do the moment I walk into a room."

"I didn't say I wouldn't fight you," Akira replied, her voice low and dangerous.

"Nor did you say you would," Kyou retorted. "All I've heard are excuses. Which, to be fair—"

Akira snatched a wooden practice sword from the rack, the heavy blade smacking against her thigh. "You need only ask."

Kyou grinned, the challenge lighting up his eyes. "This is no game for children. If we fight, we fight for real." He unhooked a katana from the wall and tossed it at her. She caught it midair, testing its weight with practiced ease.

"You've always been prone to savagery," she hissed, gripping the blade.

She shoved the wooden sword at Ryū without looking. "No problem," he muttered sarcastically. "Glad I could live out my dream of becoming a coat rack."

The two Yōsei walked to the center of the dojo, their matching sandals sinking deep into the padded floor, as if it could sense the heaviness of the room.

"Jiro said to stick to practice swords unless he's around," Jun called from the sidelines, his legs crossed and his expression exasperated.

Kyou didn't even glance his way. "And here I thought you'd finally outgrown that leash your mother tied around your neck, Jun."

Jun flinched. The glow of green light flickered along his veins, seeping from the crystal embedded in his collar. Shoji froze mid-bite, then lunged for Jun's arm. He caught him just as the glow began to pulse, and the light dimmed to nothing.

"Fools," yelled Kyou, his face now so distorted it had become red and twisted, "it is only a matter of time before the Inquisitor finds you and kills you all. Is it really worth risking your lives just so you can play around with a colored thread? And what exactly were you planning on doing Jun? Predict the weather for tomorrow? Hoping that a forecast of rain would render me catatonic?"

Shoji still held an iron grip on Jun's wrist as Kyou lunged towards Akira. Akira ducked just in time, her blade sailing through the air like a school of flying fish rushing for safety. Kyou danced back a few steps; his feet so light there was barely an indent in the mats. While Kyou swung his katana in an easy arc, Akira swung out of the way, biting her tongue in the process. She pursed her mouth as the familiar taste of metal and battle settled onto her tongue.

He turned to Akira, his katana slicing through the air in a deadly arc. "Tell me, Akira, when will you stop punishing me for something that happened over two decades ago?"

"When I no longer need to see your stupid face," she said losing her stance, her knee jarring painfully to the side. She swore under her breath but kept her eye on the prize. The prize in this case being Kyou. So not really much of a prize really.

"You could have taken me with you," Akira hissed between strikes. "You didn't have to betray everything Jiro stands for."

Akira twisted away from the other Yōsei, winning approximately three hairbreadths in distance as a reward. She sent her one-sided sword reeling towards Kyou who broke its path with his own. It was difficult to say whether the sound of clattering metal, or the burn of tensing muscles was more acute. Akira placed both hands on her sword, holding it in front of her like a barricade across her chest to ward off Kyou's barrage. The two locked eyes, Kyou's pale ones reflected back at her like the moonless night.

"You know, father was never the same after you left us," her sword clattered against Kyou's, "never saw mother's cruelty—never saw what she—" the words stuck in her throat.

"I was a kid, Akira!" Kyou shouted, his voice cracking under the weight of old guilt. "I didn't know what else to do."

Kyou lowered his sword, his breath still ragged. "I'm sorry—for what it's worth."
"Keep your apologies. I don't need them."

The room seemed to hold its breath as their wills clashed, two immovable mountains daring the other to blink first. And then—without warning—it ended.

A slip. A misstep. Akira had him.

Her knees pinned Kyou's chest as her fists came down in a fury so relentless, they blurred.

Shoji, meanwhile, had been thoroughly engrossed in the far weightier matter of whether tonight's dinner would feature salmon or chicken. It was only when the sounds of the fight began to rival the grumbling in his stomach that he stirred from his culinary deliberation.

"Enough!" he bellowed, with all the ferocity of a man whose meal has just been stolen—or whose world has abruptly ended.

"He deserves it," Akira grunted, her fists still poised to strike.

Kyou, meanwhile, was as still as a corpse. Shoji, ever the pragmatist, briefly considered checking for a pulse. But then he saw it—that grin. So smug. So obnoxious. Shoji nearly let Akira finish what she'd started.

"Enough."

The voice that followed wasn't loud, but it cut through the chaos like a knife. It was the sort of voice that didn't need volume to command. It spoke with the quiet authority of a mountain, unmoving and insurmountable.

Shoji, startled, scrambled to his feet and turned, nearly tripping over himself in an attempt to bow. The effort was—if one were feeling generous—about as graceful as a flock of pigeons attempting synchronized tap-dancing.

There stood Jiro.

At a glance, he was unremarkable: slightly taller than

average but in no way imposing, his dark hair utterly unextraordinary beside Akira's jet-black. His build was lean, honed, but not ostentatiously muscular. His attire, though well-fitted, was so plain it bordered on forgettable. Yet the room bent around him, as if his mere presence reordered its priorities.

"Enough," he repeated, this time softer but no less final. He crouched, fingers brushing the floor as threads of pink light began pooling at his fingertips. The resulting weave was not elegant—these things rarely were—but what it lacked in finesse, it made up for in inevitability.

Jiro cast the threads outward. They coiled through the air like living things, snapping around Kyou and Akira, trapping them in an incandescent net.

Silence fell. The kind of silence that feels alive, that hums with the weight of words unsaid. Akira stopped—though 'stopped' might suggest she had a choice in the matter. She was frozen, mid-motion, as if time itself had forgotten about her.

Jiro crushed the thread between his fingers, and it oozed back into the earth, dissolving as though it had never been.

"Get up," he said.

The pair scrambled to their feet with the urgency of marionettes whose strings had been yanked—awkward, jerky, and decidedly unimpressive.

Akira bowed deeply, her forehead nearly grazing her knees. Whether this was a show of respect or simply her body giving up under its own weight was debatable. Kyou, not to be outdone, bowed so low his knotted torso seemed in danger of snapping in two. "Gomenasai," he mumbled, his dark eyes disappearing into shadow. "I meant no disrespect to you, Jiro-sama."

Jiro's expression didn't so much as flicker. "And yet, here we are. Perhaps if you'd *meant* your actions, you'd have kept your integrity. Now you have neither."

He turned to Akira. "Daughter," he said softly, though

his words carried the weight of stone, "must you two squabble so? What would your mother think?"

Akira said nothing. What could she say? Her mother—six feet under—wasn't exactly forthcoming with opinions these days. Not that she'd had many even when alive. Aliko, perpetually poised yet perpetually drunk, had been a woman miscast in her own life, like a background character who'd wandered into someone else's plotline.

Even before the drink claimed her, she'd been a reluctant mother at best. Kyou's birth hadn't changed that; if anything, it had merely sharpened her indifference. By the time Akira came along, the battle was already lost. And while Akira would never speak it aloud—for fear of tarnishing her father's memory—deep down, she knew: they were better off without her.

Hell, Aliko had always seemed as if she'd landed in this life by accident, like an actor who'd stumbled onto the wrong stage and simply decided to stay.

Akira's head dipped lower, brushing Kyou's as they knelt side by side. Her voice was barely a whisper, "You should have never come back."

EIGHT

KALLAE

The incident with the island—which, as it turned out, was a hibernating dragon—was soon forgotten. As most things are out at sea. The ocean has a way of swallowing not just ships and souls, but also memories. Even if the lack of food, water, and stimulating conversation ("What do you think that seagull is thinking?" was the intellectual peak) wasn't enough to bother them, the sea itself seemed to beckon for secrets. And if you didn't have any to give her, she'd cheerfully manufacture them herself.

There had been some hubbub about this Red Lady—who she was, why she'd almost killed them—but those conversations went about as well as actually interrogating a seagull about its existential musings. Only Kilie seemed to recall the near-death experience in any detail, and the rest of the crew had collectively decided 'details' were overrated.

It had been three days—or three weeks, maybe; time at sea had a way of tying itself into knots. Despite their hope that the sticks and pebbles they'd salvaged from the dragon's horde might sustain them for months (an optimistic miscalculation at best), they were, as Kallae had predicted, doomed. Peter was the first to go. One moment, he was standing at the edge of the boat, probably contemplating something philosophical about the abyss, and the next he keeled over. Dead.

In Peter's defense, staying alive had become an entirely unreasonable request. Two others followed in quick succession. The rest badgered Kilie hourly to "use that confounded magic of yours," despite him explaining, with all the patience of a man asked to explain fire to cavemen, that his crystal had been drained days ago. Even if it hadn't, you couldn't conjure food out of thin air without at least a seed—and the sapling they'd been nurturing? Devoured.

The last piece of splinter-flavored gum had long since become a cherished memory. The crew was now subsisting on memories and spite, though not necessarily in that order. Rain, of course, would have been helpful. Alas, the merry band of seafarers had less luck than a one-legged cat in a dogfight. Still, considering they'd escaped a fire-breathing dragon with only one casualty (maybe), this might qualify as lucky. Depending on whose book you were reading.

Kilie had suggested a memorial for the most recent fallen crew member—whose name, oddly, no one could remember. It sparked a lively debate about whether he'd existed at all. Every hammock from the evening before was still filled, and every stomach still growled with undiminished ferocity. For the record, his name had been Josh, and yes, he had existed. Josh's legacy now amounted to a handful of ashes and a meager pouch of gold, neither of which would make it to his family because, well... The crew had moved on. As had the sea.

Kallae spent the endless hours sprawled on the deck in a starfish pose that seemed designed to inconvenience everyone as much as possible. A casual observer might assume he hadn't noticed the annoyance this caused. They would be wrong. He noticed. He reveled in it.

He idly fiddled with the chronocrystal embedded in his chest, the stone cool under his fingers like the comforting touch of a jilted lover. Earlier, he'd attempted to read—a task abandoned when his stomach protested the cognitive effort. Now, he was stuck in the purgatory of trying to compose an acrostic poem about despair. Which, unsurprisingly, was not something Kallae got an inordinate amount of pleasure from.

In a moment of absent-mindedness, Kallae attempted to channel magic through the crystal. He knew the result before it even came—a dull clink as the magic refused to cooperate. It was the magical equivalent of a door slammed in his face.

"What do you want from me?" he muttered.

If you keep running from the truth you will never find it.

The voice startled him—not because it was loud, but because he hadn't said the question out loud. Great. Sky voices. Just what he needed to spice up this delightful descent into madness. Then again, Amriel had never been one for 'traditional communication'.

Kallae didn't bother responding. He wasn't sure if he was relieved or disappointed when no follow-up messages from the cosmic abyss arrived. Either way, the silence was unnervingly chatty.

The rest of their voyage to Fujikura was unremarkable. No one spoke unless absolutely necessary. Even then, most conversations were confined to snarls or monosyllabic grunts. Talking to barnacles would've been a more enriching experience. Still, no one was murdered (a low bar, but an achievement nonetheless), and no more dragons emerged to ruin their day. A win, depending on how desperate you were for victories.

Their arrival at Fujikura was determinedly less emotionally scarring as the one to Lotus Island (which again, wasn't really an island, and more of a dragon named Lotus). The seas which had been raging as if they had just found out that the skies were having an affair with the mountains, took a reprieve that day. No doubt she was busy plotting her revenge with a series of borderline depressive forests, or a huddle of pebbles beset with a severe case of post-traumatic stress disorder. One could only hope she might seek out less emotionally damaged company for guidance, but that's seldom how such things go. Trauma has a nasty habit of attracting even more trauma.

Kallae leaned on the weather-worn railing, staring into the horizon with the solemnity of a man contemplating his life choices—and regretting every single one of them.

Kilie joined him, radiating an infuriating level of energy for someone who had no right to be cheerful. Kallae considered walking away but decided against it. Movement required effort, and he wasn't feeling particularly charitable toward the concept of effort.

Fortunately, Kilie did not seem particularly chatty. Which did not mean he was silent. Oh heavens no. This merely meant he did not speak in paragraph form, or extended soliloquies but rather conversed like a normal person who did not value pretention quite as highly as him.

"Did you see it?" Kilie asked, pointing toward the distant shores.

Kallae hummed in response—a sound that could've meant yes, no, or please stop talking before I throw myself overboard. Kilie, ever the optimist, interpreted it as interest and gestured more enthusiastically. Kallae peered into the distance, silently praying for patience—or divine intervention. Whichever came first.

Kallae tried to resist looking where Kilie was pointing, motivated by pure, unfiltered spite. Unfortunately, this proved as impossible as not thinking about a pink rhinoceros the moment someone mentions one. (You're picturing a pink rhinoceros now, aren't you?) With that suitably distracting thought lodged in your mind, let's return to the story.

The object Kilie gestured toward emerged from the shimmering haze of distance, sharpening into something decidedly... perplexing. What began as an ambiguous smear of red resolved itself into a wooden structure, painted a red so offensively vibrant it felt almost hostile. It clashed horrifically with the mirror-like waters below, creating a tableau that could offend even the most aesthetically indifferent sailor.

As they approached, the red construction grew—not just in size but in strangeness. It was a gate, or three gates, or possibly some avant-garde interpretation of gates that defied logic and symmetry alike. Crooked beams leaned precariously, one larger than the others, with gaps wide enough to inspire a visceral sense of unease. A ragged strip of cloth hung from the largest beam, its faded writing torn beyond legibility. It flapped weakly in the breeze, a dying gasp of significance.

The second gate came and went, and Kallae shuddered.

"There is a darkness here," said Kallae, "I can feel it in my bones."

Kallae still gazed out at sea, but Kilie (rightly) assumed that this comment was directed towards him, "Those are some pretty insightful bones you've got there."

"We should never have come here," Kallae replied grimly, still staring at the water.

"Then why did you?" Kilie asked, voice sharpening.

Kallae sighed, not breaking his gaze. "Because Amriel would have me do so."

"Amriel told you to come?"

"Not directly. And not recently."

"Your crystal is still dull," Kilie pointed towards his

own crystal which had slowly been regaining some of its usual purple hue as they pulled in closer to the island.

Kallae finally met Kilie's gaze, his amber eyes twitching so ferociously one had to wonder if he was suffering from some sort of ailment, or perhaps an electrolyte deficiency.

"Your powers of deduction never fail to astound," he spat.

"Well," said Kilie, "am I wrong?"

The other man sighed, his posture deflating like a dog told to wait at home, "Can't."

"Because you've closed yourself off to him, haven't you?"

A flash of anger marred his countenance, turning his smooth features into a mire of grooves and creeks, before melting as the snow in the rain. He shrugged.

"I just think," Kilie said, holding his hands up in mock surrender, "that if we're out here risking our necks, maybe you should consider getting over whatever personal grudge you have with Amriel."

Kallae's expression twisted—anger, guilt, and weariness waging a quiet war. He gave no answer, which was an answer in itself.

Kilie let out an exasperated sigh. "We're here for a reason, Kallae. Whether or not you want to admit it, you can't do this alone."

"Alone would be preferable to this," Kallae muttered, waving vaguely at Kilie and the sailors who were—rather ineptly—steering the ship dangerously close to the gates. The scraping of wood against paint jarred them both. "And last I checked, we were here to find Brother Calder."

"That's why I wanted to come sure. Helping Brother Calder has always been my intention. But chronomagic, the gift of Amriel, should be shared with everyone. Why not use this opportunity?"

"There are people back home who need us. Who deserve our help. These people would not recognize help if it slapped them in the face and defecated on their shoe."

Kallae began to walk away from the other fairy, his steps sinking into the floor with a great deal more gravity than was necessary. But Kilie snagged his arm before he could get much further than half-way across the deck.

"And who gave you the right to decide that? If you believe it with such certainty, then why did you even come?"

Kallae squirmed his way out of his grip, "Like I said, Amriel wished it. It was that or spend eternity underwater talking to a glowing orb like a psychotic loon."

To Kallae's simultaneous relief and irritation, the sailors finally delivered them to Fujikura's rocky shores. Their exit was as curt as their demeanor aboard the ship; they rowed away without so much as a backward glance.

"Good riddance," Kallae muttered, his tone laced with bitter humor.

Kilie, ever the optimist, shrugged. "Guess it's just us now."

"Wonderful," Kallae deadpanned.

The island was a stark, rugged thing, its forested hills rising sharply against the horizon. The air was thick with humidity, and the soil clung stubbornly to their boots with every step. The fairies had barely begun arguing about their next course of action when the sound of approaching footsteps silenced them.

"Who's that?" Kallae asked, jerking his head toward the figure sprinting toward them.

Kilie cocked his head, "Who?"

Kallae sighed and pointed haphazardly behind him, "That one."

The man was short, perhaps an average height for a woman. Which again, he was not. Because he was a man. And he was dressed in such a way that led one to believe he either had a very poor sense of hygiene, or was in fact, homeless.

"Should we run?" Kilie asked, torn between curiosity

and survival instinct.

"Feel free," Kallae replied, his tone dripping with mock encouragement. "I, however, am conserving my weevil-infested cracker energy."

In the time it took the two fairies to work out their differences, and by work out I mean, lay them all out in the open and proceed to resolve nothing at all, the man had arrived. Despite his gaunt frame, and clothing that resembled something akin to a rag given to a dog as a tug-toy, his breaths were as even as if he had merely been on a stroll, and not a breakneck run.

They proceeded to stand in a circle, or perhaps more of a triangle given it was three of them, and merely stared. It might have been somewhat comical if it had not been so terribly awkward. Several times Kilie opened his mouth to say something, but the problem with allowing silences to hang around for too long is that they begin to expect something profound to break them.

What Kilie settled on was decidedly not profound, having used all of his remaining cognitive reasoning to utter a weak, "Hello."

The man stared at him with all the recognition that a pigeon might have. Before either of the fairies could think of saying anything else he began speaking rapidly. Or at least they assumed he was speaking, for whatever it was he was saying held as much meaning to them as the song of a bird, or the cries of a dying cat.

"Do you speak Cyrgen?" Kilie asked, enunciating each word with the exaggerated clarity reserved for the otherwise illiterate or terribly stupid.

The man folded his hands in front of him and bowed towards the two fairies, "Sorry," he said softly, the word tumbling from his mouth with mis-matched cadence, "I take you. Follow."

"Seems trustworthy," Kilie said cheerfully, already stepping after the man.

Kilie shrugged and began walking behind him, only to

be pulled back by an aggressive hand to the shoulder, "What do you think you're doing?" hissed Kallae.

"What does it look like?"

"It looks like you're as dumb as you look."

"Well what else would you have us do?"

Kallae chewed his lip.

"Thought so," said Kilie pulling himself free and making his way towards the man who had now paused at the entrance to the forest and was waving rather aggressively at them.

Kallae glared, but hunger and resignation drove him forward. As they followed their guide into the dense forest, he muttered, "If we die, I'm haunting you first."

It was certainly a matter of luck, or perhaps some greater celestial force, that the village the man led them to happened to be sympathetic to their cause and not some ferocious beasts, or for that matter, some local Fujikurans who would have been more than happy to promptly separate them from their heads.

Though, to be precise (which I obviously always am), they were local Fujikurans, they also just so happened to be converts to the Way of the Light. Or if not converts at least sympathetic towards them, and not immediately set on killing them. Fortunately, a number of them possessed a primitive grasp of their language, for neither Kallae nor Kilie had thought it necessary to learn some basics before travelling thousands of nautical miles to a foreign land. They had assumed that the locals would simply understand them. It is perhaps somewhat unfortunate that this particular group of locals did not do much to disabuse them of this notion.

They were led to a small encampment by the man (who it turned out not to be homeless), with the two fairies following him blindly and entirely without any possibility of defending themselves were things to sour. He might have been leading them to have supper or he might have been leading them to a pit to *become* supper, whatever the case, Kallae and Kilie had little choice but to follow.

"Home," said the man gesturing to the ramshackle building around him. "Tshu," he pointed to himself.

Kallae frowned. Kilie smiled and repeated the gesture, "Kilie."

"Yes," said Tshu and he pointed towards the purple chronocrystal which hummed on Kilie's chest, "Threadcaster, yes?"

Kilie nodded, which quickly incited what can only be described as a minor mob, as people from all around the village surrounded the fairy and began touching his robes, prodding his crystal, and most unpleasantly, pulling at his hair.

"Show us," said one of the villagers, a small woman, or perhaps a large child, Kallae could not quite tell, from the safe distance he decided to keep. This elicited a chorus of chanting which had Kallae reminiscing about the shrieking cries of seagulls.

Kilie obliged, weaving a few threads of light from his fingertips. The display prompted a scene of sheer chaos, the villagers clamoring to touch him as though he were a deity. Tshu barked something sharp, and they scattered like startled birds.

"Excited," he said, "long time since Threadcaster come." He bowed. Kilie turned towards Kallae, who offered him all the insight of a half-hearted shrug. Kilie decided to bow back, though the movement was made somewhat awkward by the fact that he tripped on his robes when he rose back to standing.

Tshu waved them forward. "Come. I show you."

The camp was small. Insultingly small, really. In fact, it was somehow smaller than the ship they'd just spent several interminable weeks lamenting, a feat Kallae thought was only possible in some metaphysical sense—like the ship had crumpled inward, out of sheer despair, and become this place. Not that Kallae wouldn't have found something to complain about regardless of the accommodations. That much was certain.

The state of the villagers' clothing should have prepared them for what awaited them, but somehow it still managed to be a surprise. Their robes were long and brown, though it was impossible to tell if the color was intentional or just the accumulated grime of years spent tilling the earth. The fabric hung on their frames as though it had been designed by someone who'd heard the term 'clothing' once in a hazy dream and promptly forgotten it. Each robe was cinched at the waist with string—once colorful, now every variation of faded gray imaginable. They were technically functional, a loose diagonal fold preserving some sense of modesty, but 'functional' is a low bar when your competition is nakedness. As for their straw hats, calling them 'hats' was an affront to hats the world wide. They were more accurately described as tragic collections of twigs, dust, and, judging by their smell, regret.

Despite these meager conditions, Kilie and Kallae were led to a small shed—a structure so unimpressive that calling it a 'room' felt overly charitable. Several vials of a metallic substance dangled from the mud walls, glinting like tiny trapped stars. The grooves worn into the glass suggested they'd been cradled by many hands over the years, though whether that was out of reverence or desperation was unclear. Attempts at communication were about as successful as trying to teach a dog about the stock market—mostly a lot of blank stares and tail-wagging equivalents. Thus, Kallae and Kilie were left to their own devices.

That first night was not so much 'sleeping' as it was entering a semi-conscious limbo, somewhere between life and death (with a preference for death). Kallae's dreams were plagued by dark, insidious shapes that flitted against his closed eyelids like bats hunting in the dusk. When morning arrived—as mornings annoyingly tend to do—it brought with it a huddle of villagers eager to see him.

Unfortunately for them, Kallae was about as excited to see them as a cat is to attend a dog convention. The villagers' enthusiasm—bounding, puppy-like—was met with Kallae's best impression of an immovable wall of disdain.

Kilie, ever the idealistic do-gooder, decided to take this opportunity to teach the villagers a bit about chronomagic. This went over surprisingly well, causing some of them to flit about like lunatics, wide-eyed and jittery with excitement. For Kallae, this display did nothing to dissuade his belief that they were all brute savages—possibly possessed by a cocktail of malicious spirits. His patience, already stretched thin, wore even thinner when Kilie's lessons were interrupted several times by villagers frantically ushering them back into the shed with a hurried "quiet" and no further explanation. The pattern repeated over days—or weeks? Time in the camp was an abstract concept, much like happiness or adequate nutrition.

It quickly became clear that Kallae and Kilie were not particularly welcome in Fujikura. Sure, the small village was eager enough to soak up Kilie's teachings, but it was also made abundantly clear—through pointed looks and frantic gestures—that venturing beyond the village would be ill-advised. Apparently, most other inhabitants of the island would greet them less as curious visitors and more as fugitives in need of swift and preferably violent justice. Whether that justice involved prison bars or the business end of a stake was left to the imagination. Attempts to glean further information were met with stammering, murmured repetitions of something that sounded like 'The Inquisitor' or, occasionally, 'The Pacifist.' Kallae figured the former was more likely, given the villagers' terrified whispers and wide, fearful eyes. Unless, of course, they'd somehow found the one place in the world where pacifism was so taboo that even the word inspired abject terror. Knowing his luck, Kallae couldn't entirely dismiss the possibility as pure folly.

One evening, as twilight painted the sky in shades of

resigned inevitability, the two fairies sat outside their shed. This was not a popular choice among the villagers, who hovered nearby with a mixture of disapproval and thinly veiled panic. Some even climbed into the surrounding trees to keep an overwatch on the forest, an act that Kallae found both unnecessary and deeply patronizing. Kilie's attempts to remind him that they were being housed and fed 'free of charge' fell on deaf ears. 'Free,' in this case, included meals that were bland, questionably nutritious, and barely distinguishable from the dirt underfoot.

Conversation between the two had become a rare occurrence. What was there to say? Their discussions inevitably spiraled into the same dead-end arguments: Kilie, desperate to find Calder; Kallae, desperate to be anywhere else but here. What they shared was a mutual understanding that lingering here much longer served no purpose. Even Kilie's valiant attempts to teach the villagers about Amriel and the Great Clock fell flat, met with polite but uncomprehending stares. Sure, a few of them could do some basic chronomagic, it turned out these were the Yōsei of the group, but even Kilie's most valiant attempts seemed to fall on deaf ears when he tried to explain who Amriel was, and indeed how the Great Clock worked.

Kallae was halfway to a grudging nap, his straw hat balanced precariously across his forehead, when Kilie whispered, "Calder."

Kallae groaned and shut his eyes tighter. "Not this again. Can we have one evening where you don't bring him up? Get it through your skull, Kilie: this trip was a fool's errand. Calder's dead. And soon, we will be too."

Kilie ignored him and shook his arm. Kallae's hat, possibly out of sheer existential despair, chose that moment to disintegrate into its constituent twigs. "Wake up!" Kilie hissed.

"I'm up! What is it now?" Kallae snapped, half-heartedly swatting at Kilie's hand.

Kilie pointed to a figure in the distance. "There. Look."

Kallae squinted, his vision swimming from the interruption, and then froze. The figure stood just beyond the edge of the trees, spectral and still. For a moment, Kallae's breath hitched. Calder. It couldn't be, and yet… in his mind, Calder had already become a ghost. Perhaps that was what he was seeing now. Or perhaps Kallae had finally reached the inevitable destination of the grand adventure colloquially known as 'life', that is, a state of insanity so severe that one might even mistake it for happiness.

NINE 九

AKIRA

Tensions were running high—on par for Jiro's clan for any random Tuesday. Toss a bunch of high-strung A-type personalities into a dojo, teach them to fight, and it's only logical to expect some measure of chaos. What set this particular Tuesday apart, however, was that the usual simmer had reached a roiling boil.

Kyou had been sulking ever since his very public humiliation in the dojo, a feat of sustained bitterness even by his standards. Meanwhile, Shoji's culinary ambition—reinventing the humble *okonomiyaki* (a savory cabbage pancake)—had backfired spectacularly, leaving the entire building with a smell akin to decaying livestock. Unfortunately, this was a scent the clan knew all too well. Shoji's earlier escapade, an ill-fated attempt to train rabbits as spies, had ended not with espionage but with a rabbit population explosion and an infestation that, to this day, lingered somewhere deep within the walls. Three rabbits remained unaccounted for, and their legacy haunted every corner of the compound.

So, when the chance for an outing arose, even the faint promise of fresh air was a welcome reprieve from the olfactory onslaught. Naturally, the trip went about as smoothly as one might expect when herding a dysfunctional family out from the comfort of closed doors, and the distraction of other people. The novelty of the journey wore off three minutes in, at which point the 'Are we there yets' began in earnest.

The journey wasn't long—just three days—but even that was two days, 23 hours and approximately 57 minutes too long for this lot. Predictably, things devolved into an all-out brawl. Ryū and Jun, the clan's self-appointed philosophers, spent the better part of the trip pondering karmic retribution. By day two, they'd concluded that the other must have been responsible for either the untimely death of the Emperor's daughter (historically, dysentery was to blame) or the wholesale slaughter of a Tanuki village (Tanuki being raccoon-like shapeshifters inexplicably regarded as symbols of luck despite their penchant for mischief).

Jiro, ever the strategist, had prepared for this inevitability. Shoji was kept placated with a steady supply of snacks, lychees proving particularly effective as they required effort to peel—a perfect distraction on horseback. Kyou and Akira were kept civil by the simple expedient of physical distance, though even that frayed by the second day. The others were treated as the responsible adults they *should* have been. Emphasis on "should."

Of course, there was still ample amounts of bickering despite these contingencies. Kyou kicked it off with his usual flair for tactlessness. "Why do I need to come along to Tsuyoshi's compound? What am I supposed to do while you all laze around in the Sanctum, recharging those sacrilegious things?"

Akira, ever the opportunist, seized on this. "I hate to agree with anything he says, but in this rare instance he has proven that it is possible for something vaguely sensible to come out of him," and then added, "and I think we would all be considerably happier if he did stay behind. In fact, it's not too late," she turned to her brother, "look there's a lovely little shack just over there. Perfect for you, Kyou." She pointed towards a bundle of sticks some distance away that may at one point have been a house but could have just as well have been—well—a pile of sticks.

Jiro didn't bother turning around. "Enough. He's coming."

Akira wasn't done. "He isn't even a Threadcaster! He still practices the Way of the Water. He killed my fern the other day!"

"My condolences on the fern," muttered Kyou. "It was half-dead anyway. At least I'm not a heretic. Forgive me if I prefer not to disobey edicts from the Emperor himself."

"Bah!" scoffed Akira, "do not pretend you do this out of loyalty to the Emperor. Loyalty is as foreign to you as soil is to a fish."

"Enough!" Jiro's voice cut through the bickering. "Kyou is family. I may disagree with his choices, but family is what matters most. You'll see that in time."

The trip to Tsuyoshi's compound was a yearly ritual, tied to the second waning of the blue moon. Predictably, 'second waning' could mean anything from the third to the fifth, depending on the accuracy of their predictions. The compound, nestled in the province of Oto, was the largest in the region, dwarfing even Jiro's substantial domain. It was a hub for trade and subterfuge, most notably the secret practice of chronomagic, outlawed by imperial decree some three years prior.

Tsuyoshi and Jiro, rivals in almost every sense, had found common ground in defiance. When the imperial decree came, Jiro had charged for the Sanctum with no plan beyond blind fury. Fortunately, Tsuyoshi shared his disdain for the decree. Together, they concocted a plan so haphazard it should have failed outright. Instead, it succeeded against all odds, with losses limited to three men and a scarecrow. The Sanctum was declared destroyed, its ruins left as a facade for imperial inspection. In reality, the heart of the Sanctum lay intact, twelve feet beneath the rubble, and its secrets safeguarded by the clans. Despite neither being particularly fond of the other, they had clearly deemed it wise to keep some allies in the bank were things to sour. Or rather, sour further than they already had. It was only a matter of time before the both of them could set up lemonade stands and retire for good.

This shared secret was the pretext for their annual visit. Jiro's clan returned each year to recharge their crystals, which lost potency far faster than Jiro would have liked. He might have visited more often, but even once a year strained tempers and allegiances.

Which leads us back to the very apt question of why on earth Kyou was accompanying them on this yearly fabrication. Kyou, though a Yōsei, and thus potentially capable of threadcasting, was as likely to attempt the Crystal Trials as he was to willingly set foot in a nest of vipers. He had left Jiro's clan, and his family by extension, some twenty years earlier and had not looked back since. Well not until three months ago, when he had appeared in their compound, nothing save the skin on his back and a blade in his hand. Having joined a rival daimyo group, led by a stringent supporter of the Way of the Water, they had not expected to ever see him again. Unless of course, on the field of battle. Unfortunately for Kyou, this rival daimyo had gotten himself killed in series of events that can only be described as terribly unfortunate.

In the midst of fighting another rival daimyo (rival daimyos were as bountiful as sand on a beach), he had drawn upon the lifeforce of a field of daisies which he had assumed were in the prime of the life but were actually losing a rather dramatic battle of their own with an aggressive strain of invasive lichen. Having thus miscalculated by a factor of fifty (he had never been one particularly good with numbers), his conjured Shikigami had promptly turned on him, and devoured him from the head down. This left his samurai warriors leaderless and entirely without guidance (not that he had been especially good at providing either of these things when he was alive). Most had fallen upon their swords, as tradition would demand, but Kyou, having decided dying on behalf of what was essentially a man with a cognitive capacity of a head of lettuce, was a rather stupid thing to do. To hell with tradition. Of course, telling tradition to kindly sod off, was not something the other daimyo particularly respected, so Kyou was left with only one daimyo who would accept him. That of course, being his father.

When the clan arrived at Tsuyoshi's compound, they did so in record time, having sacrificed sleep to minimize time spent in each other's company. The compound was a sprawling marvel, low wooden houses connected by walkways lined with vibrant pink-flowering trees that seemed to glow in the moonlight. A stone fortress encircled the compound, its height more decorative than defensive. The red guardrails and thatched roofs gave the place a whimsical air, crowned by the enormous fountain at its center. A life-sized metal kitsune, its nine tails fanned like a peacock's plumage, lay curled atop the fountain, radiating wealth and power.

Needless to say, Tsuyoshi was a wealthy daimyo. I might have given you a similar picture by simply describing his compound as *'obnoxious'*.

Had Jiro been a man prone to jealousy or a one-uppity syndrome, he might have said Tsuyoshi's compound was only bigger than his because it was based in Oto and not the densely populated capital of Fujikura, Gedo. But Jiro was not such a man, which is for the best since Oto happened to be the former capital, and had only recently been swapped because the Emperor, being somewhat of a paranoid fellow, had fled from the blood-soaked grounds of Oto and set his sights on greener pastures. It is difficult to say whether this move had been well met, for the Emperor had not been sighted since his hasty departure, and so it had been rather difficult to ask him about his sentiments, or indeed anything else. But I digress.

Akira took it all in with a faint smirk. "Obnoxious," she muttered, earning a snort from Ryū. Even the kitsune seemed to be judging her from its metal perch, its sly expression somehow knowing.

Jiro's face remained impassive as he dismounted, but the tension in his jaw betrayed his unease. This was not a place for comfort or camaraderie. This was a battleground—a quieter one, perhaps, but no less dangerous for it.

They were met at the entrance to Tsuyoshi's compound by a greeting party that could be described as 'bare bones,' though that would be generous. It consisted of exactly one man, who, judging by his appearance, had only recently earned the right to be called man and not child.

"Welcome," he said with all the flair of someone paying their taxes, "Tsuyoshi-sama awaits you."

Jiro frowned and returned the man's bow, though only with a slight incline of his head—his right as a daimyo. "I take it Tsuyoshi was otherwise occupied?"

The man merely bowed again and opened his arms, gesturing them forward. He then led them at a pace that was nothing short of impressive, considering they were on horseback and he was on foot. As he walked, he pointed out various sights, none of which Akira retained. "Your lodgings," he said, indicating a particularly elaborate structure encircling a large tree.

He stopped so abruptly that Akira had to yank her reins to avoid a collision. "You may dismount here," he said, "and leave your things. Dinner is already waiting."

"I wasn't aware we were so delayed," Jiro said slowly,

begrudgingly handing his reins to a stableboy.

"Tsuyoshi-sama is never late," the man replied.

Jiro raised an eyebrow. "You're new here," he said. "I don't remember you from last time we visited."

The man scoffed. "I'm Akio. Tsuyoshi-sama's son."

"Forgive me. I wasn't aware Tsuyoshi had a second son. I'm well-acquainted with Haru-chan, his eldest."

Akio pursed his lips and gestured for them to follow. "Well, perhaps you're not as well-acquainted with Tsuyoshi-sama as you believe."

"And I thought Tsuyoshi-sama was the obnoxious one," whispered Ryū.

Akira snickered. "Well, the apple never falls far from the tree, does it?"

The food served excellently reflected the sentiment of 'obnoxious.' They were seated on pillows around a grand table, only to be swarmed by servants on all sides. Tsuyoshi was a man who was not used to waiting—and he wasn't about to start now. His clan were already seated, wiping their hands with steamed towels infused with a sweet-smelling flower that gave Akira an immediate migraine. She declined when offered one. Shoji, however, accepted his and promptly tried to eat it.

Akio, who sat beside his brother Haru, muttered, "I told you."

Haru shifted in his seat, nudging Akio, who swayed slightly. "Shhh," he hissed. "They are our guests." Even as the words left his mouth, a snicker slipped out.

"You know we can hear you, you pig-brained simpletons," said Ryū, his mouth full of thinly tenderized beef.

"Who are you calling a pig-brained simpleton?" Akio shot to his feet, which was no small feat considering they were sitting on the floor.

Ryū continued chewing, his gaze never leaving his plate. "Did I stutter?"

"Enough," Jiro and Tsuyoshi said in unison, their

voices trailing off into the clink of chopsticks.

Fortunately, the blur of food—served in plates so small they could have been meant for children or perhaps overfed gerbils—was ample distraction for the complete lack of conversation that followed. There was fish stewed in soy sauce, fresh lemongrass, and jasmine; eggplants dripping with a sweet glaze; fresh tuna sliced so thinly it melted on the tongue before one could even realize it had been there; syrupy red beans in sticky rice; and enough sake to intoxicate an entire village.

Time passed in a haze of food and awkward silence, and the feast continued on—so long that even Kyou's usual scowl faded as he took a bite of richly marinated beef.

Jiro grinned broadly, which did very little to convey how he actually felt, for he took politeness to an extreme that was not so much admirable, as utterly annoying.

"I see you've added some new faces to your clan, Tsuyoshi," he said, inclining his head slightly toward the recruits, lingering a touch too long on Akio.

The other daimyo grunted and nodded, his response as unenthusiastic as a stone's.

Unperturbed by the lack of response, Jiro added, "But some old familiars are missing—Daisuke, Ren, Ichiro—"

"They turned back to the old ways," Tsuyoshi cut in.

Jiro frowned. "So where are they now?"

Tsuyoshi shrugged. "Why concern yourself with such trifling matters? Surely you've had your own problems with those who refuse to accept the truth?"

"But samurai cannot leave their daimyo," Jun interjected. "Only death can release them from their vows."

Kyou squirmed, but said nothing.

"Do not take me for a fool," Tsuyoshi spat, his tone venomous. "I know our ways well enough. I have found use for these men. There is always work to be done on the compound."

Tsuyoshi's eyes swept over the members of Jiro's clan, their cold gaze reminiscent of an alligator's—or perhaps a rabbit half-mad with rabies. Akira shifted uncomfortably under his gaze, feeling as though he was assessing the very essence of her existence in that one glance. She exhaled in relief when his gaze moved on to Shoji, then Jun, but when it landed on Kyou, Tsuyoshi paused.

"I see you've been remiss in tradition," he smirked. "The resemblance is uncanny. Had I met him on the field of battle, I would have thought it was you. But never mind that," his voice dropped, chilling the room to a frosty silence. "You've always been too soft."

"Meaning what exactly?" Jiro shot back, his voice tight.

"Tell me," Tsuyoshi continued, his voice like ice, "have all of your clan converted?"

Jiro remained silent, which was all the answer Tsuyoshi needed.

"And yet you let them sit here beside you?" Tsuyoshi scoffed. "Represent your clan while basking in the decaying corpse of the past? One can be merciful to the blind, but if you show them how to see and they deny they have eyes at all, you must cast them away. Otherwise, you'll be the fool."

"If you think casting out members of the clan is the Way of the Light," Jiro said, voice steely, "then you're the blind fool."

After that, conversation dwindled to nothing, and everyone seemed eager to escape the charade of what could barely be called a reunion. The meal concluded, and most of Tsuyoshi's clan retreated to their lavish accommodations, half of them sinking into a food coma immediately upon arrival. The others, feeling particularly daring, opted for a bath in the onsen beneath the estate. The waters ran cold, trickling far beneath the surface and reaching all the way to the former Sanctum. Even without entering, Akira could hear her crystal hum with rejuvenation, though the baths were the quickest way to recharge them.

Tsuyoshi's people disappeared into whatever dark, unwelcoming hole they had crawled out of, offering neither a farewell nor a goodnight. Given the conversation had been as warmly received as a philosophy lecture by an anteater, Akira supposed this was to be expected.

Akira, finding neither a bath, sleep, or an exploration into the psyche of Tsuyoshi's team of brain-dead yes-men particularly appealing, decided instead for a stroll around the grounds. Night had long since fallen, and the lilies that had seemed too bright for the day now glowed in the gloom like stars. The curved bridges which meandered lazily into rounded pavilions were lit with flickering lanterns, though the glow from the cherry blossoms would have been more than ample to guide her path. Then again, since Akira had no destination in mind (nor a very good sense of direction even if she did), her path was not exactly defined in nature.

She'd worked out most of the knots from the long ride and the even longer dinner when she heard voices. At first, there had been snippets of conversation as people retreated to their rooms, but as the night wore on, those faded, replaced by the sounds of crickets and other less savory creatures. But now, the voices were back, their clipped words drawing her deeper into the center of the gardens.

As she rounded a corner, two figures emerged. They were tall—taller than average—and Akira soon realized that the reason she couldn't understand their words wasn't due to distance, but because they were speaking a language entirely foreign to her. Despite Jiro's lessons, her grasp of Cygren was meager at best. She could pick out a few fragments here and there, but the full flow of their conversation was lost on her.

What wasn't lost on her, however, was their appearance. They were unmistakably Threadcasters, members of the storied order from Cyrnghräir, tasked with imparting the teachings of chronomagic. Jiro himself had been taught by one of their Order. Years ago, Threadcasters had been a common sight in Fujikura—so prevalent, in fact, that in some villages, they outnumbered the Fujikurans. But that was a time long past. Akira couldn't recall the last time she had seen one, and certainly not one so openly unafraid. There were still converts to the Way of the Light—Jiro and herself being living proof of that—but the men who had once brought it to their shores had largely disappeared.

The two Threadcasters were fiddling with something small. Too small to be easily discernible, but its long chain trailed from the curled thumb of one of their hands. Akira crept closer, stopping just before she could be seen, hidden behind a large willow tree.

She had just begun to recover the fragments of her wits—most of which had been sacrificed to the seductive powers of rice wine—when a third figure joined the scene. This figure was just as tall, and Akira immediately recognized him. It was her father. He must have just come from the onsen, for his usual ornamental attire had been replaced with a thin robe, the fabric draping over his lithe body like silk still wet from the dyeing process. He seated himself on a bench beside the kitsune fountain, its surface now reflecting the moon, swollen and pink, as if it were an unblinking eye gazing back at them.

"Good evening," he said softly in perfect Cygren, crossing one leg over the other as his eyes remained fixed on the kitsune.

Before either of the men could respond—or even seemed inclined to—he added, "Beautiful, isn't it?"

His gaze never shifted from the metal sculpture, as though looking away might bring him pain greater than death itself.

"We have work to do," muttered one of the men, pocketing whatever it was he had been holding.

Jiro smiled, gesturing forward as though the situation were entirely ordinary. "Go right ahead. You won't disturb me."

"But your presence disturbs us," the other man snapped, reaching for something else within his robes.

"I'm sorry to hear that," Jiro replied, his voice as soft as one might speak to a newborn, "but I'm afraid I'm quite intent on sitting here for a while. Do carry on with your work, though."

"We've already said you disturb our work."

"Well, that's quite a shame, isn't it?"

The two cloaked men exchanged glances, huffed as though they had just been told they had two days left to live, and then pulled out axes from within their robes. The synchronicity with which they did so could have been impressive—had it not been followed immediately by them swinging those axes at the base of the statue. A sharp, high-pitched cry rang out across the compound, so lifelike it was difficult to tell if it was the metal crying or the spirit of the kitsune itself. Another clang. Then another. Akira instinctively pressed her hands to her ears, as if she could block out the noise.

Jiro, finally snapping back to reality after the cacophony had shattered the fragile silence, leapt in front of the men and began yelling. To Akira, it sounded like frantic, deranged screams—partly because her grasp of Cygren was still shaky, but mostly because the two cloaked figures paid him no mind whatsoever, continuing their assault on the fountain as if it were a mountain of diamonds beneath the stone.

It was only when pink threads shimmered across Jiro's skin, curling around the axes, that the men froze.

"Stop," Jiro's voice was quiet now, wispy as a thread of smoke, "this is a sacred place. What are you doing? Tsuyoshi would not approve."

The smaller of the two men—though still well above average—chuckled darkly. "You have no idea what

Tsuyoshi would approve of. Some things are meant to be culled."

The other spat toward the ground, ripping the thread away like it was mere ordinary string. "It's not sacred. This is just a dumb pile of scrap metal, used for sacrilegious worship to a bunch of fickle spirits who bless you one day and piss on your crops the next."

"Whatever you may think of them," Jiro responded, his tone unfaltering, "it is not the Way of the Light to destroy. Nor is it to judge those who have yet to see the Light."

The men brushed past him, one sneering, "Get out of our way, old man." It was an ironic statement—despite the two of them being Fae and Jiro a Yōsei—they looked not just older but more fatigued, as though the weight of years had bent them in two.

Jiro planted his feet firmly at the edge of the fountain. "I cannot let you do this."

"And pray tell, just how do you intend on stopping us?"

The daimyo, still holding loose threads in his hands, began wrapping them around his wrists, as the color began to flicker. It dimmed, the pink shifting into red and then something that might have passed for green until settling on a deep blue. By the time the colors of the rainbow had been thoroughly explored, the two men were also alight, blue curls of steam wafting from their body like incense. Akira, snapping out of her trance, was just feeling the hum of her own crystal respond to her will, when she caught Jiro's eye. It shone like molten amber, and even from the distance it fixed upon her like an eagle its prey. He shook his head. The movement was so small she might have missed it. Might have told herself she had imagined it, but she knew what she had seen. And more so, she knew Jiro.

"Fujikuran scum," spat one of the men. "Using and taking what isn't yours. And this is the thanks we get? You try to use what we taught you against us? Ungrateful brats, the lot of you."

Jiro's threads flickered, the blue faltering before it returned to pink.

"Bah, would you look at this old fool, Lark!" the taller one scoffed, "Can't even calculate the basic Particulars. He wouldn't have gotten within an inch of the Academy's doors back in Cargyll."

Jiro opened his mouth to reply, but before he could, the other man crept up behind him and slammed the heel of his axe into the back of his head. The Yōsei crumpled to the ground. Akira stifled a cry, clenching her fist against her mouth to keep from screaming.

She rushed forward, only to find herself rooted in place. The pink thread, sharp and biting, had wrapped itself around her wrist. The moment Jiro fell, everything inside her seemed to freeze—her limbs, her heart, her voice.

In moments, they had him blindfolded and gagged, his hands bound tightly behind him. The thread snapped free, forgotten. Akira's body thawed, but it was too late.

"Take him to the Watchtower," muttered the smaller man, "keep him there until the next shipment to Cargyll. Sadhrin will like this one. Haven't seen one of these pigs use chronomagic like him before. He'll last a few months on the farms back in Cargyll."

The man hoisted Jiro over his shoulder and walked past Akira. He was so close she could smell the foul breath of stale alcohol on him. She reached for her sword, but as she did, she saw Jiro's eyes open. He stared at her, and his lips formed soundless words: *Don't.*

TEN

KALLAE

It can't be, thought Kallae. This is *too* easy. Nothing is ever this easy. Sure, he'd spent months stranded at sea, nearly been devoured by a dragon that had mistaken him for a snack, starved so much he could practically use his ribs as a drying rack, and—oh yes—entertained the thought of hanging himself with a noose just to escape his current company no fewer than theee dozen times, but in the grand scheme of things, this? This was still *too* easy.

Calder had wandered into the exact same village that Kallae and Kilie had *randomly* stumbled upon. At the exact same time. With barely a scratch on him. It reeked of something—something fishy. And not just because they were less than a mile from the coast.

Of course, Kilie, in his ever-unwavering optimism, didn't smell fish. Instead, he was all sunshine, roses, and rainbows, and practically ran towards the stumbling figure of Calder with a jubilant shout: "It's Calder! I knew he was alive!"

Kallae might have berated him for announcing their presence to every wild animal, beast, and village of bloodthirsty villagers intent on ripping their faces off, but honestly, it seemed pointless. Not like a pack of vicious wolves would turn around and leave just because Kallae had made Kilie apologize. So, instead, he contented himself with trailing after his annoyingly cheerful friend. Begrudgingly, of course. One might even say he did so with the level of excitement one reserves for voluntarily walking into a jail cell. Which was on fire. And lined with a rotating cast of sharpened teeth. Possibly filled with a tank of starving piranhas.

By the time Kallae had dragged himself over to the clearing, Kilie was already holding on to Calder like he might fly away otherwise (despite a multitude of false messaging, advertising, and everything in-between, the Fae did not possess the ability of flight, well at least not without the assistance of chronomagic). Kallae found the scene roughly as stomach-churning as watching a pair of newly coupled rabbits go at it.

"I can't believe we found you!" Kilie practically shouted when Kallae came into hearing range. Kallae refrained from adding that they hadn't so much *found* Calder as *stumbled upon* him—after all, beyond showing up on Fujikura, their search for Calder had been practically nonexistent.

"What have you been doing?" was the first of the series of questions, which included, but was not limited to, where had he been, who had he met, what had he seen, and how was he. Essentially, the big five: Who, What, When, Where, and Why. Think of it like a needy girlfriend's twenty questions, if she had an anxiety disorder the size of a small moon. Kilie either didn't notice—or didn't care—that Calder's responses were nothing more than grunts or monosyllabic noises. And let's be clear: the noises coming out of Calder's mouth weren't words. They were the sort of guttural grunts you'd expect from someone who'd been screaming into the void all night.

Kallae, finding he had stood there for too long doing nothing, gave a small nod and a wave in their general direction, but found this did little to disperse the awkwardness he felt. Calder appeared rather unchanged. Which wasn't altogether surprising, given he was a Threadcaster, and change was something that seldom appeared in their vocabulary.

He was not a terribly tall man, nor so short as to make it memorable. His face was long, and his eyes were kind, though perhaps the most notable thing about him were the laugh lines which spread across his countenance like streaks of lightning. Even this was unchanged. A smile so broad it looked almost painful had been on display since they had found him, and Kallae was beginning to wonder if perhaps Calder hadn't escaped Fujikura unscathed after all. While his body looked reasonably intact, certainly more well-nourished than Kallae and Kilie, conceivably his mind may not have been as fortunate.

"Come, let's sit. I have no doubt you've had a wearying journey," Kilie announced, taking Calder by the arm and leading him to their 'living room.' I say living room, but really it was more like a crudely constructed box with a slab of rotting slate serving as a table. Calder didn't seem put off by the humble setup and sat where Kilie directed him.

"So," began Kilie, settling into a nearby corner, "tell us everything. I trust it comes as no surprise to you that Mr. Faber sent us here. Your last letter—" He stopped mid-sentence, looking for the right words, but the breeze whisked them away. He hesitated, then gestured at Calder, "Forgive me. I've been speaking too much. Please, go ahead."

When Calder remained silent, Kilie's brow furrowed.

Kallae, who had long since given up trying to make sense of any of this, sighed and ran his hands through his tangled hair. He'd been lucky that his hair was dark brown, because if it were any lighter, it would've been impossible to tell the difference between his hair and the mud streaks.

"Leave the poor man alone," muttered Kallae, his hands now tangled into the bird's nest his long tresses had become, "can you not see that Fujikura has left him entirely bereft of all reasonable thought?" He yanked painfully at a knot, barely suppressing a yelp. Victory was his, at the cost of a few precious strands, which he tossed to the ground.

"We should take him and board the next ship that's leaving this hellhole," he added, voice thick with bitterness. "Hell, I'd swim to the next continent before I spend another night on this cursed island."

He gestured at Calder, who had now attached himself to Kilie like a barnacle. Calder was rooting through his pockets like a madman—which, honestly, he was at this point.

"There is no saving this place—it's a wonder Calder has any of his wits left," he said more softly now, "only destruction awaits us if we remain."

Kilie frowned and tried to still Calder's hands by clasping them between his own. This elicited a high-pitched screaming sound from the man, which had it been any higher might have only been detectable by wolves. Unfortunately, it was very much so detectable by human ears and Kallae all but began yelling himself. A second later, he really did yell. A single expletive that I do not care to repeat.

Kilie slapped both hands over their mouths, silencing the cacophony, but it did little to calm Calder. Kallae, feeling like he might actually lose his mind, yanked himself away from the madness and slumped against the wall.

"Quiet, you two," Kilie hissed, though it was largely unnecessary now that they'd both slipped into silence. "I need to think."

"Pray, do tell—what are you thinking about? The

moon's alignment? How you're going to explain to Mr. Faber how you've utterly failed him? Scared that he'll be disappointed in you too, like your father was?" Kallae paused dramatically, only to be cut off as Kilie suddenly leapt at him.

Kallae never did get to finish his question, nor did he receive an answer (though, let's face it, it was rhetorical at best, and viciously vindictive at worst), for a mere second later he was thrown to the ground by a rapidly accelerating fairy. The rapidly accelerating fairy being Kilie, in case anyone missed that.

They got in a fair few punches, likely they would both end up with matching black eyes come the morning (they did), several jabs and kicks to the stomach, and a well-aimed toss of a pebble into Kallae's open mouth before either of them realized that Calder had disappeared.

The two of them stood frozen, looking around their humble hut for a whole three seconds before bolting outside into the village center.

It wasn't difficult to figure out where Calder had gone. He'd left a trail wide enough to be seen from space: baskets strewn across the ground, fruit half-eaten and discarded, and a shirt tangled on a fencepost. The whole village looked like a tornado had passed through, with Calder at the center of it all.

Kilie and Kallae exchanged a glance and then took off in a sprint. They found Calder not far from the town hall, within the only intact building in the village. He was standing there, fidgeting with a wooden statue that looked suspiciously like a dog—except it wasn't. Not exactly. It morphed into something more lion-like the longer you looked at it (Kallae later learned this was a Komainu, colloquially called 'lion dogs'- who'd have thought). The statue, though large, was mostly hollow in its center, so it was already tipping quite dramatically towards the now murmuring Calder.

"Enough!" shouted Kilie, rather louder than was

required given their close proximity as he tried to pry the man off the statue. This was met with the success one might expect of a duck challenging an ogre to an arm wrestle. Kilie, despite all lack of success continued to claw at the other man, until that was, that Calder growled. Now I don't mean the type of faux growl that is not entirely unanthropoid as to be suspicious, but a growl which would have your hackles rising. If you have hackles that is. And if you do have hackles, we are once again in the territory of questioning your anthropomorphism.

Kallae grabbed Kilie and pulled him away just as a group of villagers appeared, ushering them out of the building with little ceremony.

"Away," muttered one of them, shoving them out the door.

"Tanuki," said another, as they entered.

Kallae's unspoken question was answered when a hog-sized, furry critter came bolting out of the building. It had the body of a barrel, and the face of a mischievous toddler. Its body was round, but it was difficult to say if this was due to its obnoxious pelt or its insatiable appetite. Beady eyes shining an unnatural white were rimmed, quite appropriately, like a masked bandit, and a short yet broad tail wiggled behind it.

Before Kallae could process what was happening, the Tanuki paused, stood on its hind legs, and waved at them like it had all the time in the world. Kallae, too bewildered to stop it, stepped aside.

"Getting away!" shouted one of the villagers, which indeed the Tanuki was.

The Tanuki took off into the night with a head-start that would've made any animal rights activist proud. It stopped once again, waved, and Kallae could swear it winked before vanishing into the darkness.

"What was that thing?" Kilie asked, though his tone suggested he wasn't expecting an answer so much as venting his confusion into the ether.

The villagers muttered in fragmented, nervous phrases, offering the sort of groundbreaking insights one might expect from frightened farmers: "It's... a creature... of sorts... mythical, maybe." Kallae didn't bother rolling his eyes. The gesture would have been wasted on this audience.

Finally, the town elder arrived—a figure whose command of Cyrgen was just competent enough to elevate him from incoherent to passably cryptic. He explained, in laboriously slow sentences, that the creature was a *Tanuki*, a mischievous sprite known for shapeshifting and causing general chaos.

Kilie, predictably, latched onto this information like a starving man to breadcrumbs. "Why did it know our friend's face? What did it do to him?" he demanded, his words spilling out faster than the elder could process.

"What do you think?" hissed Kallae.

The elder blinked, unruffled, and offered a simple, maddeningly vague answer: "Seen him. Tanuki must see him."

Kilie grabbed Kallae by the lapels—or what passed for lapels on Kallae's mud-streaked, threadbare excuse for a jacket—and shook him like a malfunctioning automaton. "Did you hear that?" Kilie's face was a mask of wild hope. "Calder must be alive then!"

Kallae wrinkled his nose. "Your optimism disgusts me."

"Without it we have nothing."

"Without it, we have reason."

"We need to go and find him!" Kilie released his death grip on Kallae and spun toward the elder, launching into a stream of questions that Kallae tuned out. Watching Kilie try to communicate with the elder was like watching someone try to thread a needle with a live eel. Fascinating in a train-wreck sort of way, but ultimately futile.

Even so, Kilie managed to extract a vague sense of direction: distant villages, whispered landmarks, and more uncertainties than answers. Unsurprisingly, none of the villagers volunteered to guide them. Apparently, aiding two bedraggled fairies on a potentially suicidal quest wasn't high on anyone's to-do list.

Kallae slumped to the ground and buried his face in his hands. "We should never have come here. I should've stayed away. Maybe eternity in a black room, talking to a glowing orb, wouldn't have been so bad after all."

"You've made it this far, Kallae," Kilie said, with the kind of relentless cheerfulness that Kallae suspected would someday get him murdered. "You're not seriously thinking of turning back now, are you? Where would you even go?"

"Back to the Academy."

Kilie raised an eyebrow. "Wasn't the condition of your reinstatement as a Brother of the Academy contingent on you going to Fujikura as instructed?"

"And I have gone."

"I don't think that's quite what Mr. Faber had in mind."

"Then he should have been more specific."

ELEVEN

KILIE

It had been three days since they'd seen Calder. Well, the Tanuki masquerading as Calder. Kilie's initial excitement was wearing thin, though no thinner than Kallae's patience. Kilie was a doer—a go-getter, some might say—and sitting around waiting for something to happen was decidedly *not* his style. Especially when the "something" could be anything from Calder miraculously finding them himself (a long shot) to the elusive Inquisitor showing up to kill them all (a real mood-lifter, that). Yet, despite the dire mood and even direr prospects, Kilie went about his day with a smile so broad it might have convinced you he'd just inherited a kingdom. Of course, given his family's wealth, that would've been the equivalent of someone handing you a soggy five-dollar bill and calling it a windfall.

The days blurred together, each one indistinguishable from the last. They woke at some indeterminate hour of the morning (the Fujikurans had no clocks, nor any desire for them—a fact Kallae grumbled about endlessly). Kilie usually rose with the sun, which he considered a charming quirk but which Kallae had deemed a war crime. And Kilie's morning routine? A symphony of misery, as Kallae had outlined in excruciating detail. First, there was the stretching—a full-body contortion so dramatic it seemed designed to summon ancient spirits of irritation. Next came the groaning, a guttural yawp that drowned out even the birdsong, which fled in terror every morning. Finally, there was the sleep-talking: a nightly barrage of incoherent mumbling so dull that even Kallae's vivid imagination couldn't turn it into anything resembling entertainment.

Once Kilie had thoroughly destroyed Kallae's morning, he would stroll around the village. He'd always thought of himself as an early riser until Fujikura shredded that illusion like so much wet parchment. By the time Kilie emerged, most of the villagers had already put in hours of backbreaking work, leaving only the elderly, the infirm, and the infants—plus, of course, Kallae, sulking in the shadows like some grumpy gargoyle.

Breakfast was a modest affair: overripe persimmons, the occasional peach, and, on one traumatic morning, a handful of plums so sour Kilie's tongue nearly staged a rebellion. Today's offering was persimmons, being diced by a toddler wielding a knife with the determination of a pint-sized executioner. Kallae sat beside the child, snatching a piece of fruit for himself with the shamelessness of a starving hyena. By the time he was on his third slice, a gaggle of villagers had gathered around him. They peppered Kilie with questions in their mangled Cyrgen, none of which he could understand. He responded the only way he knew how: by weaving threads of chronomagic in his hands and performing small, inconsequential miracles—speeding up a falling leaf, slowing down a fluttering moth. The villagers clapped and murmured in awe until someone inevitably hissed, "Attracting attention," with all the urgency of a prayer.

Kilie tried to explain the principles of chronomagic—how Amriel had bestowed the gift upon their kind—but his words might as well have been rain on a tin roof. The villagers nodded politely before dispersing, leaving Kilie feeling as useful as a snowman in the desert.

Afternoons were much the same, except that Kallae would eventually slink out of their shared hovel to sulk more publicly. He contributed nothing to the day's work, choosing instead to mutter under his breath—a habit Kilie found both alarming and irritating. He briefly entertained the idea that Kallae might be losing his mind but dismissed it. Not because it wasn't plausible, but because Kilie preferred not to dwell on the fact that he might be sharing a room with a burgeoning lunatic.

Kilie tried to help in the fields once. The experience was… enlightening. His attempts at farming were so inept that he might as well have been trying to choreograph a ballet for earthworms. He did manage to make a corner of the field bloom with a bit of fleeting magic, but the panicked reactions of the villagers quickly discouraged him from any further attempts. And so, they remained in the village, waiting. Squirming at every noise, startling at every shadow. Kilie began to feel like a rabbit in a den of foxes.

Somewhere between five and ten days after the Tanuki incident (time having lost all meaning), they had an unexpected visitor.

The two fairies had retired for the night at some indeterminate hour. Kilie was already mumbling his usual nonsense in his sleep, and Kallae had finally managed to doze off with a fortress of pillows piled over his head. Then came the tapping. A faint, rhythmic knock that sliced through the silence like a blade. Kallae groaned, pressing the pillows tighter against his ears. Kilie, predictably, kept mumbling.

The tapping persisted. Kallae's patience, always on the brink of extinction, finally snapped. "Shut it, you belligerent assholes! Shove a sock in it, will you?"

He had rather lost all sense of self preservation and had actually come to think quite fondly upon the notion of getting eaten by a pack of rapacious wolves. In fact, the possibility of getting eaten by a pack of rapacious wolves had become one of the primary motivators left in his humdrum existence.

Another tap followed. It was at this point that Kilie decided to rejoin the living.

"Ah you're up," said Kallae not bothering to whisper, "welcome to anarchy. It's nice here, I trust you'll enjoy it. If not, please redirect all complaints to the nearest person who gives a damn."

"Shhhh," hissed Kilie in response, which ironically was hardly at a lower volume than Kilie's outburst had been.

"What is that sound?" whispered Kilie, having now pushed himself up on the bed. He was rubbing the sleep out of his eyes in a way that Kallae had previously only thought done for comedic effect by those otherwise lacking in any semblance of a personality.

"Oh, let's see," Kallae growled, dragging himself up with the enthusiasm of a man heading to his own execution. "Could it be…tapping? My gods, Kilie, you've cracked the case! Someone fetch this man a medal!"

The taps ceased, leaving an oppressive silence that made Kilie's ears throb. Deciding this was someone else's problem, he promptly went back to sleep. Unfortunately, his rest was short-lived. Moments later, a thin voice cut through the darkness: "Please don't shove sock."

Kallae groaned, his voice muffled by the pillows. "If you wake me up again, I will not only shove a sock down your throat but also throw in a twelve-foot pole up your ass. Free of charge."

A clunk echoed outside, followed by soft footsteps. Kilie prodded Kallae. "There's someone out there."

Kallae didn't move. "Brilliant observation. Where

would you like me to pin your gold star?"

Kilie sighed and bolted upright, banging into the doorframe on his way out—a collision that may or may not have been intentional. Outside, the source of the tapping hadn't gone far.

It was a girl. Or at least she appeared to be a girl, though her face was lined with more years than her stature suggested. Yet Fujikura was a place where few remained young for long. One either grew up or one remained young forever, buried seven feet under the ground. Her hands were calloused and caked with mud, and her eyes, narrow and feline, glimmered with a wary intensity.

"Don't hurt!" she exclaimed, holding up her hands in surrender.

Kilie lowered himself towards the ground, his tall stature and cramped muscle, making the gesture take rather longer than anticipated.

Kilie crouched, the movement awkward and slow. "I won't hurt you," he said softly. "But why are you here?"

The girl hesitated, her eyes darting between Kilie and the shadowy doorway behind him. "Help you," she whispered, her voice trembling.

From inside, Kallae's voice boomed. "Will you two *shut up*!?"

"Sock!" The girl began to tremble and tried to push herself to her feet. Kilie placed his hands gently on her shoulders, which, unsurprisingly, only frightened her more.

"Don't mind him," Kilie said as gingerly as he could manage (which wasn't very, given his voice was still scratchy from sleep). Then, raising his voice, "Kallae! Get your cantankerous ass out here before I drag you out kicking and screaming!"

"I'd like to see you try."

Kilie didn't hesitate. He scrambled back into the room and returned moments later, dragging a mat behind him. Kallae, being the cantankerous ass in question, was still lying on it, arms folded across his chest in a posture that would have seemed peaceful if not for the permanent scowl etched across his face. Kilie dropped the mat's end, letting Kallae's legs thud against the ground.

Naturally, Kallae made no effort to rise and remained sprawled uncomfortably on the floor. "You summoned me?" he asked dryly, glancing up at Kilie.

Kilie gestured toward the girl, who was now cowering so severely it was a wonder she hadn't willed herself out of existence. "Help you," she repeated, the words barely escaping her lips before being swallowed by the yawning wind.

"Yes," Kallae said matter-of-factly, "it does appear we are in dire need of help. Perhaps you could direct us to a room built sometime after the invention of chronomagic, or, better yet, some food with more calories than it takes to digest. Or maybe, just maybe, you could get us off this godforsaken island before I chew my own hand off in frustration."

The wind carried the sweet scent of jasmine, which curdled in the air alongside Kallae's sharp words. His rant, while par for the course, was made slightly ridiculous by the fact that he was still sprawled on the ground. The humor, however, was entirely lost on the girl, who was now wriggling in Kilie's grasp as though her life depended on it.

"Kallae, must you always be such a colossal ass?"

"Have I given you any reason to expect otherwise? If nothing else, you can't fault me for being inconsistent."

Kilie rolled his eyes and crouched down next to the girl, "You must excuse him. He has the perpetual habit of waking up on the wrong side of the bed—"

"Well, if someone would stop talking in their sleep like an overgrown bat, maybe that wouldn't be the case."

"Now," Kilie continued, ignoring him, his expression softening into something sweet enough to attract a hive of honeybees, "how can you help us?"

The girl averted her gaze, staring at the ground with an intensity that could melt ice in the foothills of Umelelona. "Other villages. I bring you."

The look on Kilie's face was so sweet it was a wonder a hive of honeybees didn't try and make a home out of it.

Kilie's face brightened further. "You know of other villages with Threadcasters?"

The girl opened her mouth to speak, but then shut it abruptly as Kallae finally drew himself up, accompanied with a grunt and a series of loudly uttered profanities. She opted instead to nod.

"Our friend," Kilie said hastily, barely hiding his excitement. "Calder. Have you seen him? Heard of him?"

The girl's eyes darted between the two fairies, her lips parting before she shook her head rapidly.

"But you'll take us to this village? How far away is it? Are you—"

Kallae backhanded Kilie lightly with the back of his hand. "Could we try to maintain some semblance of control? Can you not see your incessant questioning is scaring her witless? That is, assuming she had any wits to begin with."

Kilie shot Kallae a glare but stopped his barrage of questions. He crouched again. "If your offer still stands, we accept it gratefully."

The girl nodded, pulling herself free from Kilie's arms. "Tomorrow. Dusk. Bring food."

"Enough for how long?" Kilie called after her, but she was already gone, the swaying branches her only farewell.

Kallae crossed his arms. "So, we're just going to trust a random girl to lead us to an unknown location without weapons, bearings, or any clue why she'd want to help us? Brilliant."

"What other choice do we have?" Kilie hissed, his gaze still fixed on the tree line.

"Off the top of my head? Don't follow her into what could very well be the arms of the Inquisitor."

"Who's to say this Inquisitor even exists? And besides, what could she gain by betraying us?"

Kallae shrugged. "Oh, I don't know—money, a ticket off this rock, fame, prestige. Maybe they're holding someone hostage. Or maybe—and this is just me spitballing—she doesn't want the Empire to find out her village is harboring fugitives."

"Well then in that case, the best thing for the villagers is that we leave them in peace, if the Inquisitor comes to visit, we will be long gone. We will make sure no trace of our being here remains."

"Perfect plan. We'll be long gone, screwing over a different village. Fantastic plan Kilie."

"What would you do, Kallae?" Kilie's voice rose, cutting through the gloom like a bolt of lightning.

"Get off this island before it's too late."

"Unless you have a ship hidden under your pillow or wings under your robe, that's not an option. Either come with me to find our Brothers and figure out what's happening, or stay here and sulk. The choice is yours."

Kallae grumbled. "Heck of a choice."

They exchanged little more than grumbles for the rest of the day. Kallae, despite his clear distaste, reluctantly helped gather their meager supplies, and Kilie, ever the optimist, took this as a sign of agreement. By dusk, they were armed with threadbare cloaks, a single surviving sock, and a plan so vague it might as well have been scribbled on a napkin. They met Miki, who glanced at their pitiful haul with an expression that could only be described as unimpressed. She merely waved her hand dismissively and said, "You shall hunt."

It did not seem worth mentioning that Kilie was neither fond of nor skilled at hunting. And with Kallae still blocked from accessing chronomagic, he would be about as useful as a hippopotamus brandishing a harpoon gun.

Lost in the woods with no idea where they were heading, how long it would take to get there, and a guide who barely spoke above monosyllables, the two fairies lost all sense of time and space. Hours—or maybe days—slipped by in a haze. Kilie did, however, manage to retain a small sense of direction, recognizing that they were heading further inland. The salty tang of the sea and the biting wind gave way to the heavy scent of earth and the thick mist of the forest. Bamboo trees loomed around them in such oppressive numbers that the daylight barely pierced the damp ground. During the day, the frantic screeching of drymophila birds accompanied them, their ceaseless chatter a poor substitute for silence, only slightly less maddening than the endless squawking of hunting bats that kept them company come nightfall.

After what Kilie would have sworn were two days spent stumbling through the bamboo forest, Kallae's mood darkened to such an extent that it felt almost palpable. Even Kilie, ever chipper, began to feel the sharp pangs of hunger gnawing at him. He spent more time than he cared to admit wondering whether uncooked bamboo might make for a suitable snack. It was only when he started chewing on one of the hardened husks that Miki came to a screeching halt, ripped the half-gnawed husk from his hand, and tossed it back into the forest with a huffed, "No."

Miki tossed her sack aside and scrambled through the underbrush, returning minutes later with a handful of fresh shoots, which she expertly scored with her knife. After shoving the pieces into her knapsack, she swung it over her shoulder and said, "Later. We cook."

Both fairies groaned, but Miki seemed about as concerned as a fish is with the concept of an underbaked pie. She continued through the forest, which by now had grown so dense that they were forced to draw their knives and hack their way through. Kallae, having only brought his sword, was less than thrilled at the prospect of using it to cut through the stubborn bamboo.

"So, Kilie," Kallae grumbled, his voice dripping with

sarcasm, "would you rather have died at sea, or be stuck in this cursed bamboo jungle?"

Kilie sighed and glanced down at the purple crystal on his collar. It had been dim ever since their run-in with the Red Lady, but lately its faint hum had grown louder, almost insistent. "Wherever we're going, we're getting closer to a Sanctum."

"Perfect," muttered Kallae, "I imagine that is the perfect place for the Inquisitor to lay in wait for anyone stupid enough to go there."

At some point—Kilie would have sworn it was weeks—they stopped to rest. Miki pulled out the shoots she had foraged earlier and set to work preparing a small fire. She tossed a handful of dried leaves at Kilie with a grunt. "Light."

Kilie, eager to feel useful for the first time in hours, tried with all his might to start a fire. It took him one try more than he would have liked to admit, but in the end, they had a modest flame.

The meal was meager but a welcome respite. The bamboo shoots, though strange in flavor, were at least edible. Kallae, ever the pessimist, remarked that they tasted like soap—a comment that earned him a very pointed glare from Miki. Still, paired with the broth Miki concocted from wild garlic, ginger, and some mystery fish powder she carried in a pouch, it was enough to quiet their stomachs for a few hours. After eating, they agreed—through a rather eloquent series of hand gestures—that sleep should be taken in shifts, with Kallae begrudgingly taking the first.

It felt like Kilie had just closed his eyes when Kallae's voice broke through the fog of sleep.

"Kilie," Kallae hissed.

Kilie groaned and sat up, rubbing the sleep from his eyes. "Is it already time?"

Kallae lowered his voice to a near whisper. "Shhh. Listen."

Kilie, still groggy, barely caught the faint crackling in the distance.

"Probably just some bats or your favorite raccoon critters," Kilie muttered, letting his eyelids flutter shut again.

Kallae slapped him across the cheek, hard enough to sting. "Pay attention."

Another crackle came from the depths of the forest, followed by a strange, eerie cry—a sound so sorrowful it seemed to slice through the air.

Kilie sat up, his eyes wide.

"I don't know what kind of bats you have back in Iselion, but that doesn't sound like a bat to me," muttered Kallae.

"Shhh," Kilie whispered now, creeping forward.

"Shhh yourself," Kallae shot back, his voice dripping with sarcasm. "You wouldn't hold your—"

"Shhh!" Kilie interrupted, grabbing Kallae by the collar and pulling him forward. "Come on, we have to check it out."

"Do we *have* to check it out?" Kallae's voice was thick with sarcasm.

Kilie, his heart pounding in his chest, turned to Kallae and raised an eyebrow. "Are you afraid something's going to jump out at you?"

Even in the dark, Kilie could see Kallae's brow furrow. "Well, yeah!"

"Suit yourself," Kilie shrugged, already forging ahead.

Several minutes passed when Kilie heard something rustling behind him. Stifling the urge to jump ten feet into the air from utter fright he turned around slowly to find Kallae's welcoming face about two hairbreadths away from his own.

"Ho traveler!" said Kallae, "top of the morning—or shall I say butt-crack of dawn to ya!"

"You nearly scared me half to death!"

Kallae jutted out his lower lip and trekked past him,

"Well with the noise you're making, you should count your lucky moons it was me who was following you and not a Tanuki or goodness knows what other horrors call this cursed island home."

The two fairies continued, following the cries into the depths of the forest. Until it stopped. As suddenly as it had begun it disappeared. Its absence left a cool chill in the air that was filled with the haunting chirps and howls of the night.

"We should turn back," Kallae murmured.

Kilie glanced at him, a determined glint in his eye. "We've come this far. Might as well see what we find."

Kallae, his hand heavy on Kilie's shoulder, tightened his grip. Despite his layers of clothing, Kilie could feel how cold Kallae's hand was. "Kilie, I feel something."

"Well good!" Kilie said, his voice higher than usual. "Lead the way."

Kallae's eyes flickered in the direction of something ahead. Then, slowly, he turned around. "We need to go. Now."

Kilie glanced towards Kallae and then walked forward. Hesitantly. His steps, though light, pierced through the darkness like gunshots. Gently, he spread the fronds of the bamboo shoots apart. No light came through. Only a figure. From this distance they could not tell if it was human or something else, for whatever it was, it was hunched over. Kilie shot a look at Kallae and raised his brows in the direction of the figure.

Kallae turned around slowly, his dark eyes swimming. Standing still as if he had been frozen in time.

"Brother Frenick," he said.

Kilie shot forward, knees hitting the ground as he knelt beside the figure. His hands cupped Frenick's chin, desperate for any sign of life. He searched Frenick's body for injury, but his touch was gentle, almost reverent.

Kallae appeared a moment later. His figure, though never a particularly welcoming one, was as imposing as

Mr. Faber that night. His face hung in shadows, and his black robes flickered behind him as if housing a flock of pixies beneath its billows, "Look down."

Frenick's body slumped forwards as Kilie gingerly released his grip. His spine seemed to fold in on itself, curving in an entirely unnatural way. Frenick's eyes were vacant, a film of milkiness sat over them like a man many years his senior. When Kallae glanced down, his stomach heaved. His nausea overcame him a moment later and he ran into the underbrush emptying out the meagre contents within.

When he returned, Kilie had not moved from his position. Nor had Frenick. Though Frenick would never move again. For his unnatural form was not caused by shackles nor rope, nor any form of injury inflicted by metal or fire, but the very earth itself. Partially obscured by his robes and the cover of nightfall was a bamboo sapling. Nothing unusual, given they were in a bamboo forest. All around them, saplings grew. Now there's something you must know about bamboo. One, it needs lots of water. This bamboo forest happened to have an ample supply of it. Two, it grows extremely quickly. The second part becomes important because what was once a small sapling when Frenick had been shackled to the bamboo behind him, was no longer as small as it had been. Surrounded by water and the rich nutrients of the forest, it had shot upwards, as plants are meant to do. But unfortunately, for our friend Frenick, it had shot up straight through his abdomen. A preliminary examination showed that the tender sapling had yet to find exit through the soft skin of Frenick's belly, but it was only a matter of time before it did. After all, a plant needs light. The entry wound, running clear through Frenick's tunic had already begun to fester, a thick mucus desperately trying to rid the body of its unwelcome guest. Based on the smell, Kilie suspected the bamboo had already punctured Frenick's bowel.

They could not determine how long Frenick had been left here but judging by the size of the sapling it could have been anywhere between three and five days.

Kilie ran off to the stream and returned cupping water in his palms. But Frenick, if he recognized it at all, showed no signs of having done so. If it weren't for the constant drivel which spewed from his mouth at a decibel scarce recognizable, they might have thought he had been turned to stone.

"We have to help him Kallae," the other fairy was still crouched down beside the Brother, the water trembling untouched in his hands.

Kallae shook his head. "He's gone, Kilie. There's nothing left."

Kilie shut his eyes, his shoulders sagging. "Who could have done this to him?"

"Inquisitor," said a voice.

Kilie's eyes snapped open, the fresh voice interrupting the thick fog of his panic. He could always recognize Kallae's monotone drone—six feet underwater, cotton in his ears, a mild earthquake, and Kallae would still find a way to sound unimpressed. But this voice, the one that sliced through the chaos, was unfamiliar. Miki.

"I can't leave him like this," Kilie said, his voice strained, as though the weight of Frenick's suffering was more than his heart could handle.

Miki's gaze was sharp as a hawk's talon, her expression unreadable, but the sharpness in her voice was unmistakable. Kallae sighed, "Even if we could free him, he would not last long. Not even the High Healers of Heron Academy could save him now."

Kilie's hand trembled as he knelt beside the shuddering form of Brother Frenick, the wild, incoherent babbling surging with such intensity that it felt as though the very earth beneath them might start quaking in sympathy. He reached into the folds of his robe, fingers brushing the hilt of his black blade. The cool metal was a silent promise, but before he could draw it, Miki lunged forward with a speed and ferocity that startled him, knocking the blade from his grasp.

"No," she said, her voice a low, firm command that rattled the air between them, "leave him. Inquisitor will come. We must go."

His eyes locked onto the frail, shaking form of Frenick, and for a fleeting second, Kilie thought he might actually break, might collapse under the weight of it. He could feel the gnawing emptiness inside, the aching pull of helplessness. He had been in this kind of mess before, though, hadn't he? *I can fix this*, he thought stubbornly, *I always fix things*. But this… this wasn't something he could fix.

Miki's face was unreadable as she turned away, her eyes scanning the surroundings, alert and wary. Kilie wiped his sweaty palms on his tunic, glanced at Frenick one last time, and stood.

"Alright," he said with a small sigh, forcing a grin, "I guess we're going then. Off to whatever nightmare waits for us next." His tone was light, but there was a crack in it—thin enough that only someone who knew him well would hear it.

Kallae grunted in agreement, already on his feet, his steps heavy with reluctant resignation. "Couldn't have said it better myself. Let's hope the Inquisitor prefers guests who arrive fashionably late."

Kilie flashed him a brief smile, then turned to follow Miki, feeling the sting of the night air against his skin. The jungle stretched out before them like a maze, the darkness swallowing them whole. But Kilie refused to let it swallow him too. He refused to let this be the end of it. After all, *he was Kilie*. And no matter how bleak it seemed, he would find a way through.

The only thing he knew for sure was that he couldn't go back to Cargyll. Not anymore.

TWELVE 十二

AKIRA

Akira gagged as bile rose in her throat, but she ran. She ran harder than she thought was possible, her legs screaming in protest, lungs burning. She was lucky, though. Despite having no clear plan—or really, no coherent thought in her head—she didn't run into the same direction as the Threadcasters. The odds of encountering them and surviving were laughable. Jiro was gone. Akira alone could never have matched up to two fully trained Threadcasters from Heron Academy. At best, it would've been a humiliating defeat. At worst, it would've been the kind of mess even the Inquisitor would find unsettling.

The lights, which had once been charming, seemed to mock her now, their gentle undulations almost taunting her. The scent of cherry blossoms, which had been so fresh and pleasant, now lingered sickly in the back of her throat, like azuki bean paste left out too long. Tears blurred her vision, shattering the pink and blue hues into fractured jewels that tumbled down her cheeks. Her head throbbed. Her vision was so blurred from sweat and tears that she nearly collided with Tsuyoshi on the path.

They stopped, awkwardly. It took them both a beat to recover from the near miss, but Tsuyoshi, being Tsuyoshi, was the first to compose himself. His hands folded delicately before him, his voice dripping with all the unearned affection of a man who thought far too highly of himself. "Now, now, my dear," he said with unnerving softness, "where are you off to in such a hurry?"

Akira's breaths came out in sharp bursts, her mind working overtime to catch up. But, as the sharp pain settled into her aching legs and searing lungs, clarity bloomed. "Tsuyoshi-sama," she gasped, remembering at the last minute to bow before him.

"Jiro—"

Her words failed her—whether from shock, exertion, or some unfortunate mix of both was unclear. She stumbled, struggling to find her breath. Several long moments passed, far longer than any normal conversation would have allotted, before she steadied enough to repeat herself.

"He was just taken."

"Who?" Tsuyoshi asked, his thin eyebrows quirked in that way that made him look like a bored cat with an agenda.

"Jiro," she managed, her fists clenching at her sides.

The Daimyo frowned, his lips pulling into a tight, sour line as if he'd bitten into a plum expecting sweetness and gotten something far more unpleasant instead. "And who do you claim took him?"

"Two Threadcasters," Akira practically shouted, her gaze darting around the courtyard, frantic. "If we move quickly, we might still catch them."

She resisted the urge to grab Tsuyoshi's long sleeves, though it was a close thing. Instead, she started walking back along the path, desperate to put distance between herself and his irritatingly calm demeanor. But before she could get very far, she felt a heavy hand on her shoulder, turning her roughly. He directed her to a nearby bench. Before she had time to protest, she was sitting. Tsuyoshi, unsettlingly close beside her, spoke in that same sickly-sweet voice.

"There's no need to be hasty," he said. "Tell me again what happened. From the beginning, preferably."

Akira shot up, only to be slammed back down onto the bench by the weight of his unblinking gaze. She barely managed to suppress a growl of frustration. "It was two Threadcasters," she said, trying to keep her voice steady, "they were destroying the Kitsune statue." She pointed in the direction where the fountain was. Or, well, where she *thought* it was. It was actually in the opposite direction, but that's neither here nor there. "He confronted them. And then they captured him. Said something about taking him to the farms on Cargyll?"

Tsuyoshi smiled, a slow, knowing smile that made Akira's stomach churn. "It's exactly as I suspected," he said, nodding as if everything made perfect sense. "You've misread the situation entirely."

Akira blinked, stunned. A thousand sharp responses flickered through her brain, but they all fell short, caught in the snarl of disbelief and mounting frustration. She was about to shout something when Tsuyoshi interrupted with that same infuriating sweetness.

"Now, Akira—" he glanced at her, "It is Akira, isn't it?"

Akira resisted the urge to roll her eyes, since this was no less than the tenth time they had met.

Before she could reply, Tsuyoshi continued, "I'm sure this is all just some misunderstanding. You've had a long journey, and anyone would be prone to jumping to conclusions. But rest assured, this little problem will be resolved. Leave it to me." He patted her arm, his smile unsettlingly tender. "In the meantime, you and your friends are welcome to stay here in Oto. Under my protection, of course."

Akira's heart hammered against her ribs. She was fairly certain Tsuyoshi didn't notice. She was also fairly certain that she might be dying of anxiety in front of a man who couldn't even remember her name. She smiled tightly, a perfect mask of politeness.

"That is most kind of you to offer, Tsuyoshi-sama," she said, the words slipping out like oil. "Might I ask if you know anything about the two Threadcasters who took Jiro?"

Tsuyoshi's face went completely blank, like a doll someone had forgotten to carve any expression into. "Now, now, my sweet girl," he cooed. "What have I told you? It's a dangerous time for a pretty girl like you to be spreading stories. We wouldn't want anything to happen to you or your friends, now would we?"

The smile that followed was the sort that belonged to a father doting on his child—or a man who'd found a nice piece of prey. "Best you run along now and tell your friends you're all most welcome here. Indeed, I'd warmly encourage that decision."

Akira didn't wait for any more of his insipid platitudes. She bowed again, teeth gritted and hastened away.

"Thank you, Tsuyoshi-sama. Your generosity is most kind."

"And Akira," he called after her, his gaze still fixed on the drooping sakura trees, "don't take too long to decide. I don't need to remind you what would happen if the Inquisitor were to stumble upon a group of lone converts."

Akira didn't stop. She didn't look back. She ran until she reached the hut, only narrowly avoiding crashing into the door. But this time, she didn't miss. She slammed into Ryū instead.

It felt like colliding with a block of marble. While her legs buckled beneath her, Ryū stood there as if nothing had happened.

"Oi, oi," he said, voice even deeper than usual (probably due to too much sake, Akira figured), "if you want some target practice, all you had to do was ask, Princess."

Akira didn't respond. She just grabbed him and started dragging him inside, ignoring his disgruntled grumbles. When they were halfway down the hall, however, Ryū planted his feet. He wasn't going anywhere without more explanation.

"Now, I'm all for following along blindly in the right circumstance but given you could be dragging me to an open bar or the ocean trenches of Castanon I'm going to need a little bit more context before I allow myself to be herded about like a cabbage brained oxen."

"Ox," Akira corrected, not even bothering to look up.

"What?"

"Ox," she repeated, deadpan. "Oxen is the plural. I assume you don't identify as a herd of cattle."

Ryū chewed his lip, thinking it over. "And what if I do? Ever considered herding me around, Princess?"

Akira could feel a headache starting to form. She shut her eyes, taking a deep breath. "Not here." Her voice dropped to a whisper. "Gather the others. Meet me in my chambers as soon as you find them."

Ryū winked. "Usually, I'd ask you to buy me a drink before I come to your chambers, but for you—"

Akira's gaze turned icy. "Not now."

The other Yōsei frowned and raised both his hands in mock surrender, "I'll find them."

As soon as Akira tore past the screens which led to her room, she slammed them shut. Within moments, the entire contents of the room lay in shambles upon the floor. The clothes once neatly folded sat about in various piles, papers flew around in the gentle evening breeze, and the terra-cotta statues of dragons and kitsune lay shattered in pieces. By the time the others gingerly opened the screen, the once elaborate room would have been barely deemed acceptable to house the lowest-born slave.

"The décor not to your liking?" Shoji asked, glancing around, as though the walls might give him some kind of answer.

Akira ignored him, waving a hand to usher the others in. Shoji and Ryū shuffled through the door, each wearing a look of mild confusion, while Jun stood frozen, eyeing the chaos around them like someone who'd just stepped into the aftermath of a drunken house party. In the doorway, Kyou lingered, standing like a reluctant guest at a party he never wanted to attend.

"Why did you bring him?" Akira sighed, her voice carrying the weight of someone who'd just learned a new way to despise the universe. She turned to Ryū.

"He was with the others," Ryū shrugged, as if the world was full of such unfortunate coincidences. "What was I supposed to do, tie him up?"

"Fine," Akira muttered, clearly already regretting this entire situation, "I suppose you're here now. Come around, gather close."

Kyou remained by the door while the others formed a circle of confusion and sleep deprivation around her. She curled her fingers towards her chest, "And for the illiterate amongst us," she said, "I repeat. Come around, gather close."

Kyou stayed put by the door for a second longer, as if pondering whether he could leave without causing too much of a scene. Then, with a deep, dramatic sigh, he joined the circle. Akira closed her eyes, letting the chronomagic flood her veins. A chill washed over her like the first snap of winter, the kind that crawls under your skin and makes you question your life choices. But as the magic settled in, a warmth began to spread—a comfortable heat, not quite scalding, but enough to make you feel like you've been standing too close to a campfire. Blue threads materialized from her fingertips, stretching and twisting like something out of a fever dream, latching onto each of her comrades, until they all looked like they'd been chosen for a bizarre cult initiation.

"Is this strictly necessary?" Kyou asked, eyeing the threads like they might bite.

"Your calculations are slightly off," Jun added helpfully, pointing at a flickering thread. "It's the pink and blue moon waning rather than the yellow."

"Sugoi!" Shoji shouted, spinning in place like an over-enthusiastic child.

"Shut it, the lot of you!" Akira yelled, hands pressed to her temples as though fighting off a headache. "It's like being surrounded by a flock of nesting gulls!"

"Now listen up," she said, voice tight. "I don't know how long I can sustain this many threads."

Ryū frowned. A beat later, turquoise light from his crystal began to bleed down his arms, spilling out like a stream of liquid light. More threads exploded from his fingers, weaving together with hers, creating a tangled mess that would make even the most patient spider give up in disgust.

"Show-off," muttered Kyou under his breath.

"A thank you would also suffice," Ryū replied with a grin.

Kyou ignored him. "So, are you going to tell us why we're standing in this glowing orb of blasphemy?"

"Simple," Akira said, the words heavy with frustration. "As long as I'm flecting, anything that touches these threads will be sped up. To anyone outside, our conversation will come out as a garbled mess. They won't understand a word of it."

"Neat," Shoji said, twirling around to admire the kaleidoscope of colors bouncing off the walls. "I could get used to this."

"Enough with the sightseeing," Kyou cut in, rolling his eyes. "Unless someone starts talking, I'm leaving."

"No one's stopping you," Akira snapped, her tone

sharp as broken glass. "In fact, no one invited you in the first place."

"Well, that isn't strictly true, Princess," Ryū chimed in, his voice full of mock sweetness.

"Shut it."

The silence that followed was thick enough to cut with a knife—if knives could slice through the kind of tension hanging in the air.

"It's Jiro," Akira said finally, her voice low and taut. "He's been taken."

Predictably, this sparked a discordant chorus of voices so loud and disjointed it could have shattered stone. They babbled over each other, trying to make sense of what she'd said, until Akira cut them off with a shout that was so colorful it could have painted a mural.

"If you'd all just shut up for a minute," she hissed, "I could answer your questions."

When the noise died down, she spoke again, her words crisp and clipped. "Two Threadcasters, from the Order. I saw them. They were trying to break down the Kitsune statue. Jiro-sama—he tried to stop them. Before he could do anything, they took him. I tried to help, but he warped me. I didn't see where they took him, but the Threadcasters said they were bringing him to the Watchtower. If we move fast, we might catch him before it's too late."

"We should go to Tsuyoshi-sama," Jun suggested, his voice earnest. "He'll know what to do. He'll help us."

"He will not."

Jun's eyes narrowed, doubt creeping in. "I know Tsuyoshi-sama isn't the most warm-hearted Yōsei, but Jiro and him have worked together for years. He'll—"

"You're not listening," Akira interrupted, the words spilling out like a storm. "I've already been to him. He's in on it. He wants us here, with him."

"Perhaps joining—" Kyou began.

"What?" Akira snapped, eyes flashing. "Let me guess.

You think we should join Tsuyoshi-sama?"

She gestured forward, her sarcasm dripping like honey. "Well, go ahead. Be my guest. I should actually applaud you for sticking around this long. Go ahead. Leave."

Kyou frowned. "If you'd let me finish—" he said slowly, drawing out each word like it might help Akira's brain process what he was about to say. "I was going to suggest we join the others back at base in Gedo. Gather our forces first."

Jun's eyes glazed over, staring at some distant, unseen horizon. "I would not say that is wise," he said, his voice laden with doubt. "No, no. We can't trust anyone anymore." His gaze shifted around the group, and Akira squirmed under the weight of it.

Another silence, even thicker than the first, settled over them. One that no one seemed eager to break.

When Ryū spoke again, it was with the slow, reluctant crawl of someone trying to grasp a concept too big for his mind to hold. "So... what do we do now?"

Akira hung her head, her shoulders sagging under the weight of everything she'd just said.

Beside her, Shoji sputtered something incoherent before repeating himself more firmly. "Well, it's obvious, isn't it?"

The others all turned to look at him, their expressions as vacant as if they had been drawn by someone with a clinical case of depression.

"We're going to break him out of that blasted tower of course."

THIRTEEN

KALLAE

Kallae woke up feeling about as refreshed as a fish that had been left to rot under the blazing sun of Trevnesia's sand dunes. The kind of fish you find in an old boot a week later. It had taken over an hour to finally drag Kilie away from Brother Frenick's corpse. It was only when Kallae and Miki physically hauled him off that Kilie finally consented—though 'compliance' was a stretch. The whole way back, Kilie muttered nonsense like, "This isn't right. No fellow Brother should die alone." Kallae had seriously considered leaving him there to get the poetic solitude he seemed to want so much.

Kallae's poor sleep had been compounded by a series of delightful miseries. First, there was the ground—about as comfortable as being forcibly introduced to a cactus. Even when he managed to ignore the painful knots of muscle contorting in his back, any glimmer of rest was sliced through by Kilie's endless muttering. Kallae caught somewhere between three minutes and an hour of sleep before hurling his shoe at Kilie's head. (Not that it helped much, but at least it made the silence feel more earned.)

Unsurprisingly, the meager rest did nothing to lift Kallae's perpetually foul mood. Their breakfast was a rushed affair, and the rice cakes they ate could've been used to pave roads. "It's edible," Kallae muttered, "in a famine perhaps."

The conversation turned to their next move, but it was hardly a debate. Turning back wasn't an option—they were ill-armed, ill-prepared, and utterly clueless about the villages they might encounter. Forward wasn't exactly any better, but perhaps the food ahead might taste less like ash. The decision to press on was cemented when Miki assured them that the next village was less than a day's walk.

By the time they reached it, the sun had made a valiant attempt to shine, despite the obvious risk to its own health. Kallae's mood only darkened further, as if the very atmosphere had gotten the message. In fact, it was a wonder the sun hadn't decided to pack up and find a less oppressive corner of the world. He, on the other hand, vented his frustrations on the bamboo shoots lining their path, hacking through them like they had personally insulted him. If there were an award for the careless destruction of plant life, Kallae would have the win in the bag.

The village looked almost exactly like the last one. In fact, it might've been the same one, though the distinct lack of that rancid fish smell, still fresh with the faintest whisper of rot, suggested otherwise. It was small, with a few more wooden lean-tos than the last place—though honestly, if Kallae had to count the shoddy buildings to pass the time, he would've preferred to stick to the bamboo. Ramshackle balconies extended from some of the houses, with banners hanging over the edges. Though neither Kallae nor Kilie could decipher the scribbles on them, they did add a splash of color to the otherwise drab shades of grey and brown. A red gate, similar to the one which greeted them on the shores, welcomed them to the town, inscribed with a word above it that both assumed must be the name of the town (which it was).

The village had a bit more life, too, as if the population had decided to stop hiding. People moved in the streets, dragging bags of rice, gossiping in low murmurs, or milling around storefronts that looked like they'd been slapped together out of spite. Like before, there was no clear distinction between Yōsei and humans—unless you counted the odd pointed ear sticking out from a mass of unkempt hair. Kallae was only able to distinguish the two types by spotting ears that weren't entirely human, though it felt like the whole village had decided to blend in just to screw with him.

"Arrived," Miki declared when they passed under the familiar looking red gate.

Kallae's usual sarcastic remark lodged itself in his throat like a bad piece of rice, so he swallowed it back and muttered something about finding food instead. Honestly, if he was going to be here for another few hours, he'd need to keep his energy up for the vital task of hating everyone around him.

Miki was greeted like a hero, wrapped in a flood of villagers babbling in rapid Fujik. They embraced her like she was returning from a long pilgrimage, and Kallae had to suppress the instinct to roll his eyes so hard they might get stuck. When Miki finally stopped talking, the villagers turned their attention to the two fairies, and that was when Kallae really started wishing for a solid brick wall to appear so he could promptly slam his face into it. The villagers stared at them, no doubt admiring their exotic aura—or more likely, trying to figure out what in the world they were supposed to do with them.

Kallae was about to offer a pithy comment when children and adults alike began pawing at their robes and stroking their hair as if they'd been carved from some sacred tree. The whole thing made Kallae deeply uncomfortable, but Kilie seemed to enjoy it, his grin spreading wider than the distance between Kallae's patience and its breaking point (which wasn't particularly far). Then one of the villagers reached into his robe. That was when both fairies took a step back, and a collective instinct to not get mauled by the town's residents set in.

Miki raised her hands and glanced and the two respective parties, "Ok," she said, "they know you Threadcaster. They want to see crystal."

Kallae grunted and shoved his hands deeper into his pockets, ignoring the lingering sensation of hands brushing his sleeves. Kilie, with his usual enthusiasm, began to show off, summoning blue threads that split the air with electric grace, glowing in the lantern light. Kallae managed not to sigh audibly. He figured the villagers were going to stare at him until he either snapped or did something impressive. He was leaning toward snapping.

After a series of non-verbal exchanges, they were ushered towards one of the huts. Being a village of slightly more import than the one they had come from; they actually had some form of a guesthouse. It was a low-built construction, barely a story in height. On one side it seemed they had run out of materials for walls, or perhaps it was an artistic choice. Though if it was artistic (which it was) Kallae could not help thinking he would have chosen warmth over being able to see the large, curved branches of the gingko tree or hear the unsettling sounds of the twittering bats and chirping grasshoppers. Nevertheless, given their most recent accommodations, of *'the ground'*, their situation had much improved.

Kallae had been about ready to eat his own shoes, but the noodles they offered were actually tolerable, which in this context, counted as a small victory. They weren't exactly gourmet, but at least they weren't likely to give him food poisoning.

By the time he had finished two bowls, his fatigue was heavy enough to pull him into a dreamless sleep. Even

Kilie's absurd snoring couldn't keep him awake, though he was haunted by strange dreams involving killer raccoons and bespectacled men with glowing books. Honestly, at this point, a dream involving killer raccoons seemed like the least offensive part of his day.

Kallae woke again, not to the sun, or to any heroic burst of self-awareness, but to a loud, jarring slam against the door. Kilie was already sitting bolt upright in his bed, staring at the door like he could make it disappear with sheer force of will. Kallae let out a groggy sigh.

"Well," he muttered, "were you planning on getting the door, or hoping that our guest might just tear it down?"

Kilie frowned, but then hopped off the mat, pulling himself to his feet in a fashion that appeared to break several laws of physiology. When the door opened, the knocking stopped abruptly. And for a few moments, nothing happened. Then, with all the subtlety of an avalanche, Kilie was dragged out of the room.

By the time Kallae had managed to lift himself convince himself to investigate further, he found Miki standing there, looking as casually alarmed as she ever did.

"Did anyone ever tell you it's common courtesy to wait until the sun's up before banging on a door like a wild banshee is afoot?" Kallae asked, voice still thick with sleep.

Miki shushed him, the universal signal for 'You're about to die, but I'd rather you not talk about it.' Then whispered, "No banshee. Danger."

"In my book a banshee would qualify as dangerous, but—"

"Shhhh," hissed Miki and prompted ushered them to a meandering stairwell which seemed to lead into the depths of despair or perhaps *the Bedraggled Cockerel* on a particularly rambunctious evening.

It wasn't the first time Kallae had been shoved into a potential death trap, and he was sure it wouldn't be the last. The tunnels beneath the guesthouse were dark, twisting, and filled with so much dust that it could've doubled as a dust farm. And Miki had the gall to keep shushing him as if he was the problem here. They walked for what felt like hours—Kallae's mind had begun to file complaints about everything, from his sore legs to the distinctly illogical nature of their predicament—until they reached a dead-end. Kilie crashed into Miki, and Kallae followed, slamming into him like a train wreck. At this point in time there was a greater chance of Kallae becoming a professional teacup painter than any semblance of a lucid thought.

The silence in the dead-end was only broken by Kallae's most creative curses.

After a few more moments of awkward scrambling, Miki managed to open a hole in the ceiling. Dust rained down around them, and Kallae felt it was the universe's cruel joke to make him cough just as noisily as possible.

Miki, of course, shushed him again. They climbed out of the hole and into another room that defied categorization—part workshop, part meat-curing facility, part something that probably shouldn't be touched. Before Kallae could question how any of this was remotely acceptable, a distant hum of conversation began to filter through the walls.

And, naturally, Miki shushed him again.

Kallae resisted the urge to do something that would definitely not be considered polite. Instead, he crouched with Kilie as Miki gestured toward the scene unfolding before them.

"Too late," murmured Miki, "cannot escape anymore. Must wait here."

In the courtyard—if you could call the open dirt patch a "courtyard"—a gathering had formed. Why, exactly, there was a gathering at the ass-crack of dawn was utterly beyond Kallae's comprehension. It wasn't so much a meeting as it was an uncoordinated group of people who had clearly not had enough sleep and possibly needed a round of vigorous psychotherapy. But before Kallae could unleash his usual arsenal of entirely impolite observations—of which there were many—a shout split the air and cleaved the crowd in two.

The two fairies exchanged a look, and Miki gave them the universal signal to shut up. She pointed to her lips, then held up a finger.

"Quiet," she hissed, "cannot find you. Will kill you—and rest of village for keeping secret."

The crowd parted, and the scene before them came into sharper focus, like something unpleasant in the corner of your eye that you're too tired to avoid. Kallae counted five figures—though his count was dubious at best, given that he hadn't slept in what felt like days. Four of the figures wore similar garb: long, dark cloaks with red trim, and metal plates that flared from their waists like someone had decided it would be 'fashionable' to wear armor and a dinner plate at the same time. The burnished iron pads on their necks extended down to their shoulders, stopping just above the elbow—just the sort of armor designed to be both completely impractical and vaguely menacing. Their faces were inscrutable, hidden beneath black iron helmets that flared out into dark disks, with chain-link cowls beneath them that probably prevented any meaningful conversation beyond the occasional grunt and clinking of metal.

Two of them wielded curved blades, but not typical ones. Rather than tapering to a sharp point, their blades ended in an edge so lethal-looking it made Kallae wonder if their next job was going to be cutting someone's dreams into small, manageable pieces more befitting for you dirt-average Joe. The other two wandered around aimlessly, as if they were under the distinct impression that standing still made them seem mysterious.

And then there was the fifth figure, who appeared to have skipped the intimidating training altogether. The man—or Yōsei, as Kallae presumed—was so painfully thin, he could've passed for a particularly lanky stick insect. He was tall, but not tall enough to demand respect simply for existing. His face didn't shout 'terror,' like Lord Lianthorn or Mr. Faber on a particularly ornery day. No, it was... entirely unremarkable. His face was a blank canvas—no scarring, no grimace, no smile. His eyes were an unoffensive shade of brown, and his hair was arranged in a half-bun that Kallae had seen a few villagers sporting. It was so immaculately kept that Kallae briefly considered whether this guy's hair had a better life than he did.

When the man turned to his companions and gestured for them to stand behind him, Kallae realized he must be the leader—though he should have figured it out sooner, since the guy wore gold-trimmed robes that practically screamed 'I'm important.' The four men complied with the kind of immediate obedience that suggested they had no better option.

The larger group of villagers huddled together like a flock of pigeons caught in the rain, their faces twitching with apprehension. As a few of them drifted closer to the hut where they were hiding, Kallae spotted a couple of familiar faces—mostly ones he had already filed away under 'no reason to care.'

A loud crack split through the gathering, so sharp it made Kallae's eardrums briefly wonder if they were being assaulted. A thin staff, wrapped in red silk that fluttered like an offended river, was slammed into the dirt.

"Hopkaidō no murabito!" a voice called out, crisp and certain.

Kallae shot a glance at Miki, who sighed and began translating, her Cygren far from perfect but still understandable. "Villagers of Hopkaidō." *A brief disclaimer, though Miki was certainly trying her best, her Cygren, is what one might describe as elementary, so I will take the liberty of augmenting her translation for the remainder of this interaction. Now back to the story- hey I never did claim I was a competent narrator.*

The slender Yōsei, still dragging his staff along the

ground like someone who'd read too many melodramatic novels, continued. "Is this the welcome you deem acceptable to representatives of the Kitsune Emperor?"

No one answered. One villager, either particularly brave or particularly stupid, tried to sneak away from the crowd. But the Yōsei's gaze snapped onto him, like a predator deciding which part of the mouse it would eat first. With a quick glance to one of his men, the villager was grabbed and yanked back into the fold.

The Yōsei crouched down to meet the man's eyes, a disturbingly gentle look in his voice. "Ah, ah, ah," he cooed, as though speaking to a pet caught chewing on furniture, "why try to flee just as we're getting to know each other? You should be pleased. It's not every day a tiny insignificant town like this gets a visit from the Inquisitor, now is it?"

"The Inquisitor?" Kilie asked softly, his face reflecting a mix of confusion and unease.

Miki shushed him, but the tension in her voice made it clear she wasn't happy to be in the same space as these people.

The villager remained quiet, his gaze now dropping to the floor. Though after the rough handling he had received it was difficult to say if this was due to some form of obliged reverence, or if he had merely lost consciousness. The Inquisitor's eyes narrowed, and he rose back to his full height. He threaded his staff between his fingers, the red ribbon fluttering behind him like a stream of blood.

"Now, now," he said quietly, "there is no need to be frightened my dear people. I am here to protect you."

The Yōsei tilted his head, his lips curving into a smile that could've been described as 'strained grimace' if you were feeling charitable. "Who is the leader of the good people of Hopkaidō?"

Not one person stepped forward. Somewhere in the distance, birds suddenly took flight in a flurry so dense it dimmed the sun.

The Inquisitor's fingers tapped rhythmically on his staff, and his smile stretched impossibly wide. "I trust we are all capable of civilized conversation, hmm?"

An elderly man, his face more wrinkles than skin at this point, stepped forward and bowed deeply enough that Kallae thought the wind might knock him over.

"Inquisitor-sama," the man stammered, not looking up, "apologies for the… unacceptable welcome. Your presence is… unexpected."

The Inquisitor laughed. A sound which coming out of any other person might have been no more unsettling than a child with a hard-boiled sweet, but from the mouth of the Inquisitor it dripped with a darkness that clung to Kallae's skin like crude oil. "Ah, but I'm sure you'll do better. Just answer my questions, and there's no need for such… platitudes."

The villager straightened, his voice growing louder. "Long reign the Way of the Water!" His voice became discordant as it echoed around the empty houses along the street.

The Inquisitor nodded, the smile still plastered on his face like it was welded there. "Indeed."

For what seemed like an eternity, the Yōsei drifted from one villager to the next, examining their faces with a scrutinizing gaze. His staff clinked along the ground with each step, like a countdown to something particularly unpleasant. Kallae had a feeling this wasn't going to end with everyone holding hands and singing songs.

Finally, the Inquisitor stood before his guards, his smile never wavering. "Well," he said quietly, "I must say I am surprised."

The village chief looked up, panic flickering in his eyes. "What can we help you with, Inquisitor-sama?"

The Yōsei grinned, his voice low enough to make Kallae want to dive into a hole and stay there. "What do I always say?"

One of the guards, the biggest one, stepped forward. "Obedience is all."

The Inquisitor nodded, still grinning. "Indeed. And since you've so kindly offered… I would like to know why Hopkaidō opposes the Holy Emperor's will, hmm?"

The village chief gasped, eyes darting upward. "Never!" he blurted, his words tumbling out like a landslide. "Hopkaidō has always been, and always will be, loyal to the Empire."

The Inquisitor's eyes hardened. He crouched to meet the chief's gaze. "Then tell me, Chief…" His voice dropped to a growl. "Why, after the Emperor has fed you, clothed you, protected you, do you scorn him by betraying everything he stands for?"

"We would never!"

The Inquisitor slapped the chief with the side of his staff, sending the man sprawling backward into the crowd, where he was promptly swallowed up, like a hapless snack caught in a very hungry stomach. Kallae could practically hear the collective gasp of the villagers as they crammed themselves together to avoid being next.

"Do not lie to me," seethed the Inquisitor, his smile gone, replaced by a scowl that could freeze a river. The once elegant curve of his lips had given way to something much more jagged.

The Inquisitor gestured with his sharp, bony brows, signaling for his guards to move. They spread out like some macabre choreography, circling the villagers with the precision of predatory animals.

"Tell me, dear people," the Inquisitor crooned, his voice syrupy sweet, "are you all traitors, hmmm?"

The crowd shifted nervously, their eyes darting everywhere and nowhere at the same time. Some shook their heads, others muttered.

"Then am I to believe you are all merely stupid?" The Inquisitor's voice rang out with the sort of fake patience only someone truly insufferable could muster. His steps, slow and deliberate, rang against the stones like the ticking of a clock nearing midnight. He walked toward the crowd with all the grace of a man who enjoyed every second of his own drama. "Because I cannot think why else one of your own"—he pointed with exaggerated care, like he was conducting a symphony of suffering—"would help a Threadcaster."

Kallae's jaw clenched at the mention of his kind, but he bit back the bitter retort that threatened to spill out. This was not the time for moral high ground, not when it was clear the Inquisitor had no concept of what that even meant.

The crowd gasped. It wasn't as if they had much of a choice—his words had the kind of weight that broke whatever fragile resolve they had left.

"Four days ago," the Inquisitor began again, the prelude to something unpleasant hanging heavy in the air, "one of my subordinates found a Cargyllian Threadcaster heading towards this town from Oto. He was apprehended and left to think upon his transgressions. But imagine my surprise, when this morning…" He slammed his staff down on the ground with a satisfying crack, "I found someone had relieved him of his much-deserved contemplation. Freeing him from his suffering with a blade to his heart."

"Frenick," Kallae muttered, the name scraping against his throat like sandpaper. He turned to Kilie, who was staring ahead, his lips thin and tight.

The Inquisitor narrowed his eyes, drawing the attention back to him. He gestured for his guards to close off the perimeter. The villagers were herded into the square like cattle being directed toward a slaughterhouse, and Kallae couldn't help but wonder how many of them would survive the next few minutes.

"Now we can do this the easy way," the Inquisitor purred, a smile creeping back onto his lips, "or the hard way. It makes no difference to me. But I suggest you think hard on what you decide, hmmm?"

With a flourish, the Inquisitor reached into his robes and tossed a chunk of clear rock onto the ground. It clinked loudly as it hit, and for a moment, Kallae swore he saw the light around it ripple like water. The crystal was so pure, so perfect, it could have belonged to another world.

The Inquisitor turned to the villagers, his eyes gleaming with cruel amusement. "Now, my good people," he said, his voice soft, almost coaxing, "line up." Some of them complied immediately, and the Inquisitor smiled that same insufferable smile. "Very good."

He gestured toward the crystal and the first villager in line, a woman so small Kallae couldn't quite place if she was mortal or Yōsei. Maybe both. There were too many things wrong with this place to focus on just one.

The Inquisitor's grin widened. "Step on it."

The woman bowed deeply, almost too deeply for comfort, and then, with a visible tremble in her hands, stepped onto the crystal. A crack rang out, sharp and biting, but the crystal held.

And so it went, the process repeated with each villager who came forward. With every step, the cracks spread wider, the crystal's once flawless surface beginning to look more like a web of desperation.

"What is that?" whispered Kallae, watching the scene unfold with growing dread.

Kilie turned to him, his eyes rimmed a color he could not decipher, "It's a chronocrystal."

Kallae frowned. "I've never seen one this color, nor one so large."

Kilie shook his head, his voice barely above a whisper. "There are some in the vaults of Heron Academy. It's a dead crystal."

Before Kallae could respond, a deafening crack split the air, and for a second, Kallae thought the crystal had finally given in. But it wasn't the crystal—no, the sound had come from the Inquisitor's staff. A man—no older than twenty-five, if that—stood over the crystal, foot hovering inches above it, a tremble quivering at the edge of his lip.

The Inquisitor turned on his guards, and they lunged at the young man, throwing him to the ground with a sickening thud.

"You sympathize with them, do you?" the Inquisitor sneered, his tone dripping with disdain. "Well, if you care so much for the Way of the Light, then you can gladly die with them."

Kilie lurched forward, his own crystal shining its bright purple hue as it lit up the gloom. Kallae and Miki grabbed hold of him just before he could go hurtling out of the hut like a horse down a racetrack. Kilie struggled against them, but a few moments later he relented, his body growing limp as another two, then three of the villagers joined the other man who had hesitated above the crystal.

"What will happen to them?" Kilie asked, his voice ragged.

"Torture," Miki said, her tone chilling in its casualness. "Then death."

"I need to help them."

Kallae gripped Kilie's shoulder more firmly, "It is not on you to help fools. All they need to do is step on the crystal."

"Would you, if you were in their position?"

"Would you not?"

Kilie's eyes widened, his purple crystal flickering dangerously, "I would never."

"It's not even a real crystal, it's symbolic. Meaningless. What difference will it make if one person refuses? The next will crush it all the same. It is not worth leaving this world before my work is done to save a people beyond saving."

"The crystal is real Kallae. It has no lifeforce of the Great Clock in it, but that does not make it any less real."

The two fairies fell silent, turning their attention back to the scene before them. The sobs and cries from the villagers had now built into a kind of symphony, a chorus of anguish that rang through the hollow air. The sound, in its bleak beauty, might have been moving if the weight of sorrow hadn't been so suffocating.

"There is an evil in this place that even Amriel cannot penetrate," whispered Kallae.

Kilie's gaze turned upward, staring through the cracks in the roof of the hut. "He's here. As he is everywhere."

Kallae followed his gaze but saw nothing. Nothing but the shifting shadows and the relentless tick-tock of time that carried them all forward, one step at a time.

FOURTEEN 十四

AKIRA

Ryū's labored breaths echoed Akira's own as they sprinted through the dense forest. Behind them, Jun and Shoji kept pace with varying degrees of success. Kyou, still sulking—or something to that effect—lagged several meters behind. The underbrush was thick, but the tangled boughs of the ancient trees offered no comfort to Jiro's clan, as they all took turns glancing nervously over their shoulders.

"How much farther?" Shoji panted, his feet on the verge of revolt and his lungs threatening to ignite from within.

Akira, still pushing forward, managed a muffled grunt, "Just a bit further." She coughed, the rapid movement sending a bug straight down her throat. "The watchtower's right on the border of Oto. We passed it on our way in."

"That's at least another five miles!" Shoji shot back,

his voice a blend of disbelief and mild hysteria.

Ryū's voice cut through the air like a whip. "Well, the faster you run, the sooner we'll get there." To reinforce the point, he threw a tangerine at Shoji for good measure. It was a solid throw—too bad Shoji wasn't prepared for it.

Shoji's reaction was immediate: he barreled ahead, leaving the rest behind. But his triumph was short-lived. A few moments later, he was distracted by an evergreen tree, its branches laden with ripe lychees. The scent was so intoxicating that Akira almost stopped herself. Almost. Instead, she growled, "We don't have time."

Shoji, however, had no such reservations. Lychees in hand, juice dripping from his chin, he shrugged. "Bah! There's never a wrong time for lychees. Tell me one scenario where they aren't essential. I dare you."

"Now!" Ryū barked, his arms already pulling Shoji along in a half-nelson.

The five miles, thankfully, didn't take as long as they feared. Though, when one considered the distance against the backdrop of impending doom, forty minutes felt like the entire span of a lifetime.

When the tower finally emerged from the gloom, it was almost laughable. Akira had remembered it as an imposing structure, a jagged sentinel reaching up to mock the heavens. But now, shrouded in the shadows of evening, it appeared more like a stranded boat lost at sea. There was no plan. No light. Half-charged crystals. And yet breaking into the tower and rescuing Jiro seemed like the only option they had.

"Well, that was easy," Shoji puffed, his chest heaving as though he'd just crossed the finish line of a marathon.

"It was," Jun said, though his frown deepened as his eyes scanned the area. "A little too easy for my liking. Why didn't anyone follow us?"

Shoji, still bent double, raised a hand in mock protest. "I was joking."

"Well, if we weren't prisoners of Tsuyoshi-sama's, what reason would he have to stop us?" Ryū added, the logic of his words hanging in the air, doing nothing to alleviate the unease.

"Indeed," Jun muttered, eyes narrowing as he glanced around. "We'll scout the area tomorrow. But first, we need to rest."

"Yeah, I don't know about you lot," Ryū said, stretching as though he had all the time in the world, "but I prefer undertaking suicide missions after a full night's sleep."

"It's only a suicide mission if you die," Shoji added helpfully.

"Yes, that's—" Ryū sighed. "Never mind."

They made camp soon after, though 'camp' was a generous term for the haphazard collection of blankets, crushed shirts, and a flickering fire. It was far from luxurious, especially when compared to the sprawling comfort of the compound they'd just escaped. Still, sleep found them quickly. In fact, none of them bothered to set up a watch. They all slumped around the fire in a disjointed circle, like half-hearted cultists trying to decide what to sacrifice.

Jun was laying on his stomach, his face shining an unnatural orange thanks to the glow from the fire, "So I guess we're Ronin now."

Akira could sense Kyou's shadow stir as he curled himself more tightly away from the fire, despite the chill which hung in the air.

Ryū, who was one badly assembled sleeping mat away from Kyou, inhaled sharply. "We are not Ronin. Not until Jiro draws his last breath. Until then, we are Jiro's men."

Akira's heart seemed to race—whether it was from the sudden spike of emotion or the oppressive weight of uncertainty, she couldn't tell. It wasn't a restful sleep. Not by a long shot. But somewhere in the haze of discomfort, sleep did finally claim her.

Morning broke with the subtle cruelty of light seeping through her eyelids, an unmistakable signal of dawn's arrival. Most of the others were already awake, though Kyou remained still in his curled-up position, making even a fetal position look threatening.

Akira sighed as she folded up her blanket and shoved it into her bag, leaning it against a pile of rocks along with the others. She glanced around the clearing, suddenly aware of the absence. "Where's Shoji?"

Ryū waved a hand toward the bushes. "He's off collecting mushrooms."

"Does he even know which ones are edible?"

Ryū shrugged, a gesture that could mean anything or nothing at all.

"Perfect." Akira poured herself a cup of steaming green tea from the fire, eyeing the lack of food. Trust Jiro's ragtag crew to pack tea but no food.

"Jiro should have been brought to the tower by now," Jun said, his voice low.

Kyou scoffed, his tone dripping with sarcasm. "Ah, your seer-senses are finally kicking in?"

Ryū, as always, found humor where none existed. He threw a pebble at Kyou, narrowly missing his target. "So, the great sleeping giant awakens. I was halfway through planning your funeral," he said thoughtfully. "So tragic. He died so young. Stolen from us in the prime of—" He was cut off when Kyou threw the pebble back with far more force than it had been thrown.

"You'd like that, wouldn't you?" Kyou muttered, slouching down into the circle.

"Well, just who's bright idea was it to wander out here on nothing more than a hunch?" Kyou snapped. "We need more people! Even if he's in there, how are we supposed to get him out?"

He gestured at the tower, now bathed in the harsh light of morning, looking as intimidating as it had in Akira's memories. The dark wood walls seemed to stretch infinitely upward, curving platforms jutting out at intervals, resembling an enormous double-toothed saw. There was no door—except one, eternally guarded by an ever-rotating group of sentries.

Akira couldn't help herself. "And who exactly would you ask for help, Kyou? Do you have an army hidden in your pockets? Perhaps an armada of archers tucked under your robes?"

Kyou glared at her. "The rest of Jiro's men. If we return to Gedo, we can gather anyone willing to help. Even the villagers if we have to!"

"Oh yes," Akira retorted, "that's exactly what we need—ancient men with pitchforks. I'm sure they'll be a tremendous help against academy-trained Threadcasters."

"So what, your brilliant plan is for the five of us to sneak past a bunch of Threadcasters?" Kyou shot back. "Just knock on the front door and ask them to kindly let us in?"

"Don't be an ass."

"Then stop making asinine suggestions."

"Then make a suggestion yourself!"

"I just did."

Before the bickering could escalate, a clicking sound cut through the noise. They all turned to see Jun, muttering to himself as he moved a piece across a boulder.

"What in the Tanuki's tail are you doing?" Shoji asked, returning with a handful of mushrooms.

"Playing i-go," Jun muttered without looking up.

"Against yourself?"

"I thought we were trying to come up with a plan, not sit around making noise," Ryū grumbled, still preoccupied with executing a series of complicated lunging exercises off a tree.

"Helps me think," muttered Jun. He moved another piece. *Click*. "Besides, this is the only way it represents some form of a challenge."

"Ah I see," said Shoji, slamming his heavy body down

on a boulder beside Jun, a heap of mushrooms beside him.

"You are aware he's just insulted you," said Kyou.

"In fact, I insulted all of you," corrected Jun.

"Wait a second," Shoji said, standing up with a newfound clarity, "are you saying we're stupid?" He picked up a mushroom dramatically and pointed it at Jun. Unfortunately, the gesture was lost when a bird swooped down, plucked the mushroom from his hand, and flew off with it.

"No," said Jun slowly. *Click*. He replaced a piece and picked up another. *Clack*, "I'm **implying** it."

"Well stop your implying, you little—you little—" stuttered Shoji, "implicator!" he added.

"Shh," Jun interrupted, his tone suddenly serious.

"Now you shush—"

"Shhh!" repeated Jun, "something's coming," he dropped the piece he'd been holding, and it rolled to the ground disappearing over the ledge, where it would no doubt be found by some unsuspecting wanderer centuries later and would be used to draw wildly speculative claims about ancient civilizations.

The spoon Shoji had somehow produced from his robes hit the ground with a loud clatter. But just as quickly as the spoon fell, another sound followed, one that was decidedly less… culinary. It was low, throaty, and distinctly animalistic, though the creature producing it seemed to have all the grace of a rampaging bull in a china shop.

Ryū held a finger to his lips, his purple crystal beginning to hum in anticipation as he gingerly pulled himself up from the ground. Kyou followed suit, despite Ryū's silent protestations. They crept together. Not exactly in sync, but as close to an approximation as the two of them could achieve. Ryū glanced sideways at Kyou, his eyes darting forward in a barely concealed plea for cooperation. Kyou scowled, his brows knitting together like two hostile forces battling for supremacy. It took several more silent, frantic hand gestures before Ryū's patience snapped.

"Move forward, you dumb brute!" he hissed, voice just a little too loud for comfort.

Kyou, naturally, chose that moment to ignore him completely. But before any of the usual bickering could begin, pink threads snapped out, wrapping around their legs like some kind of twisted, sticky trap.

There was no hesitation. No gasp of surprise. Neither Ryū nor Kyou so much as blinked. Even in the contorted position Ryū had put himself in, no tremor flickered through him. No breath stirred in the air. His half-bound hair lay frozen, unaffected by the gentle breeze that continued to push through the clearing, as if nature itself was afraid to disturb him.

"For the love of the golden kitsune," Jun muttered, exasperated. "You'd think by now we would have learned not to be snuck up on."

FIFTEEN 十五

AKIRA

The two Yōsei perched at the edge of the thickets, their bodies so still it was as if they had transformed into part of the boulders beside them. Akira, slowly regaining her wits, shuffled forward. Her hand moved instinctively toward her blue crystal, its cold surface sending a chill up her arm. But before she could gather her thoughts or prepare her next move, another thread snagged her ankle. If Shoji and Jun had entertained any thoughts of doing something useful, they too were promptly dissuaded.

The rustling behind them escalated, the noise reaching a fever pitch as if their very helplessness had conspired to amplify the sound. Moments later, a figure emerged from the bushes, and Akira gave herself an instant migraine fighting the warping. Despite her extensive experience with warping (thanks to Ryū's occasional, uninvited 'teaching'), she was still astounded at how her eyes refused to move. Fortunately, the newcomer's position allowed her to get a clear enough look.

He was tall—so tall, in fact, that it was the first thing you'd notice about him. But oddly enough, he didn't carry the striking presence one might expect from such height. He was neither broad nor well-built, almost on the lanky side, like someone who might've missed a few meals. His face fit his frame: angular, with the kind of sharpness that looked like it had been hastily etched by a distracted sculptor. What was truly missing was a scraggly beard that would have completed his look of a travelling vagabond. However, considering he was of the Fae, facial hair was about as likely as him suddenly bursting into a rendition of "Twinkle, Twinkle Little Star."

His hair wasn't the familiar dark black of the Fujikurans but hovered somewhere between burnt caramel and auburn—yet another sign that he belonged to the 'foreign alien' category. His black robes were cinched at the waist with a plain belt, and his tunic underneath was a shade of beige that screamed, "I haven't seen a laundry basket in days.' As if that wasn't enough of a giveaway, the faintly disgruntled flicker of his purple crystal only further marked him as a Threadcaster. And based on his attire and disheveled appearance, a particularly bedraggled one.

Akira would have hissed, but her body wasn't cooperating, and quite frankly, she was terrible at it. Instead, she stared at the man's pale eyes, as though she could incinerate him with sheer willpower. Naturally, this didn't work.

The man turned to face them, slipping one hand into the long sleeve of the other, his posture eerily calm. "I mean you no harm," he said softly, in fluent Fujik, his voice as smooth as an overripe fruit about to spoil. "I will release the warping; I only ask that you hear me out before doing anything... hasty."

The purple crystal flickered again, like a child sulking over being told their favorite toy was about to be taken away.

Akira nearly collapsed into Ryū when the warping

lifted, her muscles seizing in protest like they had all taken a vacation at once.

"Yes, well," Kyou said, already brushing nonexistent dust from his navy robes. "I too find that the best way to signal 'I mean no harm' is by capturing people and holding them hostage."

The Threadcaster frowned, then turned to face Kyou. "If my intention were to capture you, I would have done so already. I merely needed you to listen."

Kyou narrowed his eyes, clearly unimpressed. "Might I suggest," he said slowly, the words dripping with sarcasm, "and I know this is a rather radical suggestion, but perhaps we'd be more inclined to listen to you if you hadn't just attacked us?"

Kyou shot quick glances at Ryū and Shoji, who were inching forward, clearly ready to participate in whatever escalating chaos was about to unfold.

The Threadcaster raised his hands, his expression patient but strained. "Now, now, friends—"

"I don't know what has given you the impression that we are friends," Kyou shot back, his voice cold as ice.

The Threadcaster's frown deepened, and his lips curled into something that wasn't quite a smile. "Must I remind you how easily I warped you all in place? Or will you insist on going for round two?"

The five of them exchanged various glances—some quizzical, some nonsensical (Shoji was responsible for most of those)—but all underlined with a solid layer of distrust.

Akira gestured toward one of the rocks near the now extinguished fire. "Then don't let us delay you. Tell us what you want."

The man smiled, and despite the agelessness of Threadcasters, a crinkling of his forehead and the sides of mouth accompanied it, "My friends—"

"Stop calling us that," Kyou ground out through clenched teeth.

Shoji, ever the optimist, offered a new olive branch. "Can I offer you a bowl of mushroom stew?" He presented a copper bowl, ridiculously cupped between both hands. How Shoji had managed to whip up a fragrant mushroom stew in the middle of a forest, with no kitchen in sight, was a mystery that would remain unsolved.

"Not now, Shoji," Ryū hissed.

The Threadcaster shrugged, unbothered. "I could go for some stew."

A round of hostile glares followed, with a few thinly veiled grunts of displeasure. Despite this, Shoji handed over the bowl with an air of proud obliviousness.

After a few bites, the man laughed—a sound that was somehow unsettling and too familiar. "Now, as I was saying. I'm not here to ask for your help, but rather to offer you mine."

Akira let out a dark chuckle, her eyes narrowing. "And pray tell, why would we want your help?"

The man casually scooped up a spoonful of rice, blowing gently across its surface. "You want to rescue Jiro, don't you?"

Shoji's eyes darted around the clearing, his brows furrowing. "Jiro is with you?"

Kyou rolled his eyes. "Shoji," he said slowly, "I do believe you've unlocked some mysterious 'seerful' insights that allow you to see things that aren't there." He waved a hand at the empty air before him. "Tell me, am I currently slapping the invisible Jiro right now?"

"Must you always be such a cabbage-brained git?" Ryū muttered as he jumped off his boulder and rejoined the others.

Before any further squabbles could break out (and they would), the Threadcaster wisely slapped a bamboo scroll onto the ground. One could say little about it, other than that it was a scroll. It was old and held together with what looked like a tattered bit of leather—maybe. But beyond that, it could have been a parchment of great importance or just something he found on his way over. Akira, already half-forgetting her rice, spread the scroll out before them. It was dense—so dense that it took all of them a moment to figure out what they were even looking at. Thin lines snaked across the page like spider webs, curving and shifting in patterns that almost felt alive. Tiny, impossibly small writing scattered across it, requiring them to practically glue their eyes to the paper.

"It's the plans," the Threadcaster said softly, as though it were the most obvious thing in the world.

"To what?" Akira asked, tracing her finger along the undulating lines.

"The tower." It was Jun's voice who answered. His voice would never be one that would send enemies running. Indeed, it seldom invited anything other than thinly veiled ridicule, as its tone was several octaves higher than one might expect for a man of his stature.

"Why do you have this?" Akira asked, her voice tight with suspicion.

The Threadcaster frowned deeply, his brow furrowing so much it looked like a caterpillar had taken up residence there. "I broke into Tsuyoshi-sama's chambers."

"Why?"

"Because I needed them, of course."

"But why?" Akira echoed Jun's question, with a heavy dose of suspicion.

"Because there are friends of mine in that tower."

"Jiro among them?" Akira probed further, her tone sharpening.

The Threadcaster shrugged with a maddening air of nonchalance. "I did not see him—though it is possible. It's been many years since I last saw him." His pale eyes drifted downward as he stirred his rice absentmindedly. "Indeed, you," he gestured at Akira, "were but a little girl. Before the Emperor's decree, your father frequented the Sanctum of Oto, as did I. As did every other Threadcaster in the Order. But few of us remain now." His voice dropped to a wistful murmur.

Akira's frown deepened as her memories stirred. "You're Calder," she said, savoring the familiarity of the name like a bitter tea. "I remember you."

Calder inclined his head with a faint smile.

Jun, meanwhile, had commandeered the blueprints, casting a literal shadow over the group as he flipped through them. "It's a fortress," he declared at last. "A prison."

Calder nodded solemnly. "A prison built to be impenetrable."

"Charming," Jun muttered, though his fingers lingered over the plans with reluctant admiration. "This will help."

The group fell into an uneasy silence as Jun scrutinized the designs. His meticulous inspection seemed to stretch for hours, punctuated only by the occasional exasperated sigh. On the back of the plans, he discovered rows of inscrutable writing interspersed with crossed-out sections, adding a cryptic layer to the puzzle.

Akira's patience wore thin. "What do you—"

Jun silenced her with a single finger pressed to her lips. The indignity left her recoiling as though the touch had burned, but she held her tongue. Barely.

So much time passed that it took them all rather longer than they cared to admit, to realize that Jun had stopped inspecting. He was sitting, quite still, staring straight ahead. So still did he sit, and for such a multitude of time they began to wonder if he was suffering from some form of nervous breakdown, or if perhaps he had died.

"Maybe he's using that seer stuff of his?" Shoji whispered loudly, pointing at Jun's green crystal.

Jun snapped out of his trance, startling everyone. "So, it's a fortress," he announced, as if the last half-hour had simply never happened.

"Yes, we got that part," Kyou muttered.

"If you can kindly hold all comments, questions and concerns until the end," said Jun not even bothering to look at the other Yōsei, "so it's a fortress, and from what I can tell it's impenetrable."

"Wonderful," Kyou drawled as he stood, stretching extravagantly. "Glad to see all your intellectual brilliance has arrived at such a groundbreaking conclusion. Bravo, Jun." He saluted, bowed theatrically, and turned to leave. "I'll see you all hanging in the Inquisitor's torture chamber, then shall I?"

Ryū grabbed Kyou's pant leg and yanked him back down so hard it was a wonder his trousers didn't rip. "Sit," Ryū growled, his teeth clenched.

Jun sighed dramatically. "As I was saying," he shot a glare at Kyou, "the fortress is impenetrable. But—" he held up a finger, "on the back of the plans, there's a detailed guard schedule. Two Threadcasters stand watch by the front gate. They swap out twice daily, during which gryphons are released to patrol the perimeter."

Akira looked up, squinting at the sky above the tower. "What's a gryphon?" Shoji asked, gnawing thoughtfully on a grilled mushroom.

"Hell, if I know!" Jun snapped. "I'm just telling you what's written here, and if anyone interrupts me again, I'll let Ryū stuff a towel down their throat!"

A stunned silence fell, which Jun took as permission to continue. "The prison is guarded by dire wolves."

"Wolves?" Shoji's brow furrowed as he reached for a handful of lychees that had somehow appeared in his pocket. "Why not… bears?"

Jun ignored him. "The cells are secured by motion-triggered locking mechanisms. Any movement in the corridor sets them off."

"Flawed design," Shoji mumbled through a mouthful of lychee. "How do the guards not set them off?"

"There are always at least two Threadcasters inside the fortress," Jun pressed on, "and a dozen more can be summoned on gryphons at a moment's notice."

"On wings?" asked Akira, wondering if it was even worth the energy of uttering a question that would likely be ignored.

"The only viable point of entry is one on the very top of the tower that is only accessible by flight."

"So, I take it the gryphons are winged creatures then?" asked Ryū.

Jun nodded.

"I thought you didn't know what gryphons are," added Kyou.

"Don't make me come over there," snapped Ryū, "because you know I will savor every moment of it."

"Tell me Ryū," said Kyou, "is it merely a savior complex that compels you to defend everyone despite no request for your help, or is it some other deep-seated need to please?"

Ryū lunged halfway across the fire before Akira yanked him back by the collar. "So," Jun resumed, unperturbed, "our only viable point of entry is a balcony at the top of the tower, accessible only by flight. We'll need to capture a gryphon."

"I'm starting to remember why we keep you around," Kyou said, his grin sharpening. "Anyone have a better idea?"

"A dragon?" Shoji suggested, stirring the soup pot with a spoon gripped between his toes.

Jun's expression froze. "You mean *the* dragon? The one locked in the Kitsune Emperor's vaults?"

"And I'm starting to remember why we *don't* keep Shoji around," Kyou muttered, snatching the spoon and tossing it into the bushes.

Calder, who had been quietly finishing his third bowl of porridge, finally spoke up. "Perhaps I can offer some insight?"

"No one asked you," Kyou snapped.

"Actually," Akira interjected, "I have a question." She

turned to Calder. "Why were you here in the first place? It's awfully convenient that you just happened to run into us."

Calder raised his hands, palms outward. The motion revealed thick grooves on his wrists. Akira's eyes narrowed.

"Tsuyoshi was holding me prisoner in the tower," Calder explained. "At least two other members of my Order are still held there. I escaped last night."

"How?" Jun demanded, his face inches from Calder's.

Calder rubbed his wrists. "There was a commotion when a new prisoner arrived. I suspect now it must have been Jiro. I used the distraction to channel a sliver of chronomagic. A dangerous thing without a crystal…"

"Why not use your crystal?" Jun pressed.

Calder tapped the grooves on his wrists. "Shackles. They sever our connection to the crystals."

"But—"

Ryū's voice broke through the argument like a cannon blast. "Would you just let the man speak!"

Jun muttered something under his breath but leaned back against his rock, gesturing for Calder to continue.

"Well," Calder began, "there's not much else to it. I managed to funnel just enough of my lifeforce into a breath of chronomagic to flect the cuffs. The movement froze them long enough for me to shatter them against the rock. Then I used chronomagic to flect the lock mechanism on the door until it inevitably gave in."

Jun's frown deepened. "And then you broke into Tsuyoshi's chambers?"

"Yes. I flected myself to remain undetected. One of the guards mentioned a disturbance as I passed, but I was long gone by the time he could act."

Jun looked unimpressed. "Seems far-fetched."

"It's the truth," Calder said firmly. "Far-fetched or not, I needed something to have any hope of freeing the others."

Jun opened his mouth to deliver what was surely going to be an exceptionally pedantic retort, but Akira turned to him with a glare that could have cracked a rock in two. "My turn," she snapped before looking back at Calder. "Why would you want to help us?"

"I've said—"

"Yes, yes." Akira waved him off. "Friends in the tower, yada yada. But after what the Threadcasters have done to our people, why even bother?"

Calder's frown sharpened, and for a moment, it seemed he might start emitting steam. Folding his hands together, he said, "Forgive me, but what exactly do you think we've done?"

Akira's laugh was deep, sonorous, and loud enough to startle a flock of birds into a panicked retreat.

Ryū, who had been playing the part of a stoic statue, suddenly sprang to life. "We don't take kindly to being treated as fools," he said, standing abruptly. His tone made the words sound less like a warning and more like a promise. "Leave, or you'll soon learn what we do to the unwelcome."

"I didn't mean to offend," Calder said, his voice as soft as an apology could make it. "I mean only to understand. Many of us—myself included—have been on Fujikura for years. We received nothing but a warm welcome...until everything changed. I've lost friends to the one you call the Inquisitor. I've narrowly escaped with my own life. I've tried to learn what sparked the Emperor's ire, but every time I get close to an answer, it slips through my fingers."

For a moment, the group hung in silence. Some members appeared to be biting down on their anger so hard it might require medical intervention later, while others simply wore the stunned expressions of those unsure if they should feel pity, anger, or indigestion.

Calder continued, "You must forgive me for assuming...and for prying into your business. But my crystal"—he gestured to the purple gem in his chest—"led me here. I thought I might find sympathizers among other Threadcasters."

"I am no Threadcaster," hissed Kyou.

Akira glanced at her own blue crystal, which vibrated faintly against her chest. "I—" Her voice faltered, unable to bridge the sentence.

Ryū, his hand tightening around his own purple crystal, snarled, "You say you want to free those in the tower. To help us get Jiro back. And yet, he was taken by Threadcasters from your Order." He pointed accusingly at Calder's dark robes, which hung loosely over his frame.

The Threadcaster's response was a comical, involuntary gasp. "You don't mean—Brother Threadcasters? From my Order?" His disbelief bordered on melodrama. "The ones I saw working for Tsuyoshi were Fujikuran converts, not Brothers from the Order. I thought Tsuyoshi...I thought he was working with the Inquisitor."

"That's exactly what I said, isn't it?" Ryū shot back.

"Technically," Jun interjected, "that's not *exactly* what you said."

Ryū glared at him, but Jun shrugged and began fiddling with a stray game piece he'd plucked from his scattered board.

"What would Brothers from my Order be doing working with Tsuyoshi?" Calder's jaw tensed, scars running like rivers along his skin.

"You tell us," snapped Akira.

Before the argument could spiral further, the soft creak of bamboo shifting in the wind trickled into the clearing, carrying the smell of blooming jasmine. Shoji, ever the opportunist, sniffed the air like a starved bloodhound and ladled himself more stew.

"I know you have no reason to trust me," Calder began.

"That's the first true statement you've made," said

Kyou.

Ignoring him, Calder continued, "But I promise on the honor of the Light within me, I have no knowledge of these events. Is this why the Emperor's decree was passed?"

Akira shrugged. "Seems likely."

"Highly probable," Jun added. "By my calculations, anyway."

Ryū sighed. "How could you possibly have calculated that?"

"Wouldn't you like to know?" Jun smirked. "Maybe then you'd realize fighting with three swords, while visually impressive, is no more efficient than two."

"In my book three is a higher number than two."

Jun clapped sarcastically. "I'm so proud of you. Didn't know you had it in you."

Calder hummed, "This is most distressing. I suspected corruption in our ranks, but this..." He trailed off. "If what you say is true, then something must be happening under Mr. Faber's nose—and the Council's."

Akira's voice softened. "What are they going to do with Jiro?"

Calder shook his head. "I don't know. Speculating won't help us. But I stand by my intention to help."

Shoji, who had been topping up his bowl of stew, grinned. "Most kind of you, sir."

Calder chuckled, but the sound died in his throat as cold metal pressed against his neck.

"Kyou!" Akira shouted, stumbling forward.

Kyou ignored her. "If your story is true, why didn't you free your friends when you escaped? Why steal plans instead?"

Shoji reached for the stew. "Relinquish the stew."

Calder carefully placed it on the ground, stepping away as though it were a loaded weapon. "Because I didn't know where they were being kept!" Calder's voice rose in frustration. "And even if I had, they were heavily guarded.

The guards would've returned before I could manage it."

"You didn't know where they were being kept," Jun said idly, "but you *did* know where Tsuyoshi's chambers were?"

"He interrogated me when I first arrived," Calder said through gritted teeth.

Kyou pressed the blade harder. "And you just assumed he had the plans?"

"I did not—"

"Then why bother?"

"It wasn't illogical."

"And there were no guards at his chambers?"

"No!"

Kyou loosened his grip slightly, and Calder's breath stalled by his throat.

Shoji, now frowning, nudged the bowl back toward Calder. "I trust him."

"A moment ago, you were stealing his stew," Kyou pointed out.

"It was my stew to begin with," Shoji replied, as though this settled the matter entirely.

"Well, it would depend," said Jun, adopting the scholarly tone of someone who's read far too many treatises on philosophy, "on whether we're discussing the bowl itself—which, as everyone here surely knows, clearly belongs to Shoji—or the stew as an entity separate from the bowl. This would need to be established prior to transfer—"

"The bowl was mine," muttered Akira, staring off as though considering whether this stew dispute was a new low in her life.

"Well then, Akira's bowl, in that case—" Jun pivoted seamlessly, "and as for the stew itself, we'd have to ask: does its ownership transfer at the moment of pouring, or is it contingent on Calder's consumption? Does the stew become his once sufficiently altered during digestion, or—"

"Do we think," Akira interrupted, her voice dripping with the thin veneer of civility people use when they're two seconds from yelling, "that we might be getting slightly off point here?"

The cabbage-brained cabal fell silent, as though collectively realizing how absurd they looked squabbling over theoretical stew ownership. They turned their attention to Calder, who now wore an expression akin to someone regretting every life choice that had led them here.

"I, for one, still don't trust him," said Kyou, releasing Calder with a rough shove.

"Thanks for that ever-insightful contribution," Ryū drawled, not even looking up from his sword, which he was sharpening with unnecessary zeal.

"Well, do you?" Kyou shot back. It was, admittedly, a valid question, but Ryū ignored it with the practiced ease of someone well-versed in avoidance.

Akira sighed and stood, distancing herself from the cacophony of egos clanging together like badly tuned bells. She walked a few paces away, glancing up at the towering maple that canopied the clearing in intricate shadow patterns. Its leaves, still mostly green, clung stubbornly to summer, though the deep purple of autumn waited patiently in the wings.

"I don't think we have a choice," she said, her voice so quiet it almost seemed meant for the tree alone.

"A choice in what?" Kyou asked, his tone sharp enough to slice.

"To trust me," Calder interjected, his voice laden with the kind of theatrical weariness that suggested he was very much done with all of this. He crossed one leg over the other and pulled his cloak around him like a particularly disgruntled philosopher.

"We can't trust you," Kyou snapped. "And why should we?"

"Because," Calder said, his words oozing out so

slowly they practically dripped, "you don't have a choice."

"We can rescue Jiro ourselves; we don't need you," insisted Ryū, having decided what this conversation needed was another dissonant voice.

"Your choices," Calder continued as though Ryū hadn't spoken, "are to try without me and definitely die, or trust me and maybe live."

"And where does Jiro factor into this little equation of yours?" Akira asked, plucking at a jasmine flower that hung low near her shoulder.

"That," Calder said, his voice taking on a distinctly ominous tone, "is up to Amriel." He folded his hands neatly in his lap, the picture of calm.

"Why can't we just get in the same way you got out?" Ryū asked, stroking his chin in a parody of deep thought.

"Tsuyoshi is not the type to be outsmarted twice," Calder replied, his tone flat but edged with something cold. "He'll have ensured it won't happen again. How, I can't say, but I can promise it'll be unpleasant."

When enough time had passed for a squirrel to walk by, find a nut, discover a horde of people around it and scuttle away in apt fear for its life, Calder asked, "So what is your decision?"

Shoji was the first to speak, predictably. "He's right. We don't have a choice."

Akira and Ryū turned to him as though he'd just announced his intention to marry a lamp.

"Very good," Calder said, his tone bright and brittle. "I assume, then, that we're all in agreement with Shoji?"

"I never said that," Ryū muttered darkly.

"So, you disagree?" Calder asked, his head tilting like a bird of prey.

Ryū grumbled something indecipherable, which Calder graciously chose to interpret as consent. "Right. So, what was the plan so far?"

"Steal a gryphon," Shoji said cheerfully.

Calder blinked once. Twice. "Have any of you ever

flown a gryphon?"

Ryū grimaced. "Considering I only learned they existed half an hour ago, I'm going to say no."

"Can't be much different from riding a horse," Jun offered.

"Ah, yes, because flying beasts and terrestrial animals are famously similar," Calder muttered. "And where, pray tell, were you planning to get a gryphon?"

"Actually, four," Jun corrected.

Calder pinched the bridge of his nose. "So, just to clarify: your plan was to avoid dying in the tower by dying while attempting to steal four gryphons you don't know how to fly. Solid strategy."

"Well, *smart ass,* what's your idea?" Kyou snapped.

"I'm glad you asked," Calder said, his tone smooth. "We won't be taking gryphons. We'll be using Hainu."

The group went deathly silent.

"No one's ever managed that before," Akira said softly, her fingers tracing the edge of a jasmine petal.

"Luckily for you," Calder replied, a faint smile tugging at the corners of his mouth, "I know someone who came close."

Akira glanced up. "Where is he?"

"Oh, he died trying."

SIXTEEN

KILIE

The Inquisitor's breathing was a show all its own. It wasn't just loud; it was *calculatedly* loud—a nasal symphony of disdain that drew eyes to him like he'd staged it for an audience. Kilie shifted uncomfortably, wedged between Kallae and Miki in the cramped hut. The smell of damp straw and fear permeated the air, but outside, it was worse. Much worse.

The villagers were herded together in a pathetic clump, surrounded by three of the Inquisitor's guards. Only three, yet it might as well have been an army. Fear had made the villagers malleable, and no one—not even Kilie, with his perpetual belief in the inherent goodness of people—thought they would resist.

"I thought tyrants liked to keep speeches short," Kallae muttered, his words sharp enough to carve stone. He had an uncanny ability to inject disdain into a whisper, and Kilie bit his lip to keep from snapping at him.

The Inquisitor, oblivious to their hiding place, paced before the villagers like a carrion bird surveying its next meal. "There is no need to be afraid," he crooned, the softness of his voice all the more sinister for its pretense. He tilted a woman's chin up with a gloved hand, his smile thin as a knife's edge. "Think of your loved ones. Hmm? The ones you leave behind? And for what? A god of lies conjured by *Threadcasters* to bind you and all of Fujikura in servitude!"

He spat the last word, his voice rising to a fever pitch just as a fourth guard emerged from a nearby hut. The small figure held something white and paper-thin, their movements hurried yet deliberate.

"What is that?" Kilie whispered, turning to Miki, whose wide eyes darted between the guard and the Inquisitor.

"Know not," she hissed back, her accent thick and her Cygren fractured. "No can see from here."

The guard passed the object to the Inquisitor, who froze mid-speech, holding the paper-like object delicately, as though it might bite. He unfurled the paper, touching only the edges to reveal something smooth and round nestled into the folds.

"Unbonded chronocrystal," Kallae murmured, his gaze narrowing as he studied the faint glow emanating from the Inquisitor's hand.

Kilie squinted, trying to see what Kallae saw. "That's just light bouncing off it, right?" he asked, hopeful.

"No. It's *glowing*. Glowing means it's chronocrystal. Which means—"

The Inquisitor turned abruptly, his grin now a venomous sneer. "Thought you could hide *this* from me?" he hissed, holding the crystal aloft. It dangled from a thin cord like a sinister charm, its glow pulsing faintly. "Thought we wouldn't look closer at a shikigami, hmmm? Clever, but not clever *enough*. I see now that I have been too soft on you," he turned to face the village chief, "truly,

I blame myself. For I see now that you will never learn through kindness and generosity, I was silly to think you could."

"Speak," the Inquisitor commanded, his voice now a growl, "or I'll make an example of you so vivid that Amriel himself will weep."

The chief collapsed fully, bowing at the Inquisitor's feet. "Forgive us, Inquisitor-sama," he begged, his voice cracking. "We—"

The Inquisitor's boot struck the man's stomach, silencing him. He rose to his full height, holding the crystal high again, his shadow stretching long and terrible. "Who does this belong to?"

No one moved.

Kilie clenched his fists. He wanted to believe someone would step forward. Someone always stepped forward. Didn't they?

"I trust I need not remind you that the harboring of Threadcasters will be punished with the same brutality as if you were one."

His snarl melted back into a smile, as he walked daintily around the fallen crystal, "In fact, my soft heart implores me to offer you a deal. Step forward willingly, and I will not punish you, nor anyone else in this village. Now how does that sound, hmmm?"

Still, none stepped forward.

The smile disappeared, and his face looked so natural, bearing the dark grimace which had replaced it, that one almost did not believe it was capable of supporting a smile.

"You have chosen silence," the Inquisitor declared, his voice dropping to a guttural snarl. "So be it. Let us test your god's strength against the *Way of the Water*."

With theatrical flair, he dropped the crystal and stomped on it. Kilie flinched, clutching his own crystal beneath his shirt. It pulsed against his skin, as though reacting to the violence.

The crystal on the ground, however, remained intact,

glowing faintly.

The Inquisitor frowned. He snatched a sword from one of his guards and brought it down on the crystal. This time, it skittered away like a startled animal.

"That's new," Kallae muttered dryly. "Shall we clap?"

Kilie elbowed him. "Not helping."

The Inquisitor glared at the crystal before throwing it to his smallest guard. "Take this to the magickers at the palace. We'll see if they fare better."

The guard stumbled but managed to catch the crystal, holding it as though it were cursed. The Inquisitor turned back to the villagers, his face splitting into a grotesque parody of warmth.

"Now," he said, retrieving the folded piece of paper from his robes, "where was I?"

Kilie leaned forward instinctively, his eyes on the paper. The Inquisitor unfolded it with exaggerated care, revealing a chain of paper figures—primitive humanoid shapes connected at their limbs. He blew lightly on the paper, and the chain seemed to animate, the figures grasping each other as they descended.

"What's he doing?" Kilie whispered.

"Something awful," Kallae muttered. "Obviously."

The Inquisitor tore a single figure from the chain, discarding the rest like scraps of meat unworthy of attention. Holding the lone paper figure in his palm, he began to fold it with precise, deliberate movements.

Kilie watched as the paper darkened, the edges thickening unnaturally. Its shape shifted and warped, and then, almost impossibly, it stood upright—a humanoid figure utterly void of features, texture, or light.

"Chronomagic?" Kallae asked, his eyes narrowing.

Kilie shook his head, his throat dry. "Can't be."

The Inquisitor's hands moved again, folding something invisible to all but him. The figure—if one could still call it that—grew. The folds of the paper seemed to devour themselves, consuming the figure into something upright and monstrous. What once was no larger than a child's toy now stood at life-size, its faceless void swallowing all light.

It wasn't black. Black was too easy, too familiar. No, it was an absence, a hole where existence itself failed. A hunger made manifest.

The Inquisitor made another series of cryptic folding gestures, then leaned close, exhaling softly against the back of the figure's neck. For an agonizing moment, it didn't move, but Kilie could feel his heartbeat trying to claw its way out of his chest. Then it lurched forward.

The creature's motions were disjointed, disturbingly human-like yet painfully wrong. It moved like a child taking its first, awkward steps—calculated, jerky, and unsettlingly deliberate.

"Good, good," the Inquisitor cooed, as if to encourage it. He rested a hand on the figure's back, guiding it forward like a proud parent. The mockery of tenderness made Kilie's stomach twist.

The shikigami grew steadier, its movements no longer the halting stumbles of a toddler but the ungraceful gallop of a newborn colt. Yet there was strength in its awkwardness, a terrible strength. Kilie imagined it could already outrun him if it chose.

The Inquisitor halted his creation near one of the women in the line. She clutched a bundle tightly to her chest, her arms trembling as though the act of holding it together might ward off the horror before her.

The shikigami stepped closer, jerking to a halt only when the Inquisitor's hand pulled it back. He gestured toward the woman with a cruel grin. "For you. Hmmm?"

Kilie barely had time to blink before the faceless figure's jaw—an opening that hadn't existed mere moments before—unhinged. It wasn't a mouth in any ordinary sense. It was an opening, a gaping void that twisted the air around it, grotesque and alien.

And then it devoured her.

It wasn't the tearing of flesh, not the savage, animalistic mauling one might expect from a monster. This was worse. The woman's form shimmered and fractured as if her very existence were being split apart. One half of her—paler, thinner, weaker—was pulled into the shikigami's maw, while the other grew heavier, denser, darker.

With an obscene *pop*, the paler half vanished, leaving only the darker shadow behind. The paper shikigami returned to its original size, lying innocuously at the Inquisitor's feet. He reached down, picking it up by one arm as if it were a child's doll.

"It's dinner time, boys," the Inquisitor announced gleefully, his grin widening.

The woman's shadow moved then, and to Kilie's horror, she swallowed the bundle in her arms whole.

For a moment, silence reigned. Even the air itself seemed too stunned to move. Then the screams began—first one, then another, until the cacophony of panic overwhelmed all sense. Villagers scattered, only to be torn down with terrifying speed.

The woman moved with a speed that could scarce be tracked by the human eye, her form seeming to blur as she tore through the villagers, one by one. Each of them began to split into two forms, a thin husk of their essence ripping away as it was slowly siphoned into the open maw of the woman. She swallowed, and thick dark liquid oozed from the sides of her mouth as she released a foul-smelling breath.

Kilie's jaw was clenched so tightly it was a wonder it did not snap in two or collapse in on itself creating some sort of time singularity. His purple crystal hummed so violently Kilie had to wonder how the Inquisitor did not immediately detect him. It alternated so rapidly between frigidly cold and frighteningly hot, Kilie was uncertain if he would be suffering from cold or hot burns. What was for sure, is he would be suffering from some form of burn come the following morning. Provided, of course, there was a following morning to speak of.

Kilie's hand shot out to grip Kallae's shoulder, hoisting himself up.

"What are you doing?" Kallae hissed, his opal crystal lifeless against his collarbone.

"What do you think?" Kilie shot back. "I'm going to help those people."

"And what, exactly, do you plan to do against *that*?" Kallae gestured toward the carnage, his voice dripping with disdain.

Ignoring him, Kilie crouched low, murmuring a prayer under his breath. The screams clawed at his resolve, but he forced his focus forward. When he opened his eyes again, the Inquisitor was strolling through the chaos like a king among ants, his shikigami tucked neatly under one arm.

Something tugged at Kilie's mind, a glimmer of recognition. His gaze shifted between the paper figure and the ravenous woman. The shikigami—it wasn't as white as before. Its edges were softer, its folds less sharp.

"The creature," Kilie whispered, his legs trembling from his crouch. "I think it's weakening."

The woman leapt onto the back of one of the villagers, clinging on to it like a feral monkey.

"Really?" Kallae snapped. "And what brilliance led you to that asinine conclusion?"

Kilie pointed. "The paper—it's darkening."

"And you're planning to fight this demon because of slightly darker stationery?" Kallae scoffed.

"What else would you have us do?" Kilie shot back.

"Nothing," Miki's small voice cut through the argument. Her tiny fists were clenched at her sides. "Nothing you can do. Only die."

Kallae gave a bitter laugh. "See, Kilie? Even she understands. This ground is cursed. Not even Amriel dares set foot on this cursed rock. Nothing good grows here—only death. Why spill our blood for soil that will never bear life?"

Kilie wavered, his strength faltering. His crystal burned against his skin, but he forced his gaze upward to the sliver of sky visible through the hut. A lone cloud drifted past, shifting into the shape of wings before dissolving again.

"I have to try," he whispered, standing despite the weight pulling him down.

SEVENTEEN 十七

AKIRA

"Even if we can get to the Hainu in time—" Akira started, her voice already tinged with doubt.

"And we manage to either convince or *force* them to help us—" Kyou interjected, crossing his arms like this was all somehow her idea.

"We don't have time for this," Akira pressed, glaring at him. "There's no telling when Jiro will be taken to Cargyll. If we wait here, perhaps we can intercept him when they move him from the tower."

Calder frowned, looking as though he'd just discovered that his cherished tea had been replaced with lukewarm water steeped in the bitter taste of betrayal. "Indeed, that is a viable concern." He began rifling through the many folds of his robes, which rustled in protest like they, too, were tired of this. Papers spilled out like leaves in a windstorm, and then—with all the grace of a child showing off a crayon drawing—he tore one in half and shouted, "Aha!"

Everyone froze.

"Something wrong with you?" Ryū asked, eyebrow

raised.

"Just excitement!" Calder exclaimed as if that were an acceptable explanation. He slapped the tattered paper down on a nearby boulder. "I knew there was something I'd forgotten!"

"It's a communication," he continued, stabbing a finger at the ripped signet at the bottom. "Tsuyoshi's trader will return to pick up wares in..." Calder glanced at the horizon, where the rising sun was chasing the moons away. "Two cycles. Ample time."

Ryū leaned in. "So the assumption is... Jiro's a *ware*?"

Calder nodded.

Jun, who had been unusually quiet (for him), piped up. "It's the only plan we have. The only viable one, anyway." He said this with the same self-satisfied finality as someone declaring the square root of 169.

And with that, the debate ended. The group gathered up their meager belongings and started their trek. As questionable plans go, this one had all the charm of diving headfirst into a murky lake labeled *Caution: Crocodiles.* But such is life.

Three minutes into what was shaping up to be a week-long journey, Shoji—blessedly unaware of the weight of the situation—bit into a pear, its juice dripping down his chin like an infant caught mid-meal. "So," he asked, voice muffled by fruit, "does anyone want to tell me what a Hainu is?"

Akira blinked, the sheer absurdity of the question momentarily derailing her train of thought. Before she could answer, Ryū, of course, found his way in. "Where'd you even *find* that pear?"

Shoji launched into a babbling explanation about pockets and serendipity, but Akira wasn't having it. "Wait. You mean to tell me," she interrupted, "that you agreed to a literal *suicide mission* without knowing what we're even looking for?"

Shoji nodded enthusiastically, mouth full of pear. A

glob of juice shot out and landed on Akira's sleeve, a perfectly timed insult.

"I can't believe this," she muttered, though her disbelief was drowned out by Ryū's ongoing interrogation for the whereabouts of more pears.

It was Calder, cutting through the chaos like a bamboo blade through underbrush, who restored order. "Hainus," he said, turning to face them with an air of dramatic authority, "are sacred beings."

Shoji perked up, wiping his mouth with the back of his hand. "Sacred like, holy? Or sacred like, don't-touch-or-you'll-explode?"

"Sacred as in unique," Calder explained, his tone softening. "Once, their numbers rivaled the stars. But now... well, now, they're all but gone."

"What happened to them?" Shoji asked, tossing the remains of his pear at Ryū like an act of appeasement.

Calder's sad smile carried the weight of a thousand unshed tears. "Some were hunted for sport. Others were taken captive for breeding. But no one truly knows." He turned back to hacking at the underbrush, his robes swishing with purpose. "They're creatures of chronomagic. At a distance, they might look like wolves or dogs, but they're larger—much larger. Winged, like gryphons. Once, they were the pride of the Imperial Guard. Few dared challenge a pack of flying Hainu. But no longer."

As Calder spoke, the forest seemed to darken, the mood growing heavier with each word. Akira tried to focus on his explanation, but her thoughts kept drifting, her mind consumed by the gnawing fear of failure.

Shoji, ever the optimist, clapped her on the shoulder mid-stride. "We're gonna get him back," he said with the confidence of someone who genuinely believed it. "I can feel it in these old bones."

Akira smiled weakly, but the gesture felt hollow. Shoji, satisfied, sprinted off toward the edge of a cliff, hollering about something nobody could understand.

But Akira's thoughts spiraled downward, dark and relentless. *It's only a matter of time, Akira. Everyone leaves. Just like your mother. Just like Kyou. You are destined to be alone.*

She shook her head, wondering if perhaps she might dislodge the thoughts from her mind like water out the ear. Finding this had accomplished nothing, she instead picked up speed, hoping the clamoring of her fatigued legs and blistered feet might drown out the sound of the voices. *Give up Akira. It's too late.*

"Agh!" she grunted as she began to run. She felt as Ryū grabbed hold of her arm, "Princess? You ok—" but she tore away from him, continuing to run. She heard someone pursue her, footsteps ringing like the beat of a gong.

You are meant to be alone Akira. You don't need anyone else. They will only disappoint you. "Go away!" she shouted, and she heard the footsteps stall behind her. She picked up the pace, the path narrowing as it ascended further up the mountain. To her left, a sharp drop extended far beyond her sight. Despite knowing what lay beneath it, she shuddered. The path continued to narrow, the paved road giving way to loose pebbles which skidded beneath her feet. She did not slow. *He's happier without you Akira. He wanted this.* Her feet slammed against the rocks, sending them tumbling down that mountain. She felt her heart hammer in her chest like a battering ram trying to escape.

Lub dub. Lub dub.

He never wanted you Akira.

Lub dub. Lub dub.

Just like your mother didn't.

Lub dub. Lub dub.

Even Kyou could not bear you.

Lub dub. Lub dub.

Akira had begun to yell at some point, but she could not say when, for the sound of her feet echoed with the same frequency as her heart, rushing blood stealing all her thoughts. *Lub dub.*

Her feet sailed in the air, at times neither foot on the floor as she scaled the mountain. Her lungs filled with fire, and her throat became like sandpaper. Her foot slipped. Her other leg twisted unnaturally trying to compensate. Her focus narrowed just as her leg steadied. Then it began to slide. A pebble dropped down the side of the path, the fall so long Akira did not hear the *clank* of its arrival. And then she was falling. She might have screamed but she could not be certain, her hands scrambled, her arms gyrating around like a swan at take-off. She glanced down at her crystal. Full and gleaming. But what use would fleeting be to her now? The last thing she wanted to do was fall quicker. And just as she was beginning to taste the acrid tears of panic, her entire body lurched upwards. She felt a thin rope bite her wrist, causing her to cry out. Her other hand fumbled at the rope but found that it only responded many moments after. Everything stalled, she could see that the wind still fluttered through the scrub growing along the mountain, but by the time she had processed this observation they had disappeared, smooth rockface taking their place. She knew something had happened. Was she still falling? She didn't think so. But she also could not quite decide why not. It was something to do with that rope. She glanced down. It was pink. It flickered, releasing a pale coral light which threw shadows against the rock. She knew what it was. It was on the tip of her tongue, but it refused to come.

She dangled there, suspended in time, as the world seemed to hold its breath. Calder's face appeared above her, his pale eyes wide with concern.

"Got you," he said, his voice steady.

She blinked, disoriented as her feet found solid ground again. Calder's hands were firm, one on each of her shoulders, steadying her as she swayed.

"Are you okay?" His voice was steady but edged with concern, his eyes scanning her for injuries.

She nodded numbly. "Yes. Thank you."

Relief flooded her, though her legs wobbled beneath her weight.

"You're sure?" he pressed.

"Yes." Her voice was steadier now, though her heart still pounded in her ears.

"We'll get him back," Calder said softly.

She opened her mouth to respond, but no words came. Instead, she simply nodded, the storm of doubts inside her head raging louder than anything she could articulate. "And we'll get your friends back, too," she added quietly. *Lub dub.*

Calder smiled faintly and pulled himself to his feet, offering her his hand. She accepted it, inhaling deeply as her vision wavered slightly.

A second pair of footsteps thudded against the ground, bringing with it the rest of the Jiro's clan, Kyou at the front. He sprung upon Akira examining her from all sides, "Are you ok?"

Akira brushed him off with a curt nod.

"We'll get him back," Kyou repeated firmly.

"Eavesdropping again, were we?" hissed Akira, her tone sharper than she intended. "You seem to be making a habit of this, Kyou. Is that all you learned with Daimyo Yamato? Perhaps if you'd stayed longer, you might've learned something useful." *Lub dub. Lub dub.*

Kyou frowned and stepped back, his hands clenched into fists. Akira knew she was being cruel, punishing him for a slight long buried in their shared past—she, a child at the time; he, barely older. But vengeance is a strange thing, isn't it? Children need to be taught to walk, talk, share, apologize. Most of us never truly master the last one. But revenge? That's instinctual, as innate as breathing. Perhaps the true surprise is not in cruelty, but in every instance someone chooses kindness instead.

I shall not bore you with the details of the rest of their journey, for though it could not accurately be described as pleasant, it would also be decidedly inaccurate to describe it as interesting.

They arrived on an altogether gloomy, misty autumn morning, the sort of day that seems to apologize for existing. Somewhere along the way, they'd not only crossed climates but also shuffled through at least three different personalities a piece, just to keep from losing their minds.

The landscape had turned mountainous and sparse. Struggling saplings clung to life alongside ornery bamboo elders too stubborn to give up and die already. Their breath curled visibly in the freezing air as they trudged up an ancient path, its last maintenance seemingly performed in the Bronze Age. Complaints were plentiful until someone pointed out that flying dogs didn't exactly prioritize roadwork.

Shoji and Ryū had nearly convinced everyone that the path was a cosmic joke designed to never end, but eventually, they reached the summit—or close enough to it. The true peak loomed ahead, unscalable by anything lacking wings (because of course), its snowbanks shedding a nebula of frost into the wind.

"Why have we stopped?" Shoji asked from the back, a lychee peel in one hand and a second mid-peel in the other.

Then he saw it.

The summit, though unmistakably a mountain, bore an uncanny resemblance to a temple. Its sharp peak replaced the typical dome, its unforgiving rock face stood in for lacquered wood, and yet... there was a weight to this place. A presence. Akira shivered, uncertain whether the cold or something more profound caused it.

Near the peak stood a rounded doorway. 'Hole' might describe it, but only in the way one might call a palace a 'cozy cottage.' Still, it seemed implausibly small to admit the supposedly horse-sized Hainu.

Beside the entrance was a golden statue, as subtle as a

thunderclap. Towering and intricate, it was so imposing that Akira briefly considered fleeing down the mountain, screaming.

"What is *that*?" Shoji asked, dropping a handful of prickly lychee shells.

"I'd pick that up if I were you," Ryū muttered, nodding toward the shells. "This is a sacred place."

Shoji sighed but complied.

Calder, who hadn't taken his eyes off the statue, spoke at last. "It depends on who you ask. Some say it honors Shogun Harukami's loyal Hainu, who died defending him. Others claim it marks the site of a battle between Harukami and a Great Hainu, a fight that nearly cost him his life. He survived—briefly. Time ultimately claimed him, and they erected this statue to honor the Hainu he fought."

Shoji frowned. "If it's meant to be admired, why put it somewhere no one can see it?"

Calder turned, his robes rustling as his hands vanished into their folds. The purple crystal on his chest pulsed faintly. "Because most who venture here—intentionally or not—don't live to tell the tale."

"A Hainu pack still roams these grounds," added Ryū, drawing one of his twin blades. Its silver edge gleamed in the pale light.

A mist hovered over them, seemingly enveloping the entire area in a shroud. Akira tasted moisture on her lips, finding it surprisingly sweet to the taste.

"How are we supposed to catch them?" Jun asked, already scanning the area for tactical advantages—or whatever else his overactive brain deemed relevant.

Calder laughed, the sound swallowed by the damp, oppressive air. "We don't catch them. We fight their alpha. Only then will they accept us."

Ryū bounced off the outcrop he had at some point jumped onto, his other sword now drawn and a knife in his mouth. "I will do it," he said. Though he might have also said, "I wado am," as the aforementioned knife in the mouth made speaking quite an insurmountable feat.

"I applaud your bravery," said Calder, his eyes now set on the entrance, which had shown no movement since their arrival, "but that would be a foolish choice. It must be me."

Ryū bristled, but before he could protest—or Kyou could enthusiastically agree that Ryū was, indeed, a foolish choice—Calder continued. "Whatever happens, do not interfere. Do not engage. If you do, you will die."

"What if we run?" Shoji asked.

"They'll chase you."

"Fantastic," muttered Akira, gripping her sword hilt. "Unfavorable odds, zero preparation, and near-certain death. Sounds about right."

Ryū, one blade still firmly clasped in his hand turned to Calder, "The Hainu demand respect. They will not take kindly to the use of chronomagic."

Calder snapped toward him, eyes blazing with uncharacteristic intensity. "Do not speak of chronomagic as if it were a cheap parlor trick! Chronomagic *formed* the Hainu, just as it formed everything else. They will respect it—or deny their very creation."

He turned to face the rest of them, "I have seldom seen a faster learner than Jiro. And I have no doubt he has taught you all well. But do not be so prideful as to think that you know everything. For even the Masters in Heron Academy cannot stake such a claim. You would be wise to remember this. Wisdom is not only knowledge itself but knowing when it is lacking."

The group wisely fell silent.

Jun, meanwhile, finished his meticulous inspection of the area—this had involved sniffing the ground, tasting the air, and mimicking bird calls—and stood. "Not to ruin the mood, but I don't see any Hainu to slaughter us."

"It's *fight,* not slaughter," Akira corrected, frowning. "Though perhaps that remains to be seen..."

For a long, tense moment, no one spoke. Then the shadows began to shift.

At first, it was subtle, as though the light itself was merely flickering. Then it darkened, spreading and swallowing everything in its path.

"I have a bad feeling about this," muttered Jun.

The shadows swirled unnaturally, coalescing into a form—a figure that defied comprehension. Akira's instincts screamed at her that this creature answered to no mortal law.

The darkness solidified into fur, white as freshly fallen snow, rippling like living silk. Massive paws moved soundlessly forward, each step exuding a lethal, unearthly grace.

The shadows swirled around in a way that was entirely un-shadow like, until they coalesced into a figure. Though perhaps figure is not the correct term, for that implies that the thing had some form of earthly boundaries that confined it to a single point in space and time. Though Akira had no grounds to believe this wasn't the case, something deep in her psyche told her this creature obeyed none who walked this earth.

The shadows finished their dance, melting into a thick, alabaster pelt that cascaded down the creature's neck like a living mane. Each strand moved as though caught in a silent, otherworldly breeze. The beast fixed its piercing yellow eyes on the group, and Akira felt her courage drain, replaced with the desperate urge to fling herself off the mountain and hope for a softer landing than the fate this being promised.

"I think I preferred not knowing what a Hainu was," Shoji murmured. His uncharacteristic stillness—a man who was never without a snack in hand—spoke volumes about the gravity of the situation.

The Hainu's face was long and wolfish, though neither 'wolf' nor 'dog' seemed adequate descriptors. Its luminous eyes weren't sly like a serpent's or soft like a doe's. They were something else entirely: eyes that seemed to carve into Akira's very essence, leaving her hollow and exposed. Intricate patterns, glowing faintly as though etched by starlight, adorned its face, and for a fleeting moment, Akira entertained the absurd thought that these markings might chart the course of the heavens themselves.

Around its neck hung what might have been a collar—a thick braid of red and gold adorned with feathers too immense and ethereal to belong to any ordinary bird. Perhaps, Akira mused with faint hysteria, they were plucked from a barnyard chicken. A chicken the size of a house.

Shoji would have laughed if he weren't frozen. Jun, ever the rationalist, tilted his head as if analyzing the metaphysical impossibility before him.

"So, wings," Akira muttered when her gaze finally caught the enormous appendages unfurling behind the creature. "Of course, it has wings."

"Wingspan's at least twenty feet," Jun whispered, his voice tinged with awe and calculation. "Twice that of a bald eagle."

It wasn't until Calder had ascended halfway up the temple steps that they realized he'd moved. The Hainu turned its head toward him, nostrils flaring, breath curling like milk in tea. Calder, robed in shadow and confidence, bowed low.

The Hainu's gaze seemed almost… curious. As though contemplating some ancient riddle. It stepped forward silently, its massive frame radiating serenity, the kind that whispered: *everything proceeds as it must.*

Despite its size, the creature seemed to hover rather than walk, its movements impossible to track. Akira wondered if the act of walking was merely a courtesy, the beast humorously indulging their mortal sensibilities.

"Do you accept my challenge?" Calder asked, his voice steady. His crystal pulsed with a terrible, violet light, its glow so fierce Akira had to look away.

The Hainu tilted its head and settled onto one forelimb, as though considering the question. Then, like a spring snapping loose, the silence shattered.

So quickly had it been broken no one could rightly say who had taken the first move. They both leaped into the air, and despite the Hainu's greater size and strength, Brother Calder was only a few feet below it. Several blue threads coiled themselves around the Threadcaster's arms and legs like a slumbering snake. The Hainu leapt onto one of the outcroppings of the temple, and sailed towards the fairy with a speed that should have only been possible for a flector. Fortunately, Calder was a pacer, and his purple crystal hummed as he sprung out of the way, the blue threads flickering across his body. But even with the help of the threads, he could not escape the swipe of a curved claw. It shattered against his thigh, and he felt as it grazed against the threads. For a moment it seemed as if it would just scatter off the surface, but then the thread snapped, and the blade sank into his flesh. Calder hissed as he felt hot blood drip down his leg, soaking into his trousers.

Calder retaliated, sending a thread toward the beast's flank. At first, Akira thought he'd missed, but then she saw the sapling. A tiny shoot erupted from the thread, rapidly growing into a towering monstrosity. Vines as thick as tree trunks twisted and snared the Hainu, glowing with blue light. The beast paused, its face almost amused, before biting cleanly through the vines as though they were paper.

"Calder…" Akira's voice wavered, but Calder cut her off with a strained grunt.

"I know!"

His quarterstaff came free from his back, an unassuming weapon, dark wood polished to a shine. Blue threads coiled around it as he spun it with dazzling speed, creating a blur of light. The Hainu responded with a snarl, its wings folding tightly to its body as it dove toward him.

Calder rolled to the side, his staff catching the beast midair, sending it crashing to the ground.

The Hainu was on its feet again before the dust settled, golden eyes narrowing. Calder unleashed a pink thread, which snagged the creature's hind leg. The Hainu hesitated, its movements slowed, but it twisted and snapped the thread with its teeth, wrenching Calder forward. The backlash shattered the thread into shards of glass-like light, which dissipated harmlessly into the air.

"Breaking a thread scales two-fold with the strength of the Threadcaster," murmured Ryū, "if Calder trained Jiro…" his voice trailed off, "its incalculable."

"Nothing is incalculable given the correct parameters," said Jun.

Akira wanted to intervene, but Calder's hand shot up. "Don't interfere," he barked, his gaze locked with the Hainu's.

The beast lunged again, its claws raking across Calder's side. Blood seeped through his tunic, and he collapsed to his knees, clutching his side. The Hainu loomed over him, breath curling from its maw like smoke. Akira screamed, her crystal flaring, but Calder's voice—despite his injuries—held authority. "Stay back!"

The Hainu's teeth descended. For a heart-stopping moment, Akira thought Calder was finished, but his form vanished. The Hainu snarled, its jaws snapping at empty air, its golden gaze flicking around in confusion.

It didn't notice Calder until the blade pressed against its throat. Perched on its withers, the fairy had one arm wrapped under its neck, dagger glinting in the light. The Hainu growled low, the sound resonating like a storm.

EIGHTEEN 十八

AKIRA

"Sugoi!" Shoji's voice rang out, so loud that Calder nearly toppled off the Hainu's shoulder in the process. "End it!"

Calder's eyes, beginning to flicker like a candle in the wind, scanned Jiro's ragtag crew. They looked like they'd crawled out of a forgotten corner of the world—clothes barely clinging to their bodies, as if they'd lost a battle with every possible stain, and enough grime coating them to suggest they were perhaps developing their own microbial ecosystems. He didn't spot a single intact garment, which—if you think about it—was a pretty impressive feat in its own right.

His gaze snapped back to the thick fur he was clinging to. With a somewhat graceless movement that was less dismount and more… well, gravity's reminder, Calder let go and tumbled off the Hainu's back. His injury, which had been oozing with the kind of resolve you'd expect from a waterfall (minus the scenic beauty), was made worse. But no matter—he clutched his side as if he were trying to strangle the wound into submission.

With a grimace, he managed to pull himself upright. He staggered around the Hainu, almost surprised to still be alive, until he found himself face to face with the massive beast. Its mouth was shut tight, but its muzzle bore a faint reddish hue. Up close, Calder noticed the strange white lines etched into the creature's fur, lines that seemed to hum like they were about to spill secrets. He met the amber gaze of the beast for just a beat, feeling both oddly calm and deeply aware that it could probably rip him apart for fun.

"What the hell are you doing?!" Shoji's voice cut through the air, and Calder was aware of the panic rising in his crew. Shoji himself was being restrained by Ryū and Akira, both contemplating whether to knock him out for his own good.

Calder's gaze dropped. And as he did, he collapsed to his knees—not so much collapsing as *falling*—his breath shallow, his hand trembling as he placed the dagger before the Hainu. His disheveled brown hair, half-tied up in a mess that looked more like a poorly executed bird's nest than a hairstyle, fell over his face as he collapsed.

Shoji was still busy trying to yammer something, and Akira had to resist the urge to remove her hand from over his mouth as moisture began to coat the inside of her palm.

Time stretched out, thick and sticky like molasses. For Jiro's crew, it felt like they were waiting for the next ice age, but in reality, it was probably no more than a few minutes. Time always had a way of crawling when the world was on the verge of turning to chaos—like when a bloodthirsty beast was staring you down or, you know, when one of your teammates was on the brink of bleeding out.

Akira's arms were beginning to tire, despite Ryū bearing half of the fumbling mass of Shoji. She was also starting to entertain the thought of running into the foray herself. The whole '*respect*' and '*honor*' thing was all well and good, but surely that mambo jumbo could be thrown into the proverbial fire when there was about a five minute interval between Calder sitting in a pool of blood and swimming in one.

Before she could finish her internal debate (she never was good at these), a crackle sounded from the trees behind the temple.

Now, you might assume Akira had some attention deficit disorder, and yes, a simple crackle might seem like an easy distraction. But it wasn't the crackle that drew her attention—it was the thing that caused it. *Things*, rather.

A spattering of evergreen trees sat behind the temple, their emerald pines stubbornly clinging to life despite the frigid temperatures. Though this unforgivable landscape was hardly suited to life, the evergreen tree had always been one to do their best to continuously one up mother nature. Though the smattering of trees could barely be called a forest, it served its purpose in obscuring the sight of those who had grown too big for their breeches. Such forests, in addition to being far removed from modest, were no strangers to harboring secrets. And this particular forest (despite not really being a forest) was no exception. In fact, I'd rather say in the ranking of secrets forests could hide, this one would certainly reach the top ten. It hid no deep dark secret, nor pirate treasure hoard, or a crippled old lady intent on taking out years of frustration on unsuspecting children. No, this forest had decided to hide a pack, seventeen strong, of Hainu.

Seventeen ordinary wolves might well send most people fleeing in terror, but the sight of seventeen Hainu would have even the sturdiest minds unraveling. It would compel many to check themselves into asylums, where they would spend their remaining days pondering, with maddening fervour, whether a spoon was in any way akin to a fork. Fortunately for Jiro's clan, select few of them could claim any degree of sanity, so instead of losing their marbles and becoming dribbling buffoons, they unsheathed their weapons, like the lunatics they were. Though they had now all seen (at least) one Hainu in their lives, they had also reached the unsettling conclusion that the creature who had almost bested one of the Masters of Heron Academy in a matter of minutes, was actually not the leader of the pack, but quite likely a youngling. To put it into context, if the Hainu Calder had fought was the size of the horse, compared to the rest of the pack, that Hainu was the size of your regular grassroots wolf. To put it lightly, Jiro's clan had about as much chance of surviving, let alone winning, a fight with this bunch as they did to spontaneously grow a set of antlers.

"By my calculations—" Jun began, but Ryū interrupted with his usual snark. "Really, Jun? What *do* your calculations say?"

Jun sighed, smoothing his hair back as if it might suddenly make him look less ridiculous. "If you'd let me finish, I could tell you."

Ryū stared, his silence more telling than any of his sarcastic remarks.

Jun hesitated and then looked away, apparently realizing that finishing his sentence might be an act of futility.

Meanwhile, the Hainu were closing in, forming a V-shape that would have been impressively strategic—if it weren't so terrifying. Akira stared at them, wishing with all her heart that they were a flock of geese instead. Anything but this.

The lead Hainu stepped forward, towering above the others, its fur a dark timber that verged on black. The intricate spirals in its coat seemed to glow with an eerie light, and its collar, braided in shades of navy, held feathers the color of golden maple leaves. For a moment, Akira was struck by the uncanny resemblance of it all to a nightmare—one not merely horrifying, but also strangely magnificent, as if it had been spun from the threads of a fevered dream.

The Hainu stopped, looming over Calder, whose blood had now pooled beneath him like a grim lake. The leader lowered its massive head to stare at Calder with an expression that could have been mistaken for curiosity—if curiosity was paired with the kind of power that could rip you apart in an instant.

And then, the air thickened. The Hainu opened its maw, revealing teeth that would make even the bravest warrior flinch.

Ryū was already moving before Akira realized it, charging across the clearing as the air grew heavy with the mist of the Hainu's breath. Akira's heart thudded in her chest as the yellow mist began to swallow the clearing whole. She tried to rush toward Calder, but the mist disoriented her, and by the time it cleared, she was facing the wrong direction entirely.

She pushed through the mist, tearing herself away from a low-hanging branch, only to find herself knee-deep in blood, but her focus was solely on Calder. Nothing else mattered—not even the Hainu hovering over them.

The yellow mist vanished so suddenly that Akira could almost convince herself it had never existed. She extricated herself from the branch, blood soaking into her trousers, but she barely noticed. Even the Hainu's looming presence couldn't distract her from Calder.

She fumbled around him, her hands shaking as Ryū and Jun arrived, helping to stem the blood. Cloth was stripped from their robes and pressed to Calder's side. It wasn't until Calder's hand rested lightly on her shoulder that she realized he'd been sitting upright this entire time.

Gingerly, she let go of his side. Despite the pool of blood around them, her hands were dry. There was a gaping hole in Calder's robes, but his flesh was untouched. She blinked in disbelief. She looked up at Calder, her confusion writ large across her face, while Ryū and Jun knelt beside her, equally dumbfounded.

Only then did Akira fully process the horse-sized

winged wolf hovering above them. She almost blurted something, but settled for a quiet, "But how?"

Calder, who had been silently inspecting his side, looked back at the Hainu with the yellow feathered collar. "You're a healer."

The Hainu lowered her head, her piercing blue eyes locking onto the fairy. "I am."

Akira should have been more shocked by the fact that the winged wolf had just spoken, but she took it in stride, as if a child had just stolen a toy. It was almost comical, the ease with which she accepted it. She glanced at Jun, whose face was scrunched up in concentration—more than usual. "Why are we not surprised?"

Calder pointed toward the Hainu's collar, now dulling to a shade of brown. "They're like our crystals." He lightly touched his own purple chronocrystal, which hummed weakly.

The Hainu released a similar hum but didn't comment further.

"But how?" murmured Jun, his face now squished up in the way it did when he was thinking too hard (which was most of the time).

"They," Calder inclined his head toward the Hainu, "are from the Great Clock as much as we are. Like everything else that draws breath. I have heard chatter and whispers of creatures of great power who have harnessed chronomagic in the past. But I had thought those were mere legends, or something of a bygone era. Perhaps only the Elder of the Light Fae can claim to have witnessed such feats for themselves. Many a tale told with too much ale and good cheer, have told of a time when the dragons wielded great crystals of their own. The age of the Dragonriders, when man and beast were made one by the crystals which bound them. Yet I had no reason to believe they were anything more than fairytales, for no mention is made of this, even in the restricted texts of Heron Academy."

The Hainu turned to Calder, "Legends are seldom just tales." She took a few steps away from Calder and glanced towards the rest of the pack, tilting her head forward. The gathering of teeth and claws hesitated, but then the first of the bunch teetered closer into the temple courtyard.

Calder his hand gently resting upon his former wound glanced towards the Hainu, "Thank you—"

"You would not be able to speak my true name," said the Hainu, "but you may call be Rul'ka." With her face-sized nose she indicated towards the rest of the pack who were still filing in one by one, "this is my pack—my family." When the smaller Hainu who had fought Calder appeared by Rul'ka's side, she bit him playfully by the thick ruff on his neck, "this is Al'ka. My son."

The look which passed over Calder's face perfectly personified the concept of confusion. If Akira had any competence in illustration, she would have sketched a drawing of his face and pasted it under the lexicon entry of 'confused'. Alas, she was no skilled illustrator, and even if she were, this was hardly the time or the place to pull out an easel and paints.

"If he's your son, why heal me?" Calder asked, still struggling to comprehend.

Rul'ka brushed up against Al'ka, breathing out another cloud of yellow mist over the Hainu's body. It swirled and ungulated until it was swallowed up into the thick folds of his fur.

Rul'ka nudged Al'ka, breathing another cloud of yellow mist over his fur. "Because you showed honor. Our ways are not so different from yours. But we demand one thing—honor."

A series of barks and yips followed which were answered by various members of her pack in a continuation of the series of barks and yips. All of this was approximately as understandable to a group of humans, fairies, and Yōsei as you would expect a series of barks and yips to be.

Once the barking ceased, only Rul'ka and Al'ka remained, their forms blending into the temple courtyard. Calder opened his mouth to speak, then closed it, likely realizing he had nothing of value to add. Only when the last fluffy tail disappeared into the darkness did the alpha once again turn to Calder, "Many have come here seeking help. There are few who deserve it."

Rul'ka, her massive paw leaving an impression in the ground, turned toward the forest. "Come," she commanded, her gaze sweeping over the group. "All of you."

They obeyed with varying degrees of enthusiasm. Predictably, Ryū and Kyou brought up the rear of the group. Neither of them having been terribly keen on the whole Hainu idea to begin with, and having met them, this sentiment had hardly improved.

Mother and son trod side by side, their colossal forms taking up much of the path even with wings tightly folded against their bodies. Calder walked only a few paces behind them. Though to say any of them 'walked' was rather misleading, for despite the gradual pace which Rul'ka had set, even this lackadaisical gait was realistically a healthy jog for all the bipeds behind them.

"I take it you did not come to the Nayagu for the scenery," said Rul'ka, as her giant paw left a footprint large enough to send a full-grown man into cardiac arrest.

Calder inclined his head, despite the fact that from her vantage point Rul'ka could hardly see the gesture, "We have a problem."

"Most do," Rul'ka answered. "And frankly, your kind tends to have more problems than most."

Akira, no longer able to contain her urgency, surged forward. Her jog was unsustainable, but she pushed herself. "Our leader, Jiro, he was taken by Threadcasters."

Rul'ka paused, the words sinking in. Akira barely managed to stop herself from colliding into the massive wolf. They quickly arranged themselves into an awkward circle, the two Hainu taking up the most space.

"So, this man," Rul'ka nodded toward Calder, "is not your leader?"

Akira shook her head. Rul'ka hummed at the response, and then allowed her blue eyes to drift away from the group. To their left was a pool, whose size was so large it might have been more appropriate to call it a lake. Its water was so blue and clear on a fair day it might have been difficult to ascertain where the sky ended, and it began. A bubbling brook, which let off jets of steam into the surrounding cold, completed the quaint picture. All that was missing was some bathing monkeys wasting away their lives cooking in their own filth.

"It's beautiful is it not?" Rul'ka was still facing the pool, and Akira had to wonder if she was about to jump into the waters and take a bath.

When none of them answered, her gaze drifted back towards them, prompting them to mumble out an answer at once.

"There is no need to fear me," she said softly (well as softly as was possible with vocal cords that were likely the size of a small child), "if I wished to kill you, you would be dead already."

Although her words were clearly meant to comfort them, Akira would not exactly say her intended effect had been achieved.

"So, tell me about these Threadcasters who have taken your friend Jiro." She had now settled down onto her haunches in a way that was rather akin to a domestic dog. Though I doubt she would have taken kindly to that comparison, nor would anyone with any degree of sanity have dared to express such sentiments to her face.

Calder gestured towards Akira, who had been otherwise occupied trying to decide if she wished to sit or to stand. She ultimately decided to stay standing, finding the height difference between her and Rul'ka more than sufficient to render any notion of pride or indeed any semblance of elegance, entirely moot.

Akira glanced at Ryū, internally cringing as his encouraging nod sprung forth the words she needed.

"It was a five days ago—" she paused, having only now realized that time had become a thoroughly foreign concept to her as of late, but ultimately determined the exact timeframe was neither of great importance nor something she could accurately provide, "—or thereabouts. We were all at Tsuyoshi-sama's camp—though I take it you probably don't need to know that, nor know who Tsuyoshi—"

"Child," interrupted Rul'ka, "speak freely. There is much I do not know, but little you know that I do not."

Akira's guttural reaction was to smile, it was only when she dissected the gentle tone in which the words had been spoken from their meaning that it melted back into oblivion. Mustering the strength not to frown, she continued the tale. "It was two men—fairies, I think," she started, cringing at the memories. "They wore the black robes of the Threadcasters, tall but... not remarkable. I barely saw their faces, but I'm sure I'd recognize them if I—"

Akira was once again interrupted by the heavy voice of Rul'ka. Akira, like most normal people, was not one who took fondly towards interruption. Especially frequent and repeated ones such as this. Yet I trust it is not entirely surprising to you to learn that she was not so devoted to this sentiment as to express it to a wolf at least five times her size.

'Child,' an endearment Akira was no fonder towards than interruptions, "I require no details such as these. Where was the man Jiro taken?"

Akira judged that she was approximately two interruptions away from doing something she would no doubt come to regret. So, still in possession of a degree of her wits thought it best Ryū answered her question. When Akira motioned towards him, Ryū jabbed himself in the chest with his finger and mouthed "Me?" When Akira nodded, Ryū looked like a man who would have rather jumped into a vat of raw sewage to escape his current predicament. His countenance was a warring faction with one side nearly buckling from terror whilst the other battled to sustain its preferred look of contempt. It settled on some alarming amalgamation which would have made a ventriloquist proud.

With a voice that sounded as if he had swallowed half a bag of sand and washed it down with liquid concrete Ryū (with many unwelcome amendments courtesy of Jun) explained the layout of the fortress where Jiro had been taken. Rul'ka listened in stony silence, the only sound came from Al'ka who had decided the pebbles by his feet must hold the ultimate secrets of the universe. There was something rather comical if not altogether confidence shattering to see the beast which had nearly bested a Master Threadcaster playing with a bunch of rocks.

By the time Ryū had finished his somewhat meandering description, which was generously punctuated by Jun's increasingly graphic accounts of all the ways they could fail, perish, or—possibly worse—be maimed, night had crept over them like a blanket too heavy to shrug off.

Rul'ka, now cloaked in fur as black as an endless void, swiveled her enormous head toward Jun, her eyes narrowing like twin moons set to collide. "You forgot one," she said, the words vibrating the air between them.

Jun's face crinkled in that delightful way it did when someone had pointed out a flaw in his meticulous calculations, which, of course, was always someone else's fault. He immediately adjusted his topknot as though it were the source of his current distress. "Oh? Did I?" he asked, the question hanging in the air with an unspoken plea for mercy.

Rul'ka emitted a sound that could've been a laugh, though it was more like a strangled growl being forced through the world's largest straw. "There is also the distinct possibility that Jiro might already have been taken to Cargyll," she said, her gaze sweeping across the group like an artist inspecting their latest piece. "Neither of you saw the Threadcasters take him to the watchtower, correct?"

Her eyes—vast and terrifying—fixed on Akira. Akira immediately regretted the fact that she could no longer remember how to breathe. It wasn't that the question was particularly damning, but there was something about the weight of Rul'ka's stare that made her feel like a rabbit caught in the gaze of a hawk. The silence stretched out, thick and suffocating, until, mercifully, a distant owl screamed its protest and snapped the Hainu's attention away.

"No," Jun answered at last, his hands entwined in what Akira could only assume was an attempt to hold himself together. "But it's logical to assume—"

"Perhaps to you it is," Rul'ka interrupted, her voice a rumble that seemed to vibrate through their very bones. "But there are always other answers. Have you not considered that they might use your logic against you?"

Jun looked as though he might combust from the sheer weight of this logic-defying statement. His expression shifted between horror and a fierce, unspoken vow to burn all of existence down with nothing but his thoughts and his sheer stubbornness. Fortunately, he didn't do that. Not immediately, anyway.

"Now tell me," Rul'ka continued, languidly licking her impossibly long paw, "what would you ask of us?"

Kyou, whose verbal contributions thus far could be summed up as I don't like this (spoken with the amount of enthusiasm one might reserve for brushing a spider off their shoulder), finally looked up from the ground. His voice was quieter than usual, but the weight of it still pressed heavily upon them. "We need entry into the watchtower."

"And you think *we* can provide this?" Rul'ka tilted her

head, as though she were considering the very absurdity of the request. Akira could almost hear the gears in her massive head grinding together.

Kyou exchanged looks with the others, his face hardening, before he sank to his knees with all the grace of a man who'd come to terms with his own lack of pride. His long black hair cascaded around his face like a veil, shrouding whatever shred of dignity he might have had left. "I know little of the ways of the Hainu," he began, his voice low but steady.

"But I know you value loyalty and honor above all else. Loyalty to your pack, to your family, is worth any price. And so I come to you, as a member of Clan Jiro, and as his son, asking you to allow us to do the same."

NINETEEN

KILIE

Kilie grunted as Kallae's nails dug into his shoulder. "Would it kill you to clip your nails once in a blue moon?" he snapped, just as a second set of claws—arguably sharper—sank into his other shoulder. Even with both Kallae and Miki restraining him, Kilie knew he could break their grip. His legs practically screamed with coiled energy, echoing the call of his chronocrystal as it alternated between searing heat and bone-chilling cold. The intensity made Kilie all but certain he'd be adding a new scar to his collection. He could smell burnt skin, a nauseating confirmation of the damage being done, but he felt nothing. Not numbness, not the dulling adrenaline might bring. No, his focus left no room for pain—every time he closed his eyes, he saw feathers, ablaze and red, seared into his memory.

"He is here," Kilie murmured under his breath.

Even without looking, Kilie could see the grimace which twisted on Kallae's face, "Now is not the time to be losing your marbles Kilie," muttered Kallae. "If you insist on doing so, may I request that you delay such antics until after we get the hell out of here."

Kallae turned to Miki, who still clutched Kilie's shoulder with bruising strength. "Is there a way out of here?"

Before Miki could answer, Kilie, eyes locked on the Inquisitor and the villagers, said, "I'm not leaving."

"By Amriel's will, I will drag you out kicking and screaming if I must, Kilie."

"I doubt any of us will make it out undetected if I start kicking and screaming," Kilie snapped back. "And last I heard, you didn't care much for Amriel's will anymore."

Kallae's hand twitched beside him, and Kilie felt a sharp breeze bite at the half-moons of raw skin left by Kallae's nails. He stumbled, narrowly avoiding a face-first plunge into the termite-ravaged plywood beneath him. Regaining his balance, he turned to Kallae. "I'm sorry," Kilie said softly. "That was uncalled for."

Before either could say more, a scream pierced the clearing. Screams had become as common as ants in an anthill that morning, but this one was different. It wasn't the scream of someone with nothing left to lose or someone about to lose everything. It was the scream of someone at war with themselves, someone who believed, to their core, that they deserved better.

The Inquisitor's forehead glistened with sweat. Despite the beads trickling into his eyes, they remained wide and dark, impenetrable. His mouth gaped open, an abyss so consuming Kilie felt an irrational urge to climb inside it. He didn't, of course. But as the scream faded, the Inquisitor's face bore its scars: deep lines etched from the corners of his mouth, running up until they converged in unnatural divots. His skin, unremarkable moments before, now seemed translucent. Kilie could see every twitch of muscle, every rush of blood surging to his head.

Kilie teetered between continuing to stare at the

unfolding horror and whirling around to purge his stomach—perhaps his brain too. He compromised by suppressing a strangled belch, which brought up a less-delicate rendition of the previous evening's chicken and rice. A flavorful dish on the way down, decidedly less so on the way up.

Meanwhile, the Inquisitor—clearly unsatisfied with the level of trauma inflicted—began to fold in on himself. He started walking… with knees bent the wrong way. This was enough to send Miki vomiting onto Kallae's boots. Kilie, succumbing to the vice of sympathetic retching, followed moments later. Kallae had the expression of a man who was on the precipice of giving into deeply suppressed homicidal tendencies.

Fortunately, Kallae's murderous urges were interrupted by the Inquisitor's abrupt collapse into the arms of a nearby guard. The guard, showing an ill-advised measure of compassion, caught him… only to be shoved aside and slapped. "Kaiyō-sama is stirring; he resists me," the Inquisitor mumbled. "What is Asa-chan doing?"

He clutched the guard's cloak with white-knuckled hands. "Asa will have to be punished for this oversight." Straightening, he shoved the guard aside. Dust streamed from the Inquisitor's hand, hanging momentarily in the air before disappearing into oblivion.

The Inquisitor, having regained some semblance of 'not nightmare fodder', righted himself as if he had merely tripped, and not just briefly defied the laws of biology.

For a moment no one spoke. No one moved. Even those who moments before had been surrounded by their family, and now found nothing but air beside them, were silent. Even the birds who had been singing in the trees fell silent, as if struck dead. Well for all Kilie knew they had died. He wouldn't blame them if they had all suffered from a heart attack and just keeled over after what they had just witnessed. He was half contemplating that option himself.

The silence was broken by a sound entirely at odds with the occasion. The laugh which shattered it was neither disingenuous nor even outlandish or cruel in its nature. No, it was a perfectly normal laugh. And yet it came from a man who had just summoned a shadow creature to kill half a village.

"So, my dear friends," came Miki's halting translation of the Inquisitor's words, "I trust you enjoyed my little show."

He waved a hand across the scene. Despite the chaos, no blood stained the earth, no bodies littered the ground, no torn clothes fluttered in the breeze. Only dust lingered, whirling on unseen currents, and the villagers' tear-streaked faces bore evidence of what had transpired.

He poked a pointed boot deep into the side of the village chief. Still on the floor from having dropped himself to his feet, reverence appeared to be the last thing on the chief's mind. Tears streamed down his cheeks with such abandon, puddles of black had appeared on the dirt beneath him. Even from a distance, Kilie could see the tendons knot and strain beneath the man's cheek.

The chief murmured something; his head still hidden beneath his long tresses.

The Inquisitor, now again resembling something closer to human than corpse, leaned down next to the chief. He pressed his ear up against him, "Hmmm," he hummed, "I'm afraid I didn't quite catch that."

The chief's head shot up, and he leapt to his feet. "We will never bow to you!"

The Inquisitor continued to smile, his cherry red lips standing out grotesquely against his pale white skin, "Well that is a shame isn't it," he patted the Chief atop the head like one would a dog or a small child, "but never mind that. I can do this again and again," he turned to face the rest of the villagers, "and again. Until you all understand that I am here to help you. Do you not see that it is the Empire who cares for you? When has the Empire ever let you down?"

He pulled a young woman towards him, gripping her chin with his hand, "Go ahead," he hissed. "Tell me."

When the woman refused to look up, making no sound besides the rapid breaths which came from her in quick bursts, the Inquisitor grabbed her again. This time by the arm. Though he soon released her, throwing her against the side of the well with a force that sent cracks running through the brickwork.

"Tell me!"

The smile had vanished as red began to cloud his face. "You, ungrateful people," he kicked dirt into the woman's face. "You do not see how deceived you truly are. But I will show you," he slipped the smile back onto his face. "Don't you worry dear people, by the time I am through with you, you will never forget again."

He gestured towards one of the guards, who trudged forward hesitantly. The Inquisitor motioned at him again, and the guard hastened to hand him a knife, "No you idiot," said the Inquisitor as he shoved the blade back, "the Shikigami."

The guard, the moment of realization written plainly across his face despite the chainmail, reached into his robes and withdrew the rest of the paper figures. The Inquisitor tore another one of the paper figures off, and tossed the rest back at his guard, who was fumbling to such a degree he dropped it and was forced to go galivanting across the clearing chasing after it.

The Inquisitor, holding the figure between two dainty fingers, began the elaborate folding procedure anew. Though he still did so with a dexterity which would have many a dancer purple with envy, Kilie could see his movements were more wearied than they had been. His fingers caught against the paper; their motions delayed as if the signal needed first to be deciphered by an interpreter who was halfway inebriated.

Kilie shifted, his legs and feet having long ago grown

numb, thanks to his cramped position. The shack from which they were viewing this horrifying scene, was not, shall we say, built to house three raccoons, let alone three people. Kilie turned to Kallae who was staring at the scene as intently as himself. Despite the fact that neither of them had taken so much as a step in the last hour, sweat shone on their foreheads.

Kilie's chronocrystal blazed with an intense purple light. He turned to Kallae, voice trembling with determination. "I need to help them."

Kallae, his eyes still fixed on the Inquisitor muttered, "And what do you think you can do against darkness such as this?" He gestured towards the Inquisitor, whose skin had once again taken on a pallor normally reserved for the dead or the perpetually fearful.

Kilie shrugged, "I must try. For is that not what Heron Academy stands for? We are the bearers of the light, if we shy away from the darkness, who else will fight it?"

Kallae reached out a hand, and for a moment Kilie thought he was trying to stop him again. But then Kallae's heavy hand merely came to a rest on his shoulder, "You are right, I cannot stop you."

"I take it you will not join me?"

A chill shivered through Kallae. "You know I can't."

Kilie frowned, releasing his hold on the chronocrystal. The intensity of the light flared up like a miniature sun, and the trio staggered back, temporarily blinded by the shock of it. They blinked furiously, squinting away spots of white that danced across their vision.

"We must all live with the choices we make," Kilie muttered under his breath, as though someone else had spoken the words, and now he was just repeating them out of some twisted sense of obligation.

He took a deep breath, his eyes drifting toward the clearing, only to feel someone moving behind him. At first, he was ready to snap at Kallae—*of course it was Kallae, who else would it be?*—but the familiar scowl on his face dropped when he realized it was Miki creeping up like a mouse in a field of lions.

"I join you?" Miki's voice was like a squeaky door that had seen better days.

Kilie's head, normally held so proudly upright like some nobleman's, dropped slightly. His eyes shifted toward Kallae, who was already opening his mouth to make some sarcastic comment, and Kilie couldn't help the eye-roll that accompanied it.

He hovered his hand over Miki's shoulder, clearly contemplating the awkwardness of it all. *Is that what we're doing now? Handing out shoulder pats like we're in the middle of a wholesome adventure?* But before the gesture could solidify, his hand retreated back into the folds of his robes. "Stay. This is not a battle you can win. Not yet anyway."

He paused, then added, "Stay here," and pointed a finger toward Kallae, who was no doubt brooding in the background. "Make sure he doesn't do anything too stupid."

Kallae spluttered something unintelligible, made all the more unintelligible by the fact that Kilie was now sailing through the air, threads of blue already swirling across his body. If there hadn't been a shadow creature currently ripping its way out of a piece of paper like the world's most horrific birth, the villagers might've had time to appreciate Kilie's acrobatic prowess. But, as it was, the current crisis made everything else seem… irrelevant.

Still mid-air, crystal ablaze with an intensity that made it look like a purple sun, Kilie watched as the Inquisitor shoved the shikigami towards one of the young men. The man's legs stalled in the dirt as the shikigami seemed to contemplate its next move. It was like watching an overgrown toddler trying to figure out what to do with a toy that didn't come with instructions.

And then—*screech*—the shikigami was off. Its face opened up with a noise that could only be described as what you'd imagine a dying horse to sound like, and the demon spawned itself straight into the man's body.

The man swayed, his face shifting into something more closely resembling confusion than horror, before he hunched forward, mouth agape. A scream like a tidal wave erupted from him as he began to consume everything in sight.

Kilie landed softly on the ground, his blade drawn, gleaming under the moonlight like an obsidian promise. It wasn't much of a weapon, not compared to those carried by the elite of his kind, but it was serviceable. No delicate engravings, no fine craftsmanship—just a solid piece of obsidian, sharpened to a lethal point. Still perhaps, it was this very lack of frills which made it even more menacing.

Kilie landed from a height that should have made his feet produce a thunderous roar, instead he landed with a tap that was more than covered by the screaming that was now spreading throughout the crowd. The man, the quizzical look long forgone, tore through the people with his mouth gaping wide open. This served two distinct purposes. The first was to let out a long droning, screeching sound that was not only ear-splitting but could be felt pelting through one's body like an earthquake. The second was of course so he could devour the other villagers starting from the head down to the toes.

His focus snapped back to the Inquisitor, whose gaze was fixed upon him. And just like that, the *other* monster in the room—the shikigami—turned its attention to him. The way they both locked eyes on him, moving as one, made his stomach churn.

The Inquisitor peered at him and then smiled a smile so broad, Kilie could see the spit which glistened across his too-white teeth. The Inquisitor said something in his uncannily high voice. When Kilie didn't respond, the Inquisitor frowned. But then he held up his finger in the universal signal of 'aha! I have an idea,' "Ah of course you must forgive my assumption," he now spoke in startingly fluent Cygren, "I am still not used to your people's lack of skill with languages." He laughed.

Kilie stood with feet spread shoulder width apart, a stance which his Master at Heron Academy had drilled into him with such fortitude the phrase 'battle-ready' still sent shivers down his spine. He held his obsidian blade in both hands, the light shattering in every which direction as he shuffled from one foot to the other.

"Let them go," Kilie growled, his eyes flicking between the Inquisitor and the shikigami. "It is me you want, isn't it?"

The Inquisitor smiled, "I see you hold a high opinion of yourself. It seems that is a shared feature of all members of your Order. Tell me," he took a few steps towards him, "is arrogance the *only* requirement to join the Way of the Light, hmmm?"

Kilie didn't respond, only tightened his grip on the sword, a muscle twitching in his jaw as he prepared for the inevitable.

Before he could move, the Inquisitor motioned for the shikigami to step closer.

"Ah, ah, ah," the Inquisitor cooed, wagging a finger in mock disapproval, "Can we not have a civil conversation? You're bolder than I expected—others of your Order have been much less… hmm… foolish? Is that the word?"

The Inquisitor lowered his hand and turned around, his languid steps leading him closer to the well, "But no need to fret. I am sure you will bow down just as all the others did in time," he grinned, "or of course, the other option is death. That is always an option." He held a finger across his lips, "In fact, I dare say that is the most common option chosen."

Kilie wasted no more time. He lunged forward, but the shikigami moved just as swiftly, slithering out of the way with a speed that was *unnatural.* His blade struck nothing but air. The next strike, however, sank into the thigh of the possessed villager, but instead of cutting through muscle and bone, the blade slid through like a knife through butter.

Kilie barely had time to register what was happening before the shikigami was on him again, lashing out with a speed that defied logic. He barely evaded it, his body spinning out of the way with threads of blue swirling around him.

"Of course," Kilie muttered under his breath, "like a damn shadow, it doesn't stop chasing."

The battle became a blur—dodging, parrying, the occasional cut, but nothing solid, nothing to show for it. Every time he thought he had the upper hand, the creature seemed to dance just out of reach. And as for the possessed man? He was no longer a man at all.

The shikigami, having chosen one of the lads from the village as unfortunate host, had no weapon to speak of. Then again it seemed to be doing just fine without one. Kilie already had a deep groove throbbing on his bicep from a bite he didn't quite manage to evade, and several scratches were sending fire shooting up and down his chest. Though the shikigami's teeth were no sharper than one would expect for an ordinary person (which of course the shikigami was not), and Kilie could see no visible teeth marks from the bite, the wound throbbed with a pain that threatened to send him to his knees. Kilie could not spare a moment to look at the damage, but even if he could, he was not entirely convinced he had the mental fortitude to deal with what would greet him.

Kilie parried another lash from the shikigami, almost stumbling over his own feet, and then a lone pebble in the process. The villager, who had started off this ordeal as a strapping young lad, now wouldn't so much be described as a prince in shining armor as much as a reanimated corpse with poor fashion sense. His complexion, which had begun a shade north of pale, was now so white it was almost as translucent as that of the Inquisitor, who had lost all semblance of health he had regained in the meantime. The next time Kilie's blade made contact, it neither sunk into the villager, but neither did it slide. Some degree of corpulence seemed to have been regained, yet rather than creating a cut, or doing some other sensible thing, the villager's skin began to slough off of him in layers. Kilie shook the layers off his blade suppressing the violent desire to run away screaming into a pit of fire.

Kilie swore violently under his breath, shaking the excess off his blade, trying to suppress the instinct to scream. This was not a fight. This was a nightmare.

Kilie, repressing every survival instinct he had (and any degree of sense) made another lunge for the shikigami. The creature, who had previously displayed reflexes rivalling that of a flector, barely reacted. It swayed, but that might have just as well have been from the wind. Kilie glanced at the Inquisitor, who still stood with arms outstretched, but even from a distance he could see they trembled. His muscles strained beneath his translucent skin, rendering his color a red so deep his lips appeared pale. His dark eyes had sunk so far into their sockets Kilie wondered if they had not been so horrified by the scene unfolding, they had simply disconnected themselves and rolled out. To say he looked haggard would be an understatement on the order of calling a mother dragon defending her offspring '*friendly*'.

Before Kilie could fully process the absurdity of his situation—having never found himself so thoroughly out of his depth—the Shikigami before him dissolved into something *worse* than a nightmare. Kilie tightened his grip on his blade, its cool steel oddly grounding him, a fleeting moment of clarity before everything spiraled. The creature, now writhing and buckling like a twisted heap of bones and sinew, began folding in on itself. Its limbs cracked and popped like dry twigs breaking underfoot, each new contortion defying every law of biology Kilie thought he knew. In less time than it would take to brew a pot of tea, the Shikigami had reduced itself to the size of a mere teacup—or at least, that's what it *looked* like at first glance.

What followed could only be described as the stuff of nightmares. The Inquisitor, who had been standing with arms outstretched, basking in his false superiority, suddenly crumpled to the side of the well, his frail body sagging like an old coat left out in the rain.

And then—then the teacup *shifted.*

It wasn't a teacup at all, of course. It was a monstrous, paper-thin approximation of one, but now it began to ooze and expand—not upwards, but sideways, as though it were alive. Its color darkened, turning a shade of sickly gray that reminded Kilie of meat left too long in the sun, and then—*nothing*. It absorbed all light, every photon of it sucked into the void of its form, leaving the world dimmer, quieter, as if the very air was holding its breath.

A puddle of black formed, and from its center rose a shape, like some grotesque dagger stabbing through the fabric of reality itself. Then it bloomed, growing into something that mere words could never fully describe. The creature had begun to grow so rapidly that Kilie could scarcely keep up with it. It had already outgrown its original shape, its once-familiar form now a mass of shifting, bulbous limbs and horrific appendages. Its head—or whatever might pass for one—was so disproportionate it could hardly support its own weight, and dark, twitching orbs that might have once been eyes now darted every which way. A tail, thick as a tree trunk, lashed through the air, knocking over rocks and debris in its wake.

Kilie stood frozen for a moment, his thoughts scrambling like a chaotic puzzle that refused to fit together. His fingers tingled, the familiar hum of his chronocrystal thrumming in his chest. Blue threads sparked to life in the air around him, flickering like lightning—almost annoyingly bright in the midst of the darkness that now seemed to suffocate everything else. A brief glance at his chronocrystal showed it still holding steady, its purple glow vibrant—at least for now.

Gritting his teeth, Kilie increased his leisurely pace, which though leisurely, was actually close to a full-tilt sprint in reality, thanks to the flection threads still wrapped around his legs, and begun gyrating blue threads in front of him. At first, the motion was rather clumsy, the threads being neither as light as they appeared, nor designed to be used in such a way. But by the time he reached the creature it was spinning with practiced ease, and with the augmented speed it had become a transparent blur of death. Unfortunately for the shikigami, that transparent blur of death made impact right on target.

Kilie not sure what to expect, was somewhat taken aback when it bit into the creature's skin, like well, skin. When he pushed harder, he was met with some resistance, and an accompanying cry of terror. Kilie withdrew, his arms heavy with exertion. A black ooze now pooled from the creature's side, staining the ground like crude oil. Kilie held the thread in both hands again and was about to lunge, when the creature made an odd chirruping noise and then ran off into the surrounding forest.

Kilie contemplated running after it but found he had little energy for such feats of stupidity. Though he soon discovered perhaps the wiser option was indeed to go running after an ooze monster rather than sticking around and taking his odds with the Inquisitor.

The Inquisitor, at some point during this exchange had extricated himself from his prone position clinging onto the well for dear life. Although he had certainly not recovered to a full bill of health, he looked decidedly less like he was having tea and splitting a scone with death. His skin was no longer entirely transparent, and he seemed almost capable of supporting his full weight without assistance.

"It seems I owe you a thank you," the Inquisitor said

to Kilie, his voice oddly cheery. His gaze flicked to two of his guards, and before Kilie could even form a coherent response, two guards had grabbed him by the arms, squeezing with a force that was downright unpleasant. The blue threads around his legs spun in a delicate arc, but before Kilie could act, a third guard slapped a cold device onto his arm.

Kilie's threads *snapped.*

The connection, once so strong, fizzled out like a dying sparkler.

Kilie glanced down in disbelief as his chronocrystal, once a deep and steady purple, now flickered and dulled, its color leaching away until it was a ghostly gray. *Impossible,* he thought, eyes widening. His breath hitched, the threads of his magic falling apart like so much sand.

"A lovely one, this one," the Inquisitor said, poking Kilie's chronocrystal with the tip of his staff. Kilie could do little more than scowl, his arms trapped, the weight of defeat settling over him.

"Let go of me," Kilie said, his voice coming out surprisingly dry, like a bear requesting a salad. Not that anyone was listening.

This request obviously went unheeded.

"What have you done to me?" he spat, testing his restraints. The cold object pressed against his arm sent shivers down his spine—it felt as though it were burning him, though at the same time it was the starkest chill, cutting into him like the press of a cold blade.

The Inquisitor made a dismissive noise, as though this was all terribly *trivial.* "Ah! Admiring our little invention, hmmm?" he chuckled, utterly undeterred by Kilie's resistance.

"Admire would not be the term I would use, no," Kilie muttered under his breath, though he was beginning to wonder if maybe a polite, *yes, sir* was in order. The Inquisitor continued, not even acknowledging the sarcasm.

"Quite brilliant, isn't it?" he said with a satisfied grin. When Kilie didn't respond, the two guards nodded vigorously, which earned them an irritable "Bah!" from the Inquisitor. "Go do something useful with yourselves," he snapped, waving them away.

"Now where were we?" he asked rubbing his fingers together, "ah yes, the cuffs. I will have to deliver my compliments to the Magickers at the Imperial Palace, for they have quite outdone themselves," he ran a finger over the contraption, and Kilie squirmed under his touch. "There's no use struggling my boy," said the Inquisitor, "it will only tighten the more you do. And the cuffs will siphon off any chronomagic your crystal manages to store."

Kilie's thoughts reeled. *A substance that could not only conduct chronomagic, but steal it from a chronocrystal? Impossible. Only a chronocrystal should have that ability. But how? The piece of metal digging into his wrist seemed to mock him with its existence, as though it were a living thing—no, a parasite. The questions began to flood him, but instead of voicing them, he found himself speaking without thinking.*

"What was that thing?"

The Inquisitor merely shrugged, unconcerned. "Just overexerted myself a little," he said with a sickening smile. "You'll be safe from the Shadow Shikigami with us. Don't you worry."

"I'll never come with you," Kilie growled, his tone resolute.

The Inquisitor raised an eyebrow. "Oh?" he mused, straightening his back with a pleased grin. "I thought you might say that, unless…" He turned his gaze to the guards, who now loomed, grinning in a way that sent a chill down Kilie's spine. "Unless, of course, you'd rather watch as I kill the remnants of this village for your refusal to follow a simple request?"

TWENTY 二十

AKIRA

Akira was falling. She snapped her eyes open and discovered, to her profound disappointment, that she was, in fact, still falling. The realization that the scenery was rushing past her at a speed far too fast for comfort should have clued her in to the fact that she was not dreaming, but wishful thinking had always been a size too big for its breeches.

Her first thought was to scream. She was fully aware that this would be approximately as useful as doing nothing at all, yet it felt somehow wrong to be plummeting out of the sky and not scream while doing so. It would have been like watching a comedy show and not laughing. It just wasn't done. At least not by those who lived their lives dictated by the customs imposed by polite society. It's debatable if her current companions could be suitably described as 'polite society,' but regardless of their designation, Akira had decided she should be screaming.

Her thoughts whipped out of her mind with such reckless abandon that she barely realized her screams were swallowed by the ravenous winds. She took a deep breath, only to discover the immense pressure on her chest made this virtually impossible. So, settling for the next best option, she began to wheeze. The wheezing, as you might imagine, did very little to improve Akira's predicament, and soon after morphed into a series of choking sounds, as she continued to plummet towards the decidedly pointy peaks beneath her.

One might wonder what sequence of events brought us to this point in time, but considering when last we left Akira, she was acquainting herself with a pack of flying wolves, perhaps you can use your imagination to decipher this particular mystery. The Hainu she had been riding—if gripping on for dear life could be described as 'riding'—had landed on a mountain ridge somewhere off to the left and looked unreasonably pleased with itself. Akira might have taken offense had she not had several rather more pressing matters to deal with. Not to mention the fact that she was still plummeting out of the sky.

Regaining a fraction of intelligence that had decided to curl up in a ball and go searching for its mother, Akira glanced down at her chronocrystal. It hummed in response, the dark turquoise hue beaming up at her, adding partial blindness to her ever-expanding list of problems. She soon tacked on another one because she couldn't for the life of her think of a scenario in which falling would benefit from her speeding up time.

Why is it always me who is falling? she thought, briefly considering whether flapping her arms like a deranged chicken might approximate flying. She quickly discarded the idea, though—if she failed, she would have died looking like a lunatic, and that was not something she was prepared to risk.

Which left her with the sole comforting fact that she was indeed, still falling.

Finding that her original thought—that being to scream—was really the only thing she could do, she continued as she had begun: falling out of the sky while screaming like a banshee who'd just sampled a wide range of experimental hallucinogens.

"Need a hand?" came a thundering voice beside her, which of course, had to be thundering on account of all the aforementioned screaming.

Ryū had mastered two expressions in his twenty-six years of life: a cheeky grin bordering on mildly maniacal, or the flavor of *I am going to kill you and everyone you love*. Ryū had decided the first was the appropriate expression to sport while riding a Hainu attempting to rescue a rapidly plummeting member of his clan. Akira contemplated if falling to her death might not just be the lesser of two evils.

Her arms were flailing about like a puffin trying to land (spoiler alert: puffins don't land gracefully), but she managed to twist toward Ryū, grasping his outstretched hand. For a brief moment, she continued to fall, but the fear of falling was swiftly replaced by the distinct possibility of her arm being yanked out of its socket. She heard Ryū grunt above her, and his muttered words were unintelligible.

"Can you stop that infernal rocking?" Ryū's voice was strained, "Or is mutually assured death your specialty when it comes to thanking your rescuers?"

"I did not need rescuing," Akira managed, just about managing to grab hold of one of the leather straps of the Hainu's saddle.

She felt the grip on her hand loosen. "Oh, is that so?" Ryū asked, his voice dripping with sarcasm, "So I take it you'd be perfectly fine if I let you go right now?"

Akira didn't deign to answer as she pulled down on the saddle, hoping that Ryū had tightened the girth sufficiently, and managed to swing a leg over the side. To say that her mounting was elegant would be like saying water buffalo are natural born dancers. She landed with a resounding *clank*, making the Hainu jerk back and snap at her feet.

"I rather think I would have figured something out," Akira said, now seated behind Ryū.

"Oh yeah, princess?" Ryū retorted, yanking on one side of the reins to get the Hainu to stop biting Akira's shoe. "And just what was this brilliant plan of yours?"

Akira mumbled something under her breath, wishing the ground would swallow her up for a brief moment of composure.

"I'm sorry, princess," Ryū said, jerking the reins again to avoid colliding with a fast-approaching pillar of rock. "I didn't quite catch that."

Akira gripped the back of Ryū's robes, nearly teetering off the side of the saddle. "Here's a suggestion for you, *princess*: why don't you pay attention to where we're flying, since clearly multi-tasking is something quite beyond your capabilities?"

"Ah yes, of course, what would I do without your expertise in flying?" Ryū jerked the Hainu back into another direction. "Where's *your* Hainu again?"

The rest of the flight was carried out in a heavy silence. The seventeen minutes it took them to return to the temple felt like half an eternity, and Akira practically jumped off mid-flight as the clearing came into view.

When they arrived, most of the others had already returned, save Shoji, who was almost certainly off scavenging for berries or attempting to hunt something (perhaps a bear).

Rul'ka stood in the center of the clearing, her head held high, an expression of amused superiority painting her features. She laughed—or at least made the sound Akira had now associated with her trying to laugh—and turned to face them. "Pa'ka gave you a rough ride this morning, did he?"

Akira frowned, still stumbling to reacquaint her aching limbs with the concept of solid ground. "He threw me off."

"Hmmm," Rul'ka took several steps toward Akira,

and then, without warning, sniffed her. The gust of wind from the Hainu's nostrils was so forceful that Akira's robes trembled across her skin. Five days in, and Akira was still wholly unfamiliar with the customs of wolfdom (as she had taken to calling it). "I would not say he threw you. Perhaps you simply do not know how to ride him."

The Hainu took a running leap, carrying herself fully across the clearing to land silently on the temple steps. "Much you still have to learn, furless child."

'Furless child' had unfortunately become the pack's nickname for them, and despite their insistence on Yōsei (or any number of other descriptors), it had stuck. Akira had once considered referring to the Hainu as 'overgrown lapdogs,' but ultimately decided against it. Calling a bunch of fanged, clawed, and proud furballs anything but their preferred name seemed… imprudent. Even if they were a bunch of pretentious furballs.

In the meantime, Calder appeared beside Akira and Ryū, his voice low. "Are you alright?"

Before Akira could reply, Ryū, wearing a grin obnoxious enough to make a jester jealous, playfully punched her in the shoulder. "Thanks to me. Not that I got any thanks for it, but that's alright. I'm used to it."

"It's for your own good," said Akira returning the punch in kind. "I'm only looking out for you. If your ego were to grow any bigger, I fear you would simply explode, and then whatever would I do without you to save me?"

"Oi, oi, princess, now is that any way to speak to your savior?"

"Enough, you two," snapped Calder, gesturing toward the temple entrance. "There'll be plenty of time later for you to insult each other until high noon."

Rul'ka, her dark eyes revealing nothing of her thoughts, gestured toward the temple entrance. "Come with me."

The temple entrance, while large, was neither ornate nor even particularly well-constructed. It lacked a door and, for all intents and purposes, was essentially just a hole. It was a big hole—enough to accommodate a pack of horse-sized wolves—but to call it 'welcoming' would be an overstatement. Perhaps it is not surprising that construction was not a skillset particularly well developed in a pack of flying wolves.

"Where are Shoji and Kyou?" Ryū asked, his tone casual, though his eyes darted around as if expecting an ambush.

Rul'ka's dark lips twisted into something that might have been a smile—if one squinted and ignored the glint of teeth that promised trouble. "They are being entertained elsewhere. The Sanctum is for Followers of the Way of the Light. Follow me." She dissolved into the shadows with an unnerving grace, her form melting like ink into water.

Despite five days camped at the temple's base, the group had yet to glimpse anything beyond its imposing rockface exterior. Whatever mysteries the Hainu harbored within remained just that—mysteries. Jiro's clan had spent their nights huddled together for warmth, curling against each other in a futile attempt to escape the biting cold. The temple entrance, a gaping black maw, yielded nothing but darkness.

Akira lingered at the threshold, one boot toeing the line between daylight and shadow. Behind her, a warm nudge startled her out of her thoughts.

"Fear is blinding," Al'ka murmured, padding past her into the darkness. His tone suggested profound wisdom, though Akira suspected it was the kind of wisdom that unraveled under scrutiny. She'd learned the hard way that Hainu idioms were a gamble—equal parts enlightening and nonsensical.

"Easy for you to say," she muttered, drawing a deep breath before stepping in. Bracing herself for... bats? A sudden fall? She wasn't sure. What she wasn't prepared for was how remarkably normal the interior seemed.

The chamber revealed itself, not as a cavern of horrors but as a room—an unsettlingly ordinary room, if one ignored the unnatural symmetry of its walls and the way the air hummed with a resonance that made her teeth buzz.

Torches—or what she initially thought were torches—lined the walls. Their alternating hues of firelight glimmered until closer inspection revealed them to be glass vials, each housing shards of chronocrystal. The jagged edges of the crystals pulsed faintly, as if alive.

The room's shape defied traditional geometry. Walls didn't meet in clean right angles; instead, they jutted into an intricate, many-sided space, almost fractal. Each facet led to curved staircases spiraling toward a central dais.

And at the dais's heart floated the orb. A shimmering, opalescent ball of chronomagic thread, except this thread wasn't destined for any grandmother's knitting needles. Its colors churned hypnotically, an oil slick caught in perpetual motion.

Akira descended the steps toward it, barely aware she was moving, as if the orb itself tugged her closer. The hum grew louder the nearer she came, resonating with a frequency that bypassed the ears and rooted itself in the chest. She clutched the blue chronocrystal embedded there, fingers gripping tight.

"I've been here before," she whispered, though the words felt alien in her mouth.

"So have I," Jun murmured, crouching to inspect the floor. His keen eyes scanned the room like a scientist dissecting an organism. He ran a finger across the dais, rubbing whatever he'd found between his thumb and forefinger before making a quick note in his ever-present notebook.

Rul'ka's face, illuminated now by the vivid markings glowing along her fur, turned toward them. Her gaze was piercing. "Neither of you have been here before," she said, her voice low and cryptic. "And yet you have."

Ryū groaned, pinching the bridge of his nose. "Must you always speak in riddles? Surely it's exhausting, inventing all these meaningless platitudes."

Rul'ka snapped her gaze towards Ryū, "You speak of things you do not understand furless child." She pulled her lips up in what Akira assumed was a smile but looked more like she was preparing to eat them, "But I will show you."

"Show us what?" Akira demanded, now standing directly before the orb. Her hand hovered unconsciously at its edge, drawn but hesitant.

Jun, in his own world, extended a hand, muttering calculations under his breath. Every so often, he punctuated the stream of gibberish with a number, his tone triumphant as though discovering profound truths. Akira, having endured countless similar scenes, could already feel the tension headache forming.

"If my est—" Jun began, only to be interrupted by Ryū's sharp exasperation.

"So, help me Amriel, Jun," said Ryū, "I love you man, but if the next words out of your mouth are estimates or calculations, I will personally kill you."

"By my estimates," Jun pressed on, oblivious to the growing threat of bodily harm, "I believe we have in fact—" His voice trailed off as he spotted something else, abandoning his thought entirely.

Ryū leapt around the orb with theatrical flair, landing beside him in a squat. "Oi! Finish a thought, would you?"

"If I am correct," Jun said, his brow furrowed in concentration, "this is... not the same orb as before. This one is slightly darker and—" he hesitated, measuring invisible coordinates in the air— "approximately a quarter inch south of the last."

Ryū threw his hands up. "Chikusho Jun! A *quarter inch*? Gods above, why didn't you say so sooner?!"

Jun nodded earnestly, "I know, the results are *quite* spectacular."

"Fascinating," Ryū replied, deadpan.

"You know he's mocking you, right?" Akira interjected.

Jun squinted at Ryū but dropped to his knees again, pulling out a piece of twine to measure the pedestal. Before he could secure it, a single curved claw rested gently against his arm.

"You furless children are deathly curious creatures," Rul'ka murmured, dragging Jun back with a casual flick of her claw. "It's a wonder any of you survive long enough to reproduce."

"If you'd stop speaking in circles and just *tell us*—" Ryū began, only for a loud crunch to interrupt him.

All eyes turned toward the stairs, where Shoji stood, mouth full of nashi pear. "Sugoi!" he mumbled, juice dribbling down his chin. "Where have we never been before?"

Rul'ka snapped, releasing a straggled sound that made Akira jump halfway out of her skin, and cemented a firm appreciation for the fact that she had forgone on the second cup of green tea that morning.

Rul'ka's growl was a sound that seemed to reverberate in Akira's ribcage. Her fur stood on end, her markings flaring brighter, turning her into a specter of wrath. "You should not be here."

Shoji paused mid-chew, swallowed loudly, and lobbed the pear core behind him with an air of innocence. "Pick. That. Up," Rul'ka hissed, her voice sharp enough to cut glass.

Akira had to fight the absurd urge to stoop and fetch something—anything—just to appease the alpha. She glanced around as if a pebble might suffice, but quickly dismissed the idea. Rul'ka didn't seem like the type to appreciate symbolic gestures.

Shoji, wearing the expression of a mildly scolded schoolboy, slowed his skipping. "Pick what up?"

"The pear, you cabbage-brained idiot," Ryū snarled, his words practically dripping with exasperation.

Shoji shrugged, bent down with exaggerated laziness, and retrieved the offending fruit core.

"Do you have any idea where you are? What sacred ground you've just desecrated?" Rul'ka was pacing now, back and forth in front of the dais like a judge deliberating over an especially idiotic defendant. On the opposite side, Al'ka mirrored her movements. Like the hounds of hell, except *exactly* like that.

"Clearly not," Shoji replied, now bouncing down the remaining steps with carefree abandon. The concept of self-preservation had never quite managed to penetrate Shoji's thick skull.

"You are in the Sanctum of Light," Al'ka intoned gravely, his voice reverberating like a church bell. "A sacred space for the followers of the Way of Light, and a portal to the Timel—"

"Enough!" snapped Rul'ka. Her interruption cracked through the air, silencing Al'ka and sending a visible ripple of irritation down his massive frame. "You will leave this place, or I will not be held responsible for what may happen to you."

Shoji shrugged again, utterly unfazed. "Well, I haven't been struck by lightning yet, so I'm liking my odds."

"So, this is the Sanctum," Akira murmured, stepping closer to the orb that now pulsed with a faint pinkish hue.

"Not *the* Sanctum," Rul'ka corrected sharply, her gaze still locked on Shoji. "One of two on Fujikura."

"So, the other one is in Oto," Jun said, clutching his green crystal like a lifeline.

"Your insights are blinding as always, Jun," Ryū sighed, which earned him a swift jab to the ribs from Akira.

"At least your aim is better than your flying, Princess," Ryū grunted, rubbing his side.

Rul'ka turned her massive head toward Shoji, her markings shifting and glowing in harmony with the orb's changing colors. "You must leave. There are things I must show the others."

For a brief, harrowing moment, Akira thought Shoji might argue—or worse, lob the pear core at the alpha's head. But something miraculous happened: Shoji complied. Whether it was divine intervention, a pang of maturity, or simple exhaustion, Shoji left the hall as he had entered, crunching another pear.

Rul'ka exhaled a heavy sigh, the gust so powerful that Akira stumbled slightly, her hair whipping around her face.

"As Jun has rightly guessed—"

"I beg your pardon," Jun interrupted, his tone sharp. "I do not guess. I hypothesize, deduce, or at worst, make an educated—"

"I think the word you're looking for is 'guess,'" Ryū interjected, his smirk almost audible.

"Enough," Rul'ka commanded, her voice laden with finality. Akira decided she rather liked Rul'ka's ability to end bickering with a single word. It was a skill she might need to acquire.

Rul'ka turned her attention back to the orb, now glowing a pale blue, almost white. She inhaled deeply and exhaled over its surface. Wisps of light escaped, spiraling upward like liberated fireflies. Akira tracked their path until they vanished into the vaulted ceiling.

At first, they were so bright Akira could not make out anything more than miscellaneous light, but then the whisps began to coalesce. Lined forms began to take shape, borrowing the shapes of wolves and then the wings of an eagle. They soared across the Sanctum walls, galloping over mountains and through creeks. Their pale blue light sent clouds of fireflies bursting through the forest, making the skies look like an ocean of stars. Soon they were joined by another winged figure. In shape it might have resembled a bird of prey. But it was so large its 'prey' could hardly have been your typical bunny rabbit or other small rodent. Unless of course the bunny rabbit was five feet tall. Then it might have sufficed as an afternoon snack.

The bird soared across the walls, setting the lofty ceiling ablaze in a shower of red and orange light as its wings brushed against the eaves. It dove back towards the ground, and despite being crafted by no more than lines of light Akira, Ryū and Jun all leapt out of the way. Rul'ka laughed, leaving them all feeling rather foolish, and with a sudden fascination for the floor by their feet.

The bird cawed—a piercing, primal sound that still carried a strange comfort Akira couldn't quite name. It swept down toward the pack of Hainu, their howls swelling into a haunting symphony that seemed to shake the very air. Even after the Hainu themselves fell silent, the echoes of their cries lingered, painting the space with a sense of ancient mourning.

Colors rippled through the spectral pack, shifting like liquid light. Coral, azure, gold—every hue imaginable swirled through their forms until only one remained a pristine white so intense it burned spots into Akira's vision. The bird hovered above them, wings outstretched in a display of majesty, before vanishing in a sudden burst of light.

Akira felt something sharp twist in her chest, a hollowness she hadn't realized was there until it expanded. Her gaze lingered on the blank space where the bird had been, mourning its absence before her mind caught up with reality. The spectral Hainu were gone too.

Well, most of them. The real ones—those with very sharp teeth and not a lot of patience—were still very much present. Lucky her.

"Now you see," Rul'ka said, stepping forward, her tone a mixture of gravity and expectation.

"See what?" Ryū asked, his voice cutting through the tension like a blade. He seemed to have recovered from the shared spectacle—or psychosis, depending on how one looked at it.

Akira glanced at Calder. The man stood motionless, staring at the now-barren walls, his silence more impenetrable than ever. Since their arrival in the Sanctum, Akira was certain he hadn't said a single word. Considering Jiro's clan had the collective self-restraint of a sugar-high child, it was a minor miracle anyone had noticed.

"They are a part of chronomagic," said Calder, his gaze still fixed upon the now blank walls. "As much as any of us. More so I dare say."

Rul'ka inclined her head in acknowledgment. "The Hainu have guarded the Sanctum on Fujikura since the Great Awakening. One here in Nayagu's foothills, the other in—"

"Oto," Calder murmured, the weight of realization sinking into his tone. "Where we have trained the Yōsei of Fujikura."

Rul'ka nodded solemnly.

"But why?" Ryū interjected, his voice rising. "Why keep chronomagic hidden from us—from the Fujikurans?"

"It was never hidden," Rul'ka snapped, her tone bristling. "It is part of every living thing. How can one hide life itself? But the act of casting it was a burden your people were never meant to bear."

Jun stepped forward, his sharp eyes scanning the stonework of the Sanctum. "There was another pack in Oto, wasn't there?" he asked. "I remember grooves like these in the stonework there." He ran his fingers along the faint lines etched into the steps. "I thought they were marks of construction, but now I wonder if they were left by the claws of a Hainu pack."

"You wonder correctly, Furless One," Rul'ka replied. "They were our brothers and sisters, as you all are brothers to one another. But they are gone now. Struck down by the winged lions of Cargyll. The Sanctum was defiled…"

"Gryphons?" Jun whispered, his voice barely audible.

"Shush," Akira hissed, elbowing him before he could

get started.

Rul'ka pressed on, her tone steady despite the ache it carried. "Our numbers are too few now to fight them alone. So we must keep our watch here at Nayagu."

Calder's brow furrowed deeply. "I thought the Brothers sent by Sadhrin before me had built a new Sanctum here. It resembles the one at Heron Academy. I had no reason to think otherwise."

"As the Threadcasters guard the Sanctum in Cargyll, so do we guard the ones in Fujikura," Rul'ka explained. "The Sanctum were not made by man or beast but formed with Narthor itself."

Calder's expression darkened, his features shadowed by a pain that seemed to crush him. He fell to his knees with a strangled sob, burying his face in his hands. "Forgive us," he choked out. "I had no idea…"

Al'ka exchanged a look with his alpha before stepping forward. With a slow grace, the massive Hainu lowered himself until his dark nose brushed Calder's bowed head.

Rul'ka's voice softened. "The darkness is hard to see, especially when the light blinds you. But we see you. You did not know this."

Calder muttered something muffled by his thick braid and layers of clothing. It might have been a 'thank you.' Or a sneeze. Who could tell?

"Now you understand why we brought you here," Rul'ka continued, her voice regaining its strength. "You must help us undo what has been done. We will aid you in retrieving your Furless Leader, but you must help us right the wrongs of your people."

Calder raised his head, his gaze steady despite the damp streaks on his face. "It shall be done."

TWENTY-ONE

KILIE

At some point, Kilie had blacked out. Whether it was the after effect of grappling with an ambiguous shadow creature, the delayed result of malnutrition, or simply a well-timed sedative, he couldn't say. Not that the distinction mattered much in the scheme of things.

When he came to, he found himself in a cage. And yes, *cage* in the most literal sense of the word: gridded metal bars forming an austere cube around him, with just enough space to crouch and contemplate his life's many mistakes. The floor, once padded—if the carpet tatters embedded in the rust were any indication—was as welcoming as a hedgehog moonlighting as a yoga mat.

Around him, other prisoners huddled in varying stages of despair, most clutching their knees in textbook fetal positions. A few rocked back and forth like metronomes set to a deranged tempo. The less restrained ones whispered incoherently or hummed songs so discordant they should've come with a trigger warning.

Others, prone and battered, lay like forgotten marionettes in various states of disrepair. If there was an award for Worst Place to Be, this cage would've been a shoo-in.

And yet, despite the oppressive squalor, Kilie had to admit one thing: the food situation was better than it had been outside. Twice a day, bowls of steaming rice and mystery meat were hurled into the cage like culinary grenades. Sometimes it was chicken; sometimes it was '*chicken*,' but Kilie decided not to ask too many questions. Hunger trumped curiosity, as it often did in dire circumstances.

The days—or hours?—blurred together in a haze of monotony and survival. Kilie's main form of entertainment was staring at the scenery beyond the bars. Wherever they'd taken him, it wasn't Hopkaidō. This was something else entirely. The houses here were crafted from polished, dark wood and lined a main street adorned with vibrant, fabric banners fluttering in the breeze. Occasionally, Kilie would count the houses, making it to fifty-six before boredom or hunger claimed his focus. Between the buildings stood tall trees heavy with pink blossoms that shed petals like confetti whenever the wind saw fit.

The street ended at a central square dominated by a large, rugged bath carved into the earth, its waters bubbling with natural heat. The steam rising from it carried a faint, mineral tang, tantalizingly close to pleasant. It might have been serene—beautiful, even—if Kilie weren't trapped in a cage surrounded by people who alternated between existential despair and shoe-eating.

Speaking of shoes, there came a point when the other prisoners grew tired of their limited diversions and began focusing their attention on him. After all, he was the novelty—the one who muttered in a strange tongue and occasionally gestured as if he might summon a miracle. It took hours to establish a rudimentary form of communication through Akato, the man with a tenuous grip on Cygren and an even more tenuous grip on reality. Akato's translations were barely intelligible, but when your alternatives were shoe-nibbling or outright madness, you worked with what you had.

Most lost interest as soon as they learned Kilie's threadcasting was blocked, but a persistent few clung to him, their wide-eyed hope both endearing and unnerving. Akato was their self-appointed spokesperson, prone to sudden questions that veered from philosophical to nonsensical at breakneck speed.

"Why do you follow Amriel?" Akato asked one day—or maybe it was night. Time meant less than nothing here.

Kilie chuckled, the sound scraping against his dry throat. "Because someday, I'd like to go home."

"To Cyngha?"

"*Cyrnghräir,*" Kilie corrected, rolling the word off his tongue like a marble. He absently touched the chronocrystal embedded in his chest. "No, not Cyrnghräir. The place Cyrnghräir was always meant to be. The place Narthor was meant to be."

This answer sparked a hushed debate among the others, their Fujik rapid and urgent. Kilie leaned back, resigned to being a spectator as Akato and his companions volleyed the featherweight of his words around like it might hold the secret to immortality.

The Threadcaster slipped a hand into his robes, which had taken on a dreary shade of brown that almost completely masked their original color. He fumbled for a moment, clearly unpracticed in any dexterity beyond the ability to shovel food into his mouth at the prescribed times.

Kilie smiled faintly, finally locating a golden feather from his pocket—a relic he had guarded through every indignity. "The crystal's dead, yes, but chronomagic is in all of us. The crystal's a conduit—a safeguard—but it isn't the source." He twirled the feather between his fingers. "Even without it, there's always a spark. Enough to remind us, we're not alone."

Akato and his companions examined the feather with the rapt intensity of toddlers confronting an unfamiliar object. Akato turned it one way, then another, before shaking it as if expecting hidden treasures to tumble out. When that failed, he dropped to his knees, scanning the ground for something only he seemed to think existed. Finding nothing, he passed it off to another, who—adding a personal flourish—tried gnawing on the shaft of the feather with three remaining teeth. After achieving no more success, the feather was tossed back to Kilie, who caught it deftly between thumb and forefinger.

It was, in fairness, no ordinary pigeon feather—unless pigeons in these parts had recently begun sporting fiery gold plumage the size of a man's forearm.

"Not crystal," Akato said, with the petulance of a child denied dessert.

Kilie chuckled. "Astute observation. It's a feather."

"Can see," Akato muttered, folding his arms. "Not stupid."

Kilie hummed as he smoothed the feather's soft tines back into alignment. "It's from Amriel," he said, his voice softening as the feather began to hover in front of him. "He's here." A faint blue thread, no longer than a finger, flickered at the tip of Kilie's hand.

Akato lunged forward, snatching the feather mid-air. "But how?" he demanded, turning it over for inspection. He jabbed a finger at his own chest, frustration twisting his features. "Crystal dead. How?"

Kilie shrugged. "The crystal focuses and stores chronomagic, but we're made of chronomagic. The crystal protects us from overuse and helps control it, but even without one, some magic is possible." His gaze sharpened. "It's dangerous, though. Without the crystal to direct it, you won't know you've used too much until it's gone—and then so are you."

"But you did it," Akato pressed. "You can escape!"

Kilie shook his head. "That was barely a spark—just enough to show it's possible. I've been a Threadcaster for an age, but even I wouldn't risk more."

Akato's shoulders slumped. His disappointment hung in the air, a tangible thing. No one spoke to Kilie for the rest of the evening, leaving him to eat his rice and questionable chicken in silence. Before long, sleep claimed him.

Kilie awoke to a chill that had him clutching his toes, checking if they'd survived the night. Then came a sound that sent a very different chill racing up his spine.

"Good morning!"

It was the type of voice that should have entirely escaped Kilie's notice. It was a voice that could have easily told stories to sleepy children. A voice which might have greeted a wife after a long day in the field or out on the hunt. It was perhaps of a slightly higher pitch than one might expect from the towering man it came from, but otherwise, it was entirely ordinary. It was the type of voice that could easily slip into the background, unnoticed and unheard. But for Kilie, that voice would haunt him till the end of his days.

The Inquisitor stood peering into the cage, his face a cherry-red slick of malice and cheer. "For the benefit of this one," he said, pointing at Kilie—who, at that moment, wished fervently for the ground to swallow him whole and spit him out in a volcano. "I will deign to speak in his primitive tongue."

He began walking up and down in front of the cage glancing at each of the prisoners in turn, "You see, there are things that he must understand."

The Inquisitor began pacing, scrutinizing each

prisoner in turn. Though he couldn't be called healthy, he seemed significantly less corpse-like than the last time they'd met—an unfortunate development. Kilie would've much preferred him dead. Or maimed. Or at least seriously inconvenienced.

Unfortunately, out of the two of them, Kilie was certainly the one closer to making death's acquaintance. He was roughly a stone's throw away, while the Inquisitor had now relocated a good few blocks south. As the saying goes, it's always best to move out when death pulls up in your street. Actually, that's not a saying at all. But you get the picture.

The Inquisitor's grin widened as he tapped on the cage bars with his staff, a shrill whine ringing out that made Kilie flinch like a cat forced into a bath. Turning to his guards, the Inquisitor barked orders in rapid Fujik, gesturing toward the cage.

The villagers, those poor, miserable souls, shrank into themselves, curling up like oversized hedgehogs—though, without the spines or compactness, they mostly just looked like they were practicing a dramatic rendition of 'resigned despair' rather than 'defensive brilliance.' The guards, unimpressed, grabbed them by the arms and unceremoniously dumped them by a series of natural pools.

Kilie found it surprising that none of them were bound beyond the cuffs on his wrist, but then again, what were they going to do? Attempt an escape with no weapon and no plan, in what appeared to be the middle of some godforsaken wasteland on a savage island? Yeah, that sounded like a brilliant idea. *By Amriel's grace.* Kilie was starting to sound like Kallae.

Kilie and the others were plonked down by the natural pools in the aforementioned godforsaken wasteland, and Kilie was forced to reassess his earlier assessment. Did he want to be here? No more than he wished to set up shop at the backend of a rutting gryphon. But was it quite the annals of all that was wrong with the world? Also no.

The blue waters swirled beside him in a way that probably followed some intricate natural law but looked completely random to Kilie. The steam—which had looked barely tolerable from the cage—was practically scalding up close. Kilie quickly learned he was still in possession of some minimal form of self-preservation, as he hurriedly stepped away from the steam's damp grasp.

When his vision cleared and he managed to convince himself that he wasn't, in fact, in some luxury spa getaway, but rather in the clutches of a psychopath in his prime, Kilie saw that in the center of the pools, great plumes of water shot up intermittently. These intervals were as random as the swirling, and Kilie found himself jumping in alarm each time one occurred.

The Inquisitor, having deigned to grace them all with his presence once more, trudged up the gentle hill to the edge of the pools, his long robes swirling around him in that mysteriously ominous way that only those with an alarmingly intact sense of ego could pull off.

"So nice of you all to join me," he said, his Cygren still annoyingly polished, "it's beautiful, isn't it?"

He gestured toward their surroundings, which, Kilie hated to admit, were undeniably picturesque. It was exactly the kind of place one might retreat to if one had aspirations of writing a book—or perhaps if one had reached the rational conclusion that the key to happiness was abandoning all hope and becoming a hermit. Kilie would've given anything to become a hermit right about now. Unfortunately, his plans for a long, scruffy beard and an ever-expanding collection of eccentric forest creatures would have to remain on hold (and not just because fairies were incapable of growing any facial hair).

The Inquisitor's smile dropped, as his gaze shifted downward, to his physically captured—but not exactly enthralled—audience. "Isn't it?"

His voice faltered, the words coming out like steel

dragged over stone.

The prisoners, at least those with enough strength left to lift their heads, nodded in agreement.

The Inquisitor nodded, seemingly satisfied by their non-verbal response, and resumed trudging up the hill, four guards trailing closely behind him. Their chainmail face coverings clinked with every step. When the Inquisitor reached the top of the hill, he pulled something from his pocket and tossed it onto the ground with as much ceremony as if it were a discarded apple core. But it wasn't an apple core—it was a dead chronocrystal. Kilie's stomach turned at the sight. Round two of a game he had never had any intention of playing.

Indeed, if it were up to him, he would burn the whole damn game to the ground, then feed it to a Y'doc for good measure.

The Inquisitor nodded toward Akato and gestured to the chronocrystal. "Step on it."

Akato looked around, his eyes flicking to the sea of faces, but none of them offered him the answers he was seeking. Slowly, he rose to his feet, each movement seeming to add weight to the air around him, as though gravity were growing more hostile with every step.

"Forgive me if I've given you the impression that I have time to spare," said the Inquisitor, his voice sickly sweet, "now step on it."

Akato hesitated, his foot trembling above the chronocrystal, a grotesque mix of awkwardness, exhaustion, and the bleak reality of his imminent demise seeping into every pore. Kilie's heart clenched as he watched tears spill down the man's filthy cheeks.

With a final, reluctant stamp, Akato crushed the crystal beneath his foot. The ground trembled slightly, and Kilie buried his face in his hands. It wasn't until a strangled cry escaped the Inquisitor that Kilie realized the crystal was still intact—and the Inquisitor's foot was most definitely not.

The Inquisitor, now hopping about like a wounded chicken, grimaced in pain, before pointing at one of the guards. "Tie him up," he ordered, nodding toward the pool, "we'll see how defiant he's feeling then."

Akato didn't struggle as two guards grabbed him roughly and shoved him toward the edge of the pool. For a moment, nothing happened, and Kilie almost allowed himself to wonder if the Inquisitor had merely punished the man by offering him a day at the spa. Then the screams began.

They were the kind of screams that would haunt a person forever, echoing in nightmares long after they'd faded from memory. Kilie swallowed the bile rising in his throat as bubbling blisters appeared on Akato's legs, crawling toward his chest.

The Inquisitor nodded toward a jug of water beside him. "Force him to drink that," he instructed another guard, "make sure he's well cared for."

The guard hesitated for a moment, then complied, soaking a sponge in the cool water and running it over the man's blistered body with all the tenderness of a mother. Except this particular mother had just dunked her hypothetical child in a vat of boiling water and offered only a drink of cold water as an apology. Then again, what parent is perfect?

The Inquisitor turned his attention back to Kilie and the other prisoners. Several had buried their faces in their arms, others had shoved their fingers so deep into their ears that Kilie wondered if they'd ever hear again. Most had vomited, leaving behind an acrid stench to mingle with the salty air.

"Who would like to go next?" asked the Inquisitor, his staff clinking against the rock with each step. He jabbed the tip of the staff into Kilie's chest, and Kilie had to resist the urge to cry out from the pain. "What do you call yourself, Threadcaster?"

Kilie considered remaining silent, but the garbled

scream of the man in the pool shattered any thoughts of rebellion. With a heavy sigh, he muttered, "Kilie."

"Hmmm," the Inquisitor said, clearly dissatisfied even with this. "Now tell me, Kilie, these people—" he pointed at the villagers, "—they're all here because of you."

Another scream shattered through the clearing, as one of the guards ran another bucket of cold water over the man's head. "You can save them, Kilie." The Inquisitor crouched down next to the fairy, and Kilie could smell smoke on his breath. Or perhaps it was on his clothes—Kilie wasn't sure anymore. To say that Kilie's observational skills were operating at suboptimal level was akin to claiming the sky was blue.

Kilie flinched as the Inquisitor laid a hand on his shoulder. "All you have to tell them," the Inquisitor purred, "is that it isn't real. That you made it all up. There is no chronomagic, no fickle Amriel that you speak of."

Akato was shaking now, his body a mess of trembling, cooked flesh—like a lobster left too long in the pot. If it weren't for the guards hoisting him up on either side, he would've collapsed into the pool, a limp casualty of the Inquisitor's cruelty. From Kilie's angle, it almost looked like Akato was trying to drown himself. But the guards held a firm grip, while a third one doused the man religiously with cool water, pretending to soothe the burns.

The Inquisitor smiled, following Kilie's gaze to the pool. "Quite brilliant, don't you think?" His voice was the type of voice you could imagine coming from someone who loved the sound of his own words just a little too much. "He can survive for days like this," the Inquisitor continued, "in a few hours one of our physicians will arrive, rub salve on his burns. Food will be brought to him three times a day. A guard will sponge him with cool waters around the clock. Quite the operation, as you might imagine," he sighed dramatically, then turned back to Kilie. "Very expensive."

Akato let out another scream, a noise that sounded like it was made in the deepest pits of hell, as the guard sponging him down applied too much pressure.

"So," the Inquisitor asked, his tone a mock sweetness, as if he were offering Kilie a second helping of supper, "what do you say, hmmm?"

Kilie gritted his teeth, almost biting his lip in the process. "I speak the truth. And only the truth. I will not deceive these people as you have. Amriel would not stand for it, and neither will I."

The Inquisitor's smile twisted into something far darker. "You think of yourself as righteous," he said, rising back to his full height. "Do you not?"

He frowned when Kilie didn't answer, but continued on as if he were speaking to an idiot. "You say you stand for the truth as if it represents ultimate morality. But is the truth truly good if the only person who benefits from it is oneself?" He paused, letting the question hang in the air, a thread of poison.

"That is not true," Kilie protested, but the Inquisitor had already turned his attention back to the villagers.

"Well, it seems your magnanimous leader is too virtuous to save you," the Inquisitor sneered at the cowering crowd. "What say you to that, dear people? The Way of the Water would never sacrifice its own to serve selfish desires. It is not so closed-minded as to see the world as purely binary." He drew something out of his robes, a piece of colored paper, which he began to fold as he paced, never once breaking his stride. "This man and his false religion cannot save you. Why follow someone you cannot see, who," he paused dramatically, "does not exist?"

He creased the red paper again, a series of sharp, deliberate folds now marring its surface. He held it up in one hand, gingerly placing it into the other palm. Opening his mouth, the Inquisitor released a curl of black smoke from his lips. The paper vanished from his hand, only to reappear hovering above the villagers. Though Kilie hadn't been able to identify its form before, he could now see it was a crane—its paper wings, though small, carried it effortlessly towards one of the women. It hovered for a moment, then landed on her fingertip. Its wings fluttered a few times, then folded neatly against its body before, with no warning, it crumbled into ash.

"So, you see now, my dear people," the Inquisitor said, taking absolutely no note of the fact that his creation had disintegrated into nothingness. "Our ways, the Way of the Water, is an ancient path, powerful, life for life." He pointed to a nearby flower, which had withered and died. "The cost is steep, but such is life. We have no need for these foreigners," he spat the word like spoiled milk, "these foreigners who use cheap tricks to control us. They laugh in our faces as we let them march through our country, taking us for fools. What will it take for you to see the demon behind the mask?"

He pointed a bony, gnarly finger at Kilie. "Will you wait until it is your brother, or your sister, or your mother who is stolen away by these demon people? Why do you think they're here? Don't think that they are here out of the goodness of their hearts, for that presupposes they have one to begin with."

At that, another villager was roughly pulled to her feet and tossed before the chronocrystal. When she, too, refused, she soon found herself offered an entirely different kind of hospitality—ample space in the pool.

With a chorus of screams ringing in Kilie's ears, the Inquisitor dropped down beside him once more. "How many will it take until you tell them the truth?"

"I cannot," Kilie managed before his voice broke into a sob.

"No, you *will* not," the Inquisitor said, his voice colder now, final.

"Amriel," Kilie cried, tears streaming down his face. "He will come for us."

The Inquisitor laughed, spinning in a circle as if the very idea amused him. "Well, it seems he's late," he mocked, tapping Kilie's purple chronocrystal with his staff. "And you," he smiled, a chilling thing, "are entirely at my mercy without your cute little trinket.

TWENTY-TWO

KALLAE

"You can't just leave," Miki whined, her voice trailing behind Kallae like a stray dog on a leash.

"Oh, really?" Kallae snapped, not bothering to slow his pace, which could only be described as the hurried, purposeless gait of someone who had no idea where he was going but was determined to get there fast. "I'm fairly certain I'm doing exactly that."

Kallae could hear Miki speeding up behind him, her footsteps now a full-blown sprint. She was catching up, of course. Because of course she was. Kallae sighed, a sound as deep and resigned as a sinking ship.

His current direction, whatever it was, felt like a random choice, but it was undoubtedly as far from that damn Inquisitor as possible. And if that wasn't a good enough reason to keep walking, Kallae wasn't sure what was. There were more efficient ways to achieve this, sure, but efficiency had long ceased to be his concern.

"So, what's the plan?" Miki puffed, her voice strained. "Stumble through forest like lost idiot?"

"Bah!" Kallae grunted, yanking a stubborn weed from

the ground like it had personally offended him. "This is working splendidly. I'm alive, aren't I?"

"So, you abandon us?" Miki's voice faltered, her tone dropping into something resembling hurt. "Abandon friend?"

Kallae didn't pause this time. He didn't need to. "He made his choice. I can't save a dead man. I knew it would end like this if we came here. He wouldn't listen."

He kept walking. He didn't need to check to know that Miki had stopped. She'd been right behind him a second ago, but now she was gone, and so was any illusion that they might've had some kind of partnership. That, too, had been a fleeting idea. A passing fantasy. It was for the best. Kallae only soured anything he touched.

Kallae's path through the forest was as erratic as his thoughts—no destination, just an overwhelming desire to move. If he kept moving, maybe the weight of his actions would disappear. The trees were nothing more than obstacles in his path now, clawing at him with their branches. And he, of course, had to destroy them—cut them down with such savage glee it bordered on pathological.

Every swing of his sword was accompanied by a grunt, the kind of grunt a man makes when he's trying to convince himself that hacking through trees somehow makes him less of a mess. But deep down, he knew he wasn't fooling anyone, least of all himself.

The trees didn't care. The trees didn't feel. And yet, in that moment, with the sound of bark cracking and splintering under his sword, it almost felt like the trees were the least of his problems.

Hours passed. Or maybe it was days. Kallae couldn't be sure, nor did he care to be. By the end of his impromptu rampage, his right hand was a minefield of splinters, and his skin had taken on the appearance of an unwashed battleground. But his hunger, that gnawing, insistent hunger, had finally overtaken everything else.

He dropped to the ground without ceremony, not even bothering to find a place to sleep. He was too tired for that. His mind was a blur, and his body, well... his body was about as cooperative as a toddler with a new toy.

With a resigned sigh, he sheathed his sword. But then, as the leather clasped around the blade, something caught his eye—a glimmer on the metal. It was his reflection, distorted and covered in dried blood. But it wasn't the blood that unsettled him. It was the eyes staring back at him. They weren't his eyes anymore. They couldn't be.

A resigned groan escaped his lips. Really, when had it come to this? His eyes were now actively conspiring against him. First, the body betrayed him, and now even his own reflection was in on the joke.

He hit the proverbial hay about as forcibly as he'd hit the proverbial brick wall earlier that day. That is to say, it had not been a great day. In fact, were he the type to keep lists it would have ranked in his top ten worst days he'd ever had the misfortune of experiencing, so perhaps it was for the best that he was altogether opposed to practices such as list keeping, finding them rather myopic at best and entirely misguided at worst.

When he woke up, it was to the horrifying realization that he'd been dreaming about making lists. This was swiftly overshadowed by a more immediate concern: his stomach, which had gone from mildly uncomfortable to something more akin to an active war zone.

The hunger was a palpable, gnawing force that left Kallae flailing through the forest like a drunken goat trying to navigate a particularly hostile obstacle course. Every step was graceless and uncoordinated, as if his legs had suddenly decided to stop being useful. The trees, of course, had their own plans. One in particular seemed to take offense at his presence, and a branch sliced across his leg, sending blood dripping like a slow, inevitable countdown to disaster. Kallae barely noticed. Food was more important. The bleeding? Well, he'd deal with it later.

Once he'd disentangled himself from the tree's spiteful embrace, Kallae, too tired to bother standing, decided crawling was the way forward. This was, however, not the elegant, army-crawling precision one might expect from a trained warrior. No, it was more akin to a child who'd just discovered the concept of crawling but had not yet figured out how to coordinate arms and legs in any useful way. In fact, his progress resembled that of a dying swine on its last legs—flailing, awkward, and, ultimately, doomed to failure.

It wasn't a huge surprise that his forward momentum didn't last long, but the hundred feet or so that he did manage to crawl brought him to the foot of another tree. Before he could entertain any ridiculous ideas of chopping it down—because honestly, when does one not think of hacking at a tree when in desperate need of food—he spotted something more promising: a cluster of mushrooms. At least, he assumed they were mushrooms. Several in fact. Kallae found he had quite lost the ability to count under present circumstances but decided that was ranked pretty low on his current list of problems. Foremost on that list was the sudden realization that he was now one of those people who kept lists.

Before his mind could spiral into existential dread at the thought of being someone who kept lists of things, he decided to shove the mushrooms into his pockets. He may or may not have crushed a few in the process, but that was a problem for future Kallae. Present Kallae was more concerned with fire.

After what could only be described as a small-scale miracle—or perhaps a divine intervention involving several gods who had clearly lost a bet—Kallae managed to start a fire without setting himself or the entire forest ablaze. The flames were tiny, almost insultingly so, but it was fire. It was something. At least he wasn't sitting in the dark, bathed in the overwhelming presence of his own misery.

Having ignited the meager fire, Kallae spent all of five minutes warming his hands and promptly forgetting why he had even started the fire in the first place. The mushrooms were still there, awaiting their fiery demise. So, naturally, Kallae, after several long moments of rotating in circles like a confused squirrel in a hamster wheel, decided the best way to cook them was with his hand. He did note, with no small amount of distaste, that a sticky red substance had appeared on his palm. He tried shaking it off in disgust, but the substance clung to him stubbornly, like a bad memory.

With a look of wild glee, the sort only a child with an infinite supply of lollipops could muster, Kallae flung his mushroom-laden hand into the fire. The result was immediate. He was thrown backwards, as if the fire itself had decided it didn't like his cooking skills. Once more, Kallae found himself on the ground, his face intimately acquainted with the dirt.

Bleary eyed, and now with a mouthful of dirt, he finally managed to push himself back into an approximation of a sitting position and was greeted with a sight that was about as welcome to him as a crocodile in a latrine.

A Tanuki. Sitting next to him. Just sitting there, like a raccoon who had absolutely no business being a raccoon, yet here it was. And to top it all off, he was wearing a straw hat. Kallae, in his infinite wisdom, did what any sensible person would do: he swatted at it. Of course, given his current state, it was more of a gesture of a person too tired to even aim properly. His swipe missed entirely. He probably would've had more luck swatting at the moon, but the Tanuki seemed too pleased by the effort to care.

"Go away," Kallae muttered, half-blind, his hands fumbling around for the mushrooms. They had scattered, as mushrooms tend to do when one is too busy trying to fry them with his bare hands.

"Aha!" Kallae shouted triumphantly when he found

one. Without hesitation, he shoved his hand into the fire again. This was Kallae at his finest—self-destructive, reckless, and in dire need of a snack.

Before he could repeat his earlier mistake, a pair of clammy, strong paws clamped around his wrist. The Tanuki—who had somehow gained the strength of an enraged toddler despite its gopher-sized frame—wrestled him to the ground. Kallae, already exhausted and irritated, shoved at the creature with as much force as a wet noodle.

"Knock it off, will ya!" he snapped, his voice muffled by the dust cloud he'd just produced with his latest dramatic tumble. "Or I'll toss you into the fire instead!"

The Tanuki made a sound—something akin to a surprised human noise—and stared at him with wide, glowing eyes, which seemed to pierce through Kallae's very soul. Kallae, feeling a distinctly uncomfortable sensation building somewhere between his chest and his sanity, muttered to himself, "My mind's playing tricks on me." He tried to ignore the creature, who had now taken to throwing mushrooms into the underbrush like an overly enthusiastic squirrel.

"Stop that!" Kallae yelled, hurling himself at the Tanuki with all the grace of a drunken squirrel. He hoped to halt the mushroom-related chaos in its tracks. But instead of landing on the soft, fluffy body he'd been anticipating, he collided with something far more solid. The Tanuki wasn't crouching on all fours as Kallae had assumed. No, it was standing upright, like some sort of muscled, upright raccoon with an odd sort of lap—one that looked vaguely human in its peculiar design. Which, naturally, made absolutely no sense. None. Zip. Zero.

The Tanuki's glowing eyes locked onto Kallae, unwavering and intense. Then it blinked, a slow, deliberate action that felt almost personal.

Kallae tumbled back, as though he'd been struck by a bolt of lightning, before sternly chastising himself for being a child. "Grow a pair," he muttered under his breath, wiping dirt from his robes—which had turned a pleasant shade of brown, giving him the appearance of someone who'd been lounging in the earth for far too long—and squaring his shoulders. His glare shifted to the Tanuki, now looking every bit like a flea-infested rat with a penchant for mischief.

Without so much as a word, the Tanuki, still glowing with a mysterious light, hefted a porcelain bottle and took a leisurely sip of its contents. It glanced down into the hole in the ground, looked back up at Kallae, and then back at the hole. Sighing deeply, it extended the bottle toward him.

Kallae, having lost most of his sensibilities saw no choice but to accept the offering, and without a further thought to the matter took a generous slug. One might have rightly thought, Kallae would have hesitated, or at least attempted to gauge what the contents were, before downing a mysterious liquid which had just been handed to him by a racoon wearing a hat, but as we've learned, Kallae was currently five eggs short of an oyakodon. Indeed, it was entirely questionable if Kallae even remembered what an egg was.

The liquid, shockingly sweet on his lips, was like a gust of honeyed wind. He swallowed quickly, lest his better judgment kicked in and caused him to spit it out. But as soon as he swallowed, the sweetness morphed into a scorching burn.

Now Kallae was no stranger to the local watering holes back in Barncowl Keep, but he had never been what one would call a heavy drinker. That title resided unchallenged with Kilie, who despite his manicured appearance and tailored words, could tidy away a good bottle or two on any random Tuesday. While Kallae could certainly tolerate the glass or two of wine, whatever was in that porcelain bottle was of much stronger stuff than wine.

Kallae stifled the urge to cringe but ultimately failed. His face twisted in a grimace, all crumpled-up confusion and reluctant nausea. He almost missed it when the Tanuki chuckled—or what Kallae hoped was a chuckle, because if that was actually a growl, then the Tanuki was preparing to feast on him.

"It's not funny!" Kallae snapped, then immediately tried to shove the Tanuki off its metaphorical high horse—or, rather, its literal and metaphorical highchair. This time, he was marginally more successful, managing to nudge the Tanuki upright before it could topple into the fire. Its cackle faded, replaced by a rhythmic blinking of its glowing eyes, fixed firmly on Kallae.

The staring contest dragged on far too long, until Kallae's discomfort grew to the point of near absurdity, like trying to sit still with ants in your pants. He turned his attention back to the fire, reluctantly gathering up the few remaining mushrooms, muttering nonsense to himself as he did.

The Tanuki followed him, like the most infuriating shadow imaginable, always in the way, tripping him at every turn.

He managed to skewer a few mushrooms on a stick, only for the Tanuki—eyes still burning with that eerie glow—to launch itself at him, knocking the stick from his hand.

"Why, you little—" Kallae grumbled, but before he could finish, he found himself scrambling to his feet, stick in hand, ready to whack the Tanuki back into whatever bizarre universe it had come from.

The Tanuki, one hand clutching its absurd hat, dodged around him, pointing at the stick with an air of exaggerated disapproval.

"Bad," it said, in an infuriatingly, deadpan voice.

Kallae finding it rather beyond him to care that this racoon, had just spoken, and Cygren no less, so proceeded to whack the Tanuki with his stick.

The Tanuki hopped around with the agility of a creature that clearly had far too much energy for its own good, making a sound like a yip with every jump, as if this were all a game. In fact, given the expression on its furry face, it was all too easy to imagine the Tanuki smiling—a fact that only made Kallae angrier.

Kallae chased after it, all thoughts of the fire as abandoned as any claim to intelligence he had once had, all the while yelling at the top of his lungs. "Get back here!" he muttered as he went crashing into the forest after the Tanuki. "When I get my hands on you—"

The Tanuki, having already leapt several feet above him, swinging from tree to tree, paused long enough to glance down at Kallae and, with a mischievous grin, said, "Cannot catch Tanuki," before disappearing into the foliage.

Kallae, gritting his teeth, snapped his stick in half—somehow managing to find an even larger, much sturdier one—and continued his warpath through the forest. His run resembled that of a tipsy moose stumbling through a maze of trees, startling no fewer than five flocks of birds from their nests along the way.

Despite only taking one swig of whatever was in that bottle, Kallae was starting to feel the effects—his reasoning was quickly being drowned in a sea of fuzziness. He would have lost sight of the Tanuki entirely if it weren't for the creature's enthusiastic leaps from tree to tree, throwing itself into the air with a mixture of joy and mockery, just out of Kallae's reach.

It is difficult to say how long this game of unhinged cat and mouse went on for, and it would have gone on for longer still had Kallae not finally succumbed to the angry cut on his leg and ache in his throat. One moment he was stumbling through the forest like a madman chasing a rabbit in a coat, and the next he was lying prone on his back, with a racoon in a hat hovering above him.

The Tanuki, with a peculiar grace, settled back on its haunches, and for a moment, Kallae half-expected it to light a pipe and start reading a book. Instead, it pointed to the stick, its eyes glowing with an almost serene intensity.

"Tanuki help," it said, its voice surprisingly gentle.

Kallae groaned and rolled over, muttering curses under his breath, but deciding (wisely) that strangling the Tanuki at that precise moment would be as productive as trying to catch lightning in a bottle.

He attempted to rise but misjudged his movements, landing face-first in a mouthful of dirt.

"Not stick," the Tanuki said, now on the other side, pointing at the stick with renewed urgency. "Poison."

The Fairy threw his hands up in the air. For this he spent the last shreds of energy he still had, but had decided, if the last thing he did on this good earth was make it abundantly clear to a flea-infested raccoon dog that it should kindly go shove itself into a log, he would die a happy man. Well maybe not a happy man. But as happy as he could, given his current circumstances.

The Tanuki now appeared at his side and promptly began to shake him with a vigor which sent Kallae's brain rattling. He pointed more fervently at the stick, "Poison," he repeated.

Kallae flung his hands into the air in exasperation. "Of all the hair-brained nonsense I've encountered on this cursed island, the insistence that a stick is somehow poisonous is truly the crowning achievement!" he said, his voice dripping with sarcasm. "Honestly, is this all you oversized rats are good for? Tormenting hapless travelers and whacking mushrooms out of their hands? No wonder—"

"Mushroom!" the Tanuki interrupted, bouncing up and down in a burst of energy. "Yes! Mushroom is poison."

It took a moment. But eventually the light bulb went off in Kallae's brain. He might have said any number of things, chief amongst them would have been a thank you to the '*oversized rat*' which had likely just saved his life, but instead he settled on a half-grunted, "Huh."

TWENTY-THREE

KALLAE

The Tanuki kept staring at Kallae with those unblinking, glowing eyes, as if he'd just announced he was a dragon in disguise or suggested the moon was made of cheese. Kallae squirmed, discomfort gnawing at him, the realization that he'd almost poisoned himself sinking in. He had only narrowly escaped the clutches of death thanks to a talking raccoon dog. If it wasn't enough that his life had taken a turn for the worse, now he was indebted to a flea-bitten rodent. Go figure. Life had a flair for the absurd.

The Tanuki blinked. It then reached down and clamped its proportionally tiny hands on Kallae's sleeve and began to tug. Kallae resisted the urge to kick it in the shin and make a run for it, but when the simple task of getting to his feet sent his stomach packing to a different dimension, he quickly dismissed this is a viable course of action and instead focused his energies on not keeling over into the dirt.

The Tanuki pulled harder, its sharp claws digging into Kallae's arm. "Come," it chirped, sounding like an overeager grasshopper. "Follow me. I help you. Now you help."

Kallae having only now acknowledged the gaping hole in his leg glanced down and said, "Considering I'm about two hours away from dying from a tree-wound of all things, unless the help you need is food in the form of extremely lean fairy meat, you're better off asking this rock for help," he kicked the rock in question towards the Tanuki.

"My name is Bo."

"Well Bo," said Kallae slowly, mulling the name over, "I'm going to be honest with you here," he stumbled, the effort of standing having sent stars shooting across this vision, "I have no need for your name, nor do I have any intentions of remembering it."

Bo's eyes narrowed in what could only be described as a curious, yet mildly alarming, fashion. When he closed them, rays of light leaked out from the corners of his eyelids like a malfunctioning lantern, as if his insides were trying to escape. After a few seconds, he blinked, and when they reopened, the glow was dimmer, though whether this was from his effort or Kallae's waning life force was anyone's guess. "Useless," Bo muttered, clearly unimpressed with Kallae's level of gratitude.

The Tanuki, undeterred, began digging around in his hat. Kallae raised an eyebrow—there was no way that hat was big enough to hold anything of value, yet it seemed to contain an endless amount of nonsense. A bottle of something that reeked of poison tumbled out, just narrowly missing Kallae's face, followed by a handful of shiny, pointless trinkets. Kallae could only assume Tanuki were taken by the same inexplicable urge as ravens to gather and horde anything remotely shiny, like some sort of second-rate dragon.

Bo muttered to himself in what sounded like a

language only a Tanuki would understand, tossing more odd items aside with alarming speed. A handful of berries flew through the air, splattering against a nearby tree with a satisfying squelch. "Good," he declared with pride, "but poison to Useless One." He pointed to Kallae for emphasis, just in case there was any doubt who the 'useless one' was in this scenario.

"You know, I do have a name," Kallae grumbled, wondering if lying down on the ground might be a good idea.

"No tell Bo," the Tanuki replied without missing a beat. "Bo give name."

"I'd prefer Bo wouldn't," Kallae shot back, barely suppressing a groan as he tried to keep himself upright.

Bo paused, blinking a few times as though trying to comprehend the statement. Then, without further comment, he dove back into his hat.

"Aha!" he exclaimed a moment later, pulling out another hat, one even more ridiculous than the first, and attempted to jam it onto Kallae's head. Along with the hat, Bo produced a piece of cloth, probably once white, now drenched in something that could only be described as 'wrong.' Kallae knocked the hat off with a swipe, sending it flying into the woods with a distinct sense of finality.

"Not nice," muttered Bo as he began to unfold the fabric. "Protect against sun. Strong in Tanuki forest."

"I don't look good in hats."

"Bah!" muttered Bo, "Useless One is good name." The Tanuki had now fully unraveled the cloth, releasing along with it a stench so potent Kallae's entire body wanted to curl up and die.

Kallae scrambled backwards with a speed that sent darts of pain shooting up and down his leg. But even this speed was no match for that of Bo, who hopscotched over several moments later and landed squarely on Kallae's stomach, which was as jarring as it was embarrassing.

"Was that entirely necessary?" Kallae wheezed,

clutching his stomach. The Tanuki, despite his size, had a surprising amount of momentum behind him.

Bo leapt off Kallae's stomach. "Now leg hurt less, yes?"

"Well, if you're going to kill me, you might as well get on with it," Kallae muttered, resisting the urge to pass out from the pain.

"Kill Useless One?" Bo looked horrified. "Useless One no use if dead."

"I do hope you see the irony in that statement," muttered Kallae through gritted teeth, the throbbing pain in his leg having reawakened.

"Bo help Useless One."

"So, you've said," grunted Kallae, "but so far all you've done is assault my nose with that horrifying thing of yours," he attempted to swat the foul-smelling cloth away, but failed spectacularly in his attempts.

"This help," Bo insisted, now pulling at Kallae's trousers. Kallae, who had always prided himself on being a gentleman, immediately resisted the idea of his trousers being molested by a Tanuki, but Bo wasn't having any of it. Instead, he attacked the fabric with his sharp teeth, tearing through it like a dog with a chew toy.

"Stop that!" Kallae hissed, but his protests were futile, as Bo's razor teeth shredded through the material with surprising ease. The only thing Kallae succeeded in doing was injuring himself further, his leg now sporting a fresh gash for his trouble.

"Stay still," Bo ordered, securing the now bloodied cloth around Kallae's leg with his surprisingly strong grip. "Paste of red beetle larvae prevent infection."

"The Timeless Realm will freeze over before I let you put beetle paste on my leg," Kallae snapped.

"Larvae paste," Bo corrected, utterly oblivious to the magnitude of Kallae's disdain.

"You're *really* not making it any better!"

Despite Kallae's protests, Bo managed to wrap the

cloth tightly around the wound. Kallae lost not only his trousers but his dignity in the process. Bo, on the other hand, nearly lost an eye.

"Useless One," Bo muttered, settling back with a look of mild disapproval, as if Kallae's attempts at self-preservation were beneath him.

Kallae tried to undo the bandages, but Bo promptly swatted his hands away—once on the hand, once on the head. With a sigh, Kallae leaned back against the tree, his head cradled in his arms. "So now what?"

"Bah," muttered Bo again as his eyes did some sort of weird dance. At first Kallae wondered if this was a result of his earlier scratching, but then concluded it was rather more likely the Tanuki equivalent of rolling one's eyes.

Kallae merely shrugged, as Bo, with the finesse of a raccoon digging through the trash, once more began rummaging in his hat.

"You know," Kallae remarked dryly, "You might consider organizing that hat of yours. Or—dare I suggest—using a bag? I could—"

Kallae was promptly interrupted by a loud sound played directly into his ear. After the ringing had subsided, he triangulated its source to what appeared to be some sort of horn which Bo was now enthusiastically trumpeting.

"Not that I am not an appreciator of the arts," said Kallae, "but this is hardly the type of music I would choose to listen to." Even with his fingers jammed into his ears, the sound of the horn felt like it was burrowing into his skull, as if the Tanuki's idea of music was an auditory siege on his very existence.

"Hey!" Kallae bellowed, over the cacophony. "Knock it off, would you? Or do you want every predatory beast in this godforsaken forest to come running?"

Bo, to his credit—or lack thereof—didn't flinch. Instead, he paused just long enough to give Kallae a look of innocent confusion that bordered on smugness. His thick fur seemed to flush a slightly redder shade.

"Yes, Useless One," he said solemnly.

"Yes what?" Kallae snapped, raising his voice more than necessary, as if sheer volume might translate the absurdity of the situation into something comprehensible.

Without answering, Bo delicately wiped the edges of the horn and tucked it back into his impossibly capacious hat. Then he began gathering the other random items he had hurled onto the ground, including, Kallae noted, what appeared to be an entire fish skeleton and half a deck of playing cards. With an exaggerated tug, the Tanuki yanked the hat back down over his fuzzy ears, leaving them poking out like twitching little hills.

Kallae briefly considered interrogating the creature further but quickly abandoned the idea when he was met with nothing but an unblinking, dead-eyed stare. It was the kind of stare that suggested Bo had transcended the need for logical thought altogether.

Before Kallae could further contemplate his if not dire, then entirely inexplicable circumstances, he felt something poke his neck. He barely had the chance to note something red, and decidedly pointy sticking out from it, before he fell into a fitful, restless sleep, lulled by the lingering stench of rotting fish and an unidentifiable cheese that Kallae suspected predated his birth.

He awoke to a sight so bizarre that for a moment, he was certain he was still dreaming. A sea of furry humps stretched out before him, bobbing rhythmically as they moved. It took several disoriented blinks for him to realize two things: First, he was moving despite being flat on his back. Second, he had been strapped to a stretcher like some prize carcass, hoisted up and carried by a chittering army of Tanuki.

"Oh, for the love of the thread," he groaned, attempting to sit up.

A firm paw slammed him back down with a force that knocked the air from his lungs. Bo, of course.

"Useless One awake!" Bo announced with the kind of enthusiasm usually reserved for grand discoveries, like fire or the wheel.

Struggling against his bindings, he couldn't help but notice the ropes were tight enough to leave an impression. The thought of being trussed up like a holiday roast did little to improve his mood. Meanwhile, the Tanuki around him chattered away in their strange language, which Kallae couldn't decide was more annoying than the horn or just equally so.

Hours later—or what felt like hours, considering the stretcher's every bounce was an exercise in bruising—Kallae was unceremoniously dumped into a clearing. The impact sent a jarring shock through his spine. He grit his teeth, muttering a string of curses that he felt were richly deserved.

The clearing, surrounded by an oddly symmetrical ring of trees, seemed unremarkable at first. But then the Tanuki scattered into the branches like hyperactive squirrels. Hammocks strung between the boughs began swaying wildly, though the purpose of their scurrying eluded Kallae entirely.

Alone in the clearing except for Bo, who perched beside him with an unnervingly cheerful grin, Kallae glanced at his bindings.

"So," he said with as much dry sarcasm as he could muster, "care to free me, or am I to assume I am the key ingredient to some sort of yearly sacrificial ritual?"

"Sacrificial?" asked Bo cocking his head from left to right with a rapidity that made Kallae wonder if he was malfunctioning.

"Yes, you know." Kallae attempted to gesture, but the ropes made it more of a shoulder twitch. "Bonfire, chanting, maybe a little drum circle to liven things up. You throw the guest of honor—me—into the flames, and everyone cheers. Ask for rain. Ask for the rain to stop. That sort of thing. Sound familiar?"

Bo frowned, ears twitching. "Useless One want to be sacrifice?"

Kallae sighed the kind of sigh that could drain the energy from a room. "No. I'm quite attached to not being incinerated, thank you very much. Bad for the complexion."

Bo seemed about to say something further, when a group of other Tanuki arrived in the clearing. His face lit up as a dozen glowing eyes fixed onto his.

He gestured towards Kallae, "Useless One is here."

The other Tanuki began chittering at Bo.

Bo held up his arms, "Cygren for Useless One," he said as he readjusted his hat, "he no understand Tanuken."

The Tanuki seemed to emit a collective sigh and Kallae thought he might have heard one mutter 'foreigners' under its breath.

A larger Tanuki wearing what appeared to be a fox skin scarf approached. Her whiskers twitched with what Kallae could only describe as unnecessary self-importance.

"Useless One," the new Tanuki began, its tone pompous.

"Let's get one thing straight," Kallae interrupted. "My name is not—"

"Tanuki give name," she said flatly, cutting him off. "Useless One your name. Mine," it pointed at herself, "Wise One."

"Of course, it is," Kallae muttered under his breath.

Wise One pointed at Bo, "He Bo."

"Why is—" began Kallae only to realize he did not care enough to know the answer, "Tell you what," he said, "I will allow you to call me Useless One if you untie me. I find it rather disconcerting to have a conversation while being tied to a plank like a skinned rabbit."

Wise One gestured for two smaller Tanuki to untie him. Reluctantly, Kallae sat up, rubbing at the red marks left by the ropes. To his surprise, his injured leg no longer screamed with pain, though it still protested anything resembling weight-bearing.

"Alright," said Kallae after he had managed to arrange himself in some form of sitting position, which still left him being a good half-foot taller than the Tanuki, "so why have you brought me here?"

Bo answered first, grinning ear to ear. "See? Useless One."

Wise One nodded serenely, her head bobbing in agreement.

"Hey!" protested Kallae, but was promptly swatted by Bo who said, "Wise One speaks. Tanuki listen."

"Quiet," Wise One commanded. Then, turning back to Kallae, it said, "Help we need."

"Of course you do," Kallae muttered, half to himself. "And here I was, hoping for a quick nap and a one-way ticket to literally anywhere else—hell, anyone have a direct line to hell? I'll trade you an almost-functioning leg and an ever-sunny disposition. No? Anyone?" He glanced at the sea of unnervingly silent raccoon-dog faces. "Your loss."

Wise One's gaze dropped to the blackened chronocrystal embedded in Kallae's chest. Its glossy surface reflected the faint moonlight like a shard of obsidian. "You Threadcaster," it said, poking him with one of its clammy fingers.

"Not anymore."

"Then what this?" Wise One jabbed him again, this time with enough force to send a ripple of discomfort through Kallae's chest.

"Hey!" Kallae recoiled, swatting at the Tanuki's hand like it was an overzealous bee. "Could we not? And clearly you know what it is wise guy," he muttered, "but it doesn't work anymore."

"You only one to help," Wise One repeated with maddening conviction.

"Oh, terrific. Here's the thing: *I don't care.*" Kallae threw up his hands—or tried to, given one wasn't fully cooperating. "Find someone else to solve your little crisis. I'm retired. Done. Finito. You know what's really calling my name? A quiet cave, maybe a nice bottle of something poisonous, and *no more raccoon dogs poking me.*"

Wise One stared at him, unblinking. Then she tilted her head in the way that only creatures thoroughly unimpressed with you could. "You help us."

"Well, then I regret to inform you, my furry little friend, that you're royally screwed."

Wise One exchanged a look with Bo, whose fur seemed to bristle with some unspoken urgency. "Show him we must," Bo said, solemn as a preacher.

Wise One nodded and then scampered off into the trees.

"What, *show me what?*" Kallae barked

Wise One cocked her head, "Not yet," she turned to Bo who nodded solemnly, "not ready yet."

"Ready for what?" demanded Kallae, attempting (and failing spectacularly) to rise to his feet. Wise One blinked once then scampered off into the darkness, vanishing like a shadow into the trees.

Neither Bo nor any of the other Tanuki deigned to answer any of Kallae's colorfully phrased questions. Naturally. Indeed, it would be several days until he would finally receive his answer.

The following days passed in a surreal blur. The Tanuki, despite being half his size and shaped like oversized bread loaves, managed to haul him—injured leg and all—into the treetops with a series of maneuvers that defied all known physics. The treehouse they deposited him in was...cozy. If by cozy, one meant 'grotesquely undersized and built by someone whose only blueprint was a vague memory of a bird's nest.'

The first meal they offered him consisted of a questionable mix of mushrooms (of the non-lethal variety) and berries in a creamy sauce. It was served in a bowl roughly the size of a teacup saucer. "Oh, marvelous," Kallae said dryly, squinting at the miniature meal. "Are the rest of my courses arriving later? Perhaps by falcon?"

After he insisted on no fewer than fifteen refills, they grudgingly swapped out his bowl for what appeared to be their communal dishwashing basin.

Days blurred into one another. Twice daily, a particularly surly Tanuki with a bone pierced through its muzzle came to replace his bandages. The process was perfunctory at best—though to Kallae's relief, they didn't try to sterilize the wounds with whatever questionable liquor was undoubtedly fermenting in some corner of their enclave. Kallae stopped trying to struggle, accepting that escape in his current condition was as likely as him sprouting wings and an eleventh toe.

Bo rarely left his side. This was not a kindness. The Tanuki's stream of chatter ranged from nonsensical to deeply irritating. "What is *wrong* with you?" Kallae muttered at one point after Bo regaled him with a bizarre tale involving fish guts, a stolen amulet, and what sounded suspiciously like a failed coup. Bo just grinned toothily, as if Kallae's misery were the punchline.

On the sixth evening, they came for him.

The Tanuki surrounded his bed like conspiratorial children about to steal a cookie jar. Kallae, half-asleep and wholly uncooperative, attempted to swat them away. "Oh, splendid," he groaned. "Are we having a midnight tea party? Shall I bring crumpets?"

Instead, they hauled him—quite literally—into the forest. Their pace was brutal, more of a jog than a stroll. The forest, dense and malevolent, seemed to conspire against him at every turn. Branches clawed at his skin. Bugs—most of which he was certain were venomous—bit him in no fewer than a dozen places. And the noises. Sweet gods, the noises. Somewhere to his left, something screamed—a sound somewhere between a banshee and a feral cat—and Kallae swore under his breath. "If we die out here," he hissed at Bo, "I'm haunting *you*. Forever."

Bo didn't respond. Of course he didn't. The racoon dog trudged along beside him, walking upright in a fashion that was both familiar and disturbing at the same time. Kallae noted that about half the other Tanuki had also opted to walk on their hindlegs, and of the remainder, another half walked on their forearms. Kallae decided it was best not to ask.

Their evening stroll, accompanied by the crazed screams of whatever else called this dreadful forest '*home*', lasted far longer than Kallae would have liked. But eventually they came upon a series of lights in the distance. It did not take long before the lights revealed a path, which opened up to a sprawling village. If Kallae weren't in the throes of exhaustion, he might have found its thatched roofs and warm lantern light quaint, even charming. Instead, he barely noticed it before Wise One shoved him onward, muttering, "Not be spotted."

They circled the village in tense silence, skirting the perimeter until the warm glow of the houses had faded into a distant glimmer. Their destination? A lean-to that made the rest of the village look like luxury architecture. Its walls were uneven stone slabs stacked with all the skill of a drunken toddler. The roof was neither intact nor well crafted, consisting largely of an odd collection of dried tree fronds and carelessly assembled bundles of straw.

Kallae, now thoroughly irritated, was nudged into the bushes nearby. Their branches jabbed at him with malicious glee, earning several muffled curses.

"Shhhh!" Wise One snapped, poking him sharply in the ribs.

"Oh, sure. Let's be quiet now," Kallae whispered sarcastically, his voice dripping with venom. "Wouldn't want to wake up whatever other horrors live out here. A shame, really—I was looking forward to tea with a banshee."

Ahead of them, almost obscured by shadow, stood two men, their long black robes marking them as unmistakably out of place. The faint glow flickering at their collars sealed it. "Black Cloaks," Kallae murmured under his breath, narrowing his eyes. "What are they doing here?" He squinted, trying to discern their faces. Strangers. Perhaps he'd passed one of them in the corridors of Heron Academy—a quick, forgettable nod exchanged on the way to the kitchens or a classroom. The type of encounter that left you wondering for hours if you'd snubbed someone important.

"Quiet, Useless One," Bo hissed, cutting into his thoughts as Wise One crept further into the bushes. By the time they reached the side of the ramshackle building, Kallae's arms were a quilt of scratches, bites, and hives. He was beginning to feel more like a patch of bramble than a person, his mood now a shade so black it could swallow light.

Wise One padded toward a gap in the crumbling stonework, cupping her hands around her face as if peering into a treasure chest. She moved from gap to gap like a child picking the best spot for hide-and-seek, then finally beckoned him with a sharp wave. "Come, Useless One," she whispered, gesturing impatiently. "Come and see."

Kallae hesitated, glaring at her. "Oh, sure. Let me just dive headfirst into—" Before he could finish, Bo shoved him forward with a force that was, frankly, uncalled for. He barely managed to catch himself against the rough stone wall, muttering a litany of colorful curses under his breath.

"Fine," he hissed, leaning toward the gap. "But so help me Amriel, if something comes out at me, I will skin you and make a hat out of you."

It took a moment for his vision to adjust to the gloom inside. When it did, his breath hitched. The room stretched out like a grotesque parody of a livestock pen, each stall separated by warped planks of wood, some sagging against the stone, others barely upright. But no animals filled these pens. Instead, hunched figures sat within, their bodies radiating eerie light. Some were tall, some were short. Many had long black hair, others shades of brown and even some with locks so pale they appeared white in the darkness. All were aglow with chronomagic.

Kallae's stomach churned. Blue, green, yellow, and pink threads of chronomagic oozed from their hands, so bright they carved harsh shadows across their gaunt faces. The threads pulsed and shifted as their hands moved in an endless, mechanical rhythm. In one stall, a man so emaciated he seemed to flicker like a dying flame collapsed, the light in his veins dimming to nothing. Something small and glowing rolled from his limp fingers—a spool, wound tightly with threads of chronomagic.

"No," Kallae breathed, his voice cracking. His stomach dropped as recognition hit. "Castian."

They hadn't spoken in years, but Kallae's memories of sharing bunk beds at Heron Academy, stealing late-night snacks, and sneaking into the library after curfew surged to the surface like a flood.

Wise One said nothing, but her presence pressed against him like a silent demand. His eyes drifted back to the spool. The threads of light coiled around what seemed to be a core of metal, capped unevenly at each end with rough, crystalline fragments. His heart sank.

"Dead chronocrystals," he whispered, his throat dry. "This… this isn't possible."

But as he peered closer, he knew he could not be mistaken.

A sharp voice interrupted his spiraling thoughts. "Get up, you lazy bastard!" One of the Black Cloaks stomped into the room, his boot connecting with Castian's side. Castian didn't move.

"He's a goner, Tamer. Look," the second guard kicked Castian's arm, "the fragment has already returned to the Source." Kallae leaned in seeing a thin wisp of black smoke leaving Castian's far too still form.

The guard wrinkled up his nose in disgust, "Tsuyoshi said we'll get a fresh batch soon. Those deemed fit for Cargyll have already been sent away, the rejects should be here within a few days."

Tamer grunted, rolling Castian's body over with a boot like he was turning over a sack of grain. His face twisted with disgust. Around the room, several prisoners had paused their mechanical spooling. The glow of their threads flickered in the dim light.

Tamer slammed his fist against a divider, sending a cascade of dust into the stale air. "Did I say you could stop?" he barked. "Get back to work! Or shall we skip meals for the next two days?"

The prisoners—Threadcasters and Yōsei alike—turned back to their grim task, the room lighting up again with their labor. Kallae shut his eyes, bile rising in his throat. *Why don't they fight back?* he thought desperately. The guards, each sporting purple chronocrystals, would be formidable, yes. But together…

A loud clink drew his eyes to one of the fairies furthest away. His ankles were encircled by metal cuffs chained to the ground.

"No," he murmured, trembling. "They have Klaus."

The chill spreading through his body was one he

hadn't felt since his early days of warping, the kind that reached bone-deep. He turned away from the gap, swallowing hard. "I can't watch this anymore," he whispered, his voice barely audible.

"Now you see," Wise One said, her voice softer than before as she appeared at his side. Her eyes shone with quiet urgency. "Help we need."

TWENTY-FOUR

二十四

AKIRA

Akira had thought training under her father, Jiro, had been difficult. Back then, bruises were as common as rice in their bowls, and sleep came only after a day's worth of bruising, sparring, and backbreaking chores. Yet somehow, in the comforting misery of hard tatami mats and groaning mornings, there was a rhythm to it. A predictability. Narthor swallowing her whole? At times, that had seemed preferable. But compared to the gauntlet Jiro's clan had endured these last weeks, her father's training felt like a sunlit walk in a peaceful meadow. Or at least, the kind of meadow where the bees only stung sometimes. Funny how hindsight always repaints hardship as nostalgia.

She hadn't realized how cushy her father's regime was until her new life under the Hainu began.

It wasn't just the pace of it—it was the complete lack of mercy. "Good morning, Furless Children!" came the call, cheerful to the point of sadism, every single dawn. They inhaled rice and a suspiciously fish-like chicken (or maybe it was chicken-like fish?) before heading to their mounts. Seven Hainu had volunteered for the mission, a number Akira suspected had more to do with dwindling sanity than actual enthusiasm.

When Rul'ka, the Hainu leader, explained the task to the Hainu, the decision on who they would carry was left entirely up to the Hainu. A solemn, silent process unfolded. Calder, predictably, was paired with Rul'ka herself—leader to leader, because of course. Al'ti, an elderly male whose silvering muzzle gave him a wise, almost grandfatherly air, chose Jun with a polite nod. Ba'ka, a massive Hainu with enough swagger to give Ryū a run for his money, immediately claimed him. Within seconds, Ryū was smacking Ba'ka on the flank like they were old drinking buddies, a dynamic that grated on Akira for reasons she couldn't fully articulate.

Two sisters chose Kyou and Shoji, bowing with synchronized grace before seating themselves. That had left Akira with Pa'ka.

Pa'ka. The Hainu who had already thrown her to near-certain death once before. Their initial 'greeting' was icy enough to frost over the Timeless Realm. While the other riders exchanged words, Akira and Pa'ka sat in mutual, glowering silence.

Her first weeks with Pa'ka were a bruising blur of betrayal and boulders. She was thrown against cliffs, fields, lakes—basically, if it existed in the natural world, she was hurled at it. Once, they even found a swarm of bees. That was a particularly creative touch. Meanwhile, the others regaled each other with tales of tranquil midnight flights. Akira, in contrast, spent her evenings slathering herself with salves and contemplating revenge.

It didn't help that her riding skills regressed instead of

improved. Every ache in her body added tension to her already clumsy grip, which only made Pa'ka's movements more erratic. This, in turn, made Akira cling tighter, until she resembled a barnacle gripping a bucking bronco mid-flight.

"Why even choose me if you're so eager to be rid of me?" she demanded one afternoon, dangling precariously after yet another divebomb-worthy incident. Her tone was sour, but the bruises on her ribs lent her some credibility.

"I do not wish to be rid of you," Pa'ka replied with maddening calm, banking sharply enough to nearly unseat her yet again. "But you are weak."

"Oh, thank you, Pa'ka. How very insightful," she grumbled, white-knuckling the harness.

"Your weakness will be your failure," he said, his voice like a chisel on stone. "If you wish to save your father, you must be strong. I can teach you to be strong, if only you would learn."

"I am trying!" she snapped, though her tone lacked conviction, especially when the Hainu swerved into a gust of icy wind.

"Trying is not enough Furless Child," said Pa'ka, "if you only try, you will fail."

And so went every morning. Akira would get up, get thrown off, cry (mostly internally), and clamber back onto Pa'ka. It was a symphony of frustration and futility, played out under the mocking gaze of her peers. Even Shoji, who could usually laugh at his own exhaustion, looked ready to collapse. By the second week, meals became quiet affairs—no quips, no barbs. Not even Kyou, who could usually summon an insult like a magician pulling a rabbit from a hat, had the energy left to banter.

The afternoons were draining in an entirely different, yet equally soul-crushing way. As soon as they had shoved some more rice and pickled vegetables down their gullet, they were met with Calder, who found ever more creative ways of showing them just how little they knew about chronomagic. Before Calder, Akira had thought of herself as a pretty decent Threadcaster, one hour into one of Calder's sessions, she decided she was as much a Threadcaster as she was a three-headed dolphin wearing a corset. He drilled them with the mercy of a dictator, and Akira left every evening with a collection of burns to add to the scrapes and bites she had earned in the morning.

He made them summon one thread at a time, adding on one after another, until there were so many wrapped around Akira's body, she felt like she was more fire than skin. Calder showed them how to summon lassos which could be swung towards opponents, this proved more useful to Ryū who could warp, causing his lassoed opponent to become sluggish, or even stationary. But when Akira complained that this was useless to her, Calder responded by lassoing an old ginkgo tree. His thread glowed a deep turquoise, quivering as he wrapped it around his hands and wrists. The thread began to vibrate, first slowly, and then so rapidly that it became a blur in Akira's eye. And then the tree fell. A groan, and then a crack, and the great tree, likely hundreds of years old, lay on the ground, cut cleanly in two.

"Useless, you say?" he asked, the faintest smirk tugging at his lips. She cursed him in every language she knew after that but didn't question him again.

Come the evening they all gathered outside the temple steps devoured a meal and spent the next few hours mediating in the Sanctum halls, recharging their crystals for the horrors of tomorrow. Only Jun was spared from Calder's tyrant-like mode of instruction, as he spent the afternoons with Al'ti, the elderly male Hainu. He spoke little of what Al'ti taught him, but Akira did notice his chronocrystal, which had seldom dulled in color as long as she had known him, looked decidedly drained when they sat down in the Sanctum.

Shoji and Kyou, though crystal-less, suffered through Calder's teachings right alongside them. While Akira and

Ryū tripped over threads of chronomagic, making knots, where Calder made beautiful nets, Shoji and Kyou were forced into grueling duels. They ran, they climbed, they did so many pushups they could count the grains of dirt beneath their noses. Despite both favoring swords, they were taught to be near-expert bowmen. And once they managed to hit their targets from an acceptable distance, they were unceremoniously plonked onto their respective Hainu until they could do it while speeding towards it on a flying wolf.

This went on for a solid fortnight. Somewhere between the second and third week of their stay at Sanctum Nayagu, they found themselves in the thick of it—preparing for the deep dives they would be forced to undertake. Now, the sheer act of sitting on a flying wolf would be enough to send most people into a full-blown cardiac arrest, but when you added the fact that said flying wolf was hurtling into the sky at a ninety-degree angle, and you were clinging to a leather harness that seemed held together with nothing more than sheer stubbornness and a prayer, well... that was enough to make Akira's heart attempt to flee her chest and dive into an untimely, and certainly fatal, escape.

They had flown several miles east from the Sanctum to a rocky spire—a formation that looked suspiciously man-made, but was apparently a result of some seismic activity. Whatever the earthquake or cosmic disturbance had been, Akira was thankful she hadn't been around for it. Earthquakes were one thing, but this particular geological mishap seemed almost personal.

Ryū, astride Ba'ka, flew beside her. For once, Akira could not bring herself to respond to his usual barbed quips. Ba'ka and Pa'ka exchanged a series of yips and yaps, their sounds somehow as unintelligible to Akira as the howling winds that tore past them.

They arrived after an exchange of no more than five words between them. Five. And that was counting the grunts and muttered curses.

Jun dismounted Al'ti with the kind of effortless grace that only came from doing something far too often. He landed on the rocky ground with a faint, metallic clink. The others followed suit, their landings forming a loose circle around the spire. They exchanged wary glances as the rocky structure loomed in front of them.

Jun, ever the one for theatrics, pointed at the spire with dramatic flair. His hand still buried in Al'ti's thick mane, he spoke with the kind of quiet confidence only a man whose plans were either genius or suicidal could muster. "If the plans Calder... liberated, are accurate," he began, pausing dramatically as he located Calder amongst the crowd of people and Hainu, "this spire is a good approximation for the tower."

He gestured broadly at the surrounding mountains, their peaks wrapped in mist. "The mountains here, are much like the mountains surrounding the tower," he continued, "the front of the tower is guarded by a rotating watch of Threadcasters. Getting through there will be impossible. Not to mention, there are two gryphons patrolling at all times. This means any approach has to be swift, or we risk detection. Should we fail—and let's be honest, this is not an entirely unlikely scenario—eight gryphons are kept in cages two miles away. Not to mention the battalion of Threadcasters that will be notified and promptly assemble."

Jun's gaze turned to Shoji with a pointed stare. "I trust I do not need to stress how critical it is that we remain undetected."

"How are we supposed to approach undetected with a fleet of gryphons circling the tower?" Ryū interrupted, voice tinged with skepticism.

Jun gave a slight, self-satisfied smile, the kind that suggested he knew something they didn't. "Glad you asked." He straightened, his robes flaring slightly. "Approaching from the front by foot is out. And if we try to approach from the sky, we'll be spotted by the gryphons in minutes, maybe less. But," he paused, allowing the tension to build, "there is an alternative path."

Ryū rolled his eyes. "Enough with the theatrics, Jun. Spit it out already."

Ba'ka grunted in what Akira took to be agreement.

Jun blinked at Ryū, a little taken aback, but then shrugged. "Fine, fine. As I was saying, there are mountain ridges surrounding the tower. The gryphons rarely patrol the peaks themselves, and if my calculations are correct, we should have about a minute of cover when the gryphons turn the other way. From there, we scale the ridges as quickly as possible and drop down onto the roof of the tower before they can circle back."

"Just how quickly are we talking here, Jun?" Calder asked, his voice calm but sharp.

Jun frowned, visibly working through the numbers. "I estimate we'll have a minute—two at most—while the gryphons are facing the opposite direction. The Hainu can get up to 250 miles per hour, which, if everything goes perfectly, means we have a shot. But if any of us fall to our deaths, then the whole plan's off." He hesitated for a moment, glancing at Rul'ka. "But strictly speaking, it's possible."

"Provided we don't plummet to our deaths?" Kyou grumbled. "Which, knowing our luck, is hardly a certainty."

Ryū narrowed his eyes. "So, we're going to play a deadly game of hide-and-seek with gryphons and mountains?"

"I'd like to think of it as more of an extreme sport," Jun replied, almost cheerfully.

Rul'ka's eyes flicked to Jun. "It's not just the gryphons," she said, her tone shifting. "The altitude alone will make it impossible to maintain that speed, let alone the climb. Even I would struggle." She shook her head. "This is near impossible."

"The calculations are based on ideal conditions," Jun admitted, though his voice remained hopeful. "But—"

"Even with ideal conditions," Ba'ka interjected firmly, "this is suicide. You're talking about scaling heights so steep, the risk of falling is as high as the tower itself."

"Can we not just flect to augment our speed?"

Ru'lka shook her head, "The Particulars would be nigh on impossible to accurately predict at such speeds. The alignments will be changing so quickly even Al'ti would be hard-pressed to keep up. No," she said with finality, "we cannot rely on chronomagic to fulfill this mission."

A chorus of voices erupted as everyone began talking over one another, the cacophony rising to a fever pitch. The noise swirled around Akira like a storm, voices interwoven, overlapping, growing louder with each second. Some were arguing about the plans, others about the feasibility, while others still were simply voicing their displeasure at being in this situation at all.

Akira's patience, already thin, snapped. She slammed the hilt of her sword into the ground with enough force to stop the conversation dead. "Please," she said again, her voice cutting through the noise, "please, we must try."

Ba'ka's voice boomed over the others. "There is nothing we must do. It's reckless to risk our lives when our duty is to protect the Sanctum."

A howl broke through the chaos—a sound that made Akira's stomach turn in unexpected dread. Pa'ka's voice followed, deep and resonant, echoing across the rocky landscape. "Our duty is to protect the Sanctum," he said slowly, "but what of the Light? The Way of the Light calls for sacrifice, for loyalty. How can we say saving those who are held captive is not part of our duty? they turn their eyes to this place as well. They might be content with Sanctum Oto for now, but it is only a matter of time before their greed turns their eyes here as well."

"You have seen for yourself what they did at the

Sanctum of Oto," snapped Ba'ka, "if we are caught, the Sanctum of Nayagu too will fall."

"You dare speak of Oto to me?" bit out Pa'ka, his hackles rising.

"Enough," Rul'ka said, her tone like steel, final and unwavering. The harshness in her voice silenced the room. "Pa'ka is right, for too long have we allowed what happened at Oto to send us cowering into the shadows. But the time has come for us to be the Harbingers of Light. We have promised them our help, we will not turn back on our word now. The solution is simple. We will not be caught."

Clearly some of the Hainu were still far from pleased with the decision, but none would dare challenge Rul'ka's choice, for to do so would be to challenge her very position. And even Ba'ka, with all of his strength, would not win that fight.

As Akira mounted Pa'ka, her hands twisted into his thick fur, she whispered, "Thank you," into one of his large, furred ears. His response was a huff, and then, without warning, he stepped off the cliff, allowing them to plummet into the void below. It felt like her heart was attempting to leave her chest again, but before she could fully comprehend the free-fall, Pa'ka's wings snapped open and they were soaring upward.

Akira exhaled shakily when her heart rate finally dropped below the level of an imminent heart attack. "Must you always do that?" she muttered, still reeling from the adrenaline.

"It's fun," Pa'ka said nonchalantly, his voice almost carefree. "And if I'm going to die, I'm going to make sure it's a good time before I do."

"Are you suggesting we're going to die?" Akira asked, incredulous.

Pa'ka glanced back at her, his eyes gleaming with that ever-present mischief. "Every day we live, there's a chance we'll die. Might as well enjoy it."

Just then, Ryū shot past them, yelling, "I'll race you to the top, Princess!"

"This isn't a game!" Akira shouted back, her voice barely carrying over the wind. But Pa'ka only chuckled, a low, rumbling sound that vibrated through her legs.

His eyes flicked to the rapidly ascending Ba'ka. "I wouldn't mind a race," he said, a playful glint in his eyes.

"Really?"

The Hainu hung in the air for a moment, his wings beating steadily. "That Ba'ka could do with a generous dose of humility," Pa'ka grinned, showing teeth. "And I would be more than happy to serve him with one."

Before Akira could even manage a smile, Pa'ka began his ascent anew. His wings sliced through the air with the ferocity of a storm, and Akira, gritting her teeth, clung to the harness with all the strength she could summon. The view around them blurred as they shot higher, and she soon learned that if she didn't look down, her stomach would only occasionally threaten to abandon her body entirely rather than do so in a constant, mind-numbing panic.

The winds howled in her ears, and with every beat of Pa'ka's wings, her stomach clenched, her chest tightening as if it, too, were trying to escape. She'd already ascended higher than they'd ever dared before, and the thought of plummeting was far too vivid in her mind for comfort.

Ba'ka was just a speck in the distance, and Ryū a mere glimmer as he clung to the beast's thick neck. But Akira could see they were gaining on them, slowly but surely.

"Come on," she murmured through clenched teeth.

"Come on yourself," Pa'ka huffed, his voice strained as the pressure of the altitude tugged at him. "I'd like to see you ascend a mountain in under a minute. See how much you like being told to come—"

"Sorry, sorry," Akira cut in, her breath coming in uneven gasps. "I just meant, you can do it."

"I know I can do it," Pa'ka barked, his irritation as

palpable as the cold air around them. "That's why I'm doing it."

Akira held her tongue after that, grateful for the silence that followed. Or perhaps she was simply too winded to speak, her body beginning to ache under the pressure. After several moments of this brutal ascent, she realized she could not have said anything even if she'd wanted to. The air was so thin now that it felt like ice had taken residence in her lungs, crystallizing with every shallow breath. She tried to glance behind her to see if the others were still trailing, but the world around her was hazy, unfocused. She couldn't even find enough air to open her eyes fully.

Frost was beginning to creep up the tips of Pa'ka's wings, spreading across his fur like a slow-moving plague. Akira wiped at it, but the ice returned as quickly as she could remove it. Pa'ka's breathing had become ragged, each exhale sounding like a gasp for life itself.

"You ok?" she managed to rasp as the jagged peaks of the mountain came into view, looming like the teeth of some great beast.

Pa'ka landed firmly on the peak with a grunt, his paws scraping against the rock as he stabilized himself. "What kind of question is that? I just flew up a mountain. What do you think?"

Akira decided the fact that Pa'ka was still about as pleasant to be around as a bear with a tooth ache was probably a good sign. A split second later Ba'ka appeared, Akira having lost sight of them behind a gathering stormfront.

"Beat you," Akira shot back with a smirk, more victorious than she had any right to be.

"You never accepted my challenge," Ryū replied, his voice ragged with exertion. "So, I'm not sure what exactly you think you beat me at."

"If we're being strictly accurate," Pa'ka interjected, his bark of laughter practically smug, "I beat you. Akira just managed not to fall off this time. Small victories."

Ryū chuckled, a rare sound that, for once, didn't have sharp edges. It pleased Pa'ka more than it probably should have.

Moments later, the remaining Hainu landed atop the spire with varying degrees of grace—or lack thereof. Rul'ka, Ka'ska, and Ra'ka touched down next, the latter two carrying Kyou and Shoji. Ka'ska grinned like she'd just personally tamed a thunderstorm, her sharp teeth gleaming with almost criminal confidence. Ra'ka, by contrast, looked one breath away from hyperventilating.

Shoji, ever the picture of chaotic goodwill, slapped Ra'ka's neck with far too much enthusiasm and boomed a jubilant cheer. Ra'ka regarded him with the same appreciation one reserves for being handed a soiled rag by a spastic monkey.

"So," Shoji crowed, grinning like an idiot, "who's ready for round two?"

Ra'ka, perhaps sensing the universe demanded balance, bit his shoe.

Akira and Ryū, still too absorbed in their bickering to notice the circus around them, carried on.

"Well then," Akira snapped, her breath finally cooperating, "I formally challenge you to a race to the bottom. Do you accept, or are you too afraid to lose? Again."

"No need to ask me twice, Princess," Ryū shot back, grinning as he ran a hand along Ba'ka's flank. The Hainu huffed in response, as if in agreement with Ryū's smugness.

"Are you not going to ask if I accept the challenge?" Pa'ka teased, his tone light, though the glint in his eye was pure trouble. "Or am I just some glorified pack mule to you?"

"Sounds like a pretty accurate description," Ba'ka muttered dryly, earning a snort from Pa'ka.

"Bite me," Pa'ka growled, and before anyone could

react, he launched himself off the edge of the spire.

"You guys are—" started Rul'ka, but her words were devoured by the wind as Ba'ka and Ryū followed Pa'ka into freefall.

Akira knew what was coming. Knowing didn't help. The freefall hit like a thunderclap, weightlessness stealing every scrap of control she thought she had. Her organs bunched into a miserable knot somewhere behind her ribs, and her stomach seemed to be auditioning for the role of throat.

Her mind briefly wondered how Pa'ka's wings hadn't snapped clean off from the velocity, but the thought evaporated like mist. There was only the roaring wind, the relentless pull of gravity, and the peculiar thrill of impending doom.

Out of the corner of her eye, she registered movement—someone else plummeting beside her. Turning her neck, however, felt like trying to move a mountain. Her body had betrayed her, stone-stiff and utterly useless.

And then the jagged edges of the rugged terrain below appeared, sharp monstrosities punching through the clouds.

"Pa'ka," she croaked, unsure if her voice had reached him over the howling air.

"Little busy here," Pa'ka replied through gritted teeth, his hind legs shifting as he adjusted their descent.

Akira's panic sharpened as she counted at least seventeen rocky protrusions, each one capable of turning them into a particularly gruesome shish kebab.

"Pa'ka," she said again, louder this time, her voice catching on rising panic. "We might want to think—"

Pa'ka didn't let her finish. He howled, a sound that could've summoned every ghost in the region, and snapped his wings open. The force of it whipped Akira's face against his neck. By the time she processed the landing, his paws had slammed into the rocky surface, and her spine had sent a strongly worded complaint to her brain.

She remained twisted against Pa'ka's withers, her body an uncooperative pretzel.

"Your hand," Pa'ka growled, "is digging into my back."

"Well, call it thanks for the *smooth* landing," Akira snapped, wincing as she untangled herself.

"The implication being that you'd do better?" Pa'ka cackled just as Ba'ka landed beside them with insulting grace.

"Ba'ka managed it just fine," Akira quipped.

"I was under the impression the goal was to win, not stroll in like you're late for afternoon tea," Pa'ka shot back. His wings ruffled indignantly, and his markings dimmed to a dull blue as if sulking.

Ba'ka barked something sharp and guttural, which Akira decided to interpret as a very specific, unflattering critique. Probably about Pa'ka's landing.

Jun, having being observing this test with Al'ti from the relative safety of a rock that looked almost smug in its stationary reliability, ambled over. He stared them down in that deeply obnoxious way scholars did when they wanted to look like they had just solved the secrets of the universe. "So, I see the both of you have paid this exercise the appropriate amount of seriousness," he drawled, voice heavy with the kind of disappointment only a perfectionist could muster.

Akira opened her mouth, unsure if she wanted to defend herself or just change the subject, but before she could decide, the others began to trickle in.

Ra'ka landed next, looking like she was barely holding it together. Her wings shuddered, her legs wobbled, and her eyes were wide with the kind of panic you'd associate with someone realizing they'd left the stove on at home—except, you know, midair.

Then the ground rumbled. Once. Then again.

The Hainu sprang upward like startled cats, wings unfurling with a suddenness that made Akira's stomach lurch.

Pa'ka jolted backward, and Akira had to grab a fistful of his mane to keep from falling. He yipped in protest, but there was no time for witty retorts.

Another low rumble rolled through the air, followed by a sharp, thunderous crack.

"Pa'ka," Akira hissed, panic clawing at her voice. "What are you doing?" She yanked on the harness like it was a leash, as if that would somehow solve the problem.

"Look up," he growled, banking hard to the left.

Akira tilted her head and felt her stomach drop. It wasn't just Ba'ka and Ryū hovering where they'd last been—it was a third shape, plummeting like a broken kite. And trailing them was an avalanche of debris that looked particularly unfriendly.

"Rul'ka," said Akira, the word leaving on acidic aftertaste on her tongue.

"Hold on," Pa'ka murmured, voice tight with focus. He angled closer to Rul'ka, whose wing was trapped against her body, pinned by Calder's arm as he dangled from her harness with all the security of wet spaghetti.

"Grab hold!" Akira shouted, reaching toward Calder as Pa'ka brought them closer.

The Threadcaster's markings glowed with flickering pink threads of chronomagic, swirling across his arms like veins of living starlight. For a split second, he hesitated, his eyes meeting hers.

"There's no time!" Akira screamed, the wind ripping the words from her throat.

Calder swung his arm, and Akira caught his fingers, but a sudden lurch from Rul'ka tore him away. "Again!" she yelled, the strain building in her voice.

This time, when Calder reached out, Akira latched onto his hand with all the desperation of someone trying to pull a winning lottery ticket from a storm drain. The pink threads on his skin shifted to blue, and with a ripple of magic, he shot across the gap between the Hainu like a cannonball, landing heavily behind her.

Rul'ka managed to free her trapped wing and snap it open, slowing her descent just before she could become a rather unfortunate splatter on the jagged rocks below.

Seated behind her, Calder was still aglow in a bluish hue, his eyes fixed upon Rul'ka.

It was only when Rul'ka managed to holler a strained, "I'm fine," that he allowed his gaze to shift.

By the time they landed, the group was gathered, their expressions a mix of exhaustion and grim determination. Akira slid off Pa'ka's back, her knees trembling beneath her weight. She didn't trust herself to speak.

"This mission is doomed," Ba'ka declared, his tone sharp as a blade. His tail flicked like an angry metronome. "Rul'ka nearly died."

"If you don't want to continue," Rul'ka snapped back, her voice laced with venom, "no one is forcing you. Just as no one forced you to volunteer." She sat down heavily, clearly favoring one leg, her wings drooping like a wilting flower.

"I gave my word," Ba'ka grumbled, his shoulders hunching. "I won't back out now."

"Then stop complaining," Rul'ka shot back before turning to Jun. "Well? How did we do?"

Jun exchanged a glance with Al'ti, whose green markings had faded to a dull gray, making him look even wearier than usual. Al'ti gave a faint nod, and Jun cleared his throat.

"Pa'ka and Ba'ka were within seconds of each other, the fastest of the group. Ascent time was fifty-five seconds; descent, thirty. That's about half a minute slower than our best-case scenario."

Akira dropped her head.

"Then it is not possible," said Ba'ka, his wings rustling in the wind as he spoke. "It is as I suspected. If even the best of us cannot make it, then this is more of a fool's errand than I already thought."

A few others chimed in, and soon enough a new chorus had formed, assenting voices each trying to drown out the other.

Akira couldn't take it. She turned away from the group, her legs carrying her to the cliff's edge. When she sank to her knees, the weight of everything came crashing down.

Her voice broke as the tears came. "I can't lose him. I can't lose someone else."

Pa'ka, having followed her, dropped his head, holding it so close to her own that she felt his warm breath curl against her cheek.

"Why do you think I have pushed you as hard as I have?" he asked as she felt the heat from his blue markings warming against her. "I am the only survivor from the siege of Oto. I would not wish for you to endure that same burden. Cry not Furless Child, nothing is impossible with hard work. We *will* save your father."

Lub dub. Everyone leaves eventually Akira.

Lub dub.

Just accept it. Everyone lets you down eventually.

Lub dub.

You are meant to be alone.

"No!" she shouted, the words coming out as a whisper despite the tone in which they were uttered. Pa'ka flinched.

Akira sniffed, wiping her face with a sleeve. "But what about the others?"

Pa'ka bared his teeth in a grin that was all mischief and sharp edges. "Leave them to me. I'll handle them."

Why trust Pa'ka's promises? He'll let you down, just like everyone else.

Lub dub.

Lub dub.

Akira stared out at the jagged horizon, her hands

pressed flat against the coarse stone. The world seemed too big and too indifferent for their mission to ever succeed. But Pa'ka's words echoed in her mind, defying the relentless rhythm of her intrusive thoughts.

Lub dub. He'll fail you too, just wait.

The warmth of his breath lingered on her cheek, a stubborn reminder that not everyone had failed her yet.

Behind her, the group's argument reached a crescendo. Ba'ka's voice rose above the others, sharp and cutting: "This is a fool's errand, and you know it! We're being sent to our deaths for what? A chance? A gamble?"

Rul'ka's voice came next, strained but unyielding. "If that's how you feel, then leave! No one's chaining you here, Ba'ka!"

Akira exhaled shakily and rose to her feet. She turned to face them, her legs still unsteady, but her gaze was hard as flint.

"Enough!" she barked, her voice cutting through the chaos like a whip crack.

The group froze. Even Ba'ka, mid-snarl, fell silent, his wings twitching as if unsure whether to fight or flee.

"None of us are here because this is easy," Akira continued, her voice trembling but resolute. "We're here because we have no choice. Because giving up means losing everything. So, if you're too scared to fight, fine. Walk away. But don't you dare drag the rest of us down with you."

For a moment, the only sound was the whisper of the wind and the distant crash of falling rocks. Ba'ka's jaw worked silently, his eyes darting between the others, searching for support. When none came, he huffed and turned away, his tail lashing behind him.

Akira didn't wait to see if he'd stay or go. She turned back to Pa'ka and placed a hand on his broad neck, drawing strength from the steady rise and fall of his breath.

"We're not done," she whispered to herself. "Not

yet."

Pa'ka gave a low rumble of approval, his markings flickering brighter. "Good."

Behind them, the group began to stir. Jun muttered something under his breath, and Rul'ka limped closer, her expression unreadable. Even Al'ti, gray and drained, straightened his posture just a fraction.

The air still felt heavy, but it was no longer suffocating. For the first time, a spark of determination cut through the fog of doubt.

Akira glanced down at the crumbling cliff edge. The rocks beneath her feet looked so precarious, like one wrong step could send everything tumbling into the abyss. She felt the familiar squeeze of fear in her chest, the rhythm of her heartbeat pounding louder.

Lub dub. You'll fall. You always fall.

But she didn't move away. Not this time.

"Let's go," she said, turning back to the group. Her voice was steady now, firm. "We've got work to do."

Pa'ka's wings unfurled, and he tilted his head toward her, a grin curling over his lips. "That's more like it, Furless Child. Now, let's see what you're really made of."

With that, she stepped forward, not waiting to see if the others would follow. The path ahead was uncertain, jagged and steep, but it was a path nonetheless. And for now, that was enough.

TWENTY-FIVE

KALLAE

"Now you see," repeated Wise One, her tone as infuriatingly calm as ever, "two sides there are to every story."

Kallae blinked, swiping at the unbidden tears clinging to his lashes like stubborn cobwebs. Without much thought—because if he thought too much, he might break entirely—he whirled toward Wise One and gripped her shoulders tightly.

"You don't get it!" he shouted, louder than intended. His voice cracked like a dry branch. "I can't use chronomagic anymore. Amriel has taken it from me!"

He hadn't meant for it to come out like that, raw and jagged. It felt like throwing a stone at a pond and realizing the ripple was a tidal wave.

The humid night pressed in on him, sticky and suffocating, but the skies chose that moment to crack open. Rain poured in torrents, soaking him to the bone. A deafening clap of thunder shook the ground, so powerful it knocked him off balance.

Before Kallae could steady himself, a half-dozen

Tanuki appeared, bedraggled and drenched like overgrown, miserable rats. An unfamiliar voice pierced the cacophony of rain and thunder.

"There! Get them!" it hollered. "You—alert the patrols!"

Wise One and Bo grabbed his arms, tugging him forward. "Must go," Wise One urged, pointing toward the dense silhouette of the forest.

Under ordinary circumstances, Kallae would have entertained the perverse urge to run in the opposite direction—just to be contrary, because authority and he weren't and had never been on speaking terms. But this wasn't ordinary. His mind was splintered, shards of himself scraping against each other, while his heart threatened to collapse under its own weight.

So, he ran.

He ran as if the shadows themselves were clawing at his heels. Two weeks of surviving on little more than walnuts and spite hadn't done wonders for his stamina, and his leg, still bearing the ugly gash, protested every step. He vaguely registered the stitches tearing and blood seeping into his already-soaked trousers. No matter. Pain felt distant, unreal. A silver lining, he supposed. Silver linings, eh?

Beside him, the Tanuki were just as fast, especially Bo. The little creature dropped to all fours, pausing only to keep his hat from flying off or to retrieve some random trinket it had spilled. Their group dashed through the forest, the warning gong fading behind them. The screeches of patrolling gryphons dimmed until the night was a cocoon of wet leaves and muffled breath.

When they finally stopped, their lungs clawing for air, Kallae collapsed onto his knees. His leg throbbed, the reopened wound protesting violently. Several Tanuki flopped to the ground, wheezing like tiny, furry bellows. Even Bo was silent, which Kallae suspected was a sign of the apocalypse.

The ache in his leg finally demanded attention, threatening to buckle him entirely. Gritting his teeth, he fumbled with the blood-soaked bandages, tightening them until the flow slowed, then stopped. He pulled tighter still, not caring when the flesh above turned an angry red and his calf paled unnaturally.

"Enough," Bo said softly, his small hand hovering over Kallae's.

But Kallae brushed Bo's hand away and pulled on the blood-soaked bandages further still, till the threads began to strain and snap. His fingers slipped, now slick with warm blood, but he kept on tightening, the bandage now a thick rope which bit deep into his calf. Water mixed in with the blood and Kallae could not tell if it was from sweat or tears.

"Enough," Wise One repeated, appearing at his side. Her tiny hands tugged at his arm with surprising force.

"Leave me alone!" Kallae growled, wrenching away from her grasp. His hand slipped, streaking blood across her wizened face. He tore at his tunic, ripping strips to fashion makeshift ties for his leg. It was only when two other Tanuki, Strong One and Brash One, joined in on the fun, that Kallae was finally forced to the ground. It appeared, Strong One and Brash One had earned their names for a reason.

"Let me go!" he snapped, fully aware he was throwing what could only be described as an adult tantrum. Somewhere in the fog of his mind, he knew he wasn't entirely sane at the moment. But sanity had packed up and left a long time ago.

Summoning a burst of irrational strength, Kallae broke free, sending the Tanuki tumbling like furry firecrackers. The clearing erupted into offended snaps and yips, the creatures too preoccupied with their own chaos to notice Kallae making a limping dash into the trees.

He didn't get far.

Tanuki descended like a plague. Some leapt from

trees, others launched from the ground, defying all known laws of physics. Kallae pried one off his arm, only for another to latch onto his leg.

By the time they pinned him down, he resembled a very disgruntled scarecrow. Four Tanuki—one on each limb—pressed him into the dirt.

"Alright!" he barked. "Fine. You win. What do you want? To roast me over a fire? Turn me into some sort of Tanuki effigy?"

Bo perched nearby, rummaging through his ever-chaotic hat. Trinkets and scraps flew out until, finally, Bo produced another porcelain bottle. He took a hearty swig before passing it around. The Tanuki drank with gusto, their tiny faces lighting up as they did.

When the bottle reached Kallae, it was nearly empty. He drained the last drop, the strange liquor burning its way down his throat.

"Empty," he muttered, licking his lips. Despite himself, he craved the numbness the drink offered.

Bo shrugged. "Last of pack Omega. You drink last."

"I'm not part of your pack!" Kallae snapped. "Why won't you fur-brained lunatics leave me alone?"

Wise One appeared before him, as if conjured from the shadows.

"You have seen now," she said, her tone brimming with the self-assurance of someone who spoke in riddles for a living.

"Seen what?" Kallae growled, his voice dripping with sarcasm so thick it could have been bottled and sold as a potion for cynics.

The whack across his head came faster than his wit, sending a burst of white lights dancing chaotically across his vision. He groaned, clutching his head as the shadows around her clarified into a figure leaning smugly on a gnarled stick that looked like it had fought the forest and won.

"Stupid One," she muttered with a sniff, the kind of

sniff that condemned an entire lineage.

"What happened to Useless One?" Kallae asked, though he wasn't remotely invested in the answer.

She ignored his question with the ease of someone accustomed to hearing far better ones. Digging into her burlap trousers—which, Kallae noted, were every bit as fashionable as one might expect burlap trousers to be—she produced a crumpled bundle of dried leaves and shoved it toward him. "Take."

"That might be a bit of a challenge," Kallae said, gesturing lazily toward Strong One and Brash One, who had decided his hands made for excellent cushions. "Unless, of course, you'd like me to grow a third hand. Which, given tonight, I wouldn't put past you."

Wise One sniffed, her whiskers twitching to one side then the other, and then nodded. Strong One and Brash One hopped off his hands as if they hadn't just cracked his every finger and perched beside him.

"Take!" Wise One commanded again, thrusting the leaves closer.

Kallae sighed, gingerly plucking the bundle. Up close, the leaves retained their resolute normalcy. If they had any magical properties, they were hiding it remarkably well. "Let me guess," he said, holding them up to the moonlight as though they might reveal something in ultraviolet, "ancient artifact of immeasurable power?"

"Eat."

"Sheesh," Kallae muttered, "we're feeling awfully bossy today, aren't we?"

"Eat," she repeated, her white eyes fixed on him with the unwavering intensity of a predator sizing up its prey.

Deciding that if this was an assassination attempt, it was the most roundabout and theatrical one he'd ever encountered, Kallae bit into the leaves. They were dry, crumbly, and tasted faintly of dirt, with an undertone of despair.

Nothing happened. Kallae did not keel over, nor did

he begin violently emptying his guts. All he felt was an odd tingling sensation spreading from his tongue down to his throat. It wasn't exactly an unpleasant feeling, but Kallae was no longer certain he would be capable of drinking something without having half of it falling out of his mouth.

"What is it for?" he asked, his words feeling sluggish and foreign as they stumbled out of his mouth like drunken tourists.

"So Stupid One not die from blood loss," Wise One said, poking his injured leg with her stick. The tiny motion sent a surge of dizziness crashing over him like an unwelcome tide.

Kallae groaned, his voice tinged with disbelief. "I never thought I'd say this, but can we go back to *Useless One*?"

Wise One shrugged, her tone completely indifferent. "When *Stupid One* stop being stupid."

Kallae gave her a flat look. "That's encouraging."

"Help us," she said, her voice softening just enough to make him suspicious.

"With what?" Kallae poked his tongue around his mouth, suddenly wondering if his tongue might not actually belong to him—perhaps it was some parasitic worm, clinging to the back of his throat. "Besides, what use is *Stupid One* to you?" He'd mixed feelings referring to himself as *Stupid One*, especially considering it wasn't exactly a title he'd earned or particularly enjoyed.

Wise One's response was swift and precise—*whack*.

"Free people," she said, pointing back in the direction they'd come from. Kallae didn't trust the gesture. For all he knew, they could've been walking in circles for the last hour, and this wasn't even the direction they'd started in. Nothing about this situation made sense, not even the slug-like creature that seemed to have made a home in his mouth.

"But they're not your people," Kallae pointed out,

crossing his arms. "I didn't see any Tanukis in those cells. Are your people even capable of threadcasting?"

Wise One wacked him. Again.

Now Kallae was what one would call, a not very tolerant person. It would come as a surprise to absolutely everyone who knows him that he had allowed Wise One to whack him as many times as she already had. Indeed, were his friends (the few he had) to guess what would have happened, they would have said he would have snapped it in two before she had even managed to hit him once and thrown her into a ravine for good measure. As it turns out, he allowed her to whack him three times before snatching the stick from her hands and tossing it into the bushes behind him. Fortunately for Wise One, he did not go so far as throwing her into a ravine. Then again this might not have been so much out of lack of desire to do so, but more so because there were no good ravines around, and his feet were still being held down by the two surprisingly burly Tanuki.

Wise One frowned, and for a moment, Kallae swore she might actually run after the stick like a dog chasing a—well, a stick. But then her gaze softened. She turned back to him, her demeanor far too patient for Kallae's liking.

"We are all one people," she said slowly, as though this should be *completely* obvious. "*Stupid One*," she added for good measure, her voice like a soft, almost affectionate poke to the ribs. They were, after all, a considerate people.

"Meaning?" Kallae asked, his brows knitting together.

Wise One shook her head, a look of pure disappointment washing over her, as though Kallae had just asked the most basic question imaginable—like, say, "What's an apple?" But she answered, condescending as ever.

"We all one people," she repeated, pausing dramatically as if she were about to add *'Stupid One'* to complete the thought, but somehow—*miraculously*—she refrained. "Threadcasters friends to Amriel. So friends to

Tanuki. But these people—Bad Ones. Not like *Stupid One*."

Kallae inhaled deeply, the cool evening breeze filling his lungs with something that felt like ice. He placed a hand over the crystal embedded in his collarbone, the dullness of its color reminding him of how far he had fallen. "Well, like I said," he sighed, "I'm no longer a Threadcaster. I can't help you."

His fingers traced the cold, lifeless surface of the purple crystal, the same way he had back on that wretched ship to Carfu. "Amriel has taken it from me."

Before he could finish, something whacked him on the back of the head. He spun around, already bracing for another sarcastic retort aimed at Wise One, but it wasn't her this time—it was Bo, wielding a frying pan as though it were some kind of weapon. How Bo had managed to carry it, much less fit it into that ridiculous hat of his, was a mystery Kallae had long stopped trying to solve.

"Not taken," Bo said, his whiskers twitching as his narrow muzzle wrinkled. "You reject."

Kallae pointed again at the dull crystal in his chest, his voice rising more than he intended. "Do you not see?" he demanded, "The portals of chronomagic are sealed off to me. I *cannot* help you."

"Happy One, Useless One's friend?" Bo asked, tilting his head like some kind of confused puppy.

Kallae furrowed his brow, genuinely perplexed. "Who's *Happy One*?"

"Other Threadcaster," Bo replied simply. "*Happy One*."

"Kilie?"

"*Happy One*." Yep, sounded like Kilie.

Kallae decided he did not have the energy to ask how they even knew who Kilie was. It probably involved a series of events incomprehensible to anyone who wasn't a Tanuki. Threads, for all he knew, Bo was actually that blasted Tanuki that had been masquerading as Calder.

Since it was already taking Kallae approximately 200% of his self-restraint not to skin Bo and turn him into a cushion, he decided it was probably for the best that he remained blissfully unaware on this one.

Kallae scoffed, crossing his arms. "Why does he get to be *Happy One*?"

"Because he happy," Bo blinked, completely unbothered by Kallae's frustration. "Is Happy One not friend? Useless One not want save?"

"How do you know that Kilie even needs saving?" Kallae frowned.

"Followed Useless and Stupid One."

"What?!" demanded Kallae, "how long have you—" the fairy deflated, realizing the answer did not matter, nor did he particularly care to hear it.

"Happy One, Stupid One's friend?" asked Bo, eyes unblinking.

He dropped his head into his hands with a heavy sigh. "Why have friends if they'll only die in the end? Easier to never have them at all."

"If do not have, cannot lose," Bo said, his voice so matter-of-fact, it made Kallae question his entire outlook on life.

"Exactly," Kallae muttered, eyes narrowed in annoyance.

"Maybe Useless One is Sad One," Bo offered, as if this were a profound revelation.

Bo stared at him, unblinking, as if waiting for Kallae to process the deep wisdom in that statement. A long pink tongue extended from Bo's mouth and licked the corner of his black nose before retracting, and for a moment, Kallae wondered if Bo had finally cracked under pressure or fallen into some bizarre, deep meditative state.

But then, the unsettling reality set in: Bo's eyes began to dim, shifting to a color that looked remarkably *normal* for a raccoon. Kallae blinked in confusion.

Several moments passed in eerie silence, and just as

Kallae began to notice the tiny ants crawling up his robes, Bo's body suddenly began to glow. Not like a firefly, or some over-glamorous creature from a storybook. It was different. Subtle. Threadcaster-like. Thin lines of light, so brilliant they almost hurt to look at, whirled around Bo's form like intricate patterns of thread. White, dazzling light seemed to dance across his fur, blinding against the dark.

Kallae's breath caught in his throat. He stared, mesmerized by the ethereal glow, and when it finally faded, he felt an odd emptiness settle in his chest—like a hole had opened inside him, something lost that he couldn't quite name.

He closed his eyes tightly, wishing for a moment's peace. When he reopened them, Bo was back to his usual self—unblinking, eyes as ordinary as any other woodland creature's.

"You're Threadcasters," Kallae said softly, his voice thick with disbelief. "But how?"

"Not Threadcaster," Wise One clarified, shaking her head as if Kallae were missing something painfully obvious. "No thread," she added, pointing to Bo with a practiced gesture.

"But you can use chronomagic," Kallae pressed, growing more insistent. "Bo just did. I saw it with my own eyes. This wasn't The Way of the Water—it was The Way of the Light." He looked down at his dull crystal. "But how?" He repeated, barely above a whisper. "Who taught you?"

"Amriel," Wise One answered, as she rummaged through the bushes for her stick. "Long ago."

"Impossible," Kallae breathed, the air almost sticking to his lungs.

"Possible," Bo corrected, now sitting down on his haunches, as if he had just been made privy to a grand secret and was content to let it rest.

"But we sent Threadcasters to spread The Way of the Light to Fujikura," Kallae said, struggling to grasp the contradiction. "We were supposed to teach them. Lead them away from their savage ways."

Wise One, who had been preoccupied with the stick, whacked Kallae on the back of his head again. Kallae supposed he probably deserved that one.

Rubbing the sore spot on his head, he scowled at her. "But if you have chronomagic, why didn't you teach them?" He pointed vaguely at the horizon, not sure exactly what he was gesturing at anymore. "Why do you need me?"

"Tanuki are of chronomagic," Wise One said, her expression oddly stern, as she jabbed her stick into Kallae's chest with unnecessary force. "Like you," she added for emphasis. "But you *chosen*. Threadcasters *chosen*. Guardians. Tanuki just friend of Amriel."

"Need you," Bo echoed, his eyes reflecting a mysterious, opalescent hue. "But Tanuki help."

Just then, Wise One appeared beside Kallae, causing him to flinch involuntarily, bracing for another whack or, even worse, a bite. Instead, she pressed something into his hand. Kallae was almost certain it would be another handful of dried leaves or perhaps that vile-smelling paste. Instead, he found a feather—*a very large feather*—and as his eyes adjusted, he realized it was no ordinary bird's feather. Especially not when the flames licking its surface didn't seem to burn him.

"He was here," Kallae whispered, entranced by the flickering silver flames.

Wise One nodded sagely. "Never left you. You left."

Kallae turned the feather over in his fingers, marveling at the silver flames. Despite their heat, they didn't singe him. A few sparks fizzled up his wrist, but they dissipated before they could harm or even warm him. His eyes met Bo's again, the Tanuki's gaze now luminous with an opalescent hue.

Kallae stared at the feather, watching the silver flames lick its surface with a kind of hungry grace. For a moment, it felt like a joke, something too absurd to be real, like a bad idea he'd pulled out of the dark corners of his mind and wrapped in flame. And then, in the hollow spaces between breaths, it shifted—just barely—but enough that Kallae noticed it.

A thread. Thin, almost invisible, but it was there. It wasn't much, barely a whisper against the weight of everything he had lost, but it was a thread. And threads, no matter how fragile, always connected something.

He closed his fingers around the feather, the heat of it seeping into his skin like a promise.

For the first time in what felt like ages, Kallae didn't feel quite so empty. There was still something left. Not a way out, not yet—but a way forward. He wasn't done.

Maybe he had forgotten what it felt like, but the threads didn't forget him. They were still waiting.

He glanced at Bo, at Wise One, and felt the faint pull of the crystal beneath his collarbone. The hum of it was quiet, barely even there, but unmistakable. "There's still a way," he said, like he was testing the words to see if they could hold any weight.

It was a thread, but maybe that was enough.

TWENTY-SIX

二十六

AKIRA

Never had a more miserable collection of bruised and battered souls stumbled onto the mountain ridge surrounding Oto. They landed with the kind of grace you'd expect from a pigeon drenched in oil, set alight, and shoved off a cliff—Shoji and Ra'ka nearly obliterating a flock of cranes in the process. A fitting arrival, considering how poorly the whole mission had gone so far.

They had set off from Nayagu some five days prior, Calder having finally been convinced that this was as good as it was going to get, or perhaps he'd simply decided that staring down death was preferable to lingering in that wretched place any longer. Who could say? But they were here, now. And to claim they'd arrived in anything resembling a state of readiness was an insult to the concept of preparation.

Kyou, after five days of ceaseless verbal assaults from

Akira, looked as if he might either hurl himself off a cliff or form a cult—a "Why I Hate Akira" cult, to be specific. Ryū, whose most important daily ritual had been the kicking of the air, now seemed a prime candidate for membership in that same group. And Shoji, who had once been a walking pantry of rations, had now found the limits of his extensive—but as it turns out, not infinite—supply. It wasn't wise to poke a hungry animal, but poking a hungry Shoji was like trying to pry open the jaws of a bear and curl up on its tongue for a nap.

They had plunged up and down that confounded spire so many times Akira was fully convinced half of her stomach had remained caught somewhere between the ravine and the spire. But they had done it. Just as Pa'ka had promised they would. It was tight. So tight that Jun looked like he was suffering from a chronic case of constipation every time they tried, but it was possible.

In your face Ba'ka. After more drills than Akira had cared to count they had returned to the Nayagu Sanctum from the spire, not exactly triumphant, for their exhaustion had not allowed for such costly displays of emotion, but quietly satisfied.

The days that followed in the Sanctum had been spent in the turquoise waters of the baths, rejuvenating their chronocrystals for the inevitable confrontation. By the time they set off again, Akira felt like her hands had become permanent fixtures of the water—wrinkled beyond recognition. But when they finally dismounted, overlooking Tsuyoshi's province, she found that her hands were the least of her worries. Her feet, on the other hand, had frozen solid, her bones ached as if someone had used them as kindling for a fire. Could bones scream? She was certain hers could.

Ra'ka had landed beside her along the ridge, riderless, as Shoji had leapt from her back and disappeared into the forest. If Akira had any energy left, she might've chased after him—at least asked where he thought he was going—but alas, that was beyond her capabilities. Shoji, predictably, had likely gone off in search of whatever edible creature would be foolish enough to cross his path.

She wasn't wrong. Hours later, Shoji returned, a large doe slung over his shoulders like it was a mere bag of vegetables. It was strange, the comfort of roasting a beast over a fire, while their fates loomed in the distance—Tsuyoshi's tower, with its towering walls, its threadcasters, its gryphons, waiting.

"So," Shoji said, with a glop of venison fat rolling down his chin like a slow-motion disaster, "when are we doing this thing?"

This thing being a death-defying mission to rescue a man from a tower surrounded by Threadcasters and gryphons. Piece of cake.

Calder looked skyward, cupping his hands over his left eye to block the sun, as though that would help him see any clearer. "Looks like rain," he muttered, "but we can't afford to stay here any longer than necessary. Tomorrow, nightfall."

Al'ti and Jun sat by the fire, distant figures, murmuring quietly. Al'ti, the aging Hainu, lifted his muzzle, sniffing the air like an old hound trying to remember something forgotten. The emerald glow from his feather began to seep into his fur, tracing glowing rivers along his face and down his back. He spoke in his usual gravelly tone, "Tomorrow's moons are waxing yellow, waning blue."

"Rain, maybe," Jun added, his own emerald veins shining through the fabric of his robes, though dim.

"You've learned much," said Al'ti.

"It's astounding," Ryū quipped, "Now we have our own personal weatherman."

Al'ti turned his ancient head toward Ryū, the bright threads of his fur fading away except for the swirling ones still present across his face. "Do not mock the course of the moon, boy. Those who do will never master the Way of Light. Only by understanding its source can you fully command its true power."

Ryū, somewhat chastised, returned to his venison, though it was hard to say if he was more focused on eating or pouting.

"So," Calder continued, his voice cutting through the tension, "we set off tomorrow evening. Shoji and Akira, you'll head to the eastern flank of the tower. Myself and Jun will be slightly to the South. If we're caught, maybe the distraction will help the others get in." He turned to Ryū and Kyou, "You'll stand watch in the southern forests, keeping an eye on the gryphon patrols. You will light a fire as soon as the coast is clear, and then monitor the gryphon's patrol. If anything changes, we will need you to throw them off the scent."

Ryū shot Calder a skeptical look. "Are you serious? Jun and Al'ti have ascended that tower exactly once. Ba'ka has done it dozens."

"He's right," Jun added. "We're better off on the ground, where we can be useful. If Al'ti sees something, we—"

"That's precisely why you must come," Calder interrupted. "If either of you sees or senses something, you'll need to be with us."

"And what?" snapped back Ryū. "This realization only came to you now? In a dream perhaps? Has my sight left me too now?" he turned to Ba'ka, "tell me, does Calder now also wear a green crystal I cannot see?"

"Why should I listen to you?" Ryū muttered, his words more dangerous than any blade. "What's Jiro's rescue to you, anyway?"

"I—" Calder faltered, his words tumbling out like dry leaves in a storm. "I hope to atone for the evil that's been done to these lands."

Akira fixed Ryū with a steely gaze. "Enough," she said, her tone sharp as a cutlass. "Calder, you atone for things you've never been part of. But that same honor might very well be what saves my father—and for that,

I'm grateful."

"We all thank you," murmured Kyou, his voice soft, but sincere.

Ba'ka snarled, showing his teeth. "We didn't train to be sidelined, Furless Child," he growled at Calder, "Nor do I take orders from—"

Rul'ka snapped at him, her teeth sinking into Ba'ka's flank. "You will know your place."

"I do not take orders from Furless Children," Ba'ka repeated, his hackles rising.

"But you will take orders from me," Rul'ka said, her voice cold and final.

Calder turned his attention back to Ryū who was baring his teeth. A formidable sight to be sure, but slightly less intimating without the sharp incisors that could tear a full-grown man into strips of confetti. It seemed their time spent with a pack of flying wolves had given them all some curious new habits.

"You agreed to my leadership," Calder said, his words heavier than they should have been. "You may not understand my reasons. Nor do you have to. But this is my choice."

"Shoji cannot even cast," muttered Ryū, "what will he do against the Threadcasters in the tower?"

Shoji shrugged. "Challenge me any time you like, fairy-man. We'll see who comes out on top." He tossed a chunk of venison to Ra'ka, who snatched it from the air.

"If the only way you can fight is with chronomagic," Calder said, his voice more serious now, "then you aren't ready. So, make your choice. But if you trust me, you'll stick with this plan."

Ryū grumbled something under his breath but kept silent.

The atmosphere had grown thick and awkward, tension threading through the air like a stormcloud. It wasn't a comfortable silence, not by any means. This was the kind of silence that pressed against you, heavy and oppressive, as though the universe itself was holding its breath.

The morning had come and gone with little fanfare. They lazed around, the sort of idle laziness that comes from having no better option, probably questioning every decision that led them here—whether it was getting involved with the Hainu, agreeing to follow Calder, or even just *existing* at this point. By the time dusk rolled around, the nervous energy had become contagious. Calder, returning from some mystical meditation ritual (or just a nap, it was hard to say), approached the camp to find the circus in full swing.

Ryū, with his trademark obliviousness to the sacredness of anything that wasn't his idea, had decided that the two-hundred-year-old ginkgo tree was a great place for a one-handed pull-up competition. Shoji, in a similarly reckless spirit, had turned the deer carcass into makeshift darts, and was now using Kyou as a target. Kyou, for his part, was grinning like a madman, even though a dart had already embedded itself into his arm.

The Hainu, having disappeared into the shadows earlier, were now lurking in the forest like specters—none of them had bothered to return, and that wasn't helping anyone's nerves.

Akira and Jun were engrossed in a bizarre game that only made sense to them, involving a rotating stack of cards and pebbles that were thrown at each other with the unpredictability of a drunk pigeon. Akira, already sporting a growing bruise under her eye, barely noticed Jun's quip about how the game was a 'reflection of their lives.' She would have retorted, but her focus was mostly on dodging more flying pebbles.

"It's time," Calder finally declared, breaking the chaotic circus atmosphere as he approached Jiro's clan. His voice was as calm as ever, though a hint of something darker seemed to cling to his words. Behind him, Rul'ka and the rest of the Hainu appeared, seemingly emerging from the very shadows themselves.

Jun and Akira hastily packed up their absurd game, exchanging vague promises that they'd 'continue later' while Shoji and Kyou retrieved the darts scattered across the ground—because nothing says preparation like stepping on one of those things halfway through a journey.

Time moved like honey. The sun, with all the punctuality of a long-suffering servant, dipped beneath the horizon, leaving the sky awash with hues of amber and pink. By then, there was nothing left to do but mount the Hainu, and even that was done in a silence heavy with the weight of unspoken things. Things no one wanted to confront just yet.

Akira found herself struggling with Pa'ka's harness, trying to keep it from tightening around her fingers in ways that felt uncomfortably familiar—like a life that just wouldn't let go. Pa'ka, who had the emotional range of a cactus, was clearly annoyed by the delay, his teeth making soft clicking noises as if mocking her inability to deal with the leather straps.

Kyou, having wandered over with all the stealth of a person who was clearly *not* trying to be stealthy, started to speak. "Akira-"

"Not now," she growled, tugging uselessly at the harness as if it could somehow solve everything. Kyou's shoulders sagged at the coldness of her response, and his eyes lowered for a moment before he muttered something under his breath.

"We'll talk when we get him back," Akira added, more gently than she intended. For a moment, Kyou's face flickered with something—hope, perhaps? But he masked it quickly with a smile, even though it barely reached his eyes. He turned, and as the last gleam of daylight disappeared beyond the horizon, the weight of unspoken promises hung between them like a veil.

Pa'ka was tense beneath her, his muscles coiled like

springs under his sleek fur. Every twitch of his body screamed impatience, as though the world was dragging its feet, and he alone was cursed to endure it. Akira tried to reassure herself—she had *some* control here, didn't she?—but the truth was harder to ignore. The harness, no matter how dazzling with its sparkling gems, was about as effective as a paper crown in a storm.

The twin moons, yellow and blue as Al'ti had predicted, began their reign, dancing together to create eerie shadows of emerald and chartreuse, "You ready?" asked Akira leaning down over Pa'ka's neck.

"What kind of question is that?" snapped the Hainu, flicking his ears back.

Akira sighed and settled into her seat, fussing with the harness out of habit. It wasn't that it would do anything—it wouldn't. The elaborate contraption was a treasure trove of glittering gems but had all the practicality of a gilded teapot at a gladiator match. *At least it's pretty,* she thought bitterly. *I suppose there are worse fates. None come to mind, but I'm sure Jiro's crew will dream something up eventually.*

Pa'ka's shoulders tensed again, shoving her further back in her seat. His tongue darted in and out, clinking against his teeth with a sound like breaking icicles. He was anxious. That wasn't comforting.

"We'll get him," he said suddenly, without turning back.

Akira let her hand rest on the coarse fur of his neck, sinking into the softer down beneath. "Yeah," she murmured, more to herself than to him.

Shoji appeared a moment later, Ra'ka practically skipping behind him, her energy filling the clearing like static electricity. She jittered, shifted, and flicked her wings like a live wire. Akira's stomach churned. Shoji's presence was steady, but Ra'ka's was anything but calming.

Before Shoji mounted, Ryū materialized from the shadows like a phantom, placing a hand on his shoulder. "Hey," he began awkwardly, "I'm sorry about yesterday.

I—"

"Don't sweat it," Shoji interrupted with a grin, swinging a leg over Ra'ka's side. "I know you didn't mean it. Not everyone can be as perfect as me. I was born brilliant. Amriel's personal gift to this sorry plane." He winked.

"Oi, oi," Ryū protested, mock indignation in his voice. "As soon as we're out of this, we're settling this once and for all. Let's see who's really the brilliant one."

"It's your funeral, mate," Shoji shot back, burying his hands in Ra'ka's thick mane. "But happy to oblige."

Ba'ka ambled over beside Ryū, ears flicking as Akira and Shoji nudged their Hainu towards the eastern cliffs.

"Good luck, princess," murmured Ryū.

"Kindly shove a sock in it!" Akira hollered back, though the corner of her mouth betrayed her with a small smile.

The descent through the trees was dizzying. The Hainus darted between trunks, zigzagging in a way that made Akira's stomach lurch. She was *extremely* grateful she'd skipped lunch. By the time they emerged from the forest, her stomach had long since made its intentions clear: it wanted out.

"Well," Shoji mused, as Ra'ka hovered beside Pa'ka, "guess Jun was wrong."

"Hm?" Akira tightened her grip on the harness, trying to focus.

"No wraiths," Shoji said, pulling a small crossbow from under his arm. "Was looking forward to giving this baby a spin."

Akira sighed, throwing him a look of disbelief. "You're *disappointed* we didn't run into any Shikigami wraiths?"

Shoji pouted, tucking the crossbow back. "It's called *Wraith Forest,* Akira. False advertising's a crime."

"Have you ever actually seen a wraith before?" she asked dryly, eyes scanning the forest's edge for Ryū and

Kyou's signal. So far, nothing. She gestured for Shoji to descend.

Pa'ka and Ra'ka let their wings fall to their side, dropping to the ground with soft feet.

"Not yet," he admitted, craning to see past her. "But they sound *awesome*."

Akira groaned. "Be thankful you haven't."

"Looks farther down than the spire," muttered Shoji, gripping his crossbow like it was a lifeline. "I thought Jun was supposed to be good at this whole numbers thing."

Akira shrugged, her armor creaking with the motion. "Well, I guess there's nothing we can do about it now." She had just begun wondering how long her ribs would withstand the battering ram of her own heartbeat when a flicker caught the corner of her eye.

"Coast is clear," she murmured, shooting Shoji a glance.

He nodded and offered her a quick, reassuring smile—the kind that almost made her believe it. "We'll get him back, Akira," he said softly. Then he winked, because of course he did, and launched off the edge with a whoop of "It's showtime!"

Akira leaned into Pa'ka's coarse fur, letting it tickle her cheek. "You ready?" she whispered.

Pa'ka angled his massive head downward, his yellow eyes gleaming with wild excitement. Below them, Shoji was already whooping like a cowboy, one hand gripping Ra'ka's harness and the other spinning an imaginary lasso.

"I was born ready, Princess!" Shoji hollered back.

"Not you too," Akira snapped, just as Pa'ka dove off the cliff with a burst of muscle and instinct. His forepaws plunged into the abyss first, the rest of his powerful body following in a controlled chaos that Akira generously referred to as "falling."

"I couldn't resist!" Shoji's voice barely reached her over the deafening roar of wind.

"Would you two kindly shut your gaping pie holes?"

Pa'ka barked, his growl slicing through the noise. "I'm trying to concentrate, and I can't hear myself think over the sheer *volume* of your stupidity."

"Sorry," Akira muttered, barely audible. She earned a disdainful grunt in return.

Pa'ka swerved around an arrogant outcropping of rock that had dared to grow too large, and Akira clamped her legs tighter to avoid sliding off. Her palms, clammy and streaked with sweat, slipped slightly on the harness, leaving smudges like accusing fingerprints.

To her left, she caught a glimpse of Rul'ka and Al'ti. Their wings were pressed so tightly against their bodies, from a distance one might have almost thought it was literally raining cats and dogs. Well, I guess it was literally raining Hainus and screaming people.

The ground rushed up to meet her far faster than she liked. Not that she ever liked it. Even after dozens of leaps off the spire, her insides still threatened to evacuate her body permanently. Honestly, it was a miracle her organs hadn't unionized against her by now.

Her chest tightened with the pressure of a thousand invisible weights, and she fought to keep her focus. Then—there! A glimmer in the corner of her eye. She squinted against the wind. Not a mirage. Not like the umbrella-wielding men who sometimes danced in her peripheral vision when the adrenaline got to her. No, this was a fire. A small one. By the forest.

A fire by the forest? Was the forest on fire? No. It was too small to be a forest fire. Wait! She recognized that fire. It was the same one from earlier. Except that didn't make any sense. Kyou and Ryū had already signaled to them that the patrol was on the far end of their route. They had agreed they would extinguish it as soon as they had set off. Why had they lit it again? Maybe they too were hallucinating.

"Shoji!" Akira managed to choke out.

"What?" he called back, his tone infuriatingly casual,

as though they weren't plummeting through the air like very well-dressed meteors.

"There!" She pointed with a trembling hand, nearly dislocating her shoulder in the process. By the time she'd re-secured her grip on the harness, the fire had etched itself into her vision like an unanswered question.

Rul'ka and Al'ti flanked them as the valley narrowed, their wingbeats aligning with Pa'ka's like some eerie, synchronized dance.

"Uh-oh," Shoji muttered.

Akira's stomach dropped further. "What?"

Shoji pointed behind them. "We've got company."

Unfortunately, Shoji wasn't hallucinating—or at least not this time. Two massive shapes cut through the air, sharp beaks and talons coming into focus like a nightmare with wings. Gryphons.

Their wingspans seemed impossibly large, blocking out chunks of sky like storm clouds. The first was black, feathers gleaming like spilled ink, while the second was stark white with splashes of brown that looked painted on by a chaotic artist. They cawed, a high-pitched screech that felt like it would split her skull in two.

Pa'ka stiffened beneath her, his muscles coiling like a spring. His wings snapped open and shut with a force that cut through the wind like a blade.

"Where did they come from?" Akira murmured, more to herself than anyone else. "They weren't supposed to be here yet."

"Nevertheless," Jun's voice chimed in through the chaos, cool and maddeningly detached. "They are here now, so we better come up with a new plan pretty quickly."

The gryphons were closing in, silk ribbons tied around their necks fluttering behind them like morbid banners. One dipped lower, free-falling briefly before its wings snapped open again.

Shoji leaned close to Ra'ka's ear and whispered

something, her response a low grunt that was almost lost to the wind. Ra'ka glanced sideways at Pa'ka, and for a fleeting moment, their gazes locked. Something unspoken passed between them—a shared understanding that twisted Akira's stomach into knots.

Then Shoji turned to Akira, his expression unreadable. "It's been a pleasure," he said, smiling softly.

"What are you—" Akira froze mid-sentence, her mind piecing together the fragments: the way Shoji had whispered to Ra'ka, the determined set of his jaw, the quiet resolve in his eyes. "No," she breathed, her voice barely audible over the wind. "No, Shoji. Don't you dare."

"We can outrun them!" she shouted, desperation cracking her voice like glass. "Just stick together!"

Pa'ka barked once, his ears flattening against his skull as his wings snapped wide, catching a sudden updraft. The movement jerked Akira forward, and she had to lunge for the harness to keep from falling. Below, Ra'ka dipped slightly, pulling away from the formation.

"Stop, Pa'ka!" Akira cried, yanking at the harness with all her strength. "We can't leave him behind!"

But Pa'ka didn't stop. His powerful strikes came faster, each one driving them higher and further away, even as Akira's fists began hammering into his withers. His ears flicked back at her protests, but he didn't turn his head. His focus was on the tower, a grim determination etched into the way he moved.

"There must be another way!" Akira yelled, her voice raw with panic and frustration.

Jun, his robes alight with a green hue, angled up beside her and whispered softly, "There isn't."

Akira looked back, her heart sinking as she watched Shoji grip Ra'ka's harness tightly, his face calm despite the chaos. Ra'ka's wings tilted sharply, veering away from the group and toward the incoming gryphons.

TWENTY-SEVEN
二十七
SHOJI

Shoji had died just as he had lived: a laugh on his tongue, a reckless grin etched on his face, and a well-worn line between bravery and idiocy blazing behind him like a comet's tail.

He had let the others fly on ahead, his hands working furiously to ready his crossbow as Ra'ka slowed to a hover, her wings fanning the fog into swirling eddies. The gryphons loomed closer, their feathers slick with dew and malice, eyes gleaming with a predator's certainty. Shoji squinted against the stinging wind, muttering a half-formed prayer and locked an arrow into place.

The string sang as he released, but the wind—a fickle accomplice—had other plans. The arrow veered off-course, vanishing into the misty abyss below. Shoji groaned, but Ra'ka tilted her head back, one ear swiveling toward him like an exasperated tutor with a particularly slow student.

"Practice shot," he assured her, reloading with alarming nonchalance. The gryphons dove, wings slicing the air with predatory precision. Shoji's next arrow struck true, burying itself in the white gryphon's flank. Its scream ripped through the skies, and it spiraled downward, a flurry of feathers and fury disappearing beneath the clouds.

"Sugoi!" Shoji whooped, slapping Ra'ka's shoulder in gleeful camaraderie. "One down, girl! We're unstoppable!"

Ra'ka responded with a guttural growl that vibrated through Shoji's boots as she twisted into a corkscrew dive, her mane whipping like a stormcloud. The maneuver nearly dislodged him, but he held fast, his grin growing wider as nausea clawed at his stomach.

"Warn me next time!" he hollered, though his voice carried more exhilaration than complaint.

Ra'ka didn't bother with a reply, her focus narrowing to the remaining gryphon. She feinted left, then struck upward, her claws raking across its back. Feathers flew like torn paper, and the gryphon retaliated, its beak snapping close enough to nick her cheek. Blood welled from the gash, dark against her pale fur, but Ra'ka barely flinched.

Shoji stood, one foot braced against the stirrup for balance. Somewhere in the melee, he'd lost his crossbow, but if there was one thing Shoji never ran out of, it was backup plans. From the depths of his jacket, he produced a blade so sharp it looked like it could carve the sky itself.

"Time for some close-range negotiation!" he quipped, lunging toward the gryphon.

Ra'ka dodged a swipe of its talons, but the abrupt jolt threw Shoji off balance. His knife slipped from his hand, vanishing into the mist below.

"Well, there goes my favorite," he muttered, clinging to the harness as Ra'ka banked hard.

"You've got another, don't you?" Ra'ka growled, her voice tinged with strain as she fought to outmaneuver their foe.

"Who do you take me for?" Shoji grinned, though he was already scanning his arsenal for alternatives.

Ra'ka surged forward, her claws slicing the air with deadly intent, her every movement a dance of brutal elegance. She caught the gryphon's wing with a savage strike, feathers and flesh tearing away in a spray of white and crimson. The gryphon screamed—a high, guttural noise that reverberated in the air, its wings faltering as Ra'ka pressed her advantage. Her jaws snapped shut on its shoulder with a sickening crunch.

Blue lines began to pulse across Ra'ka's fur, an electric glow that contrasted sharply against the pure white of her hide. "Hold on," she grunted, her voice a low rumble that vibrated beneath Shoji's feet.

"This isn't my first rodeo," grinned Shoji.

Ra'ka's wings blurred into near invisibility as she banked right, following the gryphon's erratic flight. The beast wheeled around to face her, recognizing the futility of escape. It swiped at her with its talons, but Ra'ka dodged as if she had already anticipated the move. She clawed at it with lightning speed, her body twisting in perfect synchrony, and then curved her head to bite.

Her jaws clamped down hard, but the gryphon was already pulling away, its frantic wings flapping desperately. Ra'ka spat out a mouthful of feathers and tried again. This time, her bite was rewarded with the metallic taste of blood, mixed with something far more foul—like rancid oil.

Shoji braced himself, placing a steadying hand on Ra'ka's withers as he rose to his feet. He wobbled for a moment, still struggling to regain balance on her back, but then his sword was in his grip—a wicked curve of steel that gleamed with purpose. The blade, honed to a razor's edge, could split bone like butter, and Shoji was itching to use it.

"Steady," he muttered, more to himself than to Ra'ka,

his gaze locked on the gryphon's thrashing form below. The beast was trapped in Ra'ka's death grip, its wings useless. Shoji could feel the tremor in his hands as he held the blade. The gryphon was weakening, but there was still fight in it.

Ra'ka growled under her breath, "Speed it along a little, would ya?"

The gryphon twisted violently to the side, jerking both Ra'ka and Shoji forward. Shoji cursed under his breath, his knees buckling slightly, but he grinned. "Come at me, you overgrown pigeon!" he yelled with a manic thrill as he drove the blade down through the center of the gryphon's withers. It faltered, its defiance splintering with the force of the blow. Shoji pushed deeper, feeling the blade crack through bone, and then through muscle, until it finally passed out the other side. Still, he pushed, his arms trembling with the effort.

"I think you got him," said Ra'ka, releasing her bite just as the gryphon's wings drooped, defeated. It plummeted toward the ground, a weightless corpse.

Shoji staggered back, barely managing to hold onto the saddle as the gryphon's fall dragged him down with it. The sword, still embedded in its carcass, disappeared from sight, and Shoji stared at the empty air with a half-hearted sigh.

"Awww," he muttered, leaning over the side of Ra'ka's back to peer into the abyss below. "What a waste." He straightened, his expression lightening, and placed a hand on Ra'ka's shoulder. "We did it, girl."

"That we did," Ra'ka answered, her face glowing with a soft blue light, her breath quickening in the aftermath of the battle.

But then, as quickly as the moment had passed, it shattered. The white gryphon—having been decidedly less dead than they had thought—slammed into Ra'ka from below. Shoji was thrown violently to one side, barely managing to stop himself from falling entirely by slamming his arm against Ra'ka's neck. He felt a sickening pop in his shoulder as he did, his vision flashing white with the pain.

"Balls," he muttered through clenched teeth, but Ra'ka was already spiraling, her wings locked in a frantic attempt to regain control. The air whipped around them, the wind a torrent that tried to tear them apart. The gryphon, still alive, cawed in fury and dove again, its talons snapping. Shoji scrambled, trying to reach for another of his blades, but his options were limited—most of them had been flung to the ground in the chaos.

He reached for the one in his sock, but his dislocated shoulder screamed in protest. His arm felt like it was made of wet clay, sluggish and unresponsive. The wind and Ra'ka's descent made it all the worse.

And then, just as they neared the ground, Ra'ka's blue lines turned a fiery pink, and Shoji froze. Not frozen in place, but frozen in time. He tried to move, but his muscles were slow to respond, as if his entire body had been submerged in syrup. His outstretched hand seemed to hover in the air, distant, detached from the moment. His thoughts warped and tangled into an incoherent mess as his world slowed to a crawl.

"This is amazing!" he shouted, but his words came out distorted, as if spoken through a long, echoing tunnel.

And then, they dropped.

Shoji's stomach lurched, his breath catching in his throat as time seemed to stretch, a sickening, weightless moment hanging between what was and what would be. His thoughts snapped back to the present with a jolt—but the impact didn't come. Not yet. The world seemed to spin slowly around him, a dizzying blur of rock, air, and sky. The ground was closing in, and yet, they hurtled toward an outcropping barely large enough to hold them both. He reached out in a panic, his hands scraping against his body in a frantic search for broken bones. Legs intact? Check. Organs where they should be? Check. Limbs all attached? Quadruple check. Well, minus the dislocated shoulder, of course.

Ra'ka let out a low, exhausted huff beside him. Her wings hung slack at her sides, like curtains that had been dropped from their rods. She breathed heavily, the air coming in soft, labored puffs that carried the smell of sweat and desperation.

But then it happened.

In one horrific, bone-chilling moment, the white gryphon struck.

Shoji's breath hitched as its claws slashed forward, faster than he could blink. Ra'ka's wing—so majestic, so powerful moments ago—was ripped from her with a sickening, tearing sound. The gryphon's talons caught the great, broad wing and tore it off as though it were little more than paper. Ra'ka screamed—a raw, unearthly cry that vibrated through Shoji's chest, so full of agony it made his teeth ache. Her shredded wing fluttered away from her, tossed aside like a useless thing, its feathers floating in the air like blood-soaked confetti.

Ra'ka's body buckled, her legs folding under her, sending a spray of rubble tumbling down the mountainside. Her breath became jagged, frantic, and Shoji could only watch in horror as her once-proud form crumpled.

"Ra'ka!" Shoji shouted, but his voice was drowned out by the gryphon's shrieking descent. His heart clenched as he saw her falter. The sight of her—strong and proud just moments before—now broken, her pain too much for even her to bear, sent a fire of fury through him.

"Get up, Ra'ka, get up!" he cried, grabbing at her, but she couldn't respond. The gryphon was almost upon them, its shadow swallowing them whole.

Shoji's mind raced. There was no time. Ra'ka was slipping. She was going to die if he didn't act. He glanced up at the gryphon, the beast almost upon them, its talons gleaming like knives.

"You did it girl," he whispered.

Without a second thought, Shoji jumped.

The wind tore at him as he leapt from the outcropping, his body plunging into the open air. He was weightless for a split second, his stomach left behind on the cliff, his heart pounding in his throat. Below him, the gryphon's massive form loomed, and Shoji—eyes wide, lips set in a grim line—plummeted straight toward it.

Ra'ka's scream echoed in his mind, but there was no time to think about that now. He had to save her.

The gryphon's wings flared, and Shoji's heart seized. The creature was huge, its body monstrous, its claws extended, but Shoji didn't hesitate. He reached out, stretching his arms toward the gryphon's broad chest as he fell. His hand closed around its feathers, his fingers slipping, but he held on. He could feel the heat of its body, the power radiating from it, and the scent of blood in the air—Ra'ka's blood.

Shoji gritted his teeth, the adrenaline surging through him like lightning, as he dug his feet into the gryphon's side, pushing himself up just as its claws swiped dangerously close to him. His body collided with the gryphon's ribcage, and he could feel the beast's muscles flex as it tried to twist away. Shoji pushed harder, his dislocated shoulder screaming in protest, but he didn't care. He had to stop it. He had to protect her.

The gryphon screeched in pain, twisting in midair, its wings flapping erratically as Shoji clung to it with every ounce of strength he had left. His shoulder burned, his fingers bled from the force of his grip, but the creature was bucking, desperate to shake him off.

And then, Shoji's foot slammed into the gryphon's wing. The wing snapped at the joint, the bone cracking under the force of his blow, and with a violent, disorienting twist, the gryphon began to plummet. Shoji barely held on as they dropped, tumbling together, the world a blur of wings and feathers, the wind howling in his ears.

Ra'ka's form was a distant memory now, her voice lost in the chaos as the gryphon's body twisted beneath him. Shoji's fingers slipped again, his other shoulder finally giving way, but it didn't matter anymore. He had done it. He had stopped it.

The gryphon's body finally tumbled past him, its flight no longer under control. Shoji grinned, even as his world started to close in around him. He had saved her. "We showed them, Ra'ka," he whispered, the words barely escaping his lips as his body succumbed to exhaustion. And then, with the rush of air around him and the cold bite of the world slipping away, his vision faded to black.

TWENTY-EIGHT
二十八
AKIRA

"We have to go back!" Akira cried, swiping tears away from her face with shaking hands. Her voice cracked, raw with emotion. "We need to help him!"

Jun and Al'ti flew in tight formation beside her, effectively blocking any chance she had of veering off course. Jun's face was tight, his voice soft but unyielding. "Shoji made his choice, Akira. The best way to honor it is not to let his sacrifice be in vain."

"Ra'ka and Shoji chose honor," Al'ti added, his voice as resolute as granite. "We must do the same."

Akira's throat constricted, her protest a lump she couldn't swallow. Pa'ka surged forward, his wings beating against the air with a sound like the drum of war. "Come, Furless Child," he said in a rumble that seemed to vibrate her very bones. "Let us go save your father."

The words hit her like a slap. Father. She didn't have time to unpack the searing ache in her chest before they flew past Calder. She caught a glimpse of him, his expression stoic, save for the tears glittering in his eyes, barely held at bay.

A low thrumming gong sounded from the mountain's core, a hum so deep it tunneled through the stone and resonated in her ribs. It was a warning, ancient and uncompromising.

"Quickly!" muttered Jun, his eyes darting downward as his fingers moved in a rapid series of gestures that looked more arcane than practical. "We've only got minutes before reinforcements arrive."

As they descended, the tower loomed closer, shedding its child's-toy façade and revealing its true, oppressive grandeur. Hewn from black rock polished to a sinister shine, it jutted up like a knife through the lush forest and jagged peaks that encircled it. The shape was alien, an affront to geometry. The base defied classification—a lopsided polygon that gave way to spires stabbing skyward at unpredictable intervals. Halfway up, one spire dipped downward as if it had collapsed under its own weight, only for another to rise defiantly in its place.

No windows marred its surface, no imperfections softened its edges. It was a fortress of flawless malevolence.

"Fascinating," Jun murmured, his voice tinged with academic reverence.

"If you're into aseptic, monolithic death traps, sure," Akira snapped, though she couldn't tear her eyes away.

The wind howled louder as the hainu descended, their wings flaring wide as they prepared to land. Pa'ka let out a rumbling growl, a sound that Akira could feel more than hear, as he adjusted their approach. The slick black surface of the spire offered no friendly perch, but the hainu moved with practiced precision.

"Hold on tight," grunted Pa'ka, his voice carrying over the rush of the wind. "This landing will not be gentle."

Akira clung to his thick fur as her stomach churned with the drop. She could feel every muscle in the hainu's back tense as he adjusted his wings, angling to avoid the cruel edges jutting from the tower. Behind her, Al'ti and Rul'ka, let out sharp cries, coordinating their movements to avoid collision.

The surface of the spire loomed closer, and Pa'ka's claws scraped against the stone as he finally touched down with a jarring thud. Akira winced as the impact reverberated through her body, but the hainu didn't falter. Pa'ka's wings folded tightly to his sides as he crouched low, allowing her to dismount.

Pa'ka turned his massive head toward her, the markings on his face glowing faintly in the twilight. "Quickly, Furless Child," he rumbled. "Your task awaits."

Akira swung her leg over and hesitated for a moment, gripping his fur. "Thank you," she said, her voice barely audible over the wind.

Pa'ka's expression softened, the golden glow of his eyes steady. "It has been an honor, Akira." He nudged her gently with his snout before stepping back.

Behind her, Jun clambered off Al'ti with significantly less grace, muttering under his breath about heights and poor life choices. Calder landed with practiced ease, his staff already in hand as he scanned their surroundings.

The hainu didn't linger. Pa'ka, Rul'ka, and Al'ti unfurled their wings, the force of their departure sending a gust of air that nearly knocked Akira off her feet. She shielded her face with an arm, watching as the hainu ascended into the sky, their silhouettes vanishing against the darkening horizon.

"They're leaving us here?" Jun asked, his voice high-pitched as he tried and failed to keep his footing. He grabbed onto Calder's sleeve, nearly pulling them both over.

"They've done their part," Calder replied, gripping his staff for balance. His eyes lingered on the diminishing shapes of the hainu as they disappeared into the twilight. "Now we do ours."

Akira squinted against the wind, but her focus quickly shifted as her feet slid again. She yelped, her arms pinwheeling as she scrabbled for purchase. "Oh, come on!" she muttered through gritted teeth, reaching down to pull a knife from her boot.

The surface beneath them was unlike anything she had ever encountered—sleek and seamless, almost as though it had been polished to a mirror finish. The slightest shift of weight sent her sliding perilously toward the edge. "The ground is like ice!" she hissed, jamming the knife into the surface. For a heart-stopping moment, the blade skittered uselessly before finally catching with a metallic screech.

"Watch it—" Akira began, but before she could finish, both Jun and Calder tumbled off their precarious perches.

Calder, quick-thinking as always, slammed his staff into the ground, pressing a concealed mechanism that released a spike from its base. The weapon anchored him instantly, though the force of his landing nearly wrenched it from his grip.

Jun, on the other hand, flailed wildly as papers burst from his robes like startled doves. He slid closer and closer to the edge, his legs kicking out in a desperate attempt to slow himself.

"Jun!" Akira shouted, inching toward him with her knife still embedded in the stone. "Use your knife!"

"I didn't bring one!" Jun hollered, his voice rising in panic.

"You brought a novel, but not a knife?" she snapped, her frustration barely masking her fear.

"We can discuss my packing choices later!" Jun barked, his fingers clawing at the surface as he neared the precipice.

Akira clenched her teeth, letting the familiar hum of

chronomagic flood her veins, readying herself to intervene. But before she could act, Calder lunged forward, his free arm catching Jun just as he was about to tumble over the edge. The momentum nearly dragged them both down, but Calder's staff held firm, the spike keeping them anchored.

Akira let out a shaky breath, the blue glow of her chronomagic dimming as she released it. "That was close," she muttered, her heart pounding in her chest.

Jun, pale and trembling, clung to Calder like a barnacle on a ship. "Thanks," he managed, his voice shaky.

Calder grunted, his usual stoicism tinged with exasperation. He handed Jun a blade from a wrist-guard, his expression making it clear he expected better planning in the future.

The three of them regrouped, using their assortment of knives, spikes, and sheer determination to inch their way toward the center of the spire. Each movement was painstaking, their blades leaving a cacophony of scratches and screeches on the otherwise flawless black stone.

By the time they reached the leveled-out area in the middle, their limbs screamed in protest, and their nerves were as frayed as an old sailor's rope. They paused, chests heaving, eyes scanning the oppressive darkness that had swallowed them whole.

Dusk had long since fallen, and the spire had slipped into the black void of night as though it belonged there, as though it had always been a part of that eternal abyss. But as their eyes adjusted, the shadows surrendered a few secrets.

"There," Jun said, his voice hushed but sharp, pointing. On one end of the platform, an opening gaped like a maw in the stone—a promise or a threat, Akira couldn't decide which.

"So, the plans were correct," Jun remarked, a hint of smugness creeping into his voice.

"You weren't sure?" Akira's tone was a dagger.

"Well," Jun shrugged, ever nonchalant, "the top corner had a coffee stain on it, so I couldn't quite make out the full schematics. But it worked out just fine—"

"Jun," Akira said slowly, her voice low and dangerous, "if we make it off this damn tower, I will personally drag you back up it just so I can throw you off myself."

Jun smiled, the picture of unbothered calm. "What a lovely sentiment. Shall we?" He gestured toward the yawning opening, his nonchalance practically a dare to the universe.

It was a large opening, as openings went. Having been designed to allow for easy entry and exit by gryphons. Fortunately, it was not locked, Tsuyoshi having clearly banked on the fact that no one would be asinine enough to try and enter from the top with a patrol of war-gryphons circling above them. 'Well Tsuyoshi, the joke's on you' thought Akira, you have severely underestimated our crazy. She wasn't quite sure if that was a good thing.

The room they entered was vast and oddly shaped, a twisted reflection of the haphazard exterior. The obsidian marble floor stretched out like a shattered mirror, jagged cracks cutting through the glossy surface. Portions of the walls jutted inward, others bowed outward, as if the very weight of the tower's existence had warped it over centuries.

Yet, for all its size, the room was eerily sparse. A smattering of tables stood scattered about, accompanied by chairs that looked like they'd been designed by someone with a grudge against comfort. Heavy tapestries hung along the walls, their woven scenes a chaotic montage of suffering and brutality, more befitting a sadist's gallery than a noble's hall.

Akira's gaze lingered on one particularly grotesque depiction—a battle, or maybe a massacre, embroidered with chilling detail—when her vision blurred. A flash of white burst across her eyes, a barrage of flickering orbs that danced like mad fireflies.

Beside her, Jun squinted with one eye while rubbing the other furiously. "What the—"

"Why, hello there," came a voice from the shadows, smooth and dripping with an unsettling familiarity.

Akira's instincts kicked in before her mind caught up. Her hand flew to Jun's robes, yanking him closer, while her other hand gripped her sword hilt so tightly her knuckles ached. Lines of energy rippled down her body, and blue smoke rose from her skin like steam off a hot spring.

Out of the darkness, a figure emerged, each step deliberate, each motion precise, like a predator closing in on its prey.

"Tsuyoshi," Akira said, her voice sharp and bereft of any honorifics.

The daimyo raised an eyebrow at her insolence but let it pass. "I suppose we can dispose of honorifics for now, Tsuyoshi will suffice," he replied, his tone light but his smile cold. He gestured grandly toward the center of the room, his turquoise silk robe fluttering with the movement. "Please, come in. Get out of the cold."

Akira hesitated, her muscles coiled, but before she could react further, she felt the icy press of a blade against her neck.

Guards, Threadcasters from the Order, had materialized on either side of them. One, a man Akira recognized from the Kitsune statue—Lark, if memory served—fixed her with a steely gaze.

"Move," Lark barked, his tone sharp as a sword's edge, the blade at her neck leaving no room for negotiation.

They stumbled forward into the room, and there was Tsuyoshi, seated comfortably in an ornately carved chair that looked both expensive and diabolically uncomfortable. His evening robe of turquoise silk shimmered in the light, embroidered with cranes that seemed to almost take flight with the movement of the fabric. His smile was a predator's—broad, inviting, and entirely devoid of warmth.

"Please, take a seat," he said, his voice carrying a mirth that didn't quite reach his eyes. Akira hesitated, eyeing the chair like it might be housing a carnivorous cactus, but she sat anyway. Calder and Jun followed, though the tension between them hung in the air like a storm waiting to break.

But as Calder moved to sit, Tsuyoshi's hand clamped onto his shoulder with an iron grip. "Not you," the daimyo said, his tone cutting through the room like a blade. The playful lilt in his voice was gone. "You are no guest here."

Akira's heart sank. "Calder, what's going on?" she asked, her voice trembling despite her best efforts to steady it.

"I will be asking the questions here," Tsuyoshi snapped, his hand tightening on Calder's arm, the unspoken threat in his movements clear.

Akira turned to Jun, searching his face for answers, but his eyes were narrowed in that calculating way of his, like he was solving some unfathomable equation. She dearly hoped he wasn't just trying to estimate the dimensions of the room.

Tsuyoshi gave a low chuckle, waving forward a soldier who carried a silver tray laden with tiny cups. The cups were so small they were practically useless—two sips at best, and only if you sipped politely. The soldier's expression was tight, his movements stiff, as though he were walking the edge of a blade himself.

"Please," Tsuyoshi said, his voice slick as oil, gesturing toward the cups.

Jun leaned in slightly. "I really don't drink past nightfall," he began, his voice overly polite in that way it got when he was trying to talk his way out of something. "It's terrible for my—"

"It is not a request." The weight of Tsuyoshi's tone made the air feel heavier.

The two Yōsei gingerly picked up a cup each, their

eyes still fixed upon the daimyo as they did so. Akira contemplated throwing it behind her, but Tsuyoshi's watchful gaze left her little room for such antics.

Akira hesitated, locking eyes with Jun. Neither moved to drink. The threat wasn't overt, but it lingered in the room like smoke. With a resigned sigh, they each took a cup. Tsuyoshi raised his own, smiling broadly, and clinked it against Akira's. "Kanpai!" he declared, though his tone dripped with mockery. "A toast to our guests—or at least those of you who have deigned to arrive."

Akira's grip tightened on her cup, the chronomagic humming beneath her skin, threatening to spill over. She felt Jun's hand brush hers, a silent warning. "They're all Threadcasters," he whispered, his voice barely audible. "It's suicide."

Her jaw clenched. "I have to try."

Before Jun could stop her, Akira sprang to her feet, blue threads blazing from her hands as they coiled around her arms and legs, propelling her forward. A thread lashed out, wrapping around Tsuyoshi's wrist with a sharp crack. Chronomagic surged through her veins like wildfire, the threads vibrating with a dangerous hum.

Tsuyoshi hissed as the thread bit into his flesh, blood beading at the edge of the wound. For a moment, Akira dared to hope—until Tsuyoshi's free hand gripped the thread. With a slow, deliberate pull, he yanked. The thread snapped like a dry twig, and Akira tumbled backward, her breath catching in her throat.

Akira gritted her teeth, "I have to try," before Jun could say anything further, she bolted forwards, blue threads wrapped around her legs and arms as she sailed through the air. Akira flung her hand in front of her, another thread swinging forwards and wrapped itself around Tsuyoshi's wrist. Chronomagic surged into Akira's veins, the rivers of blue now alight like the night sky. The thread began to vibrate, releasing a dull hum as it did so. The daimyo hissed as the thread bit into his skin, drawing a pearl of blood. Akira tightened her grip on the thread. Tsuyoshi, eyes pinned onto her, grasped a hold of the thread with his other hand. It tore into the tender flesh of his palm, yet he did not release it. Gripping it firmly he tugged. At first nothing happened. He tugged again. The thread snapped, and Akira tumbled backwards, her eyes wide.

"Well," Tsuyoshi said, flexing his hand as if shaking off a minor inconvenience, "is that any way to treat your host?"

Akira's gaze snapped to his hand—completely healed, not a scratch in sight. Her stomach churned. A sickly yellow hue curled from his mouth and drifted over his skin. He smiled again, showing teeth that seemed unnaturally sharp. As Ryū would say, they were about as screwed as a paper towel in a monsoon.

He turned toward her. "You'll have to try harder than that," he said, fully revealing his hands—immaculate, untouched. She could feel the weight of his gaze like a lingering threat.

The daimyo shifted his attention back to Calder. "My terms were clear, Threadcaster. All of them."

"The others are all in Oto," Calder said firmly, avoiding Akira and Jun's questioning stares, "They're just outside. I sent word last night, as soon as we arrived, just as you asked."

The daimyo sneered, shoving Calder away with a force that sent the fairy sprawling across the ground. "Do you take me for a fool?"

Calder scrambled to his feet, stumbling backward as the Daimyo strode toward him, the sharp click of his ornate staff echoing with every step. Tsuyoshi slammed the staff onto the ground with such force that the crack reverberated through the room, drowning out everything but the sound of Calder's screams. His hand was pinned beneath the staff. The pitch of his screams was unbearable, and yet, it wasn't the screams that drew

Akira's focus—it was the horror that had been building steadily, finally breaking into the light.

"Then tell me—Brother Calder, was it?" Tsuyoshi's voice oozed mockery. "Why do you bring me only two when I asked for all?"

Jun nudged Akira, and she followed his gaze. Behind Tsuyoshi, a shadowed door beckoned, the promise of escape just within reach. Tsuyoshi, however, was too absorbed in Calder to notice.

Akira tapped Jun with her elbow. Without a word, they began crawling toward the door, each movement measured and desperate.

They were halfway there when Tsuyoshi whipped around, placing a boot in their path with a swift, precise motion. "And where might you be heading?"

With a nod, he signaled his guards by the door. "Take their weapons," he ordered, pointing to Akira's sword.

Akira's heart hammered in her chest, but the real danger was in her veins. The chronomagic, wild and desperate, boiled beneath her skin, clawing for release. She reached for her sword, but the guards were already closing in. The one who gripped her sword was a Threadcaster, his face obscured beneath a black shawl, and his eyes—those stubborn, impenetrable eyes—felt like they were already a step ahead.

"Now," Tsuyoshi said with unsettling calm, "I didn't want to treat you like this, but you leave me no choice."

He turned back to Calder, a wicked gleam dancing in his eyes. "Now, tell me," he purred, "what would you do if you were me?"

"Where is Brother Frenick?" Calder's voice cracked, his hand clutching his chest.

"Ah, ah, ah," Tsuyoshi tutted, wagging his finger with exaggerated playfulness. "What did we say about asking questions?"

He dropped to Calder's level, his face hovering over the fairy's, and grinned, his breath hot against Calder's skin. "Now answer the question."

"I did what you asked," Calder muttered through gritted teeth.

"How could you?" Akira's voice broke through, the words more force than question.

Calder refused her gaze, his head hanging as though the weight of his betrayal had become too much to bear. "He has Frenick. I spoke the truth," he rasped, his words stumbling out, "He was holding me here. I escaped, but he caught me in his chambers."

Tsuyoshi smiled, the smile of someone who had won the game long before it had ended. "And I made him an offer he simply couldn't refuse."

Akira's stomach churned, and in that moment, something inside her broke. Calder had played them. He had sent them into the heart of the enemy's lair, led them down this treacherous path all for Tsuyoshi's gain. The realization slammed into her like a blow to the chest.

Akira rushed forward, fists clenched, heart pounding, but Tsuyoshi, robes shimmering with a pink glow, spun threads from his fingers. They flared out, a luminescent web that snared Akira's body in an instant, locking her in place. Pink threads, longer, brighter, more alive than any she had seen before, sliced through the air, coiling around her torso. She gasped, struggling to fill her lungs, but the air wouldn't come. Each breath felt like it had to be signed off on by some unseen bureaucrat, held hostage in her chest. Her body, suspended by an invisible hand, demanded approval before it could act.

Akira's body trembled with a quiet fury. *How had they let this happen?*

"I thought we were your friends," Jun whispered, the words heavy with a sincerity Akira couldn't quite stomach. His voice, soft but cutting, was like a knife twisting in an open wound.

Calder gritted his teeth, his hand brushing the floor as he struggled upright. "Where is Frenick? What have you done with him?"

"It's not so much what I have done as what he's done to himself," Tsuyoshi waved at one of his soldiers, who dutifully brought him a tiny cup. *Tiny.* Like an afterthought. Like a man who didn't care enough to bother with something so mundane as practicality. He sipped the liquid, smacking his lips together like a well-fed cat. "You see, Frenick couldn't see how good he had it. I offered him food, drink, protection from the Inquisitor. But am I to blame if he tried to escape and conveniently fell right into the Inquisitor's hands?"

Calder's body stiffened. He lunged forward, rage contorting his face. "But we had a deal!" His hands froze mere inches from Tsuyoshi's neck as the threads tightened, a warning.

"Hmmm," Tsuyoshi murmured, casually observing the scene like a bored god watching ants scurry about. "I suppose we did. But our deal was for you to go to Sanctum of Nayagu and bring me Jiro's clan. *In its entirety.*" He glanced at Akira and Jun, their slack-jawed faces a portrait of betrayal. "But here, I see only two."

Akira hit the ground as the threads slackened, her chest heaving with the rush of air flooding back into her lungs. She curled her fingers against the floor, grounding herself in the overwhelming surge of relief and anger.

Tsuyoshi's hand shot out like a serpent's strike, grabbing Calder by the throat. "Did you think to trick me?" he hissed. "Think you could outsmart me?"

Calder dangled in the air, choking, his face a mix of fury and panic, but Tsuyoshi let him drop as though it were a mere inconvenience. The fairy collapsed to the floor, gasping for breath.

"It seems we have both failed to honor our end of the bargain." Tsuyoshi's voice dripped with a chilling satisfaction.

He leaned down, jerking Calder's head up by the chin with cruel precision, forcing him to meet his gaze. "I suppose I should thank you, anyway. You've brought some of them. *And,*" he added, a wicked smile creeping across his face, "better still, you've brought me the Hainu. You know, I've been trying for years to get those blasted dogs out of their hole. And then Lark, bless his quick temper, provided me with the perfect opportunity. I knew you lot would do anything to get Jiro back if he were held against his will, and you," he jabbed a finger at Calder's chest, "would blindly trust whatever I told you as long as I had Frenick."

Calder's head fell, only to snap back up, realization seeping into his eyes like slow poison. "No," he whispered, his voice breaking as tears welled in his eyes. "That's why you sent us."

Tsuyoshi's smile widened. "Very good!" he turned to Jun and Akira, "This one catches on fast, doesn't he?"

Akira's vision blurred red, but she fought to keep her voice steady. "What will you do to them?"

"Oh," Tsuyoshi's laugh was almost musical, but it carried the hollow edge of a nightmare. "I wouldn't let such things concern you."

Akira's hands balled up into fists, her vision turning red.

Akira's hands balled into fists, the pressure building in her chest. Her teeth ground together. "You orchestrated everything," she growled. "But if you knew our plan all along, why not just kill us from the beginning? Why wait till we came here?"

"The Sanctum," Jun's voice was almost a whisper, but the clarity of it hit Akira like a brick. His realization echoed through the air, sharp and undeniable.

Tsuyoshi laughed again, the sound so jarring it felt like shards of glass were scraping along her nerves. "I see this one is the smart one," he pointed at Jun, "but never mind that. You know the most dangerous thing about you people?" He paused, letting the words linger in the air, thick with venom. "It's your hope. A thing for fools, and yet even a fool might stumble upon gold once in his life. But now I've given you your hope. Allowed you to taste its sweet deception, so you can see how empty it truly is. Call it a favor for a favor. I've shown you the truth, and you've lured the Hainu out from their hole. Really, I owe you my thanks."

"What did you do?!" Akira screamed, her voice cracking under the weight of her fury. Her eyes fixed on the door, her muscles straining as she fought against the guard's grip.

"Now, now, Akira," Tsuyoshi's voice was almost condescending, soothing in a way that made her skin crawl. "I assure you, no harm will come to them. Well, no more harm than came to Frenick," he added with a sickening chuckle, downing another cup of sake like it was water.

"Where is Jiro?" Akira demanded, her hands still clenched, her chest tight with dread.

Tsuyoshi turned away, his face a cold mask. "Ah yes, of course," he said, his voice now deadpan, "the reason we're all gathered here. Always the man of the hour, even when he's not in the room." He ran a hand down his neck as if brushing away the remnants of a lingering thought. "Sadhrin wanted him sent to Cargyll, but it should come as no surprise that he tried to escape. Too much of a liability. So, I killed him."

"No," Akira gasped, her heart plummeting. "I don't believe you!"

Before she could respond, the sound of something clattering, followed by a scream, echoed through the room. Footsteps thudded against wooden floors, each step a grim reminder of what was about to happen.

Tsuyoshi glanced over his shoulder. "About time," he muttered, just as a figure burst into the room. The door crashed open, and another figure, a guard, appeared, who looked rather like he'd been in a race with death itself.

"I was wondering when you might grace us with your

presence," Tsuyoshi said, as the guard stumbled in behind the first figure. The guard, panting and red-faced, barely managed to catch his breath before speaking.

"Tsuyoshi-sama," he said, still gasping, "he escaped."

Tsuyoshi's eyes narrowed, his expression darkening. "I can see that, Brante," he said, turning toward the newly arrived figure. "I don't quite know what I would do without your brilliant insights."

"Sorry, my Lord," the guard stammered, bowing quickly before he could find his breath again. "I'll return him to his cell immediately."

Tsuyoshi dismissed him with a wave, then jabbed at him with the foot of his staff. "You've done quite enough. Leave my sight before you decide to grace me with any more of your stupidity."

The guard left the room in record timing, giving even a flector a run for their money. He did trip on his way out, but he did not let that deter him. Indeed, likely nothing save a broken leg would have deterred him. And even with a broken leg, Akira would not have been surprised if he had dragged himself out on his arms.

Then she saw him.

Jiro.

The Yōsei before her was covered in grime, his crystal embedded in his clavicle, glowing faintly under the layer of dirt. His hair, long and tangled, hung in wild, unkempt strands around his face. His robes were a patchwork of dirt and despair. The man before her wasn't the one she remembered—he was someone else, someone broken.

"Father?" Akira whispered, uncertain. A tear slipped down her cheek, catching the light for just a moment before she launched herself forward.

"Father!" Her voice broke through the tension in the air, but her leap—her every move—was cut short as threads of pink shot from Tsuyoshi's hands. They wound around her like chains, locking her in place.

"On your left!" Jun's shout came a moment too late,

but it was there, a reminder that even in the darkest moments, hope could flicker—if only for a second.

Jiro's face, streaked with dirt and exhaustion, fell. "Akira," he whispered, voice thick with regret. "You shouldn't have come."

Lub dub.

Akira's heartbeat was all she could hear. *Don't. Don't you dare.*

Tsuyoshi waved his hand with an exaggerated flourish, the kind reserved for performers who'd long lost their passion but were too deep into the act to stop now. "Yes, yes, lovely family reunion, ladidadida, only slightly marred by Calder's staggering incompetence. But we'll overlook that, won't we? His voice was syrupy sweet, but his eyes betrayed a deepening boredom, like someone who'd watched this particular tragedy unfold a thousand times. Each gesture was a practiced motion, like a bored king flicking his hand to dismiss a jester who's gone on too long.

He walked toward Akira, brushing his fingers against her cheek like he owned her. Akira bit him—not fast enough, though, and she was left with nothing but the bitter taste of air in her mouth.

Jiro stumbled forward, dropping to his knees, his legs refusing to bear his weight as he collapsed to the floor in a crumpled heap. "Please," he begged, his voice cracked with a rawness that made Akira's stomach churn, "it's me you want. Let them go. I'll do whatever you want."

Tsuyoshi didn't answer at first. He just smiled that cruel smile, tapping Jiro's side with the tip of his polished boot, the sound unnervingly sharp in the stillness. "Well, Jiro," he said, his tone sweet but venomous, "how does life look from your high tower now? Does it feel good to beg for mercy? To ask for respect, like a commoner?" He leaned in closer, his eyes narrowing with malicious curiosity. "Tell me, why should I help you when you, in the same position, offered me nothing but empty promises and condescending platitudes?"

"Forgive me," Jiro muttered, his head bowed low, his voice barely more than a whisper.

Tsuyoshi let out a sound that was half a laugh, half a sigh, as if the very concept of mercy were beneath him. "Hmmm," he murmured, pacing around the room like a cat toying with a wounded bird. "You see, first Calder here"—he jabbed a finger into Calder's chest, the sound like a dull thud—"failed to keep a simple promise. And then these two, paid for my hospitality by trying to run away." He turned to face Jiro, his eyes gleaming with malicious delight. "And now, you ask for mercy?"

The sound of Tsuyoshi's staff tapping rhythmically across the floor filled the space between words, like the ticking of a clock winding toward a dreadfully inevitable conclusion.

"No," Tsuyoshi said, his voice rich with satisfaction, "I think today, I will not be merciful."

A thread of blue, thin as a whisper, began to coil out from Tsuyoshi's fingertips. It was like watching a snake unspool itself from a hidden corner of the room, slow at first, but then faster—so fast it seemed to vanish altogether, leaving behind only a quiver in the air.

Tsuyoshi released his grip on Akira, the pink thread slipping from her skin with a sickening twist. She collapsed, the world tilting sideways as her body slammed to the cold floor. A sharp crack rang through her skull, and the sensation of falling lingered long after the impact. Blood—her blood—began to pool in her eye, blurring the edges of everything.

"How the mighty fall," Tsuyoshi's voice sliced through the chaos. "Somewhat poetic, don't you think? Tell you what, I won't even take your crystal from you. Call it a token of my appreciation for the friendship we once shared."

For a moment, there was only the crushing weight of nothingness. The air hummed, the blue haze of Tsuyoshi's magic still hanging in the corners of her vision like a sickly aftertaste.

She tried to lift her head, but it felt as though the ground was trying to pull her into itself, as though her body had forgotten how to stay in the world at all. She blinked through the blood, still struggling to make sense of what had just happened—of what was still happening. Her mind scrambled, chasing fragments, pieces of a puzzle that didn't fit. The tower seemed to shift beneath her, the walls bending and folding in on themselves.

She tried to focus. "Jun!" she croaked, the name a rasp in her throat.

Her lips tasted of salt and iron, but she didn't care. She tried again, her voice cracking, "Jun—where are you?"

A voice answered, distant, like it was coming from underwater. "Akira!"

Jun. It was him. But he felt so far away. Everything felt far away. She couldn't quite place him, couldn't hold on to the sound of his voice, couldn't keep the pieces of her world from slipping through her fingers.

"Jun…" The word escaped her lips like a breath she didn't mean to take.

Her heart hammered against her ribs, but it wasn't her pulse she heard in her ears now. It was the relentless thrum of Tsuyoshi's magic, like an angry clock ticking, each beat more oppressive than the last.

Her eyes darted around. But the shapes, the sounds, everything twisted and blurred as though she were underwater, the world muffled, just out of reach.

"Father," she whispered, but the word felt foreign, like something she used to know. Where was he? Was he still alive? Was he—?

The thought cut off as she felt hands—strong, urgent—grip her arms, pulling her up. But the hands weren't warm. They weren't familiar.

Shoji? No. Not Shoji. Shoji had been torn apart by the storm. Shoji was gone.

Her body jerked with the motion, trying to escape, trying to get away, but she was weak, dizzy, disoriented. The hands pulled her further.

Someone was calling her name. "Akira! Akira!" The voice again, clearer this time. But the words sounded distant, hollow, as if they belonged to someone else.

She turned her head, but there was nothing to see. Only the shape of a figure in the periphery—too blurry, too vague to focus on. A faint shadow, and then it vanished, just as quickly as it appeared.

"Father…" she whispered again, as if saying the name might make him appear. But everything felt too far out of reach. Too broken. Too—

Her body jerked as she was yanked backwards. She fell again, but this time she didn't hit the ground. Something solid caught her.

"Akira!" a voice yelled, panic cutting through the haze. Jun? Maybe. It could have been him. She didn't know anymore.

"Are you alright?" asked Jun, his mouth contorted in a shout but his words coming out as a whisper.

She shook her head as her eyes shut, a bitter laugh on the edge of her lips. She wondered if she would ever be alright again. "No, Jun," she whispered, "I am not alright."

Lub dub.

Tsuyoshi, the blue smoke now having fully dissipated, trudged forward, a languid satisfaction in his steps. He kicked Jiro in the stomach. The body didn't even twitch, and Tsuyoshi clicked his tongue in mock regret. "I must apologize," he said, his voice syrupy sweet, the kind of clarity that made her feel like the world was slipping beneath her feet, "I must have used the wrong tense there. I meant to say I will kill him. Which I now have. Can't have people saying I'm not a man of my word now, can we?"

Akira's chest constricted, her breath jagged and shallow. Her pulse thundered, but everything felt muffled as though she were drowning in her own blood. And then, like a cruel twist of fate, her gaze—half-blurred and desperate—shifted down.

She saw him.

Jiro.

His body, her father's body, was crumpled at an impossible angle on the floor. Blood pooled beneath him, the unmistakable, horrifying outline of a body split down the middle, torn apart by the twisted blue thread Tsuyoshi still held. It was still attached to him—trembling slightly at the end, like a living thing, dripping blood. It oozed from the severed parts of Jiro, staining the floor with every beat of the thread's pulse.

Tsuyoshi twirled the thread between his fingers, a sickening grin on his face as he took a step back, admiring the work he'd done.

"No," Akira whispered, her voice hoarse, cracking under the weight of her disbelief. The blood... so much blood. It soaked the floor around her father's corpse, a cruel reminder of the irreversible reality she couldn't even process. Her stomach lurched, and for a moment, she thought she might pass out from the sheer terror and grief that clung to the edges of her mind like poison.

"Jiro," she choked, and again, the name tasted like ash on her tongue.

But there was nothing left of him. Nothing but the sickening ripple of the thread in Tsuyoshi's hands, its blood-red stain soaking into the wooden floor.

"Akira!" Jun's voice pierced through her thoughts, strained and broken, but still... she couldn't quite place it. It was like trying to remember a song whose melody had slipped away. She couldn't grasp it, couldn't make it real. Her mind was drowning, suffocated by the weight of what she was seeing.

"Jun?" she croaked. Was that his voice? It was too familiar. Too distant.

She stumbled toward him—or tried to, at least—but

her feet refused to cooperate. She felt herself falling. Then, the world went dark, slipping like sand through her fingers.

Tsuyoshi, a smug expression still painted on his face, twirled the thread between his fingers. "I do hope this was all worth the trouble, Akira," he murmured. The blood dripped, a steady rhythm, like the countdown of a clock—slow, deliberate, final. "It's always a shame when things have to end like this."

EPILOGUE

MR. FABER

A chill hung in the air. The type of chill which buried itself deep inside one's soul and leached at any warmth that might remain. Fortunately for Mr. Faber, there had not been much warmth to begin with. Not after the week he had had. Come to think of it, it was not really this week that had done it, it was the year, perhaps even this decade which had worn his bones to slivers and his hope to a knife's edge. His steps once sprite and lively might have thudded to the ground with the weariness of a man well beyond his years had he not been so deathly afraid of drawing unwanted attention. The fact fear was something on his mind at all surprised him in a way that scared him all the more. Mr. Faber could be called many things, most of them worthy of several appointments with a therapist and perhaps an extended stay at a mental hospital, but afraid was not one of them. Well until now it appeared. It seemed Mr. Faber had extended his affinity for collecting antique pipes and overpriced paintings to mental ailments (guess we all need to find new hobbies as we grow older).

His familiar path, the one that wound through streets as comfortable as his childhood neighborhood (because, of course, it was), now seemed a little off. Almost like greeting an old lover, but the kind you hadn't remained on speaking terms with. The kind who'd broken your heart and didn't have the decency to apologize.

A drop of water splashed against his cheek. He wiped it away, sighing as his chronocrystal hummed softly against his chest, protesting the rain in its own quiet way. Neither of them were fans.

By the time Mr. Faber reached *the Bedraggled Cockerel*, the exhaustion had settled deep in his bones, and he felt sorry for himself in the way only a truly miserable person can. The heavy door, adorned with a rooster-shaped knocker, swung open with a force that could've ripped it from its hinges.

"Hey," Mr. Caligan called from behind the bar, wiping something greasy from his hands. "No need to take it out on the door. It's a good door." He patted the frame with something approaching affection. "She's been through a lot."

"Well," Mr. Faber grunted, throwing himself onto one of the barstools with all the grace of a collapsing house, "so have I."

The sound of the stool hitting the floor was loud enough to register in Mr. Caligan's bones. But that was nothing compared to the pint of ale that slid down the counter and was drunk in one swift motion. "The others haven't arrived yet?" Mr. Faber asked, his voice low but edged with irritation.

Mr. Caligan gave a short shake of his head. "Nae, though I think—"

"Better have a damn good reason for dragging me out

here, Actinus," a voice cut across him. It was low, sharp, and full of the sort of unspoken threat that made you regret the moment you'd even considered getting involved. The door's bell jingled delicately as the figure entered, though it did nothing to soften the force of the man who walked through it.

This was, of course, the venerable Lord Lianthorn, the bearer of the obsidian shard blade Cazuk, leader of the Light Fae, and generally just about one of the most disagreeable people to have ever walked this good earth. I'd wager it was only his formidable skills with a blade and downright mastery of Threadcasting that saved him from being stabbed in the heart by most everyone who had the misfortune of crossing his path.

The Fairy lord's presence immediately soured the atmosphere. Not that it needed much help—when Lianthorn entered a room, the air turned cold, like a storm cloud forming on the horizon. He was tall, regal, and undeniably beautiful in that cruel way only fae could manage. He moved with the elegance of someone who knew he was above everyone around him, and it was a knowing that grated on the nerves like a blade against the skin.

Lianthorn was, as ever, the sort of beauty that demanded poetry, though his sharp cheekbones and glistening obsidian eyes might've made him the subject of nightmares instead of sonnets. His long, pale locks were crowned with a woven wreath of wooden branches, heavy with fruit, looking like something that belonged on a royal head—or perhaps a spoiled child's. The sort of thing that, on anyone else, would've been laughable. But Lianthorn could pull it off with the confidence of someone who knew they could convince an entire kingdom that a fruit salad was, in fact, the height of fashion.

"Ah, Lianthorn," Mr. Caligan said, his voice dripping with insincerity as he wiped down the counter with unnecessary force. "Lovely to see you as always. It's been a moment."

"Is it?" Lianthorn's golden eyes narrowed as he yanked a chair out, dropping into it with the grace of a predator.

"Just trying to be polite, you know," Mr. Caligan muttered, his tone strained but doing little to mask his disdain. "That's what people do, isn't it?"

"Hmmm," Lianthorn frowned, his lips curling into a smile that could have been a threat, "so shall I always assume you merely say things for the sake of saying them, or will I be needing to seek clarification every time societal custom drives you to utter something?"

Mr. Caligan sighed, poured a tall glass of violet liquor, downed it in one gulp, and then poured himself a second. He turned to Mr. Faber, deadpan. "Well, he makes you look like a field of dandelions, doesn't he?"

Lianthorn was now tapping the edge of the table with slender fingertips, his many rings clinking rhythmically with every tap.

Mr. Caligan peered over the edge of the bar, eyebrow arched in feigned interest. "Can I help you?"

"Ah yes," Lianthorn said, his voice syrupy sweet, "I would like a tall glass of the five-year vintage orange Iselionian wine. The five-year, not the six," he clarified further, "three cherries, stones removed, and a splash of lavender liquor, if you have it."

Mr. Caligan disappeared behind the counter, clinking bottles with exaggerated care, before slamming down a glass so scratched it was practically opaque. "You can have a glass of the house ale," he said, his voice a mockery of cheerfulness, "take it or leave it."

Lianthorn grumbled something under his breath but accepted the offering, slinging his feet over the corner of the table as he reached for the pint. "I would really rather—" began Mr. Caligan, but when he caught Lianthorn's piqued look, he muttered, "Ah for thread's sake, do what you want." Mr. Caligan slung the towel over his shoulder and began rearranging his liquors. An entirely mandatory task, naturally, regardless of whether the bottles needed touching or not.

"I take it Fayre has decided to once again shirk his responsibilities," Lianthorn said, idly running a finger around the rim of his glass. His voice was the epitome of casual disdain. "I suppose one might say he's reliable in that way."

A bell above the door chimed. The sound was at once a herald and a threat, announcing the entry of yet another soul determined to ruin Mr. Caligan's evening.

"Well, would you look at that, the half-dead, flea-infested cat drags itself in," said Lianthorn, just as a tall figure entered the room. The Fairy Lord twisted in his chair, using his foot to push against the table with the delicate precision of someone who'd mastered both subtlety and indifference. "Fayre," he said, voice dripping with honeyed sarcasm, "impeccable timing as usual."

"Well," the Lord of the Dark Fae said, hanging his velvet cloak upon the hook with disdain, "I wouldn't want to prolong the time spent in your company any more than necessary."

Lianthorn's face darkened a shade, leaving his pale features looking almost ghostly. "I take it the heinous hag you call a wife has been otherwise detained? Or are congratulations in order for her untimely, or shall I say timely, demise?"

Fayre knotted his long dark hair into a simple bun and leaned over the countertop, whispering something to Mr. Caligan who, without hesitation, poured a tall glass of something violet and smelling of a spring field.

"Tell me," said Mr. Caligan, elbows perched on the edge of the bar, "has he always been this insufferable, or was he less of an unbearable cullion before the Splintering?"

Fayre hummed, as if contemplating a great philosophical truth, and glanced out the window, searching for some crude form of inspiration. "You know, there was a time when Lianthorn and I were friends."

"Lianthorn, friends? Thought the only person he tolerated was that odd butler of his—Laeroth."

"Well, I can't imagine he has very many anymore, but there was a time when he did."

"What happened to them?"

"Knowing that stubborn old git, he probably drained them for their blood or fed them to his—"

"You are aware I am in the room, yes?" Lianthorn asked, his dark brow arching almost to his hairline. "Or is it too presumptuous of me to assume you both possess the basic function of sight?"

"Quite," snapped Fayre, "despite my best efforts to unsee your sorry face."

Mr. Faber, normally the one with the biggest ego in the room, found himself dethroned and stood quietly beside the bar, an observer to the sharp exchange. But Mr. Faber was never one to let adversity stand in his way. He straightened his fitted black cloak, adjusting the golden buttons that scaled its side, and strode into the middle of the room, taking a seat beside Lianthorn. He contemplated asking him to move but decided that was perhaps not the hill to die on. There would be plenty more to choose from, and it's seldom wise to go with the first option presented.

"If the lot of you are quite done enjoying the sound of your own voices," Mr. Faber said with an air of authority, "perhaps we can get on to why I have asked you here today?"

Lianthorn gestured forward, letting his chair drop to

the floor with a satisfying clank. "By all means. Don't let me keep you. I only have an entire realm to run, after all."

"And I an Order," Mr. Faber shot back, his tone cutting, "now kindly deprive us from hearing your voice for more than a few seconds."

"Very well then," Lianthorn said, pale eyes shining in the dim light, "get on with it then."

Mr. Faber chose to ignore the Lord of the Light Fae, which was generally the recommended way of handling the cantankerous fairy. That or softening him up with a generous supply of fairy wine. But since Mr. Caligan seemed about as eager to serve Lianthorn as he would be a bear, it seemed the former option was what Mr. Faber was left with to get through this evening.

Mr. Faber's gaze drifted from one end of the room to the other, scanning the innkeeper's pristinely kept space. Despite the tavern serving some of the vilest members of society, Mr. Caligan had always managed to keep everything clean enough to eat off any surface—whether that be the floor or the top corner of his liquor cabinet.

The evening had been chilly. Twin moons, yellow and blue, hung in the sky, bringing in a cold eastern front that had seeped into Mr. Faber's bones like mist. But within *the Bedraggled Cockerel*, a roaring fire had done its best to thaw him, cocooning him in warmth that should have had him sweating. He shivered.

Blue light surged into his veins, adding an eerie hue to the warmth of the fire. The tips of his fingers frosted slightly as threads of turquoise streamed from them, wrapping around his wrists, then meandering over to do the same to the others.

"Is this strictly necessary?" Lianthorn asked, half-heartedly trying to brush the threads away from his hand like an uncovered spider's web.

Mr. Caligan glanced only briefly at his own set of threads. "Don't bother," he sighed, "his paranoia has reached a height reason can no longer assail."

"You'd be the same if you had seen what I have," grumbled Mr. Faber, visibly relaxing into his seat. "It never hurts to be cautious."

The threads wrapping around Mr. Caligan quivered, then drew blood. Mr. Caligan winced, licking the blood from the wound. "A slight miscalculation, perhaps, Actinus?"

Mr. Faber readjusted. The yellow moon was waxing, not waning. Maybe he was losing his touch. The thread stopped quivering. "Too much on my mind," was all he said.

"I'll say," muttered Mr. Caligan.

The threads began to hum, and though it looked as though Lianthorn slowly sipped at his room-temperature ale with a look of dissatisfaction, to anyone spared Mr. Faber's blue threads, they would have seen a full glass of ale disappear in the blink of an eye, as the gathering of four men sat in icy silence. A slightly deranged gathering, mind you—one that could have easily risen from their seats, held hands, and danced around the room singing *Ring Around the Rosie.*

Though, if gripped with the blue threads that hummed like a hive of bees, you would not have been met with icy silence. Instead, you would have been part of a conversation that probably should have never happened.

Lianthorn plucked at one of the threads on his wrist. "You know, we could all do this for ourselves," he let the thread snap back against his skin. "Even Fayre is a capable enough flector to mount a noise shield."

Mr. Faber threw up his hands, jolting all the threads in the process. "Call it hospitality. Whatever lets you sleep at night." He turned to the others. "Now, are you all quite finished?"

A circle of nods met him.

He slammed something down on the table—a spool. It was at that point that Mr. Caligan learned his table, or perhaps his floors, were not as level as he had previously assumed. The spool rolled down the oak surface like a rogue boulder, only stopped by the edge of one of Lianthorn's obsidian knives. When exactly the blade had appeared there was a mystery, and one likely not worth solving. The Lord of the Light Fae flicked the tip of his blade upwards, plucking the spool out of midair.

"Curious," he said, rolling it in his palm, inspecting it like an oddity from a distant market.

He tossed it to Fayre, who gulped down the last of his drink as it flew towards him. "Thanks," he muttered, wiping purple liquid off his chin.

Mr. Caligan leaned in over Fayre's shoulder, leg bobbing incessantly.

"It's chronomagic threads," murmured Fayre, finding the end and beginning to unspool it. "Blue."

"Your powers of observation never fail to astound," muttered Lianthorn, flicking his knife between his fingers with an almost musical rhythm.

"It shouldn't be possible," said Fayre, brow furrowing.

"And yet it is," said Mr. Faber.

"But how?" added Mr. Caligan, his voice tinged with genuine curiosity.

Lianthorn let his head fall into his hands with a theatrical sigh. "It's like I'm surrounded by a gaggle of hair-brained squirrels," he muttered under his breath.

"The outside of the spool is made of dead chronocrystal," Lianthorn said, lifting his head again, raising his voice, "It can theoretically hold chronomagic for some time. The spool body itself is metal—though I trust I needn't explain basic chronomagic conductivity to a bunch of fairies who last had their Metaltaking over two centuries ago?"

"You got all that from just a glance?" murmured Mr. Caligan, unable to hide his surprise.

Lianthorn shrugged. "I dare say if you spent as much time educating yourself as you do wiping your countertops, you too might experience the wonder of an insightful thought once in your life." He pointed toward the spool, ignoring the scowl now adorning the Barkeep's face. "Dead chronocrystals are rare. I know of a few places that have them. And even fewer people willing to obtain them."

Lianthorn glanced at Mr. Caligan, his golden eyes glinting mischievously. "I can see you wish to ask what a dead chronocrystal is, but do not wish to show your ignorance."

"That's not true," insisted Mr. Caligan, his leg bouncing faster than ever. The floor creaked in protest.

"Is it not?" Lianthorn's gaze was sharp, his dark brows rising in an almost amused challenge.

"Fine," muttered Mr. Caligan, slamming his glass down on the table, the hollow thud punctuating his surrender. "Tell me."

"Well—" began Lianthorn.

"They're chronocrystals removed from a Threadcaster," interrupted Mr. Faber, his patience clearly running thin. He wondered, not for the first time, how the Fairy's overinflated ego hadn't caused him to burst into a million pieces. The thought almost made him smile.

"You mean to say they physically extract a crystal?" asked Mr. Caligan, his eyes widening.

"That is precisely what I mean to say," clarified Mr. Faber.

"They have to be alive too," added Lianthorn casually, as if he were discussing the weather. "The crystal becomes unstable shortly after death and turns back into pure chronomagic."

"But surely one cannot simply gouge a crystal out of someone still alive?"

"Oh," Lianthorn remarked, picking at the dirt beneath his nail with the tip of his blade, "they usually die once it's been removed. On account of the gaping hole in their chest and all," he said, nonchalantly pointing to his own opal crystal, just in case Mr. Caligan hadn't quite grasped the severity.

"There's more," said Mr. Faber quietly, almost ominously.

"Well, do spit it out, old chap, places to be and all that," said Lianthorn, sitting back with an air of exaggerated disinterest.

Mr. Faber cleared his throat. "The spool was found in the hands of Puldrick."

"Why did he have it?" chimed in Mr. Caligan.

"Where is he now?" added Fayre, leaning forward with sudden urgency.

Lianthorn's eyes narrowed. "He's dead, isn't he?"

Mr. Faber glanced at the Light Fairy, his face unreadable. "He was found dead in an alley behind *the Chanting Lard.*"

"Terrible establishment," muttered Mr. Caligan, his voice dripping with distaste. "Worst ale in the city."

Mr. Faber's jaw tightened, the words almost lost beneath the weight of his irritation.

"Was he killed?" asked Fayre.

Mr. Faber shrugged, his voice distant, "In a manner of speaking," he said slowly, "his body was sucked dry, as if every ounce of flesh had been drained. And he had the appearance of a man as old as time itself."

"Impossible," huffed Fayre, shaking his head. "He was a Threadcaster."

"Do you imply that I am lying?" Mr. Faber's tone turned sharp. "Do you doubt what I saw with my own eyes?" He slammed his fist against the table with a thundering crack. "I saw Puldrick myself. If it weren't for the emblem on his chest, I wouldn't have recognized him. It was in his hand that I found the spool, clasped between his gnarled fingers as if it was the only thing left in this world that mattered."

"I have seen something like this before," said Lianthorn, his voice quiet but heavy with meaning. "It is an awful sight, an unnatural thing. I've seen it a handful of times in my lifetime, but a draining of one's life-force can happen if too much chronomagic is drawn at once. The body is overwhelmed, unable to funnel so much energy at once."

"This was no miscalculation of power," said Mr. Faber, his voice turning hard. "Puldrick was far too careful. This was done to him."

"But who would do such a thing?" Fayre leaned over the table, his face illuminated by the flickering lantern light as he peered down at the spool.

"I think we all know the answer to that," said Lianthorn, his expression turning grim.

"Do we?" Fayre and Mr. Caligan said in unison.

"You must forgive me," said Lianthorn, his voice dripping with condescension. "I so often forget what it's like to operate at such an amateur level."

Mr. Faber gritted his teeth, his patience thinning. "Sadhrin."

Recognition flashed across Mr. Caligan's face. "You have proof now?"

"Sadhrin has seized control of Heron Academy."

"Balls," said Mr. Caligan.

"Well," Lianthorn said slowly, his voice tinged with satisfaction, "it seems, unlike what you had previously implied, you in fact do not have an Order to run.

S.D.G.

Soli Deo Gloria

Sign up for my Author Newsletter!

Join the community and find up what shenanigans I am up to at the moment at https://stwhitebooks.com/

A NOTE ON THE AUTHOR

S.T. White, regrettably, does not reside in Narnia but on the decidedly less magical planet Earth.

The Way of Threadcasting is her debut novel, though she has plenty more worlds brewing—most of which have significantly fewer talking raccoons.

ACKNOWLEDGEMENTS

"If I find myself with a desire which no experience in this world can satisfy, the most probable explanation is that I was made for another world." – C.S. Lewis

Thank you to the original and the greatest Author and Creator, without whom none of this would have been possible.

I have many people to thank for supporting me on this great adventure, and for putting up with me scribbling on napkins, sticky notes, hands, and everything in-between. Most of all, I have to thank my mother, who has been my greatest supporter and inspiration since I began this journey over a decade ago. I also owe a very special thanks to Roberto who has probably read this book more times than I have, and has put up with many half-deranged conversations about dragons and flying wolves. I also have him to thank for the wonderful cover which has hopefully convinced you all to buy this book. Thank you Allen Arnold for your priceless insights and support during this process, I could not have asked for a better coach. And thank you to my Honey Badger for all your support and the bubble teas and Zweifel chips.

To my other beta readers, Fre, Ayesha, Dieter, Skaty thank you all for your feedback and pointing out where I forget about minor details like dragons that never get mentioned again.

I am privileged to have a list of friends I should thank that would require another book-worth of space, and I am sure I have forgotten some (my apologies in advance): my old school friends Sophia (wifey), Green Peas, Matteo, Lena, Justin, Christian, Sonja; work friends Estelle, Richard, Ela, Johannes, Oliver, Isobel, Zach, Roman, Uria, Clara, Edo, Juani, and the rest of the Stocker Lab; old university friends Stasi, Julia, Oli, Angus, Hibiki, Maciej, Dimitri, Thomas (the Pagan Heretic), Hubert (sorry Trebuh hasn't made it in yet), Loic, Camilla, Vera, Kalo, Thea, Naomi; fellow chemistry survivors Ella, Fraser, Lochie, Matthew, Vesi, Reinis, and Charlie for all the great DnD nights; all my former teachers, especially Mr. Peake, Mr. Myndio, Mr. Pieri, Mr. Browning. Ms. Rossi, Mrs. Wienand (Miller), Mr. Kirkwood.

And a final smorgasbord quick-fire round, thank you Carol, Grandma and Grandpa, Aunt Hirako, Aunt Miwako, Aunt Toshiko, Desmond, Stephanie & Rosario, Nancy & Robert, Verena, Julie, Bless, Mother Hen & Coconut, Joy & Peter, Richard & Susan, Matthias, the Two Moons Team, Sacha & Ari, Dr. Schiestl, Dr. Landolt and the other doctors at KISPI, Team OceanCare (especially Sigrid, Fabienne, and James), Chalfont Horgen (especially Patrick & Iris, and Stephanie), Nick, Lauren. I am sure I have forgotten to put some people on this list, and for that I am sorry—if you read my book and this lengthy acknowledgement, you can send me an angry letter and I'll be sure to include you in the next book.

Thank you to everyone who bought and read this book, thereby enabling—and dare I say, encouraging—my deeply problematic tea consumption. Admitting it's a problem is the first step. The second step, apparently, is another cup.

Printed in Dunstable, United Kingdom

65979188R00234